PERSEPHONE'S ORCHARD

Molly Ringle

2013

www.centralavenuepublishing.com

First print edition published by Central Avenue Publishing, an imprint of Central Avenue Marketing Ltd.

PERSEPHONE'S ORCHARD

ISBN 978-1-926760-98-8

Published in Canada with international distribution.

Cover Design: Michelle Halket

Cover Photography: Courtesy & Copyright Olga Vladimirova (Shutterstock)

PERSEPHONE'S ORCHARD

PROLOGUE

THE FIRST GUNSHOT SENT ADRIAN Watts' dog, Kiri, crashing to the ground with a yelp. Ten meters ahead, in the darkness under a tree, she twitched and then lay still.

The smart thing to do would be to switch realms right away, without her. But he would never leave her.

He sprinted forward and threw himself on the grass, gathering her in his arms. He looked around the park, but the night hid his attacker. All he caught was a shadow and fast footsteps: someone taking cover behind the next tree.

As Adrian was about to dive into the spirit world with Kiri, the second shot came. The bullet tore through his back and out his front. It felt like his midsection had exploded.

Gasping and rolling onto his back, he laid his hand over his belly. The ragged wound stretched as wide as his palm. Blood soaked his T-shirt and jacket. The attacker walked over, both hands on the gun. Adrian could just make him out against the stars: medium height, muscular build. A strange shape around the eyes, and a glassy glint, suggested night vision goggles.

"If you're mugging me," Adrian said hoarsely, "I only have twenty dollars on me."

"I'm not."

"You know who I am, then?"

"Shut up."

"I see." Adrian gagged on the familiar metallic taste of blood, and cleared his throat. "What if I'd been some ordinary bloke, walking his dog in the park?"

"Then you'd be dead."

Adrian touched the wound on his stomach, where the edges were already itching and trying to pull together. "Yeah. Guess I would be."

"You will be, next time." He sounded American, or at least that was Adrian's best guess. The gun remained pointed at him, and Adrian had to wonder just how well he'd recover if a shot shattered his skull across the ground. Was this the kind of gun that could do that? He could barely see it in the dark, and even if he could, he wouldn't have any idea. His life hadn't involved such training so far, and he rather wished it would never have to.

Adrian pulled Kiri closer, curling his arm around her, gathering his strength. She didn't move. From the feel of the blood on her neck, the shot had hit her in the head, but Adrian didn't panic yet.

"Listen to me," said his assailant. "You and your friends go back to your other dimension or whatever you call it, and stay there. Show up among humans again and you're dead. Understood?"

"We *are* human." Not important at the moment really, but Adrian's offended pride couldn't let the slur stand.

"Shut up. Go away, never come back, never make any more like yourselves, or you're all dead."

"Sorry. I don't make promises to people who shoot dogs." Adrian's strength and focus recovered just enough to let him reach for the other realm. He slipped into it, bringing Kiri with him.

His attacker vanished. The city lights winked out, giving way to a sky full of stars. The grass turned into moist dirt scattered with leaves. The park's landscaping disappeared; a patchy forest of tall trees now stood around Adrian and Kiri. Some kind of monkeys or apes whooped and chattered in the branches.

Adrian rolled onto his side, wincing. Kiri twitched again and whimpered. Her breathing grew steadier.

"It's all right, girl. Just rest a bit." He stroked her ears. "We weren't going to die without getting to meet Sophie, were we? No. We wouldn't do that. We'll be okay." He lay looking at the stars, his pain receding with each breath.

CHAPTER ONE

DON'T START CRYING, SOPHIE DARROW repeated to herself as she stared into the small, empty closet in her new dorm room. True, her parents and little brother had just driven away, heading back to Washington, leaving her here at Oregon State University for her first term of college. And yes, her boyfriend was beginning college in a different city and her best friend in an even farther city. So, indeed, Sophie was all alone now, alone to a degree she'd never experienced before; and she knew nobody here, and missed her family and friends so much it felt like a fresh wound in her chest. And meanwhile, of course, panic was rapidly overtaking her at the idea of facing life as a university student.

But surely the other freshmen in the dorm suffered the same problems, and *they* didn't sound like they were about to cry. They laughed and chatted out in the hall, just past her open door, unfolding their life stories to each other with glee as if this was the best vacation they'd ever taken.

What was wrong with her?

Sophie drew a deep breath, blinked three or four times, and knelt to unpack her shoes into the closet.

All she had to do was get her stuff moved in properly, make this little room feel like home. Then her spirits would recover.

As if this could ever be home, her lonely mind lamented. Home was the drafty farmhouse in Carnation, Washington, out on the highway, the family produce stand set up at the roadside. Home was her room on the second floor, a tattered and colorful oval rug on the uneven hardwood planks, her bed with extra comforters piled up against the chilly nights. Home was Liam, her little brother making a clattering racket on his skateboard in the cracked driveway. Home was sleepovers with Tabitha—now far away in Seattle—or, lately, cozy movie nights with Jacob. Home was Mom and Dad and the dogs, and not having to procure her own food and share a room with a girl she'd never met.

Kneeling on the floor, pulling the packing tape off a box of clothes, Sophie stopped and closed her eyes. *Don't start crying.*

At that point her father's words came back to her. *Don't start crying. Start doing.*

He said it whenever she threw a frustration fit about homework, or a fight with Liam, or someone bullying Tabitha or herself. "Do something to fix it, and if you can't, then do something else to make your life better. Tell you what, crying isn't going to fix it."

Sophie took another deep breath, in and out, and wiped her eyes. Line up the shoes. There. Already did something. Now, perhaps, to take a picture of how ridiculously tiny her closet was, and send it to Tabitha, who probably had a more glamorous dorm room, since she was at an arts college.

But as Sophie got out her phone, someone wandered into her room, babbling in a foreign language on a cell phone.

Sophie rose to her feet to stare at him, regarding him as both an intruder and a welcome distraction.

He lowered the phone beneath his chin long enough to tell her, in heavily accented words, "I am sorry. This phone, it is like crap. I get signal only here."

Then he was shouting into the phone again and gesticulating at his invisible acquaintance.

"No problem," Sophie said, though he couldn't have noticed, what with his tirade.

Her homesickness subsided a bit as she looked upon this new perspective. She couldn't imagine studying in an entirely different country, where they didn't even speak your native language. Poor guy.

She sat on her still-bare mattress, between a box of books and a stack of clothes on hangers, and studied him. His dark brown hair was thick and curly, fluffing out around his head to near-Afro levels. Sophie could do that to her hair if she wished—she had genuine African heritage on her dad's side. But this boy looked more Mediterranean. Maybe that was Italian he was speaking?

Sophie reached back to scratch her neck, and found her hair was escaping from its clip, tendrils sticking to her skin. The September weather here in Corvallis, Oregon, was turning out hotter and more humid than the university brochures had advertised, and the dorms lacked air conditioning. After carrying all those boxes up two flights of stairs, Sophie was sweaty and sticky.

The boy's tan skin gleamed at the temples with sweat too, as did the triangle of sparsely-haired chest above his shirt. He was tall and fit, with a perfect complexion, and possessed a certain beauty with that symmetrical face and thick hair. And a foreign accent was usually a plus. But those clothes—*oh, honey*, she thought, adopting her best friend Tabitha's favorite condescending phrase.

His shirt was striped purple and orange, and a white drawstring zigzagged up its V-neck. His red jeans clung like tights to his body. Golden leather sandals rounded out the ensemble. Seriously, golden, as if he had spray-painted them. Even Sophie didn't own any footwear so sparkly.

When the boy swung away from her, still arguing in Croatian or Russian or whatever it was, Sophie surreptitiously snapped a photo of him with her own cell. Setting the phone on her lap, she added a message for Tabitha.

Room just got invaded by this guy, shouting on cell in foreign language. Welcome to college.

She sent the text to Tabitha, up in Seattle, and thumbed through her other messages for a minute.

Her little brother Liam had just texted her, presumably from the car, *Mom is txting some1, wtf?*, which sent her stomach into an uneasy dip. She had her suspicions about their mom's leisure activities lately, and whom she might be texting.

Meanwhile, Sophie's boyfriend Jacob had told her: *I miss you :(* at which she sighed sadly.

A text bounced in from Tabitha, in response to the photo: *Hi, the Eurotrash club called. They want their clothes back.*

Sophie grinned, but felt bad for making fun of the nice clueless visitor. Just then, the guy told the other speaker something that sounded like "Okay" and some kind of goodbye, and switched off his phone. She set hers down too.

He pushed aside her box of books and sat with a sigh beside her, resting his head in both hands. He smelled like a thrift store, as if he had just today purchased that outfit at one.

Sophie waited for an explanation, and, getting none, asked, "So, what language was that?"

"Eh?" He lifted his face. "Oh, yes. Greek. I am Greek. You have heard of Arkadia?"

"Uh…"

"Yes, is in Peloponnisos, in Greece."

"Okay."

"I am from there. Yes."

"How are things at home?"

Another big sigh. He cast a look of desolation at her window. The late afternoon sun lit up his pale green eyes. "Is difficult," he said. "My family and friends, there is problems always, between them. And my cousin, he wants me to find a girl for him."

"He wants you to find him a girl?"

"He looks for someone, a certain girl. Is my job now, somehow."

"Um. Yeah, that's difficult." Sophie decided she wasn't even going to ask.

He stuck out his hand. "I am Nikolaos. Hello."

She shook hands with him. "Sophie."

"Ah! Sophia. Is good name. Greek. Wisdom."

"Yep. That's right."

"You know. Of course. You are how old? Eighteen?"

"Yes."

"Ah, I as well. So you are freshman here too?"

She nodded. "Just moved in." Her gaze trailed along all the things she still had to unpack, and the tiny half of the room in which she had to fit them. Her roommate Melissa, a short, mousy, pale Oregon girl with brown corduroy shorts and white sneakers, had stuck around for about two minutes when Sophie and her entourage had arrived. Then Melissa had backed out of the room, flashing her student ID and claiming it was time to go use it to get dinner, and vanished. Apparently dinner took a while, as that was two hours ago. Sophie was alone.

Her mood sagged downward again as she recalled just how alone she was.

"So I am confused," Nikolaos said. "You can help me perhaps?"

Sophie lifted her head. "How?"

"You know where bookshop is? For the textbooks?"

"Yeah, I went there earlier. You go down the main street outside, and—"

"The street here?" He pointed in the wrong direction.

"No, right down there, by the parking lot."

"I go across a street?"

"Actually, you just go *down* the street, and…"

He crinkled up his eyes, looking hopelessly lost. "It is not far? You can show me, yes?"

Sophie gave up. Getting out of the dorm room would be a relief anyway. "I can show you. Sure."

He beamed and jumped up from the bed with her. "Thank you. It is good. You are very helping."

Stuffing her cell phone in the pocket of her denim shorts, Sophie led Nikolaos into the dorm hallway and locked her door. She turned and headed for the stairwell. Nikolaos followed, bobbing beside her, grinning too widely at everyone who passed.

They trotted down the stairs and emerged into the breezeway between Sophie's dorm and the next. Warm air rolled over them, smelling of dry grass and a thousand burgers being cooked.

"I see you moving in with your family before," Nikolaos said. "There was tall boy with hat. He is your boyfriend?"

Jacob had bravely worn his new yellow and green University of Oregon cap onto the Oregon State University campus, earning him jeers from a car full of OSU football fans.

"Yes. He's going to U of O, down in Eugene." Forty miles away. Not so far, perhaps. But until now, she had always lived in the same town with him, and with everyone else she knew.

"He does not know how lucky boy he is." As they entered the shade of a huge redwood arching its branches over the sidewalk, Nikolaos threw his arm around Sophie's shoulders. "I make him jealous, yes?"

Uh-oh, she thought. She faked a laugh. "Probably shouldn't." She tried to push his arm off, but it wouldn't budge. The boy was stronger than he looked.

While she tried to decide the nicest way to say *Hands off, dude*, Nikolaos swung to face her, snaring her in both arms. "Hold on tight."

Her face went hot in protest. She tried to twist away, still failing. "I'm serious, I—" At that second the ground heaved beneath her. Losing her balance, she tumbled into the tall grass, in Nikolaos' arms.

An earthquake? No, it had only been one jolt, no rolling or rumbling. And tall grass? Where had that come from? They'd been walking along the dorm sidewalk, next to short hedges and cropped lawn and a few giant redwoods—all of which were now gone.

As she debated whether to worry about that later and stick her thumbs in his eyes now, Nikolaos pinned her to the lumpy ground, grinning. "That was easy. We must teach you to be less trusting."

His awkward Greek accent had nearly vanished, only a trace of it remaining. He now spoke a fluent and rather British English.

He'd been faking! Bastard. The self-defense moves they'd taught her in high school gym class came sweeping back to her on a wave of fury. She slammed her knee up between his legs, and shoved both hands at his face.

He grunted, and rolled off her, clambering to his feet. "Ow. Careful." She had definitely made contact—her knee and fists throbbed from it—but he didn't appear to be in any pain.

Whatever. Time to escape. She flipped onto her front and scrambled to get her feet beneath her, but found herself being lifted by Nikolaos, who caught her around the ribs and set her upright as if she were light as paper.

When she got a look around, she froze. Golden fields rippled in the late afternoon sun. Trees dotted the hills. The buildings and people were all gone. The normal campus sounds—music, laughter, cars—had vanished with them. Leaves rustled, birds twittered, and the wind whispered; that was all.

Panic washed through her. Had he slipped her a drug of some kind? How? No, she'd surely been knocked out just now, and this was a dream, or a coma. But it felt so *real*.

"Who are you?" Her voice shook; she couldn't control it. "Where is everyone?"

He still held her by the arm, casually but firmly. "You don't believe my name is Nikolaos? It's perfectly true, I promise."

She swallowed, gaze darting around the wild terrain, her mind scrambling to recall all the details leading up to this. "And you're Greek. Sure."

"I *am* Greek. Honestly, I'm insulted you doubt me."

Sophie shot him another look, and now noticed the mature shrewdness in his green eyes. "I guess you're not eighteen, either."

"All right, you've got me there."

She looked around again, seeking any sign of the campus. Nothing. Just nature, and a lot of it. Something that sounded like the trumpet of an elephant echoed from far off.

Nikolaos let go of her for a moment to tap something on his cell phone. She seized her chance and bolted across the meadow. Her feet hit unsteady lumps and dips of ground, but she made decent speed. Thank goodness she was wearing her jogging sneakers rather than impractical sandals.

"Bad idea," called Nikolaos from behind her.

She slowed to reach into her pocket for her cell, thinking now might be a good time to try 911. But the phone wasn't there. *Crap.* She suspected she'd dropped it in the meadow, and good luck finding it in this tall grass if she had. Forget it. Escaping was more important. She put on a burst of speed.

As she reached a large oak tree, a growl brought her skidding to a halt. From the grass a lion emerged, staring at her with amber eyes. It was a *huge* lion, as tall as Sophie even when down on its four giant paws, its shoulder muscles piled high behind its short ears. Its fur was browner than any lion's she had seen in a zoo, and its mane was shorter.

She'd been scared already, but now pure primal terror chilled her from head to feet.

Though she might indeed have just stepped through some kind of magic wardrobe, this was not Aslan she was dealing with. From the predatory gaze and the saliva dripping from those fangs (which looked at least six inches long), she was sure this animal regarded her as lunch.

Oh, please, let this be a dream or a coma, she prayed. *Otherwise I'm about to die.*

Were you supposed to climb a tree when faced with a lion, or run in a zigzag pattern, or punch it in the face, or what? She couldn't recall.

Then a young man and a medium-sized dog darted in between her and the lion. The guy had curly black hair, tamer than Nikolaos', and wore all black: untucked long-sleeved shirt, jeans, and boots with laces. She couldn't see his face yet; he was staring down the lion, as was his dog. The dog's hackles bristled beneath its golden fur.

"Off you go, mate," the guy told the lion.

As if to back him up, his dog growled, and barked.

The threat worked. The lion hissed, turned tail, and bounded away into the grass.

Sophie's knees shook as her adrenaline subsided, leaving her weak.

The young man turned around to look at her. "You okay?"

He was rather lovely. Probably a couple of years older than Sophie, with olive skin, shapely mouth, and large dark eyes with black lashes and brows.

She parted her lips, found she was too upset to answer, and merely nodded.

"Please don't run," he added. "We're not going to hurt you. But the lions won't give you that guarantee. It's not safe out here."

Sophie detected a different accent in the slant of his words, Australian perhaps. She answered with another nod, more guarded this time.

Footsteps rustled up behind her, and she spun about.

But it was only Nikolaos. "Told you running off was a bad idea. But now you've met…Wat-son." He separated the syllables playfully, as if this wasn't the guy's real name.

Watson glared at Nikolaos. "Why are you dressed like that? What is *wrong* with you? Did you need to wear the most conspicuous clothes on the planet?"

"It worked, obviously," Nikolaos said. "So, I shall leave you two dears alone." He sauntered to Watson, and slipped something into his palm while murmuring a few words in a foreign language, maybe Greek again.

Watson nodded and tucked the item into his jeans pocket. His dog, meanwhile, sat and gazed calmly at each human in turn. It looked like a golden retriever crossbred with something darker, perhaps some kind of shepherd dog. It also looked gentle, not the type of animal who would rip out her throat upon command. She tried to take comfort in the gaze of the friendly dog.

The two men finished their discussion, and Nikolaos turned and executed a bow in Sophie's direction. "Sophia, it has been a pleasure. I hope we meet again soon."

She didn't dignify that with a response, only a cold gaze. *Yeah, hope we meet again. Thanks for kidnapping me, you lying jerkwad.*

Nikolaos, catching the glare, laughed, then waved and strolled away into the wilderness.

Sophie turned her wary attention to Watson, or whatever his name was. He was already studying her, but when their eyes met, he looked down and cleared his throat. "All right. Let's talk."

CHAPTER TWO

ADRIAN'S STOMACH CHURNED. HE HATED having to approach Sophie this way, loathed it. He dared another look at her. Streaks of dirt marked her slim white T-shirt from her tussle on the ground with Nikolaos. Her hair was shorter than last time Adrian had seen her, cut to just below her ears and partially pinned back. Bits of dry grass stuck to her dark brown curls. She hugged her small, curvy body as if trying to protect herself from him. Her hazel eyes watched him, sharp with distrust. Her full lips looked pale, and her light brown complexion had gone ashen.

She still looked thoroughly beautiful to him.

And, of course, she had no idea who he was. Yet.

"Am I in a coma?" she asked. "Or dead, or dreaming?"

"No. You're awake."

"Then where the hell are we? And what's with the lions?" Her voice was unsteady.

He'd asked similar questions when he first got dragged into this realm. Using stronger language, in fact. "It's kind of like another dimension," he said. He tried to sound gentle and reasonable so he wouldn't scare her further, though he suspected it wouldn't work. "It's the same geography as the living world—see, same mountain over there, same river over there—so in a sense we're still in Oregon. But only animals live here, species that evolved without humans around. There's no civilization, because humans don't live here."

"Except you. What are you?" Her eyes narrowed.

"People like Niko and me, we have certain abilities. We can switch back and forth between the realms. The animals here avoid us."

Sophie glanced at Kiri, sitting at attention beside him. "They avoid your dog too?"

"Yeah, her too." Adrian reached down to stroke Kiri's head, then straightened up again. "I had Nikolaos fetch you because I wanted to meet you."

"Why?"

Ah, there it was. The perfectly logical question he didn't dare answer in full. He swallowed. "You're important to me. I wanted you to see this place."

"Why would I be important to you? We've never met."

"Well. We have and we haven't."

"When? When have I met you?" She sounded tense and panicky.

He couldn't answer that either yet; and in fact, any partially true answer could make it sound like he was a common stalker. In all the time he'd spent planning how to meet her and talk to her, he hadn't realized how hard it would be to speak calmly when she stood in his presence, staring at him in alarm and suspicion.

He folded his arms as his stomach tensed again in nervousness. "Never mind. I'm sorry to have done it this way, but you wouldn't have believed us if we approached you and told you we've got this other realm, and invited you nicely to come see it. Would you?"

Sophie hugged herself tighter, looking out at the field. "Of course not."

"And in order to switch you from one world to the other, one of us has to be holding onto you, so Niko had to grab you like that."

"And getting me here was so important why?"

He hesitated. "You have to promise you won't tell anyone. I say that for your own protection. Niko and I can hide out here and no one'll find us. But if *you* try to convince people about this place, well, most of your time will be spent in a psychiatrist's office, which I doubt is what you want."

"Then I'm not crazy? Good. I was wondering." Clearly she was attempting sarcasm, but the tremor in her voice betrayed her fear.

"Also," he continued, "there are a few people who do know about me, and about this realm, and they're not fond of us. They're quite dangerous in fact. You do not want to be on their radar. So just promise you won't tell anyone."

"Okay. I promise." She sounded as guarded and uneasy as ever, but he was unlikely to get a more trusting pledge for now.

So Adrian drew in his breath and delivered the true but incomplete explanation: "This world is where souls go. People's souls, when they die. There's a place we can go to see them, though it's a long way from here."

Sophie stared at him several long moments without speaking. Then, evidently deciding he was mental, she spread her hands in front of her and said, "Look, if it's money you're after, my family doesn't have much. My parents run a fruit stand, we grow a little produce, but—"

"No. I know. We're not after money."

"Then…what?" The quiver was back in her voice. Probably she thought he was going to rape her or sell her into slavery.

"I'm not here to hurt you," he repeated. "I only want to talk to you. And you can't get back to the regular world by yourself, so please listen and don't run away. I'm not lying and I'm not crazy, all right? Can't you admit that this is…supernatural? That something very unusual is going on here?"

She pressed her lips together, glancing around. "Unless you or your buddy drugged me or knocked me out."

Adrian sighed, and squinted across at the mountain—Mary's Peak, they called it in the living world. "All right." He took his own smartphone from his back pocket. The other pocket held Sophie's phone, which Niko had swiped. "I asked about you, in the—the place where the souls go. Here's what I found. Watch this, then I'll take you home, I promise." He selected the video and held the phone out to her, his heart pounding.

Sophie took the phone, frowning, and tapped the screen to begin the video. Immediately she inhaled a quick breath.

"Hi, Sophie Sodapop," said her grandfather, who'd been dead over a year. Adrian kept his distance rather than watching at her shoulder, but having filmed it himself and previewed it, he knew how it looked. Sophie's grandpa smiled benevolently, but, like all the souls, glowed greenish and appeared translucent. Behind him milled other souls in the fields. The black of the cave's interior surrounded them all.

Adrian felt uneasy bringing photos or videos of the Underworld out of its borders, even into the rest of the spirit realm, but he had to convince her.

"This fellow here tells me it's September of 2012," her grandfather continued on the video, "and you're about to start college. Sounds like you chose OSU. Honey, I'm so proud."

Sophie choked back a sob, and splayed her fingers over her mouth. She kept her gaze riveted to the video. Adrian bowed his head, closing his eyes for a moment. Why was he doing this to her? Why couldn't he leave her alone? Well, he knew why. But couldn't he have found a gentler way?

"I miss you and Liam and your dad and mom," her grandfather went on, "but it's not so bad here. There's all kinds of interesting folks to talk to. I even found some old friends. Now, this boy says he can bring you here to see me, if you're willing. Sophie, I'd sure love that. I wouldn't be able to touch you, but it'd be a real treat to talk to you again. I hope you'll come. In the meantime, I love you so much, honey, and you take care of yourself."

The video ended.

Tears ran down her face. She handed the phone back to Adrian, holding her arm out to the side and not looking at him.

He took the phone, and handed her a clean cotton handkerchief from his front pocket.

She accepted it, and blew her nose.

"I'm sorry," Adrian said, then found himself talking rapidly, saying things he hadn't entirely planned to say: "When I was a kid, my mum died. Suddenly. In a routine surgery, one of those complications that isn't supposed to happen but sometimes does. And when I first went to the...that place, and found her soul, I...

was really shaken." *Was crying too hard to talk* would sound maudlin, he decided, although it was true. "Everyone feels that way. I mean, the few living people who've been there, and talked to their loved ones. It's normal. But you do get used to it after a while."

Sophie wiped her eyes. "I don't know how you did the video. Or why." Her voice sounded shakier than ever now. "But I want to go home."

His heart sank, but he had expected as much. He nodded. "Then come over here."

He walked past a few trees and over into another meadow, Kiri trotting beside him. Sophie followed at a distance of a couple of steps. Adrian stopped by a stake with fluorescent orange flagging tied to its top.

"Here's the spot we picked as safe to reappear. Safer than, like, the middle of the street or something."

Eyes reddened, Sophie glanced at the stake. She moved her hand to her back pocket, and exhaled a sigh. "Right, I lost my phone. Great."

"Oh. Here." Adrian pulled the purple-cased smartphone from his pocket and offered it to her. "Niko picked your pocket. Didn't want you causing a panic by dialing 911."

She grabbed it, then gazed in abstraction at its screen. "I probably ought to. But I don't know what I'd say."

"Really, don't. Please. It'll only complicate things for you."

Sophie lowered her arm without dialing anyone.

He hesitated. "Listen. The souls, your grandfather, this whole realm…it barely scratches the surface of the things I want to show you."

She met his gaze, her face tense and disturbed. "How do I know it's real?"

"How could I have faked it? That's what I want you to think about for a few days."

"Then what? What happens after a few days?"

"I'll ask you again if you want to come with me."

Her eyebrows darted closer together. "You're going to kidnap me again?"

Adrian tried a smile. "No, I'll ask you if you *want* to be kidnapped again."

Sophie looked away, declining to answer. After a moment, she glanced at the crumpled handkerchief and held it out to him. "Yours."

"Nah, keep it. Maybe it'll convince you this was real. So will this." From the breast pocket of his shirt he took a bit of white linen, and unfolded it. A violet with red petals lay within, partially wilted. He'd picked it several hours ago, in the Underworld. He handed the flower to her.

She took it and studied it, looking pensive. Maybe she'd realize you couldn't easily find a violet with red petals and a stem so pale green it was nearly white. Only in the Underworld, in fact.

"All right, then." Adrian stepped closer to her.

She recoiled a few quick steps.

"I have to be holding onto you," he repeated. "In order to take you back."

"Oh. Fine." She kept her eyes averted, but held still.

Adrian settled his hands on her waist.

The low evening sun sparkled in her eyes as she gazed past him. The wind blew the scent of her hair to him, feminine and earthy. He would have gladly laid his face in it and breathed it for hours. As indeed he used to.

He drew her up against him, feeling their bodies touch at knees and hips and chest. "Ready?" he asked. "May want to hold on."

Her lips flattened. She settled her hands on his shoulders, one hand still clutching the phone.

"Here goes." He tightened his hold on her, and the tip of his nose brushed her forehead. He reached for the living world.

The ground shoved upward beneath their feet, and flattened out into smooth concrete. Swaying in the moment of tipped balance, Adrian found himself leaning against a wall. Steadying Sophie, who had also stumbled, he stood upright, then let go of her.

She gasped, turning in circles and looking at everything: the neon signs in restaurant windows, the sheets of paper stuck to a bulletin board in the breezeway where they stood, the tamed ivy crawling out of a stone planter near their feet. The sounds of cars and distant conversations and music thrummed around them. Moving aside, she peeked out of the concrete enclosure, and the bewilderment cleared from her face.

"Your dorm's right across there." Adrian pointed toward the grassy square with an X of sidewalks traversing it.

"Yeah. I recognize it, thanks." Back to the sarcasm, evidently.

"I'll talk to you in a few days."

"Don't count on it." She started walking away.

"Sophie."

She paused to hear him, but didn't turn all the way around.

"I'm truly sorry for doing it this way. I know it's hard to believe, but hurting you, or even scaring you, is the last thing I want to do." He gave a soft laugh, as a stream of poignant memories whispered past in his mind. "We seem meant to cause trouble for each other, you and I."

She frowned at him, looking as if she honestly wanted to understand. "Will you still be watching me?" she asked, the words carrying a quiver of fright. "Are you going to come after me again?"

"Not unless you want me to."

She didn't care for the evasion in the words—he could tell by her lingering frown.

Laughter and voices danced closer; other students were approaching. Adrian inhaled a cautious breath. "I should go."

"Wait. What *was* all that? And why me?"

"If you really want to know, come with me next time. Goodbye, Sophie."

She stepped toward him in protest, but he slipped back into the spirit realm, and she vanished along with the rest of the city. The concrete gave way to meadow dirt under his boots. Tall grass brushed against his knees.

He sank into the field, stretching out on his back. Kiri yipped in delight and ran over to lick his face, then flopped down next to him. Adrian drank in the sight of the sky. Puffballs of cloud edged with gold reflected the setting sun, and on the horizon stood a bank of curdled gray thunderheads.

"But will she come again?" he asked Kiri. "Or did I scare her off?"

Kiri yawned, and delivered an indeterminate grumble.

"Yeah," Adrian said. "We'll see." He filled his lungs with the sweet meadow air, and closed his eyes. "Oh, but it was so good to see her."

CHAPTER THREE

SOPHIE CROSSED THE GRASS, HER ankles trembling. She brought up her text messages as she walked. Several had piled up in the half hour she'd been away—wherever exactly "away" was.

The first text made her eyes widen. *R U ok?* her roommate Melissa had sent. *Just saw a guy tackle you then it looked like you disappeared?? Where are you?*

"Crap," Sophie whispered, thinking of the damage control she'd have to perform.

Then her heart pounded, and she leaned sideways against the brick wall of her dorm as she reached it. To an outside observer it looked like she disappeared? Then she *had* slipped into another dimension, realm, whatever? It hadn't been a dream? Because a dream was her only explanation.

But a dream wouldn't have dropped her outside the dorm, holding a borrowed hankie and a little red flower.

Quickly she scanned the other messages: Tabitha asking what she was up to tonight, Jacob checking in, her mom and Liam checking in too. Sophie fired off responses to reassure them—*Not sure yet, still have to finish unpacking* to Tabitha; similar lines, with *Love you* included, to the other three. With her emotions shaken by that video of Grandpop, Sophie felt inclined to tell her nearest and dearest that she loved them.

As she entered the dorm and climbed the stairs, however, she realized that by sending reassurance texts and pretending everything was fine, she was covering up for Watson and Nikolaos. The smart thing to do, if you were kidnapped or assaulted, was to call the authorities right away, and to tell your friends that something outrageous and unacceptable had just happened to you.

But Watson was right, wasn't he? She couldn't explain it the way it really happened. If she did, mental health specialists would converge upon her and examine her brain. If she went down that path, she wouldn't get to be a normal student, hanging out with other dorm-mates and eating cheap pizza, let alone studying.

Maybe it didn't happen, she thought, walking down the corridor toward her room, staring at the homemade cloth signs and posters the other girls had already started decorating their doors with. Maybe she'd dreamed it. She curled her fingers around the handkerchief and the violet, feeling their slightly damp, very real textures. Except it did happen, didn't it?

"There you are," Melissa greeted. She was sitting at her desk, fingers on computer keyboard.

Sophie had entered the room almost without noticing. She put on a smile. "Hey. Just got your text. I was—yeah, I'm fine." She sat on her bed and slipped off her sneakers. Dust and dry grass seeds stuck to their laces. Maybe if you looked closely you'd find crazy huge-ass lion hairs, she thought.

"Who was the guy? What happened?" Melissa sounded placid, but vaguely concerned. She pulled the ponytail band from her hair and wove it around her fingers, flexing the elastic as she watched Sophie.

"He was just some guy I was giving directions to." Sophie turned the violet over in her palm. Violets were never red, to her knowledge, and they didn't have that whitish cast to their stems. Maybe it wasn't a violet.

"But I was behind you, near the dorm, and I swear it looked like you both disappeared into thin air when he tackled you."

Sophie chuckled, and brought up the photo of Nikolaos on her phone, though she didn't show it to Melissa. "Yeah, he was being an ass. I told him off, and then…walked around to cool down a while."

"But you *disappeared*."

"What, like into another dimension?" Sophie tried to put a skeptical spin on it, throwing Melissa a smile.

Melissa was quiet a second. She rotated the elastic band between finger and thumb. "I guess it doesn't make any sense. Must have been a trick of the light."

Sophie shrugged, lowering her gaze to her phone again, where she had caught the back of Nikolaos' head and his striped outfit. She wished she had snapped a shot of Watson. She felt like studying his face would provide some kind of answer or proof, though of course it wouldn't.

A moment later, Melissa turned back to her computer and resumed typing, evidently shrugging off the strange notion of Sophie's vanishing act.

Sophie moved to her own desk and switched on her laptop, and sat gazing at the violet while the computer started up. Violets were spring flowers, and this was September. That was another odd point, along with the color. Maybe in a greenhouse someone could grow a red violet, and could do so any time of year. Or in the southern hemisphere—it was spring down there. Watson's accent did sound sort of Australian. Not that the flower itself mattered much.

Tonight she had expected to be focusing on practical matters: finding food and textbooks, getting to know her roommate and hall neighbors, wandering around campus to locate her classrooms, deciding exactly how much she missed home and her boyfriend and what, if anything, she would do about it.

Instead, one half-hour had thrown her mind into a new orbit.

A spirit world of strange animals. A land of ghosts, where Grandpop now walked. Someone who could switch back and forth between them, and was going to invite her to come visit again soon—or possibly just show up and steal her.

What would she say when he asked?

THE NEXT MORNING, groggy after a night of inadequate sleep, she found her way to the dining hall and ate breakfast with Melissa. The coffee and cereal and banana revived her, though all tasted duller and staler than she would have liked.

With an hour to kill before her freshman orientation meetings started for the day, Sophie got onto her blog.

She found a few comments from her post two days ago, where she'd announced she was off to college and therefore probably couldn't blog about fruits, vegetables, and nutrition for a few days. The comments wished her good luck and successful studies, but they were all from people she'd never met in real life.

Still, there was one from her favorite and cleverest commenter, Kiwi Ade, who wrote, *Best of luck. Looking forward to hearing about your adventures. Hope only the loveliest things happen to you.*

His kindness eased the lump of agitation inside her, and made her smile. His comment, as always, was more mature and considerate than the ones she usually got. (For example, from some girl on this post: *Have fun Sophie, dont let the frat boys mix you a drink, there way strong lol.*)

Though she'd never even seen a picture of him, Kiwi Ade was one of those people she'd met online whose words alone made her think she could probably date him, if they were unattached and living in the same country. At some point he had mentioned being from New Zealand (thus the "Kiwi" part of his nickname, she supposed), and he came across as young, maybe her own age. Most importantly, he had good taste in music and books, not to mention produce, judging from the discussions they'd gotten into on her comment threads.

But the thought of New Zealand instantly sent her mind to Watson, the possibly-Australian, possibly-Kiwi, definitely paranormal young fellow with videos of dead guys on his phone.

Hey, Kiwi Ade, she considered answering, *do you know anyone in your country or Australia who might be interested in kidnapping me? Someone with supernatural powers, maybe?*

Without typing anything, she closed the browser window and set out for her orientation meeting.

Her day didn't improve much, despite occasional texts from Jacob, Tabitha, and Liam.

In particular, Tabitha's texts frustrated her, referencing things Sophie couldn't possibly know about. *Voice practice today. Auditions next week, & competition is f'ing fierce around here.* Tabitha was attending Cornish College of the Arts in Seattle, with the aim to become a professional singer. Cornish probably put on dozens of productions a year, and Sophie had no idea which one Tabitha currently had her eye on.

Auditions for what? Sophie texted back. *Hope you get to relax later.*

Parsifal, Tabitha answered. *Yep, some gay guys invited me to a Bdwy (CapHl) club tonight. Hope the gay gals are there too!*

Was "Parsifal" an opera or a composer?, Sophie wondered, irritated. Tabitha had to realize Sophie didn't know these things. And it took Sophie a full minute to figure out that "Bdwy (CapHl)" meant "Broadway, Capitol Hill"—Seattle's gay Mecca. Tabitha was a lesbian, and until now Sophie had been her wing-woman in the limited opportunities they'd had to go out and flirt with people. Now Tab would rely on some group of sophisticated Cornish College people Sophie had never met.

Good luck, she texted, and put away her phone, lonelier than ever.

It was only a couple of years ago that Sophie had held Tabitha sobbing in her arms, after some girls in their class had lodged snotty, "formal" complaints about having a lesbian share the locker room with them. "It makes us feel weird," they had said. And though the teachers had concluded there was nothing they could do except keep allowing Tab to use the locker room like all the other girls, and had asked all the young ladies to respect one another's privacy, the gossip had flashed throughout the town.

Tab had been out to her closest friends and family before, but now she was out to everyone, like it or not. People snickered and stared and sent half-audible whispered comments at Tab's back. Sophie had wanted to grab a baseball bat and murder the snotty girls and anyone else who made a remark, but all she could do was hold Tab and stand by her, and tell off some of the nastiest commenters. That gave her the reputation of being Tab's girlfriend, of course, which was so patently ridiculous she didn't even care—or tried not to. Tabitha's parents did their best to console their daughter too, but they were in the middle of a divorce, and had no time or energy for dealing with much else. Sophie had kept Tab from collapsing, almost single-handedly.

Now Tabitha didn't even need her anymore. She was already making new friends and living a glamorous city life.

Meanwhile, Sophie was losing her mind and being introduced to kidnappers, and needed a friend more than ever. But she couldn't tell anyone what had happened to her, not without sounding crazy.

For the next few days, she stumbled through her new college existence, her mind and heart only half in it. Every time her phone buzzed with a call or text, adrenaline shot through her body. But it was never Watson.

The things he had shown her and told her seemed real. They *felt* real. Her instincts insisted he wasn't lying. Hiding things, sure, lots of them probably; but not lying.

And he had a dog, a nice dog. He couldn't be too evil or dangerous if he had such a great dog. She smirked at herself for thinking that, yet on some level it still struck her as a reliable deduction.

She sat with other girls and boys from her dorms and classes, and listened absently as they shared stories of "amazing" things that had happened to them. Sophie could beat all their stories with her single otherworldly encounter, if she wanted. Not that anyone would believe her.

In meetings, professors and campus officials congratulated her on the academic adventure she was about to undertake, and warned her of the physical and financial dangers of campus life. Adventure? Danger? she thought. Compared to the ghost-world and its huge lions, Oregon State University didn't look so dramatic.

She did believe it was real, she silently admitted to herself on Friday night, twirling the now-dried violet between her fingers. She saw no way it could have been faked. Or perhaps she only *wanted* to believe it?

Half the time she dreaded Watson's reappearance, fearing he'd leap out and steal her again without warning. The other half of the time, she wanted to see him, to demand explanations, to learn how he did all that. To visit Grandpop in person. If she never saw Watson again, she had to confess, it would be totally frustrating.

On Saturday night, two days before classes would begin, Sophie attended a party for the students of the Nutrition department. In a crowded classroom with food spread on the table, she mingled, holding a fruit-and-vegetable juice smoothie. Within twenty minutes she was utterly tired of telling people her history and plans.

I'm Sophie. I grew up in Carnation, Washington. It's east of Seattle. My family owns a produce stand and that's why I chose Nutrition. I want to help people choose foods that are better for them, and grow their own food too. Because they'd all be healthier.

It had seemed so important when she decided upon her major—a mission to improve the health of the general populace; what could be nobler? But tonight her mind obsessed over concerns of a far more fascinating nature, and she spoke to everyone with near-indifference.

She wandered outside with her smoothie, letting the night breeze cool her skin. Sitting alone on the steps of the lecture hall, she checked her phone again for messages. Nothing.

She could go back to the dorm. Another party was getting started there. "Don't tell, but someone's bringing beer," one of the girls in her hall had whispered to her, starry-eyed, as if obtaining beer was the height of lifetime accomplishment. Tabitha and Jacob were each probably doing something similar in their new environments on this Saturday night: drinking booze and chatting with people. Like proper college students.

Sophie had drunk beer a few times, but didn't love it. She pictured the boys in her dorm, of whom she'd now met a handful. She imagined them tackling her the way Nikolaos had, with more mundane motives. She grimaced. *So* not interested.

The breeze strengthened, growing colder. Sophie sat shivering, her mind traveling to her family and friends.

A week ago, she would have said her two biggest worries in

life were relationship issues: hers and Jacob's, and her mother's and father's.

A month ago, she'd seen her mother kissing another man in a car by the Carnation public library. She'd told no one except Tabitha, who urged her to stay out of it. Sophie had obeyed, but the worry of her parents possibly divorcing had been eating holes in her stomach.

And Jacob. Five months ago, just before graduating, they had admitted in a late-night texting session to a mutual crush on one another. He had snuck over to her house and they'd shared their first kiss, on the porch at 12:30 on a spring night, neither of them able to wait until morning. April, May, and June passed in a state of bliss. Then her happiness diminished, chipping away bit by bit as arguments with him cropped up on small but annoying topics. She always attributed the disagreements to the stress of college looming ahead, and made up with him each time.

Still, the day before leaving for Corvallis, she had found herself sitting on the fence regarding whether to break up with him before going away to school. Ultimately she hadn't even brought it up. She couldn't bear the thought of arriving in a new town not only alone, but with one of her closest ties freshly severed.

Now she wondered if it would have mattered. They were growing apart anyway. The last few days, even while comparing freshman-orientation stories with him via text, she felt distantly separated from him. Their paths seemed to have diverged. So, what to do?

Her phone buzzed with a new text. She looked at the screen.

David was the sender's name.

Though she knew a few Davids, she wasn't on close enough terms with any of them to expect a text from them. She opened the message.

Are you interested in being kidnapped again, then?

She clenched her fingers around the phone. Her shivers became trembling. Breathing in flutters, she shot a look around, as if he might be texting her from ten feet away. But only a few pairs of students strolled down the nearby sidewalks, no one she recognized.

She leaped up, descended the steps, and paced back and forth under a lamp post. The air smelled of damp crushed grass. An evening star gleamed over a treetop.

What would she say? Why hadn't she decided on her answer in the past few days?

Well, if going back to the dorm or the party sounded no fun, and texting her friends was going to be equally unsatisfying, and if all she was going to do was wonder about Watson and Nikolaos the rest of her life…

Rather than text him back, she selected his number and examined it. It likely belonged to another country, to judge from the extra-long chain of digits. She tapped "Call," and lifted the phone to her ear, listening to it ring.

CHAPTER FOUR

OLDING HIS PHONE, ADRIAN PACED back and forth along the steep grassy slope atop Mary's Peak, in the light of the camping lantern he had set on the ground. Kiri raced up and down the hill, tongue flying out the side of her jaws, retrieving every stick he threw for her. Only five minutes had passed since he had texted Sophie, and already he was going mad with impatience.

Adrian had remained in Oregon—or, technically, the corresponding region in the spirit world—for most of the time since their meeting four days ago. He had chosen the nearest scenic mountaintop, because lurking in the region of Corvallis would have felt *too* close to her, as if he really were a stalker.

Honestly, how am I not? he asked himself, irritated.

Regardless, he had gone back to the Underworld only long enough to fetch some of his camping gear, then returned here. He'd forced himself to wait a few days, to let her curiosity build up and to make sure she didn't contact the police. As far as he could tell, she hadn't. In the old bus pulled by the horses, he had flown to the top of Mary's Peak and set up a tent in the forest. His only trips away had been quick jaunts to Southern California, to bathe in lakes that were warm, rather than frigid like the waters in Oregon. But living in the wilderness like this, rather than clearing his head like it was supposed to, was making him feel more like a social outcast than ever.

Up here, twelve hundred meters above sea level, the wind was chilly and the air felt nothing like late summer. Stars quivered overhead, and a faint band of blue sky lingered in the west. Mist was already forming around the mountaintop, shreds of it slipping past him.

His mobile rang, electrifying his nerves all over again—especially when a look at the screen showed him the desired name. *Sophie*.

He cleared his throat and answered. "Hello."

He heard her draw in her breath. Silence for a few seconds. Then: "What is your name? Really?"

"It's Adrian. Watson was just…an alias."

"The phone said 'David' when you texted me."

"Yeah, that's another alias. I figured it was kind of a generic name; no one would notice it. So…?"

"Before I say whether or not I'll go with you," she warned, "I have to tell you I don't like what you did with Grandpop."

"I can understand."

"You used him as a…a hostage."

A burst of static hissed across the line, in tandem with a gust of wind. Adrian picked up the lantern and walked toward the trees. "Not a hostage. A bribe. Because I want you to come with me."

"What do I have to give up, to come with you? To have you explain all this?"

Smart questions. She'd been thinking about this intelligently, as he'd hoped. "Nothing too bad," he said. "You don't have to give up your soul or anything like that. But you may give up some safety. And you have to start keeping a heap of secrets."

"So if I say I'll come, then what? You pick me up and we go to this…afterlife place? To see Grandpop?"

"Right."

"And you'll bring me straight back afterward."

"Yes. But…"

"But what?" she countered.

"You'll have a couple more choices to make on the way."

"Such as?"

"Um…" He leaned against a tree trunk. Kiri loped toward him

and circled the tree, sniffing the ground. "I'd rather show you in person. It'll make more sense."

"And you swear I won't be in any danger."

"Well. No one can ever promise that, can they." They were both silent a second, then Adrian added, "I promise *I* won't hurt you. And I'll do my best not to let anything else hurt you either."

"Why should I believe you?"

"No good reason. Except that you're curious. Aren't you?"

Longer silence. Then she said, "Fine, come get me."

"Tonight? Now?"

"I'm not busy. Might as well."

He began breathing faster. "Fifteen minutes, at the spot where I saw you last?"

"All right."

"Oh, and Sophie—dress warm."

"Fine. I'll be there." She hung up.

Tingling with excitement, Adrian shoved his phone into his coat pocket. *You can't swoop in and kiss her when you pick her up, you know*, he reminded himself. *Not today, likely not even this month.*

Nevertheless, he jogged back to the bus's parking spot beneath the swaying fir trees, and dug through his stuff to find his electric razor to get rid of his scruffy three-day beard. Least you could do when going to meet a girl.

I'M CRAZY, SOPHIE thought. *This is incredibly dangerous.* Going off some inaccessible place with a guy she barely knew? It was not her usual style and not an activity she'd recommend to anyone she cared about.

Then again, several people at tonight's campus parties were probably hooking up with strangers too—though in a more sexual and less supernatural fashion. Risky either way. So maybe this was Sophie's method of going wild at college.

She jogged back to her dorm room to change into jeans and fetch a zip-up hooded sweatshirt, then ran across the quad to their meeting spot. It was a dead-end corner off a breezeway, beneath a tall building with restaurants on the street level and student housing on the upper floors. Only the planter with the ivy and a few faded flyers tacked to a utility pole shared the space with her.

She bounced up and down on her toes in nervousness, pretending to read her texts as an excuse for standing alone in a dark corner. It surprised her when a new message crystallized before her eyes.

Coast clear? Adrian texted.

She glanced around, and answered, *Yes*. Then she kept her gaze fixed on the phone, hardly daring to breathe.

A gust of wind swirled around between the walls. A pair of black boots, their edges and laces mud-splattered, materialized a yard from her feet. She moved her gaze up the dark jeans, past the thigh-length hem of a black wool coat lined with plaid flannel, to the solemn face of the young man standing there. The loose curls of his black hair stirred in the wind. His jaw looked tensely set, and his dark eyes glimmered from their shadowed hollows. The red neon light in the nearest shop window cast a glow across the planes of his forehead and cheeks, making his skin look perfectly smooth and strangely beautiful.

Her memory hadn't failed her. He was one of the hottest guys she had ever met. But unlike Jacob or the other boys she had found "hot" in her life so far, Adrian was attractive in a different way—a more mature way. More like a man than a boy.

He stepped closer, sliding his hands around her waist cautiously. "Hi."

"Hi." She looked aside as he hugged her tight for a moment and performed that trick where the civilized world vanished. They wobbled in the tall grass, clutching each other for balance. Sweet forest-and-meadow air blew across Sophie's face, and swirled up a whiff of Adrian's scent too—the enticing and healthy smell of a young man who'd been walking in the fresh air. Uneasy, she wriggled her arm to get free.

He let go of her. A camping lantern sat on the ground, its LED bulb illuminating the orange-flagged stake. His dog sat next to it, tail wagging.

Sophie stretched out her hand to let the dog sniff it. "Is your dog a he or a she?"

"She. This is Kiri."

After receiving a calm lick on the fingers from Kiri, Sophie folded her arms and looked around. "No lions tonight?"

"None that I've seen. Saw some mammoth-type things earlier."

"Mammoths?"

"Yeah. They took off when they saw Kiri and me."

"Do they keep away because of your 'abilities'?"

"I assume so. We must smell strange to them, is all I can figure."

"If this is the ghost world, why are there living animals?"

"Same way there are living plants, I guess. They evolved here. Differently than they evolved in our world—that's why the weird species."

"Then why didn't people evolve here?" she asked.

"Maybe they did, long ago, then died out. Or maybe the only humans meant to be here are spirits."

"And people like you."

He shrugged, looking away.

Beneath the starry sky lay the same wilderness she remembered from the day Nikolaos nabbed her, or what little she could see of it in the dark. The trees and grasses bent in gusts of wind. A streak of greenish light shot from one horizon to the other, like a long-lived meteor or an extremely fast plane.

"What was that?" Sophie asked.

"A soul. Someone on their way to the—the place where they go."

"You mean someone who just died?"

"Yeah."

Chilled, she turned to scan the rest of the sky. "So that's the direction we go if we want to visit Grandpop."

"Yes. But it's kind of a long flight."

She looked at him. "Flight?"

He picked up the lantern. Pale blue beams forked upward onto his face. "Come see."

He led Sophie across the field, swinging the lantern between them. She picked her way carefully through the long grass, which covered an uneven ground on which you could easily twist an ankle. Adrian rounded a stand of trees, and stopped.

A team of four ghost horses waited there—or at least she assumed they were ghosts, as they were glowing green and translucent the same way Grandpop had in the video. The horses were harnessed to a small rusty bus, which looked as if it had been recently borrowed from a junkyard. All its window glass was gone, and nothing was left of its paint except a few flakes of green and what seemed to be the remains of a letter X in blue. The three tires she could see from this side were completely flat. The horses' harnesses were entwined in vines of some kind, with a few dried leaves still hanging on in spots. Where the harnesses met the bus, thick metal cables took over, so heavily welded that they had melted into the bus's exterior and become a part of it.

After taking in this strange contraption, Sophie looked at Adrian.

"So your first big decision is," he said, "are you willing to climb into this bus with me and fly across the world at incredibly high speeds?"

She gave a laugh of half-panic, half-disbelief. She walked around the back of the bus, touching its dented exterior. It felt solid enough. "What is this thing?"

"Something I built, to attach the horses to."

"Is it safe?"

"Well, it's held together so far."

She circled to the other side, finding those tires flat too. "Is there any other way to get to the afterlife place?"

"Not realistically. This realm isn't set up for living humans. We'd have to walk across the continent, then build a boat to cross the ocean, all of which would take months and be far more dangerous, so—yeah, this is it. This or ride directly on one of the horses."

Circling around to the front, Sophie examined the horses. She approached one and reached out slowly. Her hand slipped straight through its glowing neck, but stopped upon the solid harness that secured it to its team. She tried it again, watching her hand glide through the animal as if it were made of mist. Fascination was starting to push out uneasiness, at least for the moment.

"It's not as comfortable, riding the horses for that long," Adrian added. "Especially if we're both sharing a saddle. The seat in the bus is nicer."

She kept passing her hand through the horse's body. "So it's across an ocean? What part of the world?"

"I'd rather not say yet. I don't want to plant ideas in your head."

His answer didn't make much sense, but she was growing used to that. "How long is the trip?" She tried stroking the animal's nose, but her fingers went straight through that too. The horse twitched its ears and whickered patiently.

"About three hours each way," he said. "So, if you want to sleep on it, you can go back to bed tonight, and we'd take off tomorrow morning. Or—"

"Let's go," she interrupted. She moved to the open door of the bus and peered up into it.

"Now?" Adrian's pitch rose in surprise. "You'd be up all night."

"I'm not tired. You wanted me to come. Let's do it." Though fear fluttered again in her belly, she felt a bit steadier when she took control. She climbed into the bus. The horses' glow lit the vehicle well enough for her to see its interior. The door was missing, and none of the original seats remained inside. Instead it contained two mismatched bench seats, looking like they'd been pinched from other cars, one bench in the region of the driver's seat and the other behind it. Some bundles and bags were strapped under the seats. The rest of the bus was empty, its floor rusty but more or less clean.

"Okay." Adrian walked around to the door and climbed in too. Kiri leaped in after him, taking the steps in one bound.

"Just going to let my friends know I'll be out tonight." Standing beside the seat, Sophie tapped a text that she copied to Tabitha, Jacob, and Melissa: *Staying with some people from the party tonight. M, don't expect me till morning. All is fine though. See you.*

Tabitha and Jacob, of course, were in different cities and

wouldn't know if she slept in her dorm room or not, but it felt safer to let a few various people know where she was.

Not that she was telling them the *truth* about where she was.

Sophie watched the text whoosh away, then glanced around at the dark landscape. "How come you can text and call the regular world from here, but can't see it? Or hear it or touch it or anything?"

"Certain frequencies of electricity or radio waves get through to here. Just another oddity." He buttoned up his coat to the neck, then handed her another bundle of black cloth, which looked to be a wool blanket when she unfolded it. "You'll want that," he said. He sat on the driver's seat, gathering up a riding whip from the floor. Behind the seat, Kiri turned around in a complete circle, then lay on the floor, chin on her front paws.

Sophie sat next to Adrian, the blanket bunched up on her lap.

"Buckle up." He fastened his seatbelt, and nodded to hers.

She found the two ends of the lap belt, which was the kind you'd encounter in an old pickup truck, and clicked them together over her lap.

He hooked his arm into hers. "The seatbelts are old and don't work terribly well," he explained, "especially at the speed we'll be going. So it's really important you hold on and stay near me. Ready?"

Suddenly terrified, she only nodded.

Adrian snapped the whip out the empty windshield, saying the word "Home" as he did so, evidently a directive to the horses.

They launched off, shooting up into the sky like rockets, pulling the bus with them.

The force crushed her back against the seat and stole her breath away. This was what G-forces must feel like to jet pilots, she thought as the world blurred past in blue, black, and flashes of reflected starlight. The notion of looking for signs of human habitation became laughable. She could barely distinguish one entire forest from another at the rate the landmarks were flying past.

"So if I die here," she said, raising her voice to counter the roar of the wind, "do I die in real life?"

"Unfortunately, yes." He clutched her arm tighter against his side.

As the horses reached their cruising speed, or so she assumed, the force eased, and she was able to move a bit more freely. But the shapes of mountains ahead still approached at a reckless speed. "How fast are we going?"

"The speed of souls. From doing the time-and-distance maths, I'd say it's a bit over three thousand kilometers an hour."

That scared her into shutting her mouth and holding still.

The bus tipped up, up, up into shockingly cold air, and skimmed over the snowy caps of a mountain range before plunging down again. Her ears popped with the altitude change. Sophie realized the mountains had been the Cascades, which should have been at least an hour's drive away by car, yet they'd zoomed over them within a few minutes of take-off.

She stared at him. "How can we possibly be going this fast? I mean, without the wind or the G-forces or whatever ripping us to pieces?"

"Not really sure." He kept watching the horses, but tilted his head closer to hers as he spoke. "Our best guess is some kind of aura. Either from the horses or from us. Or a combination of both."

"From you? Who *are* you guys?"

"We're on your side," Adrian said. "Try not to worry."

"How long have you been doing this? Coming to this other world and flying around?"

"Couple of years."

"And you're sure you know what you're doing?"

"Well. Mostly sure."

She watched the continent flow past beneath her. The horses kept the bus just above the treetops, but not a single car headlight or street lamp sparkled anywhere around them. It really did seem to be a world free of humans.

She shivered in the cold air. The wind, though not as strong as it should have been, still hit hard and stripped away the summer warmth from above the land. No wonder Adrian had buttoned up his coat. She shook open the blanket and wrapped it around herself. The blanket's wool felt scratchy against her hands and neck, but it took the chill off.

"So before you started hanging out with ghosts, where did you live?" she asked. "Australia?"

"Close."

"New Zealand?"

He glanced halfway in her direction, not meeting her gaze, then looked forward again.

The insight sparked to life in her mind with a jolt. "Adrian from New Zealand," she said. "*Kiwi Ade*?"

He held his spine stiff. "I *was* going to tell you."

"Why didn't you tell me right off the bat, the other day?" she said, infuriated.

"I didn't want you to go looking me up, sending police to my house, anything like that."

"I thought you said the police were no threat," she accused. "You said you could hide out over here and they'd never find you."

"I could, and they wouldn't. But it'd cause a lot of worry for my dad, and I'd rather not have a police record even if no one does find me."

"So you follow my blog. That's why you decided to come steal me?"

"No. I—"

"All these months we were posting nice comments back and forth, you were planning on how you'd reel me in with your weird skills?" Why it angered her, she couldn't say. It wasn't like he could have explained to her about this other world and his weird skills. But the dishonesty and sneakiness still creeped her out and made her genuinely angry.

Adrian huffed out a short breath. "You make it sound like I found you on the Internet and got obsessed and decided to stalk you. That's not how it is at all."

"Then why don't you tell me how it is?" She scooted farther from him, and in his agitation, he let her.

"Trust me and wait, all right?" Adrian said.

"Trust you? That's—"

The bus jolted; possibly the horses were dodging a hill. Sophie's seatbelt unsnapped itself, and she toppled over, catching a frightening glimpse of dark hills rolling past beneath the open door before Adrian yanked her back up. Even in her terror, she noticed he lifted her with seemingly no effort at all, just as Nikolaos had.

"For God's sake, stay close." He sounded scared, if gruff. He held her firmly, this time with his arm all the way around her. The steel grip of his muscles lightened to a warm human hold. The scent of his skin, swirling around her in the wind, somehow made her feel calmer. And, after all, he *had* just saved her.

She sucked in a deep breath, refastened her seatbelt, and leaned back on his shoulder.

"Is super-strength one of your abilities?" she asked, as her heart slowed down from its mad gallop.

"Yeah," he answered, but didn't elaborate.

Stars by the thousands gleamed in the sky. The bus pitched over the next range of hills, then leveled out again over the lowlands.

She stayed silent, still processing the fact that this was her online friend Kiwi Ade, now with her arm close around her, carrying her away in a flying bus drawn by spirit horses.

Adrian seemed to be thinking along the same lines. "You're important to me," he finally said, "for reasons far beyond your blog. And I know that sounds insane and stalkerish, but I promise you'll understand eventually. If you choose to."

"If I choose to?"

"It's your next decision."

One more mountain range passed beneath them, in a bumpy swath and a breath of pine-scented air. Then the land gave way to ocean, and the smell of saltwater drenched her nose. The bus ride smoothed out flat again. They shot forward through the star-strewn darkness like a comet. Adrian stayed silent, his arm around Sophie.

A glow beside the carriage caught her attention. She looked

aside and blinked in wonder. A person flew beside them, like Superman, at the same speed as the horses. It was an old woman in a polka-dotted dress, with her sparse white hair in a braid down her back. And, like the horses, she glowed.

A human ghost. Up close and in person this time.

The old woman looked at them and smiled, then accelerated and zoomed ahead, her glow soon vanishing in the distance. Now that Sophie looked around, she saw other streaks from time to time, all headed the same way across the ocean.

"Souls," she said.

Adrian nodded. "We'll see more and more as we get closer."

She was about to visit the afterlife. Suddenly it sounded ghastly instead of intriguing. She let her head sink back onto the stiff, cracked leather seat. She closed her eyes and tried merely to breathe.

CHAPTER FIVE

THE GLOW OF A SUNRISE penetrated her eyelids. Sophie opened her eyes and looked around, disconcerted. She wondered if those minutes spent tucked under Adrian's arm had been longer than she realized. However, at the speed they were traveling, they could have covered several time zones and swung around the Earth to meet the sun again. She squinted at the bright green and brown mass of land that swept forward from the misty ocean.

"Europe?" she asked. "Africa?"

"Really, I shouldn't tell you." Adrian sounded tired.

Annoyed, Sophie drew an inch away from him, though keeping close enough this time to stay safe.

The air warmed as the sun rose. Wherever they were going, it wasn't the Arctic. Adrian pulled up on the reins, and their speed slackened. She caught glimpses of dark blue sea, white beaches on a curving shore, green hills, and expanses of beige earth.

"Hang on." Adrian tightened his arm, gripping her close. The horses dived straight down in a vertical descent, pulling the bus with them. It was like being dropped in the world's highest roller coaster, and Sophie's heart rose to her throat. Watching the ground swoop up to meet them, she couldn't help making a squeak of terror. He wouldn't crash them straight into the ground, right? Would he?

At the last second, she made out the crooked black shape of a cave mouth in the rocks below. The horses and bus plunged through it. Darkness engulfed them.

With a thud and an echoing splash, and not nearly as much bone-breaking clatter as she expected, they landed. Everything went still. She sat up and tested her limbs, stretching each one. Nothing injured. Incredible.

While Adrian tucked away the whip, Sophie leaned out of the glassless windshield and looked around. They were in a deep cave, at the edge of an underground river. A blue piece of sky glimmered a hundred feet above them at the cave's entrance. A stream of transparent humans—souls, like the old woman she'd seen—flowed steadily down into the cave, and flew along the river into a tunnel. Her jaw dropped.

Adrian nodded toward the doorway. "Hop out."

Sophie dropped the blanket on the seat. The cave air was mildly cool but comfortable, with an occasional breath of warmth blowing down from above. She gripped the door frame and descended to the stone floor. Ghosts continued flying past, sending curious glances or smiles toward the two of them. It gave Sophie goosebumps.

Adrian jumped out of the bus, dragged the reins along the floor, and tied them to a large metal ring chained to a stalagmite. The ghost horses, meanwhile, stood calmly, with an occasional toss of their immaterial manes, as if content to have arrived home.

Kiri leaped down too, and stood watching Adrian, head lifted.

Adrian finished tying up the horses, and turned to Sophie. "Come on." He walked toward the tunnel.

It looked thoroughly dark in there, the pure blackness of a cave. But she had nowhere else to go, and would rather stay near Adrian and Kiri than be left alone. So she followed, picking her unsteady way along the narrow riverbank. The smell of damp stone surrounded her. The sound of Kiri's toenails on the rocks echoed close behind. After a couple of bends, the daylight from the entrance vanished, leaving only the fluctuating glow of the souls to light their way. At points Sophie and Adrian had to duck, bending almost double to walk beneath the low rock ceiling, causing her a tremor of claustrophobia. Relief spread through her when they turned one last bend and the tunnel opened out into a huge cavern.

In fact, "huge" didn't begin to describe it. "Vast," more like. Colossal. She stopped at the river's edge, taking it in.

The cave's ceiling rose so high she couldn't even see it. The largest stalagmites and columns stretched up at least a hundred feet before disappearing into darkness. The few stalactites that hung down from above showed only their tips; shadow engulfed their bases. Kiri trotted ahead to the edge of the black river, which formed a barrier separating them from an expanse of rolling hills. The light suffusing the landscape didn't come from the sky, but rose from the ground, from the thousands or probably millions of glowing souls milling in the fields.

Grass, flowers, trees, and other plants grew here, underground. Their colors were mostly pale, like a world covered in frost. The souls themselves looked washed out by their own glow, the tints of their clothing and hair fainter than they would be in life. The grass, though alive, was more white than green, like the stem of the violet Adrian had given her. Some trees and bushes grew blue-white leaves, others yellow-white or violet-white, and a few black. The flowers were the only vivid spots: bursts of scarlet and purple and lime-green (and yes, white), forming pools or pinpoints of color at the feet of the souls. Sophie watched as the ghost of a little girl tried to grasp a red tulip, her transparent hand passing through the stem over and over.

"This is it. The afterlife." Sophie meant to make it a question, but it emerged a soft statement.

"I couldn't believe it the first time I saw it, either."

"When was that?"

"Three years ago."

"Did you die or something?"

"No." He tipped his head to look up into the darkness. "Someone brought me."

"Nikolaos?"

"No. Someone else." He turned and walked along the bank. "This way."

She followed. "You're sure I'm not dead?"

"You're not. And neither am I." He led her to a post sticking up at the river's edge. A square wooden raft was tied to it, bobbing against the post in the stream's current. Kiri leaped onto the raft and sat, watching Adrian. He stepped onto the raft, and took Sophie's hand to help her down. "I'd kneel unless you have excellent balance." He dropped to his knees, untying the rope from the post. "Wouldn't want to fall in the river."

Sophie folded herself down, feeling the damp, splintered wood against her fingertips. If this was indeed some kind of magical afterlife, she could only imagine the fate that might befall someone who touched its eerie waters.

"What would happen?" she asked.

Having freed the mooring rope, he reached into the river and picked up another length of rope, this one dripping wet. "You'd be soaked and freezing."

Oh. At least that made sense.

"It's all kind of mythological, isn't it," she observed.

Adrian glanced at her. "Interesting word choice."

"Well, a cave of souls, with a river and everything."

He only said, "Hm," and returned his attention to the ropes.

The river did look cold and swift, but it wasn't huge. It was narrow enough that she could have lightly tossed a rock across it, but wide enough that she couldn't have jumped it.

The River Styx, she thought, her mind retrieving the name at last. And the Elysian Fields. That's what it reminded her of: Greek mythology. As a kid she'd owned a book of the myths, with beautiful bright illustrations. But considering the odd look Adrian had given her at the word "mythological," she kept the thought to herself.

The wet rope he held, she observed, stretched from one shore to the other, looped around a post on each side like a pulley and attached to the raft in between. She supposed it was so you could fetch the raft if it was on the wrong side of the river. Pulling the dripping rope hand over hand, Adrian maneuvered the raft to the other side. Catching the post there, he tied the mooring rope to it, then stood and stretched a hand to her.

She took it. He led her up the grassy slope to the fields. Once on level ground, she pulled her hand away.

Kiri shot past them, sprinting around the fields and up and down the hills, adroitly dodging the souls even though she likely could have cut straight through them. At the sight of the living dog barreling past, the human souls smiled. Soon Kiri had picked up a string of ghost dogs, streaking along after her, all sizes and breeds. For alongside the human ghosts, some animal souls walked too: mostly dogs and cats, with a few horses or other pets. Nothing more exotic, as far as Sophie noticed.

"Pets come here, but wild animals don't?" she asked.

"Seems to be the pattern. I'm not certain, but I think animal souls usually go some other place—maybe another realm altogether. But those that were attached to humans follow the human souls here. Handy for us. We can use horses for transport."

"Wow. I wonder if my old dog is here."

"Could be."

Sophie folded her arms, looking around. "And my grandfather."

Adrian nodded. "Do you want to find him straight away, or…?"

"Yes." She tried to look brave, though her heart thudded, and her limbs went cold with fear and love.

Adrian only looked reluctant, not defensive. "Are you sure?"

"I won't be able to believe in this place until I see proof that someone I know to be dead is *here*."

He sighed, closing his mouth, and turned to survey the crowds of souls. Kiri catapulted over, leading the stream of ghost dogs in a glowing circle around them, and took off again.

Adrian lifted his arms to attract the souls' attention, and raised his voice to address them. But whatever he said, it wasn't in a language she understood. He spoke a few words, sandwiching "Louis Alfred Darrow" and "Sophie Darrow" between them.

After delivering this announcement, he waited, and the souls murmured and whispered.

As Sophie and Adrian watched, the message moved through the crowd, spreading outward. A minute or two passed. Then a gap opened in the multitudes, far away on one of the hills, and someone walked forward into the space. Adrian nodded in that direction and led Sophie across the field.

The soul moved toward them and met them halfway.

Grandpop.

He stood before her, smiling the wide, loving smile he reserved just for his grandchildren. His white hair grew in its bushy half-circle on his balding head, exactly as she remembered. His dark brown skin retained some of the deep wrinkles he'd earned in his long life, but now contained a certain serene smoothness from the glow emanating from within him. He wore his favorite green checkered shirt and khaki pants pulled up too high, as usual. It was all just as he had looked in the video.

"My goodness, Sophie-Sodapop. You made it."

His nickname for her. His deep voice. *Him.*

Sophie blinked back tears and tried to answer. "I'm…v-visiting…" God, what a stupid thing to say. She laughed.

"It's all right, dear," said Grandpop. "You just take a minute."

She found a tissue in her pocket, and wiped her eyes. "I…I didn't know if this was real, if souls were really here, so I had him find you."

"Who knew, huh? All those wars about heaven and religion and it turns out we all go to a big cave." He chuckled.

She blew her nose, and grinned. "Hey. Did you know Dad grew a mustache?"

They talked for perhaps half an hour. Of course she tried touching him, but her hand passed straight through him. She ended up sitting in the pale grass with her legs folded, and he sat in front of her, looking more comfortable than she'd ever known him to be in his life. Even before a stroke cut his life short, he'd been riddled with arthritis. But he seemed free of pain now and stretched his legs easily out in front of him. That comforted her.

He was naturally curious about how she and Adrian and other living folk were able to visit here. She didn't know the answer. All she could say was Adrian brought her, and wanted to show her around—she didn't know why yet. She looked back at where Adrian paced in the field, out of earshot, throwing a stick for Kiri. One of the souls stood near, talking with him, a young man whose features and dark hair suggested he was from India or the Middle East. They both looked over at her, as if talking about her. She turned away, facing Grandpop once more.

"Maybe I'll be able to come see you again," Sophie said, standing as their conversation wrapped up. "I don't know. I don't quite understand what I'm doing here. I'm a little freaked out."

"Oh, don't be. *I* have a pretty good idea what you're doing here." Grandpop stood too, and winked.

"Really? Can you tell me?"

Grandpop smiled in Adrian's direction. "I think I'd better leave that to him. I wouldn't want to get the etiquette wrong."

The soul of the young man said goodbye to Adrian, smiled at Sophie, and wandered off. Adrian walked over to join them. He nodded deferentially to Grandpop, then looked at Sophie. "Ready to move along?"

She nodded.

Grandpop waved her onward. "Love you, Sophie, honey."

"I love you too." Her voice cracked, but she smiled for him before following Adrian down the slope. She looked back only once, to see Grandpop still watching her, waving. She waved back.

After steadying her lungs with a deep breath, she asked, "So he'll be here forever, waiting for the rest of the family?"

"Probably not forever. It's likely he'll wait for some of you, but the souls—well, come see." Adrian led her toward the river and walked alongside it, following it downstream.

In a few minutes they came to a rock wall, bumpy with stalagmites. Into a tunnel in the wall the river flowed, its bank disappearing. The only way to keep following the stream would be to jump in and let it carry you along, which, Sophie supposed, would be extremely dangerous.

But the souls were what commanded her attention. A thick crowd of them milled near the rock wall. Every few seconds, a soul stepped off the bank as if to plunge into the water, but instead of falling, they began to soar. And, like birds, each swooped downstream, flying above the river, their glow reflected in the ripples. A glimmer in the tunnel, then they were around a bend and gone.

The souls in the crowd, Sophie noticed, were saying goodbye to each other—those who were flying away bidding farewell to those who were staying. Most did, at least. Some walked up to the river and dived away without a final word to anyone. On the faces of those left behind was a poignant smile, not grief or terror. The scene struck a quiet awe in her heart.

"Where do they go when they leave?" she asked.

"They're reborn. We were all here, heaps of times. You, me, everyone. And when we were ready, we left and were born into a new life. Over and over. Never remembering this place till we died again."

Sophie watched the souls in their migration. "This is what they've told you?"

"Every one. Ask someone if you like. Or you can go back and ask your grandfather. He'll tell you."

Sophie remembered Grandpop's strange comment about having a good idea what she was doing here, as if he had indeed gained a lot of otherworldly knowledge lately. She lowered her gaze to a clump of pale-leaved blue wildflowers growing next to a rock, and touched them with her sneaker's toe. This impossible realm was real down to every atom, it seemed. "That's okay. I believe you."

"Well, that's a first." He sounded wry. When she glanced up, he cracked a grin. And that was a first too, she realized. She'd never seen him smile before. Though it only lasted a second, she caught a glimpse of dazzling straight teeth, and a youthful sparkle of merriment in his eyes.

Definitely handsome. Not that this should affect her judgment.

She cleared her throat and looked around at the souls. "So everyone gets to leave whenever they're ready?"

"Well…not everyone." The smile was gone now. Suddenly he looked sober; even disturbed.

"What do you mean?"

"If people have done enough bad things in their life, hurting others, killing…there's a place they go. Which I'm not going to show you today."

A sickening dread curled in her belly. "Hell?" she said softly.

"Not as bad as that," he assured. "It isn't sheer torture, as far as I gather. But…it's lonely and they aren't contented like the souls here are, and they can't leave. Not till the—the cave, I suppose, decides they've served their time." He nodded toward the river. "Then they can walk away, and leave, with the rest."

She swallowed against her dry throat. "How long? How long do they have to stay there?" She thought of Hitler, of mass murderers, of people who kept kids locked in basements for years to torture them…how did the universe pick a sentence for that?

"I don't know how the place decides." Adrian kept his eyes lowered, his brows tensed and grim. He picked a blue flower and batted it absently against his palm. "I'm glad it's not me who has to decide, I'll tell you that. But from talking to the souls, it seems it's related to however long you lived, or maybe it's however long you were hurting people, or maybe some combination of that plus something, I don't know, but there's some sort of formula for how long you have to stay out of the living world."

Sophie found she was shivering, already fearing the afterlife, even as she stood in the middle of it and saw that most of it was harmless. "How bad do you have to be? I mean, for smaller stuff, for saying something mean, or lying, or…"

Adrian sent her a reassuring glance. "You don't go there for that. Everyone's done those. And the system seems to account for how much good you've done as well, to balance out the bad things. In any case, *you* can breathe easy; you're fine. There's a line drawn, and you're far on the good side of it. You always are."

She tried to smile. "How do you know I always am?"

He only looked away. "Well." He was silent a little while, then glanced at her again, and lifted his eyebrows. "Ready for today's last big decision?"

Only one more? She could handle that. "Sure."

Adrian led her over the hills and turned onto a path that twisted down into a valley. A grove of black trees lay far ahead. The souls watched Adrian and Sophie, and even drew close to reach out and let their hands pass through Sophie's arm. After the encounter with Grandpop, she found it more moving than spooky.

As she observed them in return, she noticed some of them holding hands. At least upon death you and your fellow departed could still touch each other, even if you couldn't touch the world of the living.

"Grandpop seemed to have an idea why you brought me here," she said as they drew closer to the dark forest. "Am I going to find out soon?"

"Some of it. If you choose."

"That's my decision? Whether or not to learn what I'm doing here?"

"Partly. It's more complicated than that." He entered the grove.

Sophie followed. A whisper of wind, smelling of dank rock, swished through her hair and rustled the leaves. She shivered and folded her arms. Kiri slowed down to sniff the ground. Dead leaves crackled under Sophie's shoes as she walked. Branches thick with black foliage and red fruit formed a low ceiling over their heads. The souls didn't enter this grove much, she noticed—they seemed to prefer the open spaces—and without their glow the forest was dark.

Adrian switched on a tiny key-ring flashlight, sending a wedge of bright LED light onto the tree trunks and the ground. "The number of flashlights I've had to buy since coming down here," he murmured.

"You don't *live* down here, though?"

"Um. I kind of do."

"Why?"

"It's headquarters, for me."

"You're, what, some kind of messenger between the dead and the living?"

"That's part of it."

Adrian stopped and shone the light up into the canopy, as if searching for something.

She looked up too. The red fruits might have been apples, though she couldn't get a close enough look to be sure.

Reaching up, he plucked one off the tree. The branch whipped back. "This, Sophie, is your big decision." Adrian regarded her, his dark gaze barely straying from her face as he sank his thumbnail into the flower-like protrusion at the bottom of the fruit.

Not apples. Pomegranates. As soon as she recognized the fruit, another Greek myth snapped into place in her head: Persephone, kidnapped by Hades and brought to the Underworld, was tricked into eating a few pomegranate seeds, and therefore had to return to the land of the dead for part of every year even after she was rescued and brought above ground by her mother Demeter.

The recollection of the myth gave her a chill. She stared at the pomegranate in the hand of a man who'd brought her to an underground land of the dead.

Adrian ripped open the fruit, and held out a ragged quarter of it to her. Ruby-red seeds studded its interior.

She looked up into Adrian's eyes. They were imploring, sad, hopeful. Keeping her gaze upon his, she took the piece of fruit and cupped it in her palm. A single drop of juice ran down her fingers.

"Will you eat some?" he asked her.

"What happens if I do? Do I get trapped here for half of every year?"

He blinked and hesitated. "No. It unlocks your mind. It makes you remember everything you used to know about this place—and about me, and about your past lives. You gain the knowledge you'd have if you were one of the souls, only without dying."

Her hands went cold with apprehension and sharp curiosity. "Is that what happened to you three years ago? When you first came here, with someone else? They fed you one of these pomegranates?"

"Yeah. She offered it to me, and I accepted, and it started everything off."

Sophie wondered who "she" was, but that question could wait. She eyed the dark, shining seeds. "Is this what gave you your super-abilities?"

"Not really. That's a different story. Part of which you'll know, if you eat it."

She tilted the piece of pomegranate back and forth on her palm, trying to reason out what he was after. "Why not bring me the pomegranate at the dorm? Make friends with me, offer me a piece of fruit one day, like a normal person?"

"Lots of reasons. Most important being, the magic only works here. Eating it outside the cave wouldn't do anything."

She continued holding the piece of fruit. "Okay. I still don't see why you're doing this to me."

"But you *will* see, if you eat it."

"What if you're trying to poison me?"

"I'm not. Here, I'll eat some too. See?" He tore off a small section from the fruit, bit into the array of seeds with a crunch, and wiped at his mouth with his sleeve.

"But you have super-strength. Maybe you're immune to it while I wouldn't be."

"If I wanted to kill you, I'd have let you fall out of the bus. Or let the lion eat you. I promise, I'm not out to hurt you."

Sophie looked at the pomegranate again, touching her lips with her tongue. She hadn't eaten since dinner, and that was hours ago, and she *was* hungry. But a hallucinogenic snack wasn't what she'd had in mind. Then again, she did want to know all the answers he kept withholding. She loosened a few of the seeds and let them roll into her other palm. "Will it hurt?" she asked.

"Physically, no," Adrian said. "But unlocking all that information in your brain—well, it does send a lot of ripples through your life."

Sophie stared at the plump red seeds in her fingers. She swallowed the saliva gathering under her tongue. Then she overturned her hand and let the fruit and its seeds drop onto the ground. "No. I'm not eating it."

He groaned, and for a moment turned into an impatient adolescent. "Come on. Seriously?"

His derision only fortified her stubbornness. She dusted off her hands. "I came down here to see Grandpop, not take drugs."

Adrian sighed, glaring off into the forest. "But all those questions you had, this would start answering them." He thrust the remaining piece at her.

"I think I better go back to the regular world. You *will* take me back, right?"

He stared at her a few seconds, then dropped the rest of the pomegranate on the ground. "Right. Fine." He wheeled around, and tromped forward on the path. "This way."

Sophie followed him out of the grove. That was it? That was the whole big decision? Saying yes or no to a mouthful of pomegranate seeds? She began suspecting she'd fallen victim to an elaborate hoax put together by someone who was a little too obsessed with the Persephone myth.

She followed Adrian out of the forest and back into the grassy fields. After a few minutes of stony silence, he started to look calmer again, so she ventured a question.

"How does anything grow down here? Does it ever get sun?"

"No sun. This place just has its own…magic, I suppose is the word."

Considering she got here via flying ghost horses, and was surrounded by millions of glowing dead humans, she was willing to accept magic as an answer. Provided it wasn't all some sort of hallucinogenic hoax.

"What was the language you spoke when you asked the other souls to find Grandpop?" she asked.

"The language of the Underworld." Immediately he closed his mouth and darted a glance at her, as if he hadn't meant to say that. Then he added, "It's a Tower of Babel down here. People from all over the world. So the way they communicate is with one language everyone knows. Everyone dead, anyway."

"And you."

"Yeah."

She filed away the word "Underworld" in her head. Interesting. That matched Greek mythology too.

A little tributary stream, no wider than her hand, tumbled along the base of a valley. Sophie stepped over it, following Kiri and Adrian. She glanced over her shoulder at the stream, and bumped into Adrian, who had stopped.

He stood frowning, head turned as if listening to something far off.

"What?" said Sophie.

Adrian sighed after a moment. "It's only...I'm afraid I'm in for a lecture."

"A lecture?"

"Adrian!" called a woman, somewhere beyond the hill. Her voice echoed in the cave, and the souls whispered in a ripple of quietly interested remarks. Kiri gave an excited yelp, and bounded away in the direction of the voice.

"Adrian!" The voice was closer, and soon was followed by the woman herself, striding angrily over the crest of the hill. Kiri circled her, tongue hanging out, as if herding one of her favorite cows into the pasture.

The woman was tall and leanly muscular, and her long sheath-style red dress flapped against her bare legs as she approached.

"I know, I'm sorry," Adrian said by way of greeting.

The woman stopped to infuse him with a look of serious exasperation, which was a powerful expression on an already striking face. Sophie guessed she was perhaps thirty, but it was hard to say. Tightly spiraling dark brown hair made a cloud around her face and shoulders. She was brown-skinned, darker than Sophie by a few shades, making her look properly African.

She turned to Sophie, and her gaze softened into compassion. "What has he shown you?" Her accent was fairly strong, though whether it was from Africa or Europe or elsewhere, Sophie couldn't gauge.

Sophie glanced in hesitation at Adrian. "Well...my grandfather's soul. And the pomegranates."

"Did you eat one?"

"No."

"Good." Hands on hips, the woman turned to glare at Adrian. "Now? So soon? Like this?"

"I was about to return her," Adrian said.

"What ever made you think this was wise?" The woman exhaled through her nose, and turned again to Sophie. "My dear, I am sorry. He was wrong to do this to you."

"It's okay." Sophie wasn't sure what else to say.

"He will return you at once. We will do our best to protect you against the opposition, as Adrian calls them, but I hope it won't be a problem."

Sophie cleared her throat. "Um, I don't really understand who that is. The opposition."

"If we are lucky, you won't have to worry about it," the woman said. "Not if you go about your normal life, the way you should at your age." She directed the last statement at Adrian, though seemingly it still referred to Sophie.

"I was her age when you found me," he defended.

Sophie's ears perked up. So this was the person who'd brought Adrian here and fed him the pomegranate?

"Your circumstances were different," the woman said. "There's nothing wrong with her life."

Sophie could have argued the point. Her mom, in all likelihood, was involved with another man. Also, the family needed money, what with the farmhouse's dilapidated condition, Liam's frequent doctor bills for broken limbs due to skateboarding injuries, her mother's tuition for the M.B.A. she was pursuing, and now Sophie's own tuition. The fruit stand had never brought in much profit, but it was all her parents had done for the last couple of decades, and was all they wanted to do. Even the M.B.A. was intended only to improve the family business.

In addition, Sophie needed to find a job and balance it with her classes, settle into dorm life and make new friends, and decide what to do about Jacob now that they were forty miles apart.

But she had no idea what Adrian's life had been like before all this, except that his mother had died when he was young. Maybe her life really was a walk in the park so far, in comparison.

"I'm taking her home," Adrian promised the woman.

"Good." The woman laid warm hands upon Sophie's upper arms. "Don't worry. We're your friends. It will make sense eventually. Try to forget about all this in the meantime."

Forget about this? The most bizarre, amazing thing that had ever happened to her? Not a chance. Still, something about the woman compelled reverent answers, so Sophie nodded and said, "I'll try."

The woman answered with a firm nod as if Sophie had spoken wisely. Then she turned and glared at Adrian. "*Now*, if you please."

CHAPTER SIX

IVEN HOW LONG SHE KNEW the flight to be, Sophie was glad when Adrian suggested visiting the restroom first. He helped her across the river on the raft, then picked up a camping lantern sitting next to a tunnel, switched it on, and guided her into the passage. The tunnel descended via uneven steps in some places, turned a few times, ascended in more steps, and had several sub-tunnels branching off it along the way. Sometimes she caught the sound of trickling water, accompanied by a smell of wet rock, as if the river or one of its underground tributaries was near. In the lantern's glow, the walls and floor sparkled and flashed in all colors. She realized the cave was studded with gems. For all she knew, those pebbles crunching under her shoes were literal diamonds in the rough.

Despite that attractive quality, the tunnels gave her the creeps. They were so dark, dark as only a cave could be. She already knew ghosts were down here, so what else lurked down these passages?

In a minute or two, they entered a room with modern furniture and a high ceiling, though not as high as the one above the spirit fields. A four-poster bed with dark blankets stood against the far wall. It looked fairly new and clean, not the moldering, dusty antique she might expect in a world of the dead.

While Sophie paused to look in curiosity at the bed, Adrian pointed toward the right. "Bathroom's back there."

She stepped that way, glancing again at the bed. "This is where you sleep?"

"Yeah, when I'm here. I, um, did put in plumbing, but no electricity yet. So grab one of the flashlights in the box by the door."

Sophie walked to the "door," which was actually a curtain, and picked up a button LED light from the cardboard box beside it. With a click, it came on, and she pushed through the curtain to find herself in a small dead-end tunnel. Toilet, sink, tub, and water heater all looked new and standard, thank goodness. She gladly made use of the first two, setting the light on the granite counter.

While washing her hands a minute later in the tap, she noticed a gleam of green on the wall, catching the light of the LED.

Thinking it might be an emerald, she dried her hands with the red towel sitting on the counter, and picked up the light to shine it at the green spark. She found it was a set of dog tags sitting on a tiny ledge. One of the tags was green and shaped like a diamond. The others displayed identification numbers and vaccination proofs, as dogs usually wore, but the green one said:

```
KIRI
Adrian Watts
18 Titan Street
Wellington
```

It carried a phone number as well, but the name and address were all Sophie could reliably commit to memory on the spot. She read the inscription over and over for half a minute, fingers tingling. Then she set the tags back on the ledge, careful not to let the metal clink audibly, and went out. She switched off the LED and dropped it in the box on her way to Adrian. He handed her the lantern and walked to the bathroom himself.

Watts. That perhaps explained "Watson" as an alias—"Watts-on," Nikolaos had playfully pronounced it.

She wandered over to Kiri and petted the dog's head, then combed her fingers through the thick fur at her neck. It was enough to verify that Kiri wore no collar, and thus no tags. Sophie wondered a little why they'd been removed, or whether maybe the tags didn't belong to this dog. But mainly she wondered how fast she could get home, get online, and find out everything she could about Mr. Adrian Watts of 18 Titan Street, Wellington, New Zealand.

So SHE'D REFUSED the pomegranate. Well. Adrian did have one trick up his sleeve, if he dared use it. As he emerged from his turn in the bathroom, his gaze traveled to the plastic crate of food by the bedchamber wall.

Impulse triumphed. He veered over there.

"Midnight snack?" Adrian pulled a pair of granola bars and two small juice bottles from the crate, and held them up. He tried to look aloof, not letting his eyes give anything away.

She studied the snacks, and shrugged, noncommittal.

He twisted the cap off a bottle and handed the juice to her, along with a granola bar.

"I think I could've handled the cap myself," she remarked, but took it, read the label, and sniffed at the juice.

"Should be fresh." He sipped from his own bottle, heart thumping. "Just bought it last week."

He knew she was checking for copious amounts of alcohol or noticeable drugs. Her first sip was tiny, and she licked her lips and examined the label again before evidently deciding it was safe, and taking another drink.

Panic and remorse leaped up in his chest for a moment, and he almost knocked the bottle out of her hand. But it was too late. She'd swallowed it. Swallowed the juice he had doctored, at Nikolaos' suggestion, pouring out half of it and replacing it with juice squeezed from the Underworld's pomegranates. The tart cranberry-grape juice masked the taste; she'd never guess. Just as Niko predicted.

Adrian lowered his face, wiping a spilled drop off the outside of his bottle, his fingers trembling.

Would it even work, the juice alone? Did you have to eat the whole seed? They had no idea. But what had originally struck him as a clever if sneaky idea now seemed like a horrible date-rapist maneuver. Why did he ever listen to Niko? It was surely illegal, experimenting on someone without her consent.

"It isn't a drug," Niko had assured him. "It's just fruit juice, which stirs up knowledge her soul already had." Oh, he knew how to manipulate people, all right, that trickster.

The worst of it was, Adrian couldn't help feeling elated. *Please let it work*, he begged, against all his better counsel.

He lifted his face. "Shall we get back, then?"

Biting off a corner of granola bar, she nodded.

He led her back through the tunnels and into the bus, and they launched upward through the cave mouth, into the bright sky. A minute or two and they were soaring over the Atlantic Ocean again.

The morning sun reflecting off the sea dazzled Adrian's eyes as he guided the bus. Sophie squinted too, leaning back to stay beneath the shade of the rusty roof. Despite the brightness, the speed of the wind made the ride as cold as ever, so Adrian wore his heavy coat and Sophie had rewrapped the blanket around herself.

This time it was just the two of them for the transcontinental ride. Kiri awaited him back in the caverns, staying with Rhea, who was surely preparing further cutting remarks for him upon his return. But he barely cared. His mind whirled in a chaos of excitement and apprehension. He said nothing and waited for Sophie to speak first.

A few kilometers off the American coast, she finally did. "Since the souls can't touch anything, how do you get the riding gear to stick to the horses?"

"A lot of plants from the cave have magical properties, not just the pomegranates. A couple of the right ones woven together can stick to souls."

"Only horse souls? Or human souls too?"

Adrian focused on the hazy continental horizon. "Human too. If need be."

"You said you'd only been going there for three years. Did you learn all this in that time, or do you know it from remembering *your* past lives?"

"Some of both."

The coast swept in beneath them, then a row of green hills, growing darker as they left the sun behind and entered the shadow of the Earth again. It was still the middle of the night where she lived.

"The pomegranate myth," she said. "Persephone and Hades. Does that have something to do with all this?"

Hearing her say the names sent a thrill through him. He tensed up. "How do you mean?"

"It's a Greek myth. And Nikolaos is from Greece, and it looks like we crossed the Atlantic, so we might've been near Greece."

Adrian only shrugged.

"Is there a good reason," she demanded, "that you won't tell me the most basic things?"

"There *is* a good reason. Namely, I want you to figure it out on your own so you won't ever think I planted the ideas in your head. Power of suggestion, and such."

"Well, how am I supposed to figure it out on my own?"

He shrugged. "Eating the seeds would've helped."

Sitting back with an indignant snort, she hugged her blanket tighter. "Okay, so can you tell me this? Why send Nikolaos to get me? You're the one who seemed to have this plan, the one who knew me from online. Why not grab me yourself?"

"I didn't want to be seen near you. There are dangerous people who know who I am and what I look like. Plus I wanted it done fast, but I didn't think I could pull it off. Niko's good at tricking people, so he volunteered to help."

"Even though you knew it would freak me out."

"Yeah."

"And even though you knew bringing me to the cave would make that woman mad."

"Yeah," he said.

"Who was she? Your boss or something?"

"In a way."

"This is sounding like a mob kind of thing. Only paranormal."

Adrian pulled his smartphone from his pocket and tapped the

GPS app. "There are certainly people who'd tell you we're the bad guys."

"This 'opposition'? I still don't understand who they—what are you doing?"

"Navigating." Consulting the arrows and numbers on the screen, he twitched the reins and directed the horses to the northwest.

"You need GPS to get me home?"

Feeling sheepish, as if a real man would be able to steer by the stars and landmarks, he closed the app. "Yeah."

"You didn't use it on the way to that cave."

"The horses can get there on their own. Spirits are like homing pigeons, and that's home for them. But to get anywhere else, you have to navigate the old-fashioned way."

"Or rather, the new-fashioned way."

"Right."

As they crossed the plains and traversed the Cascades, he slowed the horses with a pull on the reins. He checked the map again. Their destination was only twelve kilometers ahead now. He slowed the horses to barely fifty kilometers an hour. The blur of dark landforms around them resolved into the silhouettes of individual trees and lighter patches of meadow. The air warmed. Beside him, Sophie let the blanket slip down around her elbows.

Consulting the GPS, he guided the horses across a field and pulled them to a stop next to the stake. The orange flagging fluttered from its top in the breeze, catching enough light from the horses' glow to be easily visible.

He stepped down from the bus and looked up. The stars and planets shone so thick and bright they nearly throbbed. The air smelled of the freshness of an Earth practically untouched by humans.

Sophie unwound the blanket and climbed out of the bus, immersed in checking her texts.

"Anyone missed you?" he asked.

"No. Thank goodness. I guess I'll sneak back into the room and try not to wake up my roommate."

"Okay. Listen…" He waited until she looked up from her phone. "It's serious, this business of not telling anyone."

Her phone's screen dimmed automatically, the light dying from her face. "These people who are after you—are they a gang or something? And they'd really come after me?"

"They're not a gang so much as a…a secret society. And I don't know exactly what they'd do. Except that they've already killed one of us, and tried to kill me."

Her breath hissed inward. "Who—why—"

"We go against their religion, I suppose you could say. They're scared of us. They shouldn't be, but they are."

"So, wait, do they know you're Kiwi Ade, online?"

"I expect they do."

"Then why'd you go commenting openly on my posts? They could *already* know we know each other." She sounded outraged, for which he couldn't blame her.

"That's true. But if you pretend you don't know what I am or anything about this realm, then they shouldn't have any cause to bother you."

She sighed, glancing again at her phone. "Well, I don't know what you are, that much is true." She stayed quiet a few seconds. "Why was it so important to leave comments?" she echoed.

"I wanted to connect with you." God, did that sound lame. But he kept on. "There was no way I *couldn't* reach out to you, once I…" He forced himself to stop. Even the suggestion that they'd known each other in past lives, or that his compulsion to find her had anything to do with the pomegranates, could be enough to make her doubt the validity of the memories when they started streaming into her mind. "You're probably right," he said. "I shouldn't have commented. But if you knew how lonely it was, hiding out over here…"

Now he sounded desperate and pathetic. Shut up, Adrian, just shut up.

Sophie cleared her throat. Her voice became meticulously tactful. "I have a boyfriend. I should have mentioned. I thought you knew."

"No, I do know. You've said, on the blog. It's fine."

"I came because of Grandpop, and because I was curious. But in case you thought it was a date…"

"Well, it would be a pretty strange date, wouldn't it." He tried to laugh.

She agreed with a polite laugh of her own.

"Ready to go back, then?" he asked. "Last chance. I could whisk you away to Hawaii instead, if you'd like to sleep on a beach or something."

He won a smirk from her. "No, thank you."

"All right." He gathered her close, letting himself breathe the sweet scent of her for a stolen second, then pulled her back into the living realm. The artificial glare of a streetlight seemed to light up the world after the dark star-studded realm of the spirits. They both swayed as the ground reshaped itself under their feet. When they'd caught their balance, he let her go.

She backed out of the concrete enclosure. "Thanks. It was… interesting, to say the least. But if I decide I can't handle it again… well, I don't know if it's for me."

Oh, it's for you. More than you know.

Adrian nodded. "Get some sleep. You might have some interesting dreams."

And rather than drag out the farewells—or allow himself to say anything pathetic again—he waved goodbye and vanished into the spirit realm.

Darkness washed down around him. His eyes adjusted, and the stars shone out again. Night birds and insects chirped in the grass and trees.

What if the juice worked?

Then Sophie would dream, and remember, and learn she'd been tricked. She'd be even more confused, scared, and angry than she already was. But one of the main things she would remember was him. Both of them, in living bodies and able to remember who they had been before—that hadn't happened in thousands of years, because only lately had living people rediscovered the

Underworld. He was one of the lucky souls, and he longed for Sophie to be another.

He leaned back against the bus, and checked his messages. Zoe had left him a voice mail an hour ago; merely, "Hey, wondering if there's any news. Ring me."

It was nearing midnight in New Zealand by now, but she sometimes stayed up late. She'd turn off her phone if she was asleep, so he called back.

She answered at once, sounding anxious. "Ade! How are you?" Zoe had tended to fret about him ever since he was attacked in February. Natural reaction, when your best friend tells you he's been shot and needs to leave the country, perhaps the living world altogether.

"I'm good. You?"

"Fine. Did you meet her again?"

"Yep. It went…well, I guess."

"And the pomegranate?"

"She turned it down. But I, um…" He shut his eyes. "Gave her some juice from it. She didn't know that's what it was, and she drank it."

"*Adrian.*"

"I know. It was Niko's idea. I don't know why I listen to him."

"Maybe because you're dying for her to remember you."

"Okay, a little." Adrian looked out at the horizon, watching a soul streak by. "Ah, Z. When are you going to join us, eh?"

"Not till you've rounded up every last crackpot and nut-job who's trying to kill you, and killed them yourself. Or at least locked them somewhere in that cave of yours."

"You know that isn't how I operate."

"Some god of death you are."

"That isn't exactly my title, either." He shifted his back against the cold rusty bus. "You're probably smart to refuse. So was she. What have I done?"

"It was only the juice, you said? Maybe it won't work."

"Maybe. But if it does…when all that enters your mind, and builds up, it changes everything."

"Which is *why* I refuse."

"Okay, but it does change everything in a fun way, sometimes."

"You're crazy."

"Yeah." He lifted his face, and found a bright evening planet shining upon him between clouds. "But maybe now I'll have someone to be crazy with."

CHAPTER SEVEN

Sophie crossed the quad quickly, shivering as the breeze kicked up. Thunder rumbled in the distance, though the sky above was clear. The air smelled chilly, like dew on grass. Summer was giving way to fall, she thought, irrelevantly.

Or maybe it wasn't irrelevant. The myth of Persephone had been on her mind. And when Persephone was kidnapped into the Underworld, her grieving mother Demeter ranged all over the Earth looking for her, and in doing so dropped her care of the world's growing plants. She only let spring be reborn when Persephone was freed to rejoin her. And every year, when Persephone had to return to Hades, Demeter repeated her withdrawal of fertility in the Earth.

The myth explained the seasons. That was all Sophie had ever gotten from it as a child. Tonight Persephone's story suggested a cavern full of other issues, deeper and grimmer.

The smart thing to do was clear: politely say, "No, thank you" to every invitation Adrian issued from now on, and take care of her regular life, like a grown-up. That was why she'd refused to eat the pomegranate—it could have been some kind of drug, which would perpetuate her falling for this hoax, if indeed the whole thing was a hoax.

But that spirit world seemed so real. Ignoring or forgetting it would be impossible.

In the dorm room, Melissa breathed in quiet snores. Sophie

took her pajamas and toiletries to the bathroom to change. But upon returning and climbing into bed, she only lay wide awake.

Finally she sat up, bunching the pillow behind herself, and carefully drew her computer off the desk and onto her lap.

She got onto her blog and looked for the comments he had left as Kiwi Ade. But she couldn't find them—every one of them had vanished. She hadn't deleted them, so he must have.

Frustrated, she moved on to a search engine.

adrian watts wellington new zealand, she typed. For good measure, she added *kiri* to the string.

It popped up within the first ten hits: a news story from five years ago. A Wellington paper had run an article titled *Assistance dogs go to school.*

She clicked on it, and found that it discussed various students in Wellington who used service dogs to help in their disabilities. Near the end she discovered this paragraph:

    Adrian Watts, 16, has been a paraplegic since an
    accident at age 5. He got his dog Kiri when he
    was 9, and "Life improved right away," he says.
    "She picks things up for me if I drop them, helps
    carry my books and stuff, and opens nearly any kind
    of door, which can be really hard when you're in
    a wheelchair. And she's constant company. I can't
    imagine life without her."

They included a photo: a teenage boy in a wheelchair—sure looked like Adrian, though skinnier and younger—and a dog who resembled Kiri, her paws on his lap, licking his face. If he was sixteen five years ago, he was twenty-one now, which also seemed accurate.

Sophie re-read the article, piecing the big picture together. Clearly he wasn't a paraplegic anymore, but it appeared he used to be.

"Your circumstances were different. There's nothing wrong with her life," the woman in the red dress had said to Adrian.

Did Adrian make some kind of magic deal, giving him superpowers and a cure for paralysis? And now perhaps he was in the crosshairs of someone dangerous because of it. But what did that have to do with past lives and pomegranates? And why was he living in the cave with the ghosts? Was that part of the deal? And again, why did he insist on bringing Sophie into it? Her blog posts couldn't have been *that* fascinating.

None of it made any sense. She needed sleep. She closed the laptop and slipped it back onto the desk. Rain began tapping on the windows. Thunder rumbled again. The wind rustled branches outside the dorm.

She'd known her life was about to change when she arrived at college, but she hadn't imagined it would veer straight into the surreal.

She clearly should avoid Adrian from now on. But how could a person go on with an ordinary life after an experience like this?

Upon Adrian's return, he found Rhea in the entrance cavern, sitting on a rock, running her bare foot over Kiri's fur. The dog snoozed on the floor, next to the sandals Rhea had removed.

Adrian climbed out, adopting an expression of humility as he tied up the horses.

"Why would you disrupt her life that way? You know the dangers."

Rhea's question was gently spoken, but he felt the seriousness of the words. He'd tussled with the quandary a long time now himself.

He knelt beside Kiri, who lifted her head and licked his hand, her tail thumping the floor. "I wanted her to know before she got too deep into a regular life," he said. "College, career, husband, kids. It's better to start early if you can."

"You only say that because *you* started early."

"Maybe." He eased down to sit upon the floor, picking grass seeds out of Kiri's coat. "Um, I should tell you, Sophie did eat the pomegranate. Or at least drank some of the juice. I...kind of tricked her into it."

Rhea pulled in a long and evidently furious breath.

Cutting in before she could expel it in the form of a tirade, he said, "Yes, it was horrible of me. But she could be an ally. She will be, I'm sure of it."

Rhea stood and paced barefoot to the river's edge, hands on hips. The passing souls flashed green light upon her figure. "Does she know she's eaten it?"

"Not yet."

"Well. You must be rather content."

He didn't dare say yes, but remained quiet, flicking aside the grass seeds and feeling the tumultuous happiness surface as a smile.

Rhea turned and saw it. She snorted and turned her back again. "Given who she was to you, I suppose I can't remain angry."

"Given who she was to us all, you could even be happy."

"I will be, if she doesn't run from us in horror. And if you keep her safe." Rhea pivoted and gave him a warning stare. "Handle her carefully. Help her see the beauty. The rightness."

Rightness was a word Rhea liked to use to describe their unique condition, and he understood its appeal, given that the opposition was entirely convinced of the wrongness of people like Adrian, Rhea, and Niko. Honestly, he doubted their rightness at least once a day himself. Still, for the chance to have Sophie stay around forever...

"I'll do my best," he promised.

FOUR HOURS OF sleep was really not enough, Sophie observed in the morning, stumbling along to the communal bathroom to wait her turn at the showers. Her head ached from insufficient sleep and oppressive amounts of stress, not to mention weird dreams.

As she lathered up the soap, she reflected upon the dream she'd woken up from. In it, she had been in her thirties, married, and living in Germany in the mid-twentieth century. There was a man she felt drawn to, but he wasn't her husband. She sat with him in a coffee shop with framed pictures of trains on the walls.

They spoke German together, not that Sophie actually knew German. In the dream she did. And the man, though he didn't look a whole lot like Adrian except around the eyes, seemed to be Adrian nonetheless. The only thing that made sense was that she'd be thinking of him in her dreams, given he was the man who "kidnapped" her last night.

As she sat in orientation meetings, the dream kept unfolding and strengthening in her head, presenting new details about the life of this last-century German dream-Sophie. Strange. Usually dreams faded until you couldn't remember them by mid-morning.

So her Kiwi friend's name was probably Adrian Watts, she mused while she jogged back to the dorms through a cool rain shower. She had that much on him.

In the last life it was Karl Hirrmann, her mind helpfully added.

Wow. That was odd. Dreams didn't usually invent entire names for their characters. She didn't know her own German name from that dream.

Sure I do, she thought. *I was Grete Sommer Meier.*

Hmm.

As she climbed the stairs in the dorm, she wondered whether anyone with that name had ever existed. Even if reincarnation was real—which it certainly might be, she suspected, given her glimpse of the Underworld—she wasn't supposed to be able to access those lives. Not without eating the magic pomegranate.

In the dorm room, Melissa and another girl sat on Melissa's bed, watching an episode of a TV show on the computer. Sophie exchanged hellos with them, then dumped her backpack on the floor and settled down at her desk with her own laptop.

Grete Sommer Meier, she typed, putting quotation marks around it to search on the phrase as a whole. Before hitting "search," she paused to think of some other indicator that would prove it was a real memory and not a coincidence.

What year was Grete born? she considered.

1901, her mind supplied with ease. *And I died in 1985. And Meier was my maiden name; my married name was Huber.*

Nervousness twisted her stomach. The search wouldn't turn up anything. No need to get antsy.

She added "1901" and "Huber" to the search, as extra terms outside the quotation marks. She hit "search."

At once the page listed several dozen links, mainly to genealogy sites. Clicking on two or three of them was enough to prove that, indeed, a Grete Sommer Meier had been born in Germany in 1901, married a Franz Huber, and died in 1985.

Her fingers felt icy. She clicked another link, which turned out to be a brief obituary copied in from an old newspaper. Only after reading the whole article did she realize it was written in German, which she was reading with as much ease as she read English.

She quit the browser with a quick keystroke and jumped up from her desk.

Melissa and the other girl sent her a glance. "Going out?" Melissa asked.

"Yeah. I'm going to walk over to the, uh, library." She shut her laptop, tucked it into its case, and hustled out.

CHAPTER EIGHT

ADRIAN HUDDLED IN THE BACK of the bus with his laptop computer, draining its battery by looking up places he could buy some kind of caravan to live in. He wanted to stay near Sophie, rather than commuting back and forth from the Underworld. But camping in the chilly damp outdoors was growing uncomfortable, and would only get worse as autumn advanced.

His phone interrupted, vibrating with a new text message. Seeing it was from Sophie, he closed his computer and read the text.

Hey, random question, it said. *Why the hell can I speak German? ANSWER ASAP.*

Rapture and guilt braided themselves together to form his new mood. A low chuckle flowed from his throat.

The pomegranate juice had worked.

Kiri lifted her head to look at him, and he ruffled up her neck fur. "All right, here we go," he told her.

Ah. Indeed, he texted back. *I take it the dreams have started. Grete Meier and Karl, is it?*

He waited. His phone rang with an incoming call in less than a minute.

"Hi," he answered.

"What is happening to me?" She sounded really, really angry.

"Yeah…about that."

"How did you know the name Grete Meier?"

"I think you can answer that."

die." While the chilling words skittered over her, he added, "That is…we don't know of any other way to clear the slate. Sorry. You're stuck with these memories till next time you're reborn."

"Well. Crap."

"Therefore try to make peace with them. I did this so you can get some of the answers you want—and so I can talk to you about them. The answers are in there, most of them."

"Answers. Right." Sophie wandered aside, hugging herself again in the wind, distracted by the mélange of thoughts about Grete, Karl, herself, Adrian, and this world of ghosts. A grove of huge gnarled oaks nearby looked like a possible refuge from the wind, and she moved toward it as she sorted through her confusion.

Adrian walked with her.

Beneath the trees, she found a calmer patch of air and leaned against a mossy trunk. "You were Jewish. I helped you escape the Nazis."

"You had the money. We bribed the right people."

"I got you a ticket on a train to France. Then…"

"A boat to New York," he finished. "Sailed in May of 1939."

Exactly the date she was about to say. Feeling weak, she rested her weight against the tree. "This is crazy."

"We never saw each other again. Just letters." He looked down at his boots. "I remember missing you so much, knowing I shouldn't be unhappy; I should just be thankful to be alive."

The ache in Sophie's chest told her a similar truth: as Grete, she had loved Karl. But she had been married, with children, and couldn't ever be with him. The tragedy, the sweetness, and the increasing conviction that she really had been Grete (and he really had been Karl) all began swaying her toward forgiving him.

She could see herself searching him out too, if she had this knowledge and he didn't. Not that she'd admit it out loud.

"I'm sorry I hit you," she said, grudgingly.

"It's all right. You had good reason."

"Grete and Karl—is that why you went looking for me? Because we were them?"

Adrian hummed a dismissive note, glancing up into the tree. "They're only the tip of the iceberg. Come up here, let's sit." Before she could accept, he had hooked his arm around her middle and hoisted her up to where the branches split out from the trunk, six or seven feet off the ground. Though this time she anticipated his strength, it still impressed her. He lifted her as easily as she would have lifted a kitten.

As she seized the nearest branch, he pushed against the soles of her shoes, and she scrambled into the tree's central cup. It was soft under her hands, carpeted with moss and small ferns. She chose a seat on a mostly-flat area with one of the branches against her back. Adrian pulled himself up and sat opposite her. They both bent their knees up, but the confines of the oak crowded their feet against each other. From below the tree came the contented sounds of Kiri chewing on a stick.

"We can sit in the bus if you'd rather," he said. "I promise I won't drive it anywhere."

"I'll take my chances with the tree."

"All right. So…" He spread his palms over his knees. "We've both lived many, many lives and seen all kinds of things. But there's one particular life, a long time ago, that's especially important. It's the main reason I came looking for you, and got you to drink the juice, and it's the one I want you to remember."

She closed her eyes to concentrate. "Okay. I don't—everything's all jumbled in my head, but—how far back? What year?"

"Uh…I can't be sure exactly. A few thousand years."

Her eyes flew open. "*What?*"

"And here's the trouble: you won't be able to remember it right here, today. Your memories only just got opened up, and the first ones to come back are the most recent."

"So it's going to take days, weeks—longer?—before I get to this ancient life you're talking about?"

"Not necessarily. See…" He shifted in the tree, straightening his back. His fingers danced upward from his kneecaps as he explained. "This huge collection of memories, of lifetimes your soul has lived through, it's like a big bag of—of pomegranates."

"Enough with the pomegranates."

"Oranges, then. Now, the first orange you pull out is the one on top, the last one that was put in."

"Yes…"

"You *could* sit down with that orange, peel it, pull it into sections, examine it all day. Or you could put it aside, reach into the bag, and get the next one. Then put that aside, and take out the next, and the next, and so on, until you get to this amazing, shining, huge, golden orange. *That's* the one you sit down and open up."

"How will I know which one it is?" she asked.

"Oh, you'll know."

She grunted in impatience.

"Although," Adrian added, and drummed his fingers on his knees, thinking. "Yeah. Okay. I can give you a hint. Another thing the pomegranate makes you remember is the time you spent *between* lives."

"Between?" She suddenly understood. "In the Underworld?"

He smiled. "You're even calling it the right name now."

Whispers of images sprouted at the back of her mind, ideas and memories moving like shadows, just out of reach. She sighed. "Great. Now I'm remembering the language of the Underworld, too."

He answered in the musical, vowel-rich words of that language, *"Congratulations. You can now talk to anyone who's down there."*

"Just what I always wanted," she responded, in the same tongue. The sounds felt strange in her mouth, but she knew the translation was right. She closed her eyes again and furrowed her eyebrows. "So what is it I'm supposed to remember from the Underworld?" she asked, switching back to English.

His low voice guided her. "Not very long ago, before being born into this life, after dying as Grete, you and I met there, in the fields. We mostly stayed with our families—the souls of our children, spouses, siblings, and so on—but there was one day we took a walk together, just the two of us."

The image blossomed in her mind: Karl grayed and elderly,

like herself, but still dear to her eyes. "We walked to the trees," she said, keeping her eyes shut. "That forest, where the pomegranates grow."

"Yes." He sounded almost breathless. "What did we say?"

She exhaled, massaging her temples, letting the memory unfold. "I said...something about the trees being neglected."

"And I answered, *The orchard needs you...*" he prompted, in a whisper.

"...*Persephone,*" she finished. With a gasp, she opened her eyes and stared at him.

He held her gaze, his dark eyes sparkling. "Right."

CHAPTER NINE

ADRIAN'S HEART DRUMMED MADLY. SOPHIE'S heels skidded against the trunk as she shoved herself upward until she stood, hands braced against two large branches. She stared down at him, wearing the same expression of astonishment he must have worn when Rhea guided him to the same truth. He still remembered the feeling—like Earth and heaven had been broken into jigsaw puzzle pieces and rearranged into a completely new picture.

"But that doesn't make sense," she protested. "We couldn't have *been* Persephone and Hades. The myths weren't real." Even as she said it, her gaze wandered away from him, as if her own thoughts were contradicting her, which he knew they must be.

"True, the myths largely aren't real," he said. "None of us could throw lightning bolts, or walk on rainbows, or turn into animals. But the things we did do—well, I think you'll be impressed."

"Hades stole Persephone. It wasn't a happy marriage. Why would you want to be him, or have me be her?"

"Being them isn't an option. We *were* them, period. We can't change it. As for the kidnapping, the unhappy marriage—those are part of the myth, which, again, wasn't quite accurate."

"Persephone *liked* being kidnapped?"

He almost smiled, but managed not to, reckoning it could look creepy. "I shouldn't explain today. I'd be giving away too much."

"But—what does it matter now? Even if it really happened, it was thousands of years ago. No one's going to worship us and I don't want anyone to."

"I don't want anyone to, either. But it matters now because, for the first time in centuries—in millennia—we can both remember while we're alive. We could only remember between lives before, in the Underworld. All those other lives when we knew each other, we couldn't remember what we were; we were just ordinary people. But this time, we can be like Hades and Persephone again."

Sophie breathed in shallow gusts, looking up and around at the tree branches. "What does that mean, be like them? I can't remember anything about being her. Only talking about it, after being Grete. I can't remember…"

"No, of course you can't," he assured. "It's buried down deep in that bag, beneath all the other oranges. You've got to do some digging before you get to it."

"But when I try to remember, it's all confused. I can't concentrate. Real life keeps getting in the way—and by the way, I have a *lot* of real life to concentrate on right now."

"I know. That's why I said to look to your dreams. Dreams are much more reliable for this exercise. You can really live in the memory, and if you go to bed thinking, 'I'm going to control what I see,' you can skim backward and forward much faster."

"How long will that take?" she asked. "Before I get to whatever-it-was B.C.?"

"My best guess is 1700 B.C. We're talking something like seventy-five lifetimes between then and now, so even if you get skilled at skipping backward through the lives, it'll probably still take you several nights."

She leaned back against a branch, looking stunned. "Thirty-seven hundred years?"

"Hard to wrap your mind around, yeah." Adrian picked a fern frond and brushed it back and forth against his hand. "Honestly, I'm not sure of the exact figure. I've tried to work it out—how long each of my lives was, how long I spent in the Underworld between them—but I just can't be sure, especially in the earliest lives. Back in the old days, people often lost track of exactly how old they were. So that's my rough estimate. The year itself doesn't matter much, anyway. We don't need to punch a date into a time machine."

"But..." She frowned. "If we were gods, how could we have died?"

A chill shivered through Adrian. How he wished he could spare her that memory. "That, I shouldn't explain. You'll trust the memories better if they come from your own head."

"Oh, fine."

"You'll know soon. Really. So..." He dropped the fern and laced together his fingers, taking on a humble expression. "You forgive me for the pomegranate stunt?"

"I'm going to need more time for that," she grumbled. But the flicker of teasing in her tone gave him hope. She sighed, and pulled out her phone to glance at the screen. "I need to get back soon, if you're not going to tell me anything else."

"All right. I've given you enough to think about today." He clambered down the tree's trunk, and held up his arms to her.

She sat at the edge of a branch, swinging her legs down. "Do I jump?"

"Sure. I can catch you."

Still frowning, she sprang out of the tree. Adrian caught her around the middle, her arms colliding with his shoulders and head, her breasts in his face for one pleasantly distracting second. He lowered her to her feet, and they dusted bits of moss off their clothes.

"Did you used to be in a wheelchair?" she asked abruptly.

Caught off guard, he felt the old defensiveness lock across his face like a shield. "How'd you find that out?"

"The Internet. There was an article from a while back, about you and Kiri, and other assistance dogs."

"But how? I mean, I never told you my last name or what city I was from or anything."

"I saw your name and address on Kiri's dog tags, in your bathroom. In the Underworld."

Realizing he'd left those in plain sight, he spread his palm over his face. "I am so bloody stupid."

"So when you got your superpowers…that made you able to walk?"

Ugh. This was a can of worms he did not feel like reopening. "Yeah," he said, dropping his hand and looking off at the horizon.

"Sorry. Maybe it's none of my business."

It was kind of her to apologize, when she was under no obligation to do so. He pushed a smile to the surface. "I think I did nothing but run for about two weeks when I got cured. Must've run a thousand kilometers in all. Gave Kiri a nice workout."

She smiled down at the dog. "I can imagine."

"Come on, let's take you back." He reached out and clasped her hand, not even thinking what he was doing until he felt her fingers tense in his grasp. Rather than pull his hand away, though, he lingered to see what she'd do. And in a moment she relaxed, and allowed him to hold her hand as they walked back to the stake with the orange flagging.

When they reached it, she gasped and dropped his hand, staring at him.

"What?" he asked, alarmed.

"I *slept* with you!"

"Oh. Which time are you thinking of?"

"As Grete and Karl—I was married and I slept with you!"

"Just the once. I was leaving forever. It was our only chance."

"Hang on, what do you mean, 'which time'?" She sounded shocked. "How many other times—other lives—"

Now he couldn't keep from grinning. "How many? In all the lives together? Oh, my. I'd have to be counting a long time to come up with an answer to that."

With a short shriek of outrage, she turned away.

"You're only *just* remembering this?" he asked.

She spun around to him again, shaking her fingertips as if to get something off them. "This is weird! You have no idea how weird it is to remember doing something you haven't done."

"Actually, I have a good idea what that's like."

Sophie scowled. "Yeah, I guess you do."

"I'm sorry. I wasn't laughing at you, or at the memories. In fact, I quite like those memories. But I don't mean that in a sleazy way."

"I know. You're a guy." She grumbled the words in resignation.

"Well. I'm human."

She lifted her face to study him. "Yet you're Hades."

He gazed into her eyes, almost shivering at how familiar they were. "Pretty much."

"You're Hades and you kidnapped me—Persephone—and dragged me away to the Underworld in a chariot pulled by black horses. Then you tricked me into eating a pomegranate so I'd have to come back to you."

"Funny how that worked out, isn't it?"

"Is that how you did it the first time around?" she asked.

"Go to sleep and find out."

CHAPTER TEN

HAT ADRIAN REMEMBERED OF HADES' life, he was at first inclined to doubt, because how could anything so far-fetched, from so long ago, and so influenced by his own knowledge of mythology be accurate? But comparing his memories with those of Rhea, Nikolaos, Sanjay, and others showed him it was real, for they all matched up. Soon Sophie's memories would fall into place too.

Hades was born on Crete sometime around 1700 B.C., to Adrian's best estimation. Adrian knew the island was actually called Keftara by its citizens at the time, and his own name was Aidisi—or those would be Adrian's guesses at the spelling, since he rarely wrote at all back then, and when he did he used his civilization's hieroglyphs rather than the modern Latin-based alphabet. But the familiarity of mythology and geography led him and the other immortals to refer to their past selves and countries by the names found in modern books. "Hades" had a certain cachet to it and Adrian had come to like it.

Besides, he didn't fancy an eternity of correcting people: "Actually, it's 'Aidisi.'"

Hades' parents grew barley and figs, and kept pigs and goats, in a village half a day's walk from the palace city of Knossos. Hades was married at age fifteen in an arranged match, and, following the local custom, moved to his wife's village on the other side of the valley. His bride was nearly a stranger when they underwent the rites together, but they quickly grew fond of each other. So it devastated him when, barely a year later, she died in childbirth, and their baby son with her.

Hades blamed himself, and suspected his wife's family blamed him too. Hades had always been unusually and unnaturally strong. He had never once been ill. A huge sow bit into his wrist when he was a child, and everyone expected his hand would be crippled for life. But it healed completely within a day. At age ten he could lift the sow by himself. It frightened his parents and cousins to see him do such things, so he hid his abilities whenever he could. He knew his family loved him, but they seemed relieved to see him go when he married and moved away. Having him around made them uneasy.

His strength grew along with him. When a scaffold broke during the construction of the house he was helping build for his new wife, and a giant cube of stone went tumbling down the slope, Hades leaped forward and stopped it before it flattened a little boy. His new neighbors appreciated his strength that time, but they still feared him. He heard muttered invocations to their household goddesses, thanking them while requesting protection from eerie forces—which he knew referred to him, not to whatever force made the scaffold break. The accident wasn't unnatural; that kind of thing happened from time to time. But Hades' invincibility most certainly didn't.

So couldn't his bizarre strength be the reason his son was too much for his wife to bear?

It was a bad year already for the island. The winter had brought only a few showers of rain, the spring even less, and now, in the baking heat of summer, the springs and wells were drying up. Animals, crops, and people languished. The usual supplications to the goddess of the harvest and the god of weather garnered no divine response. So the high priestess at the palace of Knossos took drastic action, and put out a call for a human victim to be sacrificed.

In Hades' memory this had only happened once before—when he was a small boy—to end a series of earthquakes that had rattled the island. A young woman, one of the junior priestesses, had stepped forward to offer herself. Hades and his parents had joined the crowd in the palace grounds to witness the rite, and his father had held him up on his shoulders so Hades could see over the heads of the citizens. But when the high priestess had raised her knife and the masked male attendant had stepped forward with his shining axe, small Hades covered his face, shuddering so dramatically that his father lost his grip and the boy fell to the ground. He was, of course, unhurt. Meanwhile the crowd's voices rose in a wail as the young woman collapsed in a pool of blood.

And the earthquakes, as far as he remembered, stopped.

When he was a child he could not fathom why anyone would volunteer to become the sacrifice. But now, not quite seventeen years old, widowed, lonely and dispirited, he did understand.

After the two palace messengers delivered the announcement and moved on to the next village, Hades spent the afternoon in thought. While the rest of his wife's family took their daily nap, he lay awake, making his decision.

He grieved for his wife and child. Her family mourned them too, and made no effort to embrace him as their own son. He felt shunned and alone. Rather than viewing his extraordinary strength as something to be cherished and explored, he felt it a curse that would forever set him apart from others. If the goddess could destroy his body at last, and summon him to the spirit world where he might find his young wife and child, then she was welcome to do so.

When his wife's parents awoke, he told them he wished to offer himself as the island's sacrifice.

They showed the shock and fear anyone might upon hearing a person say this, but made only weak efforts to dissuade him. He held firm. They relented. Then he went out to the road and awaited the return of the palace attendants, on their way back to Knossos. When they came, he stepped forward and volunteered.

The two attendants, a man and a woman some fifteen years older than himself, stood and talked to him in concern a long while. Was he sure? Would he not wish to stay, be of use to the village, perhaps marry again and have children?

"No," he said. "This is the only way I can be of use."

So he said farewell to his wife's parents, and accompanied the attendants to the palace.

In Knossos they let him bathe, and brought him fine food, and gave him a private room with rugs on the floors and a deeply soft bed, in which he tried to sleep without much success. He felt as if he had already died, and was numb to the world.

The next day they gave him a feast. Four attendants, two male and two female, wrapped him in linen robes and strings of flowers as if he were a new bridegroom. He was brought to a table full of priestesses and city officials—including the island's king—all talking and celebrating. The king, a proud middle-aged man, summoned Hades to him. Hades knelt before his chair, eyes turned down and hand upon his own forehead in obeisance. But the king bade him rise, and thanked him in ringing tones for his courage. Smiling, he then waved the surprised Hades off to take a seat along the table.

Hades tasted the roast lamb, the figs and grapes, and the excellent wine, and paid close attention to the sounds of the flutes and lyres, knowing he wouldn't have full enjoyment of his senses anymore in the afterlife. The religious leaders always had been quite clear on how the afterlife worked. Those who had been good or heroic—which certainly must include his wife and son and himself—went to a beautiful island, bathed in gentle sun and resplendent with gardens and mountains, where they needed do nothing but relax in comfort, feeling forevermore as if they were drifting in a dream. Those who had been wicked went to a dark realm at the bottom of the sea, but Hades didn't bother worrying about that. One who offered himself as a sacred sacrifice would no doubt end up on the island of cherished souls.

It was a pleasing image. Still, dread of the transition from life to death chilled his entire body, and rendered him mute with terror.

The following day was the sacrifice. The same attendants prepared him at dawn. They bathed him and massaged scented oil into his skin. They combed out the tangles in his hair and sliced off his black curls above his neck, to make it easier for the executioner's axe. With an adroit touch, the elder of the men shaved Hades' still-thin beard off his face. They dressed him in a tunic, sleeveless and knee-length like the ones he'd always worn, but of the snowiest white he had ever seen, and tied an embroidered cloth belt around his waist. They slipped clean sandals onto his feet, and fastened a long purple cloak by a slender silver chain around his neck. Then they led him outside for the procession through the open court.

People filled the court and lined the wide steps that rose to the palace, their cries of appreciation drowning out the thumps of the drums. Two shining black bulls, his fellow sacrifices, walked on either side of him, snorting and tossing their horns while the attendants guided their reins.

Young women wept as if Hades were their own doomed sweetheart, and reached out to touch his bare arms as he passed. Children, wives, and grandparents stepped forward and placed their offerings upon him and upon the bulls. They slipped rings onto his fingers and draped necklaces around his neck. Households who couldn't afford precious metals or jewels brought garlands of poppies, which still bloomed in the meadows despite the drought, and placed them upon his head or around his shoulders. Soon both he and the bulls were ablaze in blossoms with red petals and black hearts.

The procession descended the steps and moved between the rows of desiccated olive trees. The cloak stretched out behind him, dragging along the pavement and growing heavier as he walked, for people tossed their offerings upon it. Plates, knives, silver cups—all were for the temple, the goddess, not for him. He didn't care. He wouldn't need riches where he was going. He only felt, through his frigid shock, a whisper of gratitude that so many people finally appreciated him. As the procession turned and began climbing the steps back to the palace, the attendants gathered up the cloak's corners and helped carry the net of offerings to the high priestess.

Before Hades knew it, he was kneeling on the step before her. He smelled the incense and the bulls, and heard his heart pounding and his ears ringing. The open court, though packed with hundreds or even thousands of people, went silent as the priestess raised her voice in her eerie, supplicating song, of which he understood not a word in his mental haze.

He had seen her only rarely, and always at some distance, even during last night's feast. He knew her name was Rhea, and that she was tall and frightening. She usually wore a live venomous snake wrapped around her arm, its tongue flicking in chilly interest at anyone who came near. That alone would have made him keep his distance. Today she looked taller than ever in the high cone-shaped headdress she wore, its gold bands and jewels glittering in the sun, making her unearthly and fearsome.

But when she placed a cool hand under his chin and lifted his head to look at her, he found her face was that of a kind young woman, her brown eyes sorrowful. "Don't fear," she whispered. "The goddess will carry you home soon."

The snake looked him in the face and flicked its forked tongue at him. From behind, someone's hands lifted away the necklaces and garlands, leaving his neck bare.

The masked attendant stepped up beside Rhea, cradling the axe in his muscled arms.

Rhea raised her knife. The snake glided its head back and forth just behind her knuckles. In the moment before she slashed her own arm, Hades noticed how smooth her limbs were, how completely free of scars; and he thought it strange, because she regularly drew her own blood for ceremonies.

Then her blood began to drip upon his forehead, and she swung the reddened knife and plunged it into his heart. The pain took his breath away. As he gasped and stared down at the hilt sunk in his chest, Rhea stepped out of the way to make room for the masked attendant. The axe went flashing. The world tumbled upside-down. Hades' mouth filled with hot blood, and his consciousness passed from pain into darkness.

HADES OPENED HIS eyes to the starry night sky. Straight walls closed off the horizon on all sides. He seemed to be in a small courtyard open to the air. The taste of blood saturated his mouth. Pain throbbed in his chest and throat with each beat of his heart. He desperately wanted to draw a deep breath, but upon trying to do so, coughed so violently that fresh blood gushed up against the back of his tongue. He rolled over to spit it out, gasping for air, and found he was lying on a raised stone platform, rectangular and just large enough for a body—a slab for cleaning and dressing the dead. He had been stripped of all clothing except a blanket that covered him from navel to knees, as if his body were indeed being prepared for the funeral pyre.

But he wasn't dead.

"It's all right," whispered a female voice. "Lie down. Rest a little longer." The woman knelt and clinked something metal near the ground. A flame flared into life, and she stood again, holding the oil lamp. It was Rhea, now without her snake or her ceremonial headdress. She wore a simple dark gown and a crescent-shaped pendant on a leather string. Her hair was braided back. She could have been any woman selling grapes at the market.

"Am I dying?" he asked.

"Actually, for someone whose head was cut almost clean off, you're doing quite well."

"How…"

"I suspect you are what I am. I heard stories about you, your strength, your power. Your village fears you, yes?"

He nodded. "But…I wanted to die. For the land. To be with my wife." Tears filled his eyes, stinging and then cleansing.

Rhea touched his neck. "You were very brave. Believe me, what we did should have sent you to the spirit world. But the goddess sent you right back. As I expected, your neck has joined itself together again." Her fingers moved to his bare chest and traced the line of the wound over his heart. "Yes. You're healing. That's what I suspected would happen. That's why I ordered you to be left alone during the night."

Blinking away his tears, he examined her warm brown face. Now that he thought about it, she looked too young to be the priestess who had presided as an adult since before Hades was born. "You said you're this way too?"

"Yes. And there are others like us. Not many, but enough. I'm going to send you to them. Tonight. Can you travel?"

"I…" He coughed again, but found he could breathe more easily now, and lifted his hand to test his ability to wiggle his fingers.

"We'll let you recover a little longer. But you must be out of the palace before morning, before it's discovered you aren't dead. We'll tell the people you were cremated in the usual way, in a court within the palace. The bulls will be burned anyway, so the smoke will be there to assure them."

She beckoned to someone near one of the walls. Another young woman, already dressed for travel in a hooded cloak, hurried over with a large cloth bag.

"Put these clothes on," said Rhea. "Tanis will take you across the sea to Greece. Pretend you're married and traveling together. I must return to my chambers before the dawn prayers, but you'll hear from me again, Hades. May the goddess travel with you both." Rhea kissed his forehead and Tanis', then handed Tanis the lamp and darted away.

Tanis set the lamp on the slab beside him. She set about cleaning his face with a damp cloth, and giving him water to drink from a goatskin flask. "Truly, it's amazing how fast you're healing," she said. "Do you think you can sit up?"

He planted a hand on the slab and tried to rise, but the pain flared up again in his neck and he winced and fell back down.

"No, all right, we'll wait a bit," she apologized. Her hood fell back to show a lovely face in the flickering lamplight. Her skin was paler than that of Rhea, who, rumor said, came from Egypt. Tanis appeared to be paler even than the olive-tan of the islanders. Though her hair was dark, her eyes were light, possibly green—the flame's warm color made it hard for him to tell.

"Where are you from?" he asked.

"The north of Greece. That's why I'm to be your guide. I know my way around."

"Are we still in the palace?"

"Yes." She squeezed out the damp washcloth and poured another splash of water onto it. "You're lucky. Most citizens never see these courts."

"I was meant to be dead when they brought me here," he supposed.

"Indeed." She stroked the cloth along his hairline and across his ear. He felt the sticky blood get wiped away, a cool trail of water taking its place.

It took a long while, and many sips of water, but he gradually grew strong enough to sit up and put on the tunic, cloak, and sandals she had brought. Leaning heavily on her shoulder, he slid off the slab of the dead, and planted his feet upon the ground.

Tanis extinguished the lamp, wrapped it in a small skin, and tucked it into her bag. "Come."

With their hoods drawn over their heads, they tiptoed through corridors, beneath ceilings and out again into the open. They moved inside, outside, over and over, making so many twists and turns that Hades would have been totally unable to find his own way back to the court where he'd awoken.

The palace slept around them. Torches burned in sconces to light the way, and as Hades hurried past, supported by Tanis' arm, his eyes drank in gorgeous murals on the walls: blue dolphins arching over waves, athletes leaping over black bulls, and fanciful creatures he couldn't put a name to, with bodies like lions, but wings and crests like birds. Like the court they had just left, he supposed these paintings were sights most citizens would never see; they were only for the eyes of the priestesses and their attendants.

At the end of one corridor, Tanis pushed her shoulder against a stone wall, which gave way, rotating and opening to let in a gust of fresh night air. They emerged onto the sandy ground, and Hades helped her shut the hidden door silently. The pain in his throat and chest had dulled to a moderate ache, and he could walk upright on his own now. He followed Tanis up the hill, dry scrub crunching under their feet. Tall trees soon surrounded and hid them.

Before stepping into the forest, he looked back at the shimmering torches outlining the great square shapes of the palace. He knew he might never see it again, and the thought brought him both sadness and relief. Thinking of Rhea, he could swear he actually sensed her down there, like a particular note plucked on a string, though it wasn't a matter of hearing, nor any of his other senses.

If it were a piece of magic, it would only be one of many tonight. Accepting it, he turned and followed Tanis.

At the crest of the hill, a breeze washed over them, cooler than he had felt in months. It smelled like the sea.

"There, look." Tanis pointed to the north, where the wind came from. Clouds blotted out the stars along the horizon. "Your sacrifice worked. The rain's coming."

CHAPTER ELEVEN

A KNOCK RANG BRISKLY ON SOPHIE'S dorm room door. It had only been two hours since she parted with Adrian, and her mind was not in the least ready to focus on the general chemistry textbook she was attempting to inflict upon it. Seeing her boyfriend, even in her current confusion, was a diversion she was happy to embrace. She leaped up and opened the door.

Jacob stood there in his denim jacket, broad-shouldered and stocky, waiting with his thumb hooked into his belt loop. He smiled at her. The familiar grin, and the way his light brown bangs swooped down to cover one eye, stirred a burst of affection in her. She laughed and leaped into his arms.

"Hey, babe." He gave her a lingering kiss on the lips, tasting of tropical-fruit gum. "Missed you."

"You too. Thanks for driving up." She led him into the room. "Melissa, you remember Jacob?"

Melissa unplugged one earphone, looking up from her laptop. "Oh, yeah. Hi."

"Hey." He aimed a pointer finger at her, thumb up. "We didn't get a chance to talk when I was helping Soph move in. What are you planning to study?"

"Biology. Maybe a women's studies minor."

"Right on."

"You?" Melissa asked.

"I'm hoping to get into the J school at U of O." Upon seeing her blank look, he clarified, "Journalism."

She nodded, returning to her screen-watching. "Cool."

Jacob lifted his eyebrows at Sophie. "So. Where can we grab some pasta?"

They wound up at a diner that served food from all over the globe, with decor to match. African-inspired rock music played, Italian-style red-checkered cloths covered the tables, and a mural of what might have been Cambodian temples sprawled on the wall. After ordering his pasta, Jacob fell quiet, flicking his butter knife over the flame of the votive candle on their table.

Sophie let her thoughts wander too, and they instantly journeyed to Adrian. Or Karl, or Hades—whatever name best fit him. A lot to wrap your mind around, indeed. Though, as she'd recalled with a shock this afternoon, it wasn't much of a hardship to wrap your arms and legs around him. It had been romantic and poignant as well as hot, if Grete's memories could be trusted.

What details did Adrian remember about her? How did her face look to his eyes; how did her body feel in his arms? Not just in past lives, but this one, too. What did he think of her, and what did he want from her?

Jacob kept tilting the knife over the flame. "Have you met a guy named Adrian Watts?"

If Sophie had been holding any silverware herself, she would have dropped it. She blinked, ducking her head to scratch the spot where her barrette held back her curls, thinking fast. How the hell had Jacob found out his name?

"I don't think so," she said, trying to sound indifferent. That lie felt safest at this moment.

"Are you sure?" Jacob's voice held a chilly edge. "What if I said 'Kiwi Ade'?"

Holy crap, she thought. "Oh. Then in that case I think he comments on my blog." She still tried to sound casual. "Lives in New Zealand or something. Why?"

He clunked the knife's handle against the table, between beats of the music. "Have you met him in real life? Like recently?"

"Why—what—" Sophie drew in her breath, aware she now had to make a major choice: lie to protect Adrian, a guy she still couldn't figure out; or tell Jacob the truth, possibly putting Adrian in danger. As she weighed her options, Jacob watched her, his brown eyes guarded and uneasy.

It's serious, this business of not telling anyone, Adrian had said.

She proceeded with her calm tone as best as possible. "No, like I said, he lives in another country. Why are you asking? Where did you get his name?"

Jacob glanced around nervously, tongue flitting along his teeth. "I'm—look, I'm freaked out, Soph. I'm worried for you."

She stared at him. Had these superpowered people contacted him too? Or was it this "opposition" Adrian mentioned?

"Why?" she asked.

"These people found me at my dorm the other night. Investigators—I guess detectives of some kind. And this Adrian guy, he's apparently wanted for, like, lots of scary stuff. They said something about girls missing or killed, girls who had been connected with him…I don't know all the details. But now it looks like he's trying to get close to you."

Sophie found she was shaking—partly fright, partly a sense of outrage she couldn't account for. "Why were they asking *you*? Why not me?"

He ducked his head, folding his hands over the back of his neck with a sigh. "I wasn't supposed to ask you right out; it's just that I got freaked out. Look…" As he lifted his face, the waitress brought Jacob's pasta and Sophie's soup and salad.

The couple sat in stony silence as she set the plates down and asked if they needed anything else.

"No, thanks," Sophie told her.

Once she had returned to the kitchen, Jacob picked up his fork and stabbed at a piece of bow-tie pasta, but didn't eat it. "They didn't know if they could trust you to turn him in. Like, maybe you'd become his friend, and believed what he was telling you. So they wanted me to find out if you'd met him, and maybe they could get a lead on him."

She dipped her spoon into the corn chowder, but didn't feel

like eating. "Are you sure they were detectives? Did you see badges or anything?"

"Why would you ask that? Yes, they showed me ID. Look." Jacob pulled out his wallet and handed a business card to her.

Bill Wilkes, Oregon State Police, it said, with a phone number, email address, and official-looking sheriff-star logo.

"I'm supposed to call him if you can help me bring in this Adrian guy," Jacob added.

Sophie returned the card, not looking him in the eye. She felt violated by this conversation—oddly more violated than she'd felt by Adrian himself. "Well, I'm not hanging out with criminals, so chill," she said.

Maybe the business card was forged, and these "detectives" were the opposition. Or maybe they weren't, and Adrian *was* a dangerous stalker on top of having supernatural powers. That was entirely possible. With a shiver, she considered that Jacob's warning might fit into what she already knew.

"Don't answer his comments anymore, all right?" Jacob asked. "Please. I just don't want you to get killed. Like those other girls." Jacob's voice almost broke on the last sentence. He let his fork drop onto the plate, clearly as uninterested in food as she was.

Sophie pulled in a long breath and released it. Jacob's stress and worry were genuine; she was convinced of that, at least. She reached across and covered his hand with hers. "Okay. Relax. Listen, I'll be careful. I'll ignore him, I promise. It's good that you warned me."

Not that she could ignore what was going on in her head, but she would at least put off talking to Adrian a few days, until she found out more.

Jacob nodded. "Thanks. And if he pesters you online, or if you see him around town or anything, just call the cops."

"I will."

And she meant it—at least for now. What she'd experienced with Adrian might have been some kind of illusion or hallucination. Abuse or death at the hands of an insane stalker might have befallen her, and still could. *Dear God*, she thought shakily, trying one more time to eat a bite of chowder. *I am seriously lucky to be alive.*

THEY DID MANAGE to eat, and the food calmed them down enough that they were nearly smiling again by the time they paid the bill. Back in her dorm room after the meal, they found Melissa had cleared out. She texted Sophie to say she'd be studying late with some other students.

"So we're alone." Jacob drew Sophie close, kissing her neck.

She supposed it was his form of making up and feeling safe. She tried to match the feeling and grow warmer toward him, and succeeded at least partway.

But he sabotaged the mood several minutes later when he asked, "Have you been to the student health clinic yet?"

They were lying on her bed, shirts and shoes off, kissing and nuzzling. Sophie turned her face away, annoyed. "I've only been here a few days, J."

"I know, but we agreed when we went to college you'd see about getting the pill or an IUD or something." He sounded petulant, which made her angrier.

She sat up, nudging his arm off her waist. "Why do you make such a big deal about it? We do other things. We satisfy each other."

"We talked about it. You said you would. I want us to be together."

"How is it not 'being together' to do these other things?"

He grimaced, and flopped onto his back. "Fine. You don't want to."

"I didn't say that. Look, I'll tell you when I talk to the clinic. I haven't had time. I'll get to it when I'm ready."

"Yeah, when you're ready."

"Damn it. Is this how you want it to happen? Because you guilt-tripped me?"

He sat up too, folding his arms around his knees. "Maybe this isn't our night."

"No, maybe it isn't." They sat sulking a moment, then Sophie added, "I'm sorry. It's all that stalker stuff you were talking about. It creeped me out. I kind of don't want *anyone* to touch me tonight."

She wasn't lying. Being alone to untangle her strange thoughts, dreams, and memories appealed most strongly this evening.

Her reciprocal guilt-trip worked, in any case. Jacob looked abashed, kissed her once more, and said, "Okay." A few minutes later, he declared it time to drive back to Eugene. Classes would begin tomorrow for them both.

As soon as he left, she booted up her computer and ran a search on Adrian's name with the terms "criminal" and "wanted" added. She found nothing. For over an hour she searched in every way she could think of, seeking some proof that Adrian was a known danger according to the authorities. Not a single crumb of evidence presented itself.

Both frustrated and relieved, she shut the computer and trudged to the bathroom to get ready for bed. All she could do now was dream, and hope the answers arrived that way.

CHAPTER TWELVE

*H*ER DREAMS WERE LINED UP in wait for her, bombarding her with images surrounding her soul and Adrian's—or at least, that's what her mind insisted they were.

After wading through the life of a woman in northern India in the late nineteenth century, she managed, in the midst of her dream, to remember Adrian's analogy about the bag of oranges. Stepping back from the scene, she mentally gathered up that life into a whole and set it aside. New images flooded in upon her from what she presumed was the life before that one—China this time. After allowing a minute to examine her silk trousers and the taste of the green tea in her small painted mug, she wrapped up that life too and moved it to the side.

Though she approached the memories backward, the most recent events arriving first, she found her mind tended to flip each individual life into the proper chronological order if she wished. All she had to do was think of it as a book, and start at the first page rather than the last, and the story unfolded in the right sequence. She preferred it that way; it made more sense. The backward direction wasn't how people tended to think about life.

Six or seven lives passed in that one night, with brief intermissions in the Underworld, where she visited people she had known. Souls remembered everything. Living mortals only remembered if they'd eaten the pomegranate from Hades and Persephone's orchard. To judge from the conversations she'd held with other souls in the Underworld, no living humans had done that for thousands of years.

"Everyone misses having you immortals around," another soul said to her once, between lives.

She awoke to the golden, cloud-streaked September morning, startled into consciousness by the word. *Immortals*.

Are you immortal? she texted to Adrian—or started to, but stopped and deleted the message. Trusting him still didn't strike her as safe, not with the rumor that he was responsible for the disappearance or murder of several girls.

Meanwhile, she had the first day of classes to tackle. Trying to pretend she was an ordinary college freshman, she armed herself with notebooks and textbooks, and plunged into the hordes on campus.

But her mind wouldn't leave the past alone. Even as she absorbed the lectures and assignments, she analyzed her memories for patterns, and immediately found at least one. In all those six or seven lives, Adrian's soul had resided in someone near her—a good person every time; almost always someone she loved.

Fine, but what if he was born into this life twisted, and was looking to use his superhuman powers to keep her in a closet and enact weird fantasies upon her before ultimately killing her?

He texted her a while later. *Everything OK today?*

She didn't answer, too rattled and uncertain.

Sophie? he added a few hours later. *No one new kidnapped you, I hope?*

She was sitting in a lecture hall, waiting for her Writing class to start. Making sure no one could see the screen, she tapped a hasty reply. *I'm fine. Just busy. Still figuring it all out.*

He must have been satisfied with that response, for he didn't text her again all day.

THE CONFUSION OF working out how long it took her to walk to each class, and the shock of how much homework they were assigning her, managed to take center stage in her mind for a week or so. Still, even as she struggled to ace her assignments and get used to the dreary dorm food, a handful of foreign languages she hadn't previously known evolved in her head, bits of grammar sticking together into long perfect chains. Moments from those lives flashed into her mind at odd times, triggered by everyday movements.

In the happiest lives she was married to the person with Adrian's soul, and in the unhappiest, they had to spend most of their time apart, attached to other people. It was both romantic and unsettling.

More nights, more dreams. More languages. More check-ins and warnings from Jacob.

On the following Monday, the first of October, she walked back to the dorm after class, navigating the crowds of texting-and-walking students. The wind sent spicy-smelling maple leaves swirling off the trees to land around her feet, reminding her of the myth of Persephone, whose abduction kicked off autumn.

So what if I really was Persephone once? she thought. As she recalled from high school literature classes, myths endured because *all* women could feel they were Persephone, Demeter, Aphrodite, Hera, the Virgin Mary, Kali in destroyer mode, or a multitude of other choices, depending on their circumstances. And men could cast themselves as Hades, Zeus, Adonis, Jesus of Nazareth, the Coyote Trickster, or whoever else fit.

Adrian had probably drugged her, making her imagine all this past-life nonsense. In particularly vivid detail, true, but who knew what kind of drugs they were dealing with here? Maybe a trip to the student health center *was* next in order.

Still, she felt a tender beat of her heart every time she dwelled on those old names. *Persephone, Hades.* Indistinct flashes of images flitted in her mind. A large purple flower, a fruit with sky-blue flesh like no other fruit she'd ever seen, a slim golden crown with amethysts on it.

Melissa was out somewhere when Sophie entered their room. Sophie dropped her backpack on the floor, pried off her shoes, and stretched out on her bed, letting her spine recover from hauling textbooks around.

Her phone vibrated, startling her.

I confess I'm dying of curiosity about what you're dreaming and remembering, Adrian texted. *How's it all going?*

It had been over four days since their last text interaction, which had been another brief *Everything okay?*, with her answering, *Yep, just busy. Classes and all.*

Sophie felt she owed him a more detailed answer, but her heart pounded in fear. Who to trust? Adrian, who was apparently also Hades—a mythological god of the dead and a selfish abductor? Or Jacob and his detectives? Or neither?

Her stress burst its restraints and took the form of boldness. She dialed Adrian's number.

"Hi," he answered.

"I've been told you're wanted for kidnapping several girls. Maybe killing them. Give me a good reason I shouldn't call the police and get you the hell out of my life."

After a second of silence, he snorted. "Killing girls now, is it? Ah. This from the nice people trying to kill *me*."

"They approached my boyfriend. Actual detectives, wanting him to look out for you, to protect me."

"Right, I doubt they were actual detectives. Do you have a minute? Can we meet?"

Sophie leaped up to pace the room. "I think I should hang up and call the cops." But she didn't, and knew she probably wouldn't. She was too keen on hearing what he had to say.

"If I'm wanted for crimes," he explained, "it'd be easy for you to find out. Go ahead, call the police in Wellington. Ask them about me. Ask the FBI, ask Amnesty International if you like. There's nothing, because I haven't done anything."

"Except drug me. Whatever you put in that juice is making my brain go nuts. How do I know it isn't all hallucination? You could have planted these memories in there."

"I couldn't plant the entire German language in your head,

could I?" he returned. "Or Hindi, or Cantonese, or all the others you're surely remembering now."

She stayed silent a moment, already knowing he was right. In addition, those web searches verified lots of the historical information she had remembered so far—details she had certainly never known before. "So why would they say you're dangerous?" she asked. "Why scare Jacob like that?"

"To recruit people to catch us. To draw them in with tales of— of poor innocent girls raped and murdered by sadistic maniacs. Who wouldn't protect their daughters and girlfriends from that?"

"But—" She whacked her fist against her closet door in frustration as she paced by it. "What do they really want, then?"

"I told you. *They* want to kill *me*. And Niko, and the few others like us. But they wouldn't get a lot of help from normal people, would they, if they led with, 'We want to hunt down immortals and blow them up into tiny pieces.'"

The silence thrummed between them on the line. Sophie's feet slowed at the image of people getting blown up, but it was a different word that brought her to a stop altogether. "Immortals?" she repeated.

Another few seconds passed, then he breathed a quiet laugh. "Haven't you got that far back in the dreams yet?"

Legs weak, she sat on the edge of her bed. "I kind of have. Not as far back as Persephone, but from what people have said between lives, I'm getting hints…I don't know. I'm so confused."

"Will you let me come see you?" His voice was gentler, kindness taking the place of sarcasm.

"First tell me…if destroying you is what *they* want, then what is it *you* want?"

"We want to help people. Really we do. The souls in the Underworld, people who were murdered—we can give them the justice they never got in life. The plants in the other realm, there's all kinds that don't exist in the living world. There could be a cure for cancer. We just have to look and learn. No one alive has been in that realm for ages. There's so much we could do."

"Okay. But what do you want *me* for?"

It took him a moment to respond. "I want a few good people to spend eternity with. And I want Persephone to be one of them."

Something in the words, and the way he said them, struck a chord deep inside her. Tears welled in her eyes, unexpectedly. She blinked them away and tried out a laugh. "You're not going to get much help if you lead with *that*."

"Don't I know it, love."

CHAPTER THIRTEEN

ADRIAN SLIPPED INTO THE LIVING world and found himself face to face with Sophie. The Oregon sky was gloomy gray overhead. It was dinner hour here, and the smells of the busy restaurants surrounding their designated corner made his mouth water.

Sophie held up a white paper bag solemnly. "Sandwiches."

"Cheers." He gathered her in his arms and switched them to the spirit realm. This time she didn't feel so stiff and resistant; she let herself lean on him as her balance shifted.

Kiri wagged her tail when they appeared. The poor dog had never quite reconciled herself to his new habit of vanishing into thin air. She didn't like it much better when he carried her along, either. He reckoned the sudden change of smells, to a sensitive dog nose, was too jarring.

He let Sophie go and knelt to ruffle Kiri's fur. "It's all right, girl. Here we are."

Rain fell in a quiet but soaking drizzle. Sophie drew her hood up. "Why is it raining here when it wasn't in the other world?"

They set off across the meadow. "My theory is that cities and traffic affect the weather, putting stuff in the clouds. Here there aren't cars or people, so the weather does different things."

"I'll buy that."

Kiri darted ahead, running until only the tip of her tail was visible in the high grass. They followed her through a thicket of evergreens. Adrian stopped on its other side, turning to Sophie with a proud smile.

She took in the shiny, rounded silver caravan sitting there, alone in the wilderness. "An Airstream?"

"Yep. Picked it up yesterday. Don't worry; it can't go anywhere. The horses aren't hooked up to it." He opened the door for her and was gratified when she climbed in after only a second's hesitation.

Kiri leaped in after her, and flopped onto the dog bed he'd bought as part of the preliminary furnishings.

Sophie pushed back her hood and looked around the caravan's interior. "Did you steal it?"

"Not at all. I paid for it." Adrian shut the door, and unzipped his coat. "Niko and I rented a truck, hooked this up to it, and drove it to that car park near your dorm in the middle of the night when no one would see us. Then we each picked up one end and transferred it here."

"Ah." She set the bag of sandwiches on the table, and peeled off her wet coat. He took it and hung it on a hook inside a closet. Settling onto one of the bench seats, she ran her fingers over the dated but clean upholstery. "Psychedelic orange and yellow flowers. I think my parents used to have a carpet with this pattern."

He pointed inside a kitchen cabinet. "Contact paper to match. All quite retro. Of course, I don't have electricity. Have to pick up a generator for that. But for now..." He pulled a pair of white pillar candles from the cabinet and brought them to the table.

She peered out the tableside window to where the bus and horses were parked, a few trees away. "Well, it's definitely an improvement over that pathetic bus."

He grinned, and sat across from her. "You dare to suggest the bus isn't a choice vehicle?"

She looked at him with a skeptical lift of her eyebrows. "Isn't Hades supposed to drive a chariot?"

"Yeah, but there weren't any left over from the old days, so I'd have to build one." He scratched a match against its box and lit the two candles. "I decided something bigger would be better, to transport large items—like taking furniture to the Underworld.

Niko and I found the bus in an Auckland wrecking yard and nicked it."

"So *that* was auto theft."

"Not technically. We left money. No one was ever going to drive it again. It's got a fabulous new life most buses will never experience."

Sophie smirked, opening the bag of food. "Fine. It's a sweet ride."

"Speaking of money—for the sandwiches..." Adrian plucked a ten-dollar bill from his wallet and slid it across the table to her.

"You sure?"

"I can't bear to steal from a uni student. Besides, I owe you. Last food I gave you was um, tainted."

She acknowledged that with a shrug, and pocketed the bill. "How do you pay for stuff? Or buy food, or trailers or things? If you can barely enter the real world without these people coming after you? Doesn't seem like you could hold down a job."

"I can't hold down a traditional paying one. I consider 'Underworld bloke' to be my job now. But the opposition, the secret society, they're small, and they don't have spies everywhere. I try to avoid spots they might expect me to be, but I can usually get into the living world long enough to buy groceries and things without anyone noticing. Plus Niko sometimes runs errands for me in exchange for a diamond or a sapphire. There are parts of the Underworld with gemstones literally falling out of the walls. We use those if we need money."

"I thought I saw that. Handy." Sophie pulled out two wrapped sandwiches, a bag of corn chips, and a pair of Fuji apples. "That's in the mythology. Hades owning the world of riches. Because mines are underground."

"They got that bit right, sort of. I only take stuff from the Underworld, though, not mines in the living realm."

Sophie glanced at the food. "So even though you're immortal, you do eat? And everything."

"And everything."

"Would you die without food?"

"No, I'd just become weak. Knackered. I *prefer* to eat. And I don't like human blood at all, so that puts me above some immortals."

She looked startled. "Vampires are real?"

"No. I was only joking. At least..." He paused and frowned. "I don't *think* they're real."

"Forget them for now." She took two bottles of water from the bag and set them beside the food. "I want to hear about you. How did you become immortal?"

He picked up the bag of chips. "Well...like you learned on the Internet, I was hit by a car when I was five. Was never supposed to walk again. Naturally that was hard enough on Mum and Dad. Then when I was eight, Mum died. I don't have any siblings, so it's just been Dad and me."

Sophie looked sympathetic, as people usually did when presented with his history.

Adrian cleared his throat, and dumped the chips into a pile on a paper napkin. "But I got Kiri around the same time, and she improved things." He tossed a chip to the dog bed, where Kiri snapped it up. "By the time I graduated high school she was getting old, and I wasn't sure what I'd do without her. I mean, I'd get a new dog, but it would be horrible to lose her."

Sophie picked up the paper-wrapped sandwiches. "I cried for a month when our dog died. Even though we already had a new pup. Um, roast beef or ham?"

"Roast beef. Thanks. Then one day when Kiri and I were at the park, this tall African woman walked up to us. At least, she looked African, and had some kind of accent I couldn't place, so I assumed African."

"The woman we met in the Underworld," said Sophie, unwrapping the ham sandwich. "Rhea."

Adrian glanced at her, smiling. "I never told you her name."

She took a bite, and pondered that as she chewed. "I've talked to her in the Underworld between lives. She knew me as Persephone. But she wasn't a soul down there—she was alive. The only one alive." Her voice went quiet in wonder at that sentence.

It was too sad a story, how Rhea had come to be the only living person in the Underworld. Adrian was glad to stick to the subject of his own recent immortality instead.

"So, in the park, she sat down in the grass and talked to me," he continued, peeling the wrapper off his own sandwich. "I kind of suspected she was mental. Some of the things she asked me were bizarre, old-fashioned, especially when it came to modern technology and medicine. And how traffic worked." He chuckled. "But in other ways she seemed so wise. She was interesting, the countries and people she talked about. We talked a while, then she said, 'Can I show you something?' And she had me get Kiri up on my lap. She picked us up like we hardly weighed a thing—wheelchair, me, and dog—and, pop, away went the civilized world."

Sophie nodded to the window. "She brought you here?"

"The spirit realm, yeah. Untamed New Zealand. I was freaked out, of course. But I also thought it was sweet as."

"Sweet as what?"

He grinned. "Just sweet as. Kiwi slang. Means brilliant, excellent."

"Oh." She lifted her eyebrows a moment, chewing a bite of her dwindling sandwich. "So did she take you to the Underworld?"

"Not right then. She let me look around a bit, and explained that this was a world most people never saw until they died. She said she'd take me home whenever I liked, but if I wanted to meet her again, she had somewhere even more amazing to show me. So the next day I arranged to be gone a few hours, and she came and fetched me. She hooked us all up to a spirit horse with these vine things—no bus or anything, just us hanging on to the wheelchair—and off we launched. The journey itself was amazing enough. But then we got to the Underworld, and that was the coolest yet. Even *without* knowing I was Hades."

"But you did eat the pomegranate that day?"

"Yeah. She took me into the forest—the orchard. She said most of the original trees had died, and the ones there now had sprouted up on their own from the fallen seeds. She wasn't sure if these pomegranates would still work the way she expected. But if they did, they'd make me remember it all."

"How long did it take you to decide?" Sophie sounded a bit sad, and he felt a flash of guilt again for taking away her choice in the matter.

"I didn't hesitate. I said, 'Give it here,' and ate it. My life...it'd been quiet, kind of lonesome. A lot of reading, thinking, wishing I could do more. I only had a couple of friends, and felt like I should keep Dad company when I could. But he's quiet too. And besides, I was growing up and would have to find my own way. Basically, when Rhea offered me a fruit that would give me interesting new dreams, I felt I had nothing to lose. Only excitement to gain."

She thought about that as she picked up an apple and polished its skin with her sleeve. "Were you right?"

He raised his eyebrows as he considered. "I did gain excitement. I don't regret knowing everything I know, overwhelming as it is. But later came the problems." He paused and took a long breath. "More on those in a minute. So—I was trying to go on with my ordinary, sleepy life in Wellington, still in the chair, while my mind was exploding with all these past lives. When I got to the one about Hades, I could hardly keep still. His lifetime was... amazing. And I was getting really frustrated, being able to know so much yet still be unable to *walk*—or explore that other realm. Only immortals can switch over; I couldn't get to it unless Rhea brought me. And I had her take me over a lot, all the way to the Underworld, just to explore. That's where I remembered something.

"There was a time once when we—Hades and Persephone— put some keepsakes in a clay jar, and sealed it, and hid it in one of the caves."

"A time capsule?" She bit into her apple with a crunch.

"Basically, though we didn't call it that. We'd heard of kings and queens doing such things, to commemorate who they were, and their...love for each other." He practically spluttered the words, and focused on pulling the cheese and the tomato slice off his sandwich and eating them. *Go easy on that stuff. She has a boyfriend, as she kindly reminded you.*

"What did we put in it?" She sounded interested, at least.

"Oh, a number of small things, which I'll let you remember in your own time." He smiled at her, accurately predicting her eye-roll and grumble. "But one of them was this plant. See—I guess I can tell you this—most immortals back then were born that way. Just a thing that happened to a small number of people. No one knows why. But there was one other way to become immortal, and that was through eating a certain...food. A plant." He glanced guardedly at her. "You'll dream about that soon too. Thing is, that plant had died out in the Underworld long ago. And, like the pomegranate, it only worked there.

"But when I remembered we had put some of it in the clay jar, then it hit me: people can sometimes take seeds they find pre-served in ice, or in archaeological sites, and plant them again and grow them, even after thousands of years. It had been done. I'd seen articles. So I told Rhea, and we went to the tunnel where it was hidden.

"The passageway, the tunnel, was really narrow and full of rocks, and she had to pick me up from the chair and carry me in until I pointed out the right spot. The hole was still all blocked up with big rocks that I couldn't move, but she could. She cleared them away, and...it was there. The clay jar." His heart beat faster, just as it had that day, knowing he held an object that was last touched millennia ago by their hands—Persephone's and Hades'.

Sophie's hazel eyes were round and stunned. "Did it have owls on it?" she whispered.

Their gazes met. Affection and pride for her swelled up in him. "Yes. We'd painted owls on it, amongst other things."

She blinked, looking overcome, and lowered her face. "I can't remember much, but these little flashes, they keep happening."

"They'll get stronger. That's how it works."

"Tell me what color the owls were." She stared at the middle of the table.

"Why?"

She looked at him. "I remember what color they were. But I want you to say it. I want to see if the memory's real."

He held her gaze. In that moment, the wonder and the longing for wisdom in her face transformed her into the Persephone he had loved. Souls could do that, surfacing and shaping a person's features so that if you looked closely, you recognized a long-gone face. He'd caught glimpses of it on Sophie before, but never as strong as this, and it took his breath away. He recovered by carefully drawing another breath, and answered, "Purple. They were purple. We...were going for dark blue, like the evening sky, but paint colors didn't always dry the way we wanted back then. Blue was hard to make."

She seemed unable to speak. The reflection of the candle flames glimmered in her eyes. She only nodded.

Their glances separated. Sophie sat back, and gazed in abstraction at the apple she still held.

Adrian cupped both hands around his water bottle, as if it were the clay jar. "When Rhea and I opened it, we mostly found shriveled-up dusty things, impossible to recognize. But the seeds were there. They have an unusual shape, so I knew them right away. They were as dusty and mummified as everything else, but we figured it was worth a shot. We took them back to the orchard, found the area where they used to grow, and planted them. Gave them water from the river."

"And they grew."

"One did. Two years later, it produced the first...parts you would eat."

"Fruit," she filled in softly. "I know it was fruit."

"Yeah. Fruit. So I had two years to decide whether I'd eat one. But I knew all along that I would. And one day I finally did." He let a pause fill in for the day of cramps, burning sensations, tingling pains, and aching thirst while the fruit took its effect. "It healed me. Went through my whole body and changed me into something almost invincible. I stood up, out of the wheelchair. I could walk. I could run. I could lift those big rocks I couldn't move before. I could do...everything."

He snapped his fingers at his side, and Kiri got up and came to rest her chin on his lap. He fed her part of his sandwich bread. "Once I made sure it wasn't going to kill me, I gave Kiri some too."

Sophie gasped, scooting over toward Kiri. "You have an immortal dog? That's so cool!" She reached down to stroke Kiri's ears. Kiri serenely licked Sophie's fingers.

Adrian smiled, tossing Kiri a slice of roast beef from his sandwich. "I didn't want to live forever if I couldn't bring her along. She deserves it more than any of us."

"Rhea must have been happy. More immortals to keep her company at last."

"She was. You can ask her about it yourself sometime. But nowadays there's a danger in hanging out with us. In fact, there always was. We just didn't realize it for a while."

Sophie settled back into her seat again, looking troubled once more. "The opposition?"

"Yeah." He decided he might as well give her more information, if they were trying to get to her through Jacob. "They're called Thanatos. It basically means 'death' in Greek, or maybe 'mortality' was more their idea. They started in ancient times, and have been around all these centuries. Basically they think no one, ever, should be immortal."

Sophie crunched on her apple, brows furrowed. "It *is* a dangerous thing you've discovered. Easy immortality—what if that got out? The world would be overpopulated in no time."

"Absolutely, and I agree, it shouldn't get out. But does that make immortality wrong altogether?" He rested both elbows on the table. "If you surveyed the world on the question, about half— if I estimate right—would say they like the idea of immortality and would like to have it themselves, please."

"That's way too many immortals."

"Right. But another, say, forty percent would say they don't want to be immortal themselves, but they wouldn't mind a few people being immortal, just for variety."

"I assume you like those people. They've got your back."

"We do like them, whoever exactly they are. But the last ten percent are against immortality for anyone. And a tiny portion of them are *freakishly* against it. Some for religious reasons, some for practical concerns like overpopulation. And they have, in fact, tracked down immortals and…killed them." Adrian's voice faltered. He wasn't sure he ought to burden Sophie with this yet. Then again, she'd best know what she was up against.

Her face tensed as she gazed at the table, the line of her cheekbone as lovely as any marble statue of a Greek goddess. "That's what happened to the gods in the old days," she said. "They were killed."

He nodded. "Not to give you nightmares, but it takes a lot of force and effort. These people have to be determined. Basically, immortals have to be burned up in very high heat, or torn to pieces, or both. These days, explosives do the trick."

She looked at him. "Who's been killed these days? You said someone had."

He swallowed, debating how much to say, then gave in. "Apollo. He was reborn in India. He was a journalist, rather famous. Had a wife and grown-up kids. You might have seen me talking to him in the Underworld, while you were with your grandfather."

She nodded. "Guess he was interested in seeing me."

"Indeed. Reminded me I shouldn't be sharing the secrets, but said he could hardly blame me, given how cute you were."

She smirked at the compliment, and Adrian continued, "Rhea found him not long after finding me. It didn't take much convincing for him to eat the pomegranate. We met a few times and became friends; stayed in touch online. He was the next, after Kiri and me, to eat the immortality fruit, even though it meant becoming strangely young, which kind of freaked out his wife and friends.

"He didn't care. He thought it was awesome, and wanted to share the news with people. And that was where he got really unlucky. See, being Hindu, he went to some of his gurus to tell them about it, figuring they'd be able to appreciate stuff like a spirit realm and an immortality fruit better than most." Adrian scraped together his sandwich crumbs, then let his hands fall still.

"Turned out one of them was in Thanatos. He confronted Sanjay in private and made some threats, but none of us understood how dangerous this cult was until too late. Until after they…planted a car bomb and murdered him."

"You're sure it was them?" Sophie sounded shocked.

"The guru visited his widow afterward and told her it had happened because he 'defied nature.' It sounded dreadfully like claiming credit for the attack."

"He should have been arrested."

"There wasn't enough evidence. We've tried, and we can't find it. It's maddening. Sanjay was in Afghanistan at the time, for work, and we suspect the group used local terrorists, whose names we don't know and whose language none of us speaks. Even if we did know who they were, there's no guarantee anyone could find them and get them to confess. Those people are good at hiding. Just ask the CIA."

"But why didn't this make bigger news?" Sophie asked, outraged.

"A car bomb in Afghanistan? It was just taken to be part of the fighting. And the notion that Sanjay was immortal, well, that'd be insane-tabloid material, wouldn't it? News like that wouldn't get out unless some immortal was really determined to prove their abilities to the world. Trust me, after what happened to him, none of us are. The only ones who believe it are this select group of fanatics. And Sanjay's widow."

"Wait, what about *your* family? They must know you were healed. How much else do they know?"

Adrian nodded, a flicker of homesickness stinging him. "I kept it secret from my dad as long as I could. I didn't think he'd understand. He's always stressed; and anyway, he's a devout Christian and I wasn't sure he'd like this notion of me hanging around with a Greek goddess. And when we started growing the immortality fruit, well, I didn't tell him that either, because I didn't want to get his hopes up—that I might get cured."

"So when did you tell him?"

Adrian smiled faintly. "The day I got my legs back. After eating the fruit. I walked in, no wheelchair, and said, 'I have some things to tell you.' He was, um, gobsmacked."

"But happy, I would think."

"Yeah. Happier than I ever realized he'd be." Adrian ran his fingertips along the table's surface. "After explaining everything, I asked him, 'But doesn't it bother you, from a religious standpoint?' And he said, 'As far as I'm concerned, this *is* the work of God.' Of course I emphasized that we shouldn't tell people the truth. We spread it about that I'd got some fancy new 'treatment' that got me walking again. But then the real trouble started."

"Thanatos," Sophie guessed.

He nodded. "They started sniffing around Wellington, looking for me. Probably they tracked me through messages between Sanjay and me."

"And you said someone tried to kill you?"

He looked into her anxious eyes, then lowered his gaze. "A guy shot me and Kiri, in the park one night." While Sophie sucked in her breath, he added, "Clearly it was just a warning. If they wanted me dead they'd have used a rocket launcher, not a gun. He incapacitated me long enough to tell me they knew about us and that we'd better get lost and not make any more immortals, and that if I showed up in the living world again I *would* be dead."

She emitted an unsteady sigh. "Okay, I see why you avoid our realm so much."

He leaned down to pet Kiri again. "Also I suppose they were testing us. Seeing what would happen if we were shot. They still might not know Kiri's immortal—she didn't regain consciousness till after I'd switched us to the other realm. But now they definitely know I am."

"And that's why you moved to the Underworld."

"Yes. And it's why I can't visit Dad much anymore." Adrian chewed the side of his lip, recalling the whole mess. "I crept back in that night, Kiri and me covered in blood, and unfortunately he was right there, and got the whole scary visual. So I couldn't break it to him gently. The long and short of it is, I was terrified someone would kill him too—maybe bomb our house—so I told him I had to leave. 'We have to pretend we've had a falling out,' I said. 'Tell everyone I'm an ungrateful, arrogant sod who's gone off on his own, and you're having nothing to do with me. Tell them whatever you have to.'"

"But you do still see him?" She sounded sad on his behalf.

"Occasionally. And I have my mate Zoe transfer messages between us, texts. Her parents are a software engineer and a security expert, so she's pretty certain she'd catch anyone trying to spy on her."

"So are you guys keeping track of what Thanatos is doing?"

"We're trying. But we ourselves are not terribly good at being hackers and spies. Except Niko—he's got the knack."

"How many of you are there?"

He lifted an eyebrow. "Now we're getting into things I shouldn't tell you yet."

"Why not? You've told me about the fruit of immortality and where it grows."

"Yeah, but they learned that from Sanjay already, and they can't get into the spirit realm. Nor can you."

"But from Sanjay they probably know how many of you there are, and what your names are."

"No, they don't seem to be sure about those things. They know about me, because of my correspondence with Sanjay. And they know about Rhea, though they can't find any current record of her, because there isn't one. And they have strong suspicions about others. But I shouldn't tell you all their names either, or how many there are, because...it's dangerous information." He decided against specifically saying they might torture her to learn it. If they did, he vowed silently, he would go against his decision not to instigate violence, and kill the torturers himself.

She stayed silent long enough that he suspected she had guessed about the torture scenario. "I'll definitely avoid them. But I don't know yet if I'll become one of you, either." She set her apple on a napkin. "This is a very deep and difficult offer you're making me, you realize."

"I do realize."

"I'd need more time to think about it even if I knew everything."

"Yes. Which you don't."

She nodded, tracing figure eights on the table with her pinky. "This is sure making me want to dream about Persephone, though."

"You'll get there soon. I'm eager to have you reach those memories myself." And not just because they were highly likely to put her in a romantic mood...but that was the larger part of his motivation.

She looked out the window. "I'm pretty sure Jacob, at least, doesn't know the truth about those so-called detectives."

"Oh, I agree," said Adrian. "I doubt he does know."

"He did honestly seem to think you were stalking me to kill me, or something ordinary like that."

"Well, I promise I'm not."

She tried to smile, but nervousness evidently wiped it out. "I don't know if I'd trust you one bit, if it weren't for all these dreams and memories."

"Yeah. That's why I had to get the pomegranate into you."

Her smile stretched more this time, and she looked at him with fresh curiosity. "How *did* you find me? Or how did Rhea find you, and all the others?"

"Another immortal ability. We can sense certain souls, ones we've made a deliberate connection with in the past, as long as the connection was made when we were immortal." He decided not to explain about how it required an exchange of bodily fluids—either by a blood-brothers kind of process, or the rather more fun and clothing-free way. "If I concentrate, I can single out a sort of hum, or vibration, and home in on it, for those select people. It was easy enough to track you that way."

"So the day you kidnapped me, that probably wasn't actually the first day you saw me in person. You must have tracked me and found me before that."

"All right, a little."

"Tell me again how you're not stalking me?" But she grinned as she said it.

Bowing his head, he smiled. "I was at your high school graduation, because that was a big crowd and no one would notice. And I bought fruit from you once at your fruit stand. That was all. No peering into windows or anything."

She looked intrigued. "From me personally, you bought fruit?"

"In July. You were working the cash register."

"Why don't I remember this?"

"You remember everyone who buys fruit?"

"No. I just feel like I should have noticed you."

"It was a busy day. Heaps of people. And I was disguised, hat and sunglasses and stuff." Also, he hadn't dared speak more than a few words to her, for fear she'd notice his New Zealand accent and pay too much attention to him.

Someday he might even tell her how hard his heart had pounded at being closer to her than ever before.

"What did you buy?"

Her question surprised him. "Er…apples. Plums. Strawberries; you guys had a special on those. Oh, and tomatoes."

"Good memory."

Regarding her? Of course. Clearing his throat, he crumpled up the sandwich papers into a ball, and blew out the candles. "I've told you enough for one day. You need to go to sleep and find out more."

She watched him stuff the napkins into the paper bag. "And in the meantime, keep dating the guy who's being approached by people who might try to kill me? Plus go to class and maintain at least a 3.5 grade point average? And be there for my family when they need me?"

"You've got it." He stood and offered his hand to her.

She scowled, but took it, and let him pull her to her feet.

As she picked up her coat, Adrian added, "Text me whenever it gets too much. You're my priority for now—making sure you adjust all right." Actually she was his priority forever, and had been in life after life. But again with the problem of sounding like a stalker if he said that.

Adrian held her coat while she slid her arms in, then put his own coat on. He opened the Airstream's door, letting in a gust of air that smelled of wet fields.

Sophie followed him outside. "By the way, who was Nikolaos, back in the Greek god days?"

"Haven't you guessed?"

She thought about it a moment, then laughed. "Of course. Hermes."

"Yep." Adrian felt an ages-old glimmer of envy at the fondness and amusement on her face. The trickster's charisma always drew people to him, women especially. Even when he was screwing with your life just for laughs.

"What was he in this life?" she asked. "Before you found him."

"A con man." Enjoying her gasp of surprise, he took her hand and led her toward the stake with its fluorescent ribbons hanging sodden in the rain.

CHAPTER FOURTEEN

Sophie exchanged a few texts with Jacob that night while they both did their homework, she in Corvallis and he in Eugene. But her mind thrummed with everything Adrian had told her. She longed to know more about Hades and Persephone.

And Hermes. He had darted across their lives on an irregular basis, forever mischievous and causing trouble, but nonetheless their ally. A valuable person to have at your back, he also excelled at dodging repercussions for his behavior. A con man? Of course; what else would he have been?

Niko had been sixty-six years old when they approached him, Adrian told her as they lingered next to the stake. After avoiding arrest for his swindles in his native Greece and half a dozen other countries in Europe, he was living in England under one of his many assumed identities. Upon receiving the offer to become eternally young and strong, and gain a whole undiscovered realm in which to hide and explore at his will, he accepted immediately.

"Turning from a paunchy, balding old guy into a fit, young-looking bloke made him insufferably vain," Adrian said. "He kept dragging me to pubs and challenging me to contests—who could get some girl's phone number first, stuff like that. Which I never took him up on."

Adrian had been quick to add that last bit, Sophie recalled. It was cute, his wanting to impress her with something as trivial as that, when he had so many other massively impressive qualities at hand.

She finished her homework, and, exhausted, fell asleep after mumbling goodnight to Melissa.

Each night she had gotten a little better at this lucid-dreaming thing. Tonight she leaned harder on the skip-backward button, shoving entire lives past her into the heap of beautiful, terrible, ordinary human things she had experienced, and searching with a physical exertion for that one life that held so many answers.

She was far enough back now that history had given way to prehistory, which meant she must be getting closer, but also made the era difficult to pinpoint.

Groggy in the morning, she picked up her phone to text Adrian. *Native America, I think*, she typed. *Our village was learning to build a new kind of boat and there was a big argument about it. One man killed his brother.*

Ah yes. Think that was the American southeast, he answered. *You're very close now. Maybe 3 more lives, then you're there.*

Her body tingled with excitement as she hurried into her clothes and walked through the cool fog to her classes, bumping elbows with other students. Jack o' lantern and bat decorations leered at her from windows. It was already Halloween season. The year was passing her by while she lived this strange inner life. But how, she wanted to demand, was she supposed to concentrate on classes and ordinary life with the prospect of unlocking Persephone's secrets dangling in front of her?

After class she treated herself to coffee on Monroe Avenue. Ignoring the other students crowding the cafe, she sat at a small table and gazed at the steam rising from her coffee. She was practicing moving backward in her mind toward the next life while awake. Thus occupied, she didn't notice the person beside the table until she spoke.

"Would it be all right if I sat here?"

Sophie looked up to find an elderly woman wearing an OSU Beavers sweatshirt, orange lettering on black.

"Oh. Of course." A quick glance around showed that, indeed, the chair opposite Sophie was one of the only empty seats in the cafe. "Sorry. I was in my own little world."

The woman chuckled, showing straight, faintly yellowed teeth. "That's all right." She eased herself into the seat, leaning a cane against the window beside her. "I'm Betty Quentin."

"Hi. Sophie. I'm a freshman."

"Pleased to meet you." They shook hands. Betty Quentin's hands were dry, her nails varnished cotton-candy pink.

"Do you teach?" Sophie asked.

"Only occasionally. I'm an emeritus professor now—retired." The professor regarded her with pale blue eyes. "What are you studying?"

"Nutrition. Or that's the plan so far." *But evidently I was a Greek goddess once, so maybe I ought to switch to Classics,* she thought, half-seriously.

"Useful field. Very good." Quentin removed the plastic lid from her coffee, releasing a curl of steam, and bent her head to take a sip. Knotty white hair covered the top of her head, a few pink patches of scalp showing in spots. "I teach philosophy. Not nearly so useful, but it's always fascinated me."

"Sounds interesting."

"It is. Also, I keep an eye on unusual people. Like your Adrian Watts."

A chill flashed through Sophie from ears to feet. She forced down another sip of coffee, trying not to let her hand shake, and offered a frown as if the name meant nothing to her. "Sorry?"

"What he's offering you isn't natural, Sophie." Professor Quentin gazed at her with concern, as if Sophie were her grand-daughter.

"What are we talking about?" Sophie asked quietly.

"The golden apple. The holy grail. *Immortality.*" Quentin said the word in a stage whisper.

Sophie tried to smile as she were amused, while her mind clamored in a panic that this might be one of the exact people who'd had Sanjay murdered. She smoothed the hem of her jacket over her trembling legs. "I'm sorry, I really don't understand."

"I know you've been talking to him. A few messages here and there, maybe some meetings. Beware, dear. I've made such people my life's study. They exist. They're not supposed to be in this world, but they've been coming in lately. I warn you, for your own safety, turn this man—this *creature*—over to us right away."

Sophie jumped to her feet, scrambling to pick up her backpack and keys; making sure she had her phone in her pocket; grabbing her half-full coffee cup. "I'm sorry, I need to get to class. It was nice to meet you."

"Contact my associate if Adrian proposes meeting you in person." Quentin held out a business card. Sophie took it. A glance at it showed the same name Jacob had received: Bill Wilkes. "If you keep talking to Adrian, and you don't let us know," Quentin added, "you're going to be caught in the middle of a fight you don't want to be in."

Clutching the card, Sophie stepped back. "I have to go."

"I've scared you. I apologize, but there was no other way. He's a monumental danger, Sophie. Don't let him seduce you. Oh, by the way…" Quentin held up her cell phone, its screen displaying a photo. Sophie leaned a few inches closer. It was a picture of her parents' fruit stand back in Carnation. "Looks like a nice place," said Quentin. "I'll have to visit."

Sophie didn't even say goodbye. She felt nauseated and cold. She backed away from the table, crashing into someone else's chair and dropping her coffee, then spun and rushed out of the cafe. She ran the whole way to the dorm, sneakers slapping the pavement, pack thumping her back, her breath tasting like acid.

Once she was safe in her dorm room—if she was even safe there—she pulled out her phone and called Adrian's number.

"Hey," he greeted.

She sat on the floor against her bed and pulled up her knees, still breathing fast. "This old woman in a coffee shop—she warned me about you. She knew what you are, and told me not to take what you were offering. And I think she threatened my family." She blinked against a sting in her eyes, and realized tears were rising.

"Who was she? Did you get a name?" Alarm had sharpened Adrian's voice.

"Yeah, she was a professor. Started with a Q. Quinn, or…"

"Quentin?"

"That was it. You know her?"

"Professor Quentin came to meet you in person? Old woman, white hair, blue eyes?"

"Yes. Who is she?"

"She basically *is* Thanatos. The head, the boss, the obsessed one who keeps them all fired up and gets them to kill us. People in the Underworld, who used to be in the group, they've told me about her. She's been doing this a long time."

"Oh, my God. So that 'freaky' vibe was right on."

"What'd she say about your family? What was the threat?"

"She flashed me a picture of the fruit stand. Said, 'Nice place; I should visit.'" Sophie tried to steady herself with a deep breath, but it wasn't helping.

"Okay, for now, try not to worry about that. She's probably just trying to scare you. But you can warn your parents that some weirdo mentioned the place to you, and that they should call the police if anyone's lurking about. Now, what did *you* say? About me and how much I've told you?"

"Not much. I acted like I didn't have a clue what she was talking about. But she said she knew about 'messages' between us."

"Hmm. Maybe just because of our comments on your blog." He paused to take a breath. "Okay, go back, tell me everything she said. And what you answered."

It wasn't hard; the conversation hadn't lasted long. Sophie did her best to repeat it in full.

"All right," Adrian said afterward. "You did the right thing, pretending you didn't have a clue. I figured someone would approach you before long, since they've already tried to go through Jacob. But Quentin personally coming all the way to see you… that's not good."

"What do you mean, all the way? I thought she taught here. At OSU."

"She doesn't. Was a professor somewhere on the East Coast. Lives in New Jersey, we thought."

Sophie hugged her knees tighter. "She came to Oregon just because I'm here?"

"Probably. As a way to get to me." They were silent a second. Adrian sighed. "God. Why am I doing this to you? Putting you in the crosshairs of people like that?"

"But if I stay...mortal...they wouldn't hurt me. Would they?"

"I hope not. Okay. Um, it's possible someone's seen us together, or stolen a look at your texts or something. Be really careful with your phone."

She groaned. "Oh, hell, I'm an idiot. They could be listening right now."

"I doubt it. If they'd done a really choice job of bugging or tracing your phone, they'd have followed you straight to one of your meetings with me. Still, look very closely at it after we hang up."

"Yeah. I'll Google how to catch spyware."

"Do that. And," he added, "I hate to say I shouldn't see you very often, but..."

"No, we can be careful," she insisted. "If we go to the spirit realm, they can't get there, can they?"

"They can't," he assured. "As long as they don't actually see you with me, we should be all right. We'll find new places to meet and switch over. Also, I'll let the others know about Quentin. I bet Niko would be happy to do some surveillance on her and this Bill Wilkes. I'll ask around in the Underworld, too. Everyone's got contacts and secrets to share down there."

"Can I tell the cops I'm being stalked?"

"At this point I doubt you could. She hasn't quite made any explicit threats, and it'd be hard to explain it without bringing up what we are. But if she—or anyone—takes one step closer to you, makes any sort of dangerous move, then yeah. Get their arse arrested." He sighed. "Don't suppose I could lend you Kiri, to guard you as you walk around."

"Nope, can't keep dogs in the dorm. But I do have pepper spray."

"Good. Carry that. And, hey, um..." His voice went shy.

"Thanks for telling me right away. For still wanting to talk to me at all, in fact."

She smiled, though he couldn't see it. "Well, I need to hear how this Hades story ends up. I can't ditch you till I find that out."

"Quite right. You can't."

After they hung up, she gazed frowning at her window. Why *had* she immediately called Adrian? Could she prove he wasn't out to hurt her — that he wasn't just as dangerous as Quentin claimed? Not really. Unless you could trust thousands of years of memories and instincts brought on by an Underworld fruit.

With a smirk, she hauled herself to her feet. Everything had turned insane in her life. All she could do was go along for the ride.

CHAPTER FIFTEEN

AFTER SNEAKING HADES OUT OF the palace, Tanis led him north toward the seaside. By dawn it was pouring, and so cold they both shivered in their soaked cloaks. But their island was receiving its much-needed rain at last, which made them exchange grins as they ducked into an abandoned sheep-herder's shelter to rest and eat breakfast.

Near evening, they entered the port town on the coast. The rain was finally letting up, allowing in warm rays of sunlight. Hades had been here only a few times as a boy, with his parents, to buy certain rare types of fish. But he had never set foot on a boat, and thus had never left the island. His contact with the sea was limited to wading and swimming near the shore on those rare visits, where he marveled at both the saltiness and the sheer might of the ocean.

Despite the new evidence that he was more or less indestructible, he quaked as he climbed aboard a ship at the docks and stared out at the fuzzy blue horizon. The vessel was huge, at least the length of ten tall men and the width of five, but even in harbor, it rocked alarmingly with the waves. The sails rippled and snapped with each gust of wind. The oars looked like thin splinters, no match at all for the sea's power.

Tanis, who had arranged their passage and paid the ship's captain, came on board with him.

"If there's going to be a storm, shouldn't we wait?" he asked.

"The sailors know the weather. They say it'll likely rain again, but not hard enough to worry about. Besides, tonight's winds are excellent for carrying us to Greece."

He gazed at the sea, where fish large and small broke the surface in energetic leaps, catching golden flashes of sun on their scales before plopping back into the depths.

If the ship overturned and sank in the middle of the Mediterranean, and sharks or other sea monsters ripped him into hundreds of pieces, wouldn't that finally kill him? He saw no way it couldn't, if various parts of him were in the stomachs of different fish.

Oh well, did it matter? He had been prepared to die anyway.

But as the crew untied the ropes and freed the ship from its moorings, and the wind swept them out upon the sea, Hades' heart lifted with excitement. The sensation of sailing with the wind was the closest thing to flying he'd ever experienced. Holding onto the edge, he watched the sea spray splash into the air while the hull danced through the waves.

Then he turned and watched his island, his only home and entire world, dwindle in their wake. Aside from Rhea, everyone there thought he was dead, killed for a good cause. He whispered a prayer to his old household gods and goddesses to keep watch over his family and neighbors. After the prayer he stopped and wondered, for the first time in his life, who or what those gods and goddesses really were. He had always assumed they were spirits who sometimes took the form of fantastical beasts (or part-beast-part-humans), the way the old stories had taught him. And of course they were invincible. But if he himself was invincible, then what did that mean?

It felt sacrilegious to think of himself as anything like a god. He couldn't be. Gods were supposed to know everything, and he knew virtually nothing. He hoped these others, to whom Tanis was taking him, could tell him what he was. And he hoped the real gods and goddesses were still up there, in their intangible, omniscient spirit forms, watching over him as they sent him on this journey.

Tanis leaned on his arm. "Let's find a spot to sleep."

They lay down behind a stack of lashed-down crates carrying cargo to Greece. Like the other passengers, they used their bundles as pillows. An extra cloak covered them both for a blanket. A spare sail had been strung overhead to keep off the rain and wind, but in the space between it and the walls of the ship, Hades could see a deep blue line of sky, sparkling with stars. The sea spray left the taste of salt on his lips. His senses full, he fell asleep.

The journey took several more days, their progress slowed by the many ports the ship stopped at. Hades filled the hours marveling at the Greek landscape and at the vast sea and its frolicking creatures, and talking to Tanis, who had made the voyage several times by now. As the ship sailed along the coast, she pointed out villages and landmarks. Finally they disembarked at a bustling port, its narrow docks so full of people that Hades was almost knocked into the water a few times as they walked toward shore.

Shouts and conversations filled his ears. The Greek language dialects were similar to that of Crete, but pronounced differently enough that he couldn't decipher half of what he heard. Tanis, being a native, took care of the trading for them, procuring them breakfast and extra food. From the heavy pack Hades carried for her, she brought out Egyptian jewelry and jars of Cretan honey and oils, and bartered them for fruit, cheese, and yogurt.

They ate in the shade of an olive tree overlooking the sea, then she led him out of town and into the mountains.

It was another few days' journey, interrupted by overnight stays in the homes of villagers and shepherds, before they reached their destination. In the shreds of a late-morning fog, they stood at the foot of a great mountain, its top hidden in clouds. The chilly, pure air rolling downward suggested snow at its peak.

"Here's where mortals like me stop." Tanis pointed at a grassy, narrow track between the boulders. "Follow that goat path. The immortals live on top of the mountain."

Hades stared with consternation into the fog. "But what if I get lost? What if I can't find them?"

"You will. Or they'll find you. And if the clouds clear, you'll see their houses easily enough."

He turned to look into the face of the brave, sweet woman who had brought him farther into the world than he'd ever been. He halfway loved her already; the painful memory of his young wife had faded further with every day he spent in the company of someone so lively and charming. And besides, it was now clear he'd never find his wife again. He had knocked upon the door of the spirit realm and had been denied entrance. He felt he'd been given permission—even encouragement—to restore his interest in living women.

"Will I see you again?" he asked Tanis.

"I'm not sure." She sounded regretful. "I will if I ever have reason to bring anyone else here, or deliver a message from Rhea. But it's not likely to happen often."

"If you do come back, try to find me. And if I ever return to Crete, I'll find you."

"Again, not likely." Despite the discouraging words, she stepped up and kissed him on the lips. "But I hope to see you. You have great things ahead of you, Hades." She glanced upward at the slopes of Mount Olympos, her eyelashes lifting. "Climb."

He climbed. Alone, in eerily silent, cold fog, he wound upward along the goat track. He found no living thing along his way, only rocks, tough little trees, and ferns. The air thinned and chilled, feeling bizarrely light in his lungs, but his legs carried him up the mountain without effort.

When he reached a pass between two boulders, a voice arrested him.

"Halt!"

It was accompanied by the unmistakable creak of an arrow being stretched into a bow. An arrow wouldn't kill him, of course, but he didn't like the idea of being impaled by one, all the same. He halted, hands out at his sides, and looked up.

A woman, her dark brown hair cut to her earlobes, rose from her crouch atop one of the boulders. A gray cloak the same shade as the rocks camouflaged her. Her dark eyes stayed aimed at him, as did the arrow from her long bow. She stepped soundlessly from rock to rock, descending until standing in front of him. "And you are?"

"Hades. From Crete. Rhea sent me."

The woman lifted her eyebrows for a moment. "Did she? Why?" She sounded to be from the Greek mainland, and he found it difficult to understand her.

"Because I'm like her. She said I'd find more of you here."

She lowered the bow. "You're immortal?"

Though still uncomfortable with the word, he nodded. "I offered myself as the sacrifice at the palace, at Knossos. But the axe and the knife failed to kill me."

She bobbed the arrow, still nocked. "I could test again with this."

"If you must. I'd rather not."

She gestured to a rock the size of a full-grown cow. "Lift that."

He stepped to it, crouched, slid his arms around it, and picked it up.

Finally she lowered the bow. "All right. Put that down and come meet the others."

CHAPTER SIXTEEN

WHAT ADRIAN REMEMBERED ABOUT THE next two to three decades was a mini golden age of learning. The immortals educated each other and taught the new ones who arrived, all the while expanding their understanding of their own powers and of the world at large.

Hades was the youngest immortal, of course, when he entered that collection of stone dwellings atop Mount Olympos. The two oldest, who were obviously a couple based on both their affection and their constant arguments, were Hera and Zeus. They hailed from Crete as well, and had been sent to Greece by Rhea—who, they maintained, was far older than they. Even Rhea herself wasn't sure how old she was, but it certainly extended into the centuries. That boggled Hades' mind, being barely seventeen himself.

Hera and Zeus were in their seventies. Poseidon and Demeter, another couple, at least off and on, were in their sixties, as was Athena. Artemis and Apollo were in their forties—Artemis had been the one aiming an arrow at him that first day, and she and Apollo behaved like the closest of siblings, though technically they weren't. Despite their various ages, all of them looked nearly as young as Hades, and were all beautiful and fit.

"If you're immortal, why bother posting guards?" he asked that first night.

Hera snorted. "We're tired of big-muscled mortal idiots ambushing us just to see if they can defeat us and steal our belongings. They can't, of course, but they're such a distasteful intrusion."

As things stood, legends and fanciful stories circulated about the group of "gods" living on Olympos, who sometimes made mundane appearances in nearby villages to buy food or wool or building supplies (or to visit lovers), and who invited only the most exotic and mysterious visitors to their dwellings. These guests were usually scholars or travelers who could tell them things about the world, or teach them new languages.

Sometimes the immortals were summoned by royalty in various cities, and hired to defeat a marauder or rival with their superior strength. Merely a few such jobs had supplied the little group with more jewels, clothing, and fine weapons than they would need in twenty years, and kept their homes luxuriously outfitted. Nonetheless, the average Greek's fear and mistrust surrounding their existence made them stay apart, hidden away on the mountain.

Hera and Zeus proposed changing all that, a few months after Hades joined them.

"If we go down and live among them," Hera insisted, "we can improve the people's lives with our knowledge and get some proper respect. And not have to live up here among the snow and fog." She brought up the argument regularly, tugging her woolen cloak around herself in disdain for the inhospitable weather of the mountain. The others always conceded the appeal of her proposition, but put her off by insisting on gathering more wisdom and enjoying their freedom a while longer. For, surely, if they descended to live in palaces, with mortals crawling all over as servants, their lives would quickly become a series of petitions and tedious ceremonies.

"Just ask Rhea," Athena pointed out.

"Yet she stays on Crete, enjoying her power as priestess," Hera returned. "Why shouldn't we do something similar, but more openly? Proclaim ourselves as the immortals we are?"

"It seems wise to investigate our powers and limits further," said Demeter, "rather than seek glory."

"Speaking of powers," Hades ventured, "there's an odd sensation I have regarding Rhea sometimes. I can somehow tell where she is—I mean, in which direction, and roughly how far. It's like isolating where a birdsong is coming from, sort of." Feeling young and foolish, he blushed as they stared at him, and he added in almost a stammer, "Does—does anyone know what I mean?"

"Oh, yes." Hera sounded almost bored, and smoothed a fold of her cloak. "Zeus and I have that. Don't we, dear?"

"Indeed." He smiled.

"I think we all do," Demeter said, "with people we've—loved." She and Poseidon exchanged uneasy glances and looked away again. Hades gathered their relationship was rocky at best.

"But I don't love Rhea," Hades said. "We barely know each other."

Zeus chuckled. "I don't think love is technically required, only a certain connection. If you understand me."

Hades' blush deepened. "No, we never…did that either. I was married, but my wife is dead, and with her…" He paused, thinking. "I suppose I felt it when she was alive, but I can't be sure."

"Yes," said Demeter. "It was the same for me and my children, though it comes and goes." She'd had children at a younger age, as had many of the others; they were grown up now and living elsewhere, probably assuming their missing parents were dead. "Perhaps there's some kind of blood connection."

"Oh," Hades said in sudden understanding. "A blood connection. That could make sense. Rhea's blood and mine must have mingled. When she sacrificed me, I mean."

Zeus laughed. "Next time, lad, put the knives away and try it the other way. It's much more fun."

"But for me the sensation comes and goes, for no apparent reason," Demeter reminded him.

Hades and the others admitted it did for them as well.

"So all we know is that our understanding and powers clearly have their limits," she concluded.

The mystery of the sensation vanishing and reappearing was solved within the year, though. One day Poseidon strode in and announced, "Oak."

When the others stared at him in incomprehension, he clarified, "Oak blocks the feeling of sensing one another at a distance. When the person enters a thick oak forest, or goes behind a wall of oak planks—in short, when oak is between the two of you, that's when you can't sense each other."

He had, he explained, discovered this while walking through a grove of oaks and thinking of various loved ones. The group of immortals easily tested it with nearby trees and wooden boxes, and found it true. It wouldn't be the first time a plant turned out to have significant properties, but it was one of the most ordinary and commonly found examples.

Meanwhile, as far as the little group could tell, nothing could kill them. They didn't know why they had been born this way. (And never would know, Adrian could attest from millennia in the future.) But each of them had undergone at least one injury or attack that should have killed them, only to recover miraculously fast; and none had ever caught so much as a sniffle even when plagues swept their towns. In the villages, people were already calling them "gods," and the immortals were beginning to consider the idea. Obviously they weren't the old gods, who'd been around forever (not that anyone had personally met them), but maybe they were some kind of new gods.

There were downsides to this invincibility. While they seemed to be able to master the living world, they had no way of knowing what happened to those who died. They all had relatives and friends who had passed on, whom they grieved for. They posed the question to each of the wise philosophers they pulled off the travelers' road, and gathered a world of theories, but no definite answers.

Among those departed souls, Hades was sad to learn, was Tanis. Two years after arriving in Greece, Rhea herself paid a visit. He asked after Tanis, only to learn her ship had sunk on her journey back to Crete just after leaving here. All lives were lost.

As he felt the pang of grief, he acknowledged with gloom another downside to being basically young forever: there wasn't much point in getting involved with someone who wasn't.

Not that this stopped him or his new companions from dallying with mortals from time to time, whether chastely, romantically, or carnally. It rarely ended well.

After several years of comparing personal histories, they discovered that immortal women had no trouble conceiving or giving birth—as with other physical traumas, there was no permanent danger in it for them. But there was heartache, as they always gave birth to mortal children, who were no healthier than the average. And for the mortal women who became pregnant by immortal men it was far more dangerous: those women nearly always miscarried or underwent stillbirths, and frequently died themselves in the process. Hades' young wife had been just one of many sad examples. The blood of mortals and immortals, it seemed, did not mix well when the mother was the mortal.

"I'm not saying we can't have companions," Demeter insisted to the group after they had digested this conclusion. "But for mercy's sake, men, don't get the girls with child."

"It's not as if we meant to kill anyone," Apollo said quietly. His latest paramour had died earlier that month in a miscarriage—one of the final clues that brought the truth home to them all.

"I know," Demeter said. "But your sorrow and apologies won't bring them back. There are other things you can do as couples. Just do those, or we'll have young women's angry fathers and mothers forming an army against us."

"All the more reason for us to live among them," Hera pressed. "If they knew us better, they'd be less likely to fear or hate us, and likelier to forgive us our mistakes."

"I think you just want a mortal bedmate yourself," joked Zeus. "What, I'm not enough for you?"

The rest stayed tactfully quiet. They all knew the situation was rather the reverse: Hera was unlikely to dally with anyone, but Zeus did so almost shamelessly. If she wanted to be down among the bustling towns on a more permanent basis, it was probably to keep a closer eye on him.

Hera and Zeus performed the experiment themselves: they went to a few distant villages and pronounced themselves gods, proving it by shows of strength and invincibility. Fear soon turned to awe and delight among the villagers, especially as Hera and Zeus promised to use their knowledge and power to help the citizens improve their crops, their health, their war-waging, and whatever else concerned them, as long as the people showed them proper reverence and didn't attempt to overthrow them. The deal was struck, and Hera and Zeus returned to Olympos to tell the happy news. It took only a few days before the rest were all convinced, and the pack of immortals descended to live among humans in a new and much grander house on the outskirts of a prosperous city, farther south on the shores of a warm gulf. They sent word to Rhea in Crete, and she soon turned over her title to one of the junior priestesses, and sailed to join them.

Hades was now in his mid-twenties, with a thicker beard and stronger muscles than before, but otherwise he looked nearly the same as he had at seventeen. And he was already being hailed as a god, and living in a more regal house than he ever expected to, with immortal and fascinating companions. Life dazzled him.

In the next several years, their searches turned up another half-dozen immortals, whom they brought back to add to their household.

Athena found Hestia, a quiet, humble servant who'd been living without aging in a rich household for decades, and emancipated her at once. Hestia, in turn, led the group to a lonely blacksmith she had heard of. He was named Hephaestus, and kept turning out beautiful jewelry and knives year after year, his skin rapidly healing all the burns he suffered from his work. Artemis brought home Ares, a soldier whose tendency to stay alive even after being run through with spears or swords had begun to look suspect in the eyes of his fellow warriors.

One morning Apollo shot an arrow through a young ruffian trying to steal his cattle. He watched in surprise as the lad climbed to his feet, yanked the arrow out of his back, and walked off without even a limp. The thief's name was Hermes. Apollo chased after him and dragged him to meet the rest of the group—bloodstained tunic, healed arrow wound, unrepentant smile, and all.

Though Hera, in particular, raised loud objections about keeping a common thief in their midst, Zeus and Apollo talked her down. Hermes was immortal—better to have him on their side than working against them.

The immortal women accepted with a mixture of interest and irritation, for Hermes enjoyed nothing more than teasing, flattering, and attempting to seduce them, generally making himself a nuisance. Actually, Hades could attest, he did the same with some of the men. Hades shoved him off his bed more than once in the middle of the night, to which Hermes always laughed and said, "You'll give in someday."

No one could even ascertain his age. To one person he said he was eighteen, to Hades he claimed thirty-five, and to someone else he said seventy-two. But Hermes' roving eye did win them a great treasure. He went out traveling soon after meeting the other immortals, and was quick to discover Aphrodite, on the island of Kypros. His charm succeeded: she agreed to come back with him.

The pair then reduced half the household (including Hades) to shocked blushes, and the other half to peals of laughter, by relating the story of their meeting.

Aphrodite, having abandoned her home village decades ago like the rest of the immortals, took up solitary residence on Kypros, and became a local legend. It was said that adolescent boys desiring to be turned into men could journey to her hut of clay and leaves near the crashing surf, and call her out to see them. If she liked a lad, she would invite him inside for the night, and dismiss the others. Her invitation was the only way into her bed. Men trying to sneak in and forcibly take what had not been offered had suffered maiming injuries or quick death at the hands of the usually gentle woman.

Those were the irresistible stories Hermes heard when he landed on Kypros, tales of beauty laced with danger, whispered to him by adolescents with lust-glazed eyes. Fearing nothing, and desiring everything, Hermes strolled out to where this legendary lover lived—a full day's walk from the nearest town on the island—and found the hut of clay and leaves, just as promised. He circled it at a distance for a while, until a tousle-haired youth backed out of the hut, smoothing down his tunic and speaking enraptured to the person who followed.

She was stunningly beautiful, and completely naked. Even the unflappable Hermes was caught off guard. Untangling her long dark hair with a comb, she leaned forward to kiss the lad one last time before turning him toward home. As the youth walked off down the beach, looking back to wave every few steps, Hermes regained his breath and approached the woman.

"You're early," she said when she saw him. "It's only morning."

"I've traveled a long way to meet you. But I can certainly wait until you've recovered from the night's adventures."

She smiled. "I need no time to recover. I'm immortal. I can last as long as you need me to."

He stepped closer. "I'm also immortal. We shall have a contest of stamina."

She laughed, slipped her arms around him, and accepted the challenge, not believing he really was immortal until (Hermes claimed) three days later, by which time she and he were both duly impressed.

Hermes being a habitual liar, Hades would have been skeptical of his story if she hadn't been there before his eyes, across the room, helping to fill in the details as he related them. In figure and face, standing still and fully clothed, she was no more beautiful than any of the other goddesses. But there was something in the flick of her eyes, the lilt of her smile, and the movement of her limbs that made it distractingly easy to picture her without clothing.

A giant contest of male vanities ensued. Nearly all the gods vied for Aphrodite's attention day and night. Hades tried not to get involved, but couldn't help glancing at her whenever she was near. She noticed and took pity on him. He awoke one night to find her slipping into his bed, kissing his face and whispering sweet invitations. He needed no further convincing.

He later thought he could have lasted three days too, if it

hadn't been for Artemis pulling him away at dawn to help her go hunting as he'd promised.

After that, not fancying the competitive attitudes his friends were taking toward him, Hades counted himself contented with one night with such a lover, and detached himself from the scene.

It was a wise choice. Romantic turmoil kept stirring up trouble among his companions. One evening after dinner, he walked down to the seashore and found Demeter sitting alone on the beach, tears on her cheeks.

He sat beside her, recounting in his mind all the possible reasons she might be crying, and came up with several. But having reached the age of thirty-six now, he knew he was better off asking than assuming when it came to a woman's mind.

"You haven't been at our meals lately," he said. "We've missed you."

She smirked, dabbing the corner of her white cloak against her eyes. "I'm sure Hera hasn't."

Yes, that was one of the rumors he'd heard. He gazed at the clouds over the sea, dyed red by the sunset. "She's over-jealous with every woman. I wouldn't let it worry you."

"Nor would I. If I weren't carrying Zeus' child."

Hades winced. "Ah. So that rumor's true." They exchanged rueful smiles, and he added, "How are you feeling?"

"Nauseated. Being immortal doesn't guard against that, probably because the cause of the sickness never goes away until the birth. It's why I haven't been at meals."

"And Hera's making you feel unwelcome? That's unfair. You're hardly the first Zeus has done such things with." He realized a moment later that it wasn't gallant to speak of someone's lover that way, and amended, "He's a good friend to me, of course. To us all."

She chuckled wearily. "I'm not in love with him. I only gave in to his attempts because...well, I can't marry the one I do love."

Poseidon, a few years earlier, had gotten a mortal woman pregnant, and by some miracle she delivered the child safely. Feeling it was his duty, and also perhaps because he loved the woman and his daughter, he had married her. Hades supposed all Demeter needed to do was wait a few decades for Poseidon's wife to age and die, but a few decades felt just as long to an immortal as they did to anyone else. He easily understood her bitterness.

"Well, your child will surely be beautiful and smart," Hades said. "And no matter what kind of snit it throws Hera into, I'll always be a friend to you and to the little one."

"Thank you." They watched the sky darken to twilight. "Zeus will never acknowledge it's his, you know. Just to placate her."

"Doesn't matter. You're more than enough parent for any child. And the baby will have lots of aunts and uncles, plenty around to help you."

"A child of two immortals," she mused. "Has that been done before? I wonder."

He wondered the same thing, though neither voiced it: would the child be immortal?

But the baby, a girl named Persephone, turned out to be as prone to fevers and injuries as the average mortal. It increased Demeter's anxiety, but the love and delight she found in her daughter outshone her concerns. And as Hades predicted, all the other immortals (with, perhaps, the exception of Hera) loved the little girl as a niece, and regarded her as part of the household.

Zeus, also as predicted, treated her as if he were a fond uncle, but never claimed the role of father.

Demeter's anxiety over the inevitable death of her daughter, and Hades' affection for his friends and for young Persephone, led him further into deep consideration of his life and his own losses. He learned to practice meditation when he was thirty-nine. An old woman taught him the poses and chants. She was tiny and skinny, with straight gray hair, and eyes like shining dark beads. She hailed from a country so far to the east that none of them had even heard of it. Enamored of Greece, she had stayed in the region several years and learned the language, and explained to Hades that meditation was the only known path by which humans could look into the world of the spirits—a world which, she attested, did exist.

The longer he practiced, year upon year, the more he sensed some other realm hovering behind that of the living. He felt if he reached just a little harder, he would slip into it. While his immortal companions debated material-world issues, he took to sitting alone on a mountainside, eyes closed, stretching his mind toward the unknown.

One autumn evening, in crisp, calm air, he sensed a hill or crest hovering just in front of his mind. Eyes shut, he reached with his whole consciousness toward the hill. With a sudden rising-and-falling feeling, he felt himself slip over the crest and slide a short distance down the other side.

The feeling had been so physical and concrete, he opened his eyes with a start. The sea, mountains, clouds, and forests were all still there. But the harbor city had vanished. A field below, which had been cleared for the planting of crops, was now a tangle of bushes and trees. In short, everything human was gone. And in the dwindling twilight, as the sun sank below the hills, Hades caught glimpses of green glowing streaks just above the ground, all flying toward the southwest.

In awe, he rose on unsteady legs, knowing he had entered the spirit realm.

CHAPTER SEVENTEEN

Sophie jolted awake in the middle of the night, shaking and sweating. Her glance took in the angular shadows of the sidewalk lights that cut in around the edges of the window shades, and the lumpy shape of Melissa sleeping across the room. Sophie pulled in a breath, trying to relax.

The dream flashed through her mind, still brighter and more real than anything in this room.

Walking through the Underworld at Hades' side, both of them ghosts. Gazing sadly at the trees she had cultivated and now couldn't touch or tend. Turning to look at her husband, who looked young as ever, his curls black and his dark eyes large and beautiful as they regarded her. Though the recent memory of some kind of awful violence hovered in their minds, they didn't speak of it. Instead they kept saying to each other, "As long as she's all right," and "If only we knew what happened to her."

Who was "she"?

Sophie closed her eyes and ran her wrist across her forehead, wiping off the sweat. God, he did look like Adrian then. Not so much as to be an identical twin, but enough to be a brother.

She pulled her cell phone from where it lay under her pillow, warmed from her head. After their conversation yesterday, she had spent the afternoon running every test and procedure she could find online for debugging and removing spyware from a phone. She hadn't found any suspicious programs or bits of hardware, so it could have been a waste of time, but it eased her mind about the safety of texting Adrian, at least for now.

Lying on her side to face the wall, she tapped in a message to him, heedless of it being 2:38 a.m.

I've gotten to just after Persephone's life. Us in the Underworld as souls. That means her life is next, huh? God, I'm shaking.

He'd likely be asleep and not answer till morning, which was fine. She felt better for having sent word to one of the only people who would understand and not think her crazy.

But as she closed her eyes again, hand folded around the cell phone, it buzzed in answer.

Yes, then that's next. Ready? Wow, now I'm shaking too.

Sophie smiled. *Don't you sleep?*, she texted.

Yeah, but I'm on standby for you, he answered. *This is important stuff.*

She shifted into a more comfortable texting position on her side. *What happens if you force yourself to stay awake? Could you?*

Like anyone else, we get grumpy and weak and kind of mental, he typed. *Not important right now. Sleep! Dream! Or just start remembering if you can.*

I'll try, she responded, and obediently closed her eyes.

She didn't expect to be able to sleep at all with her mind bouncing around like it was on caffeine, so she concentrated on remembering. Thinking of Persephone. Reaching for that extraordinary life. Trying to start at the beginning so it would make sense.

And she must have fallen asleep after all, because then she was there. Greece. Sun on white stones. Sparkling blue sea. The ground rumbling and her mother shrieking for her.

PERSEPHONE WAS FOUR years old when the earthquake hit. Sophie's memories of the event and the few years after it were patchy, the way anyone's memories of early childhood were. But she put together the important points easily enough.

Her mother Demeter, face and voice distorted in panic, pulled Persephone out from beneath the fallen stones of the house where they'd been visiting someone. Sobbing, she clasped Persephone to her chest, then whisked her to a soft patch of earth to examine her injuries.

Persephone's head and leg both pulsated with pain and were bleeding heavily. Demeter dressed her wounds in wet leaves and strips of cloth. From the bustle and shouts around them, Persephone gathered that houses had fallen on lots of people. Men and women, including her aunts and uncles, the other immortals, were digging into the rubble to rescue people.

Holding Persephone in one arm, Demeter leaped onto a horse and they galloped off, following the road along the coast. Persephone endured the ride in a storm of agony, her leg throbbing and her head thundering. Finally they stopped at the magnificent stone house where the immortals lived together. It must have been built stronger than average, for it still stood, only a few flowerpots overturned.

In one of the rooms, her uncle Apollo helped set Persephone's broken leg and, with gentle probing of his hands, ascertained that her skull hadn't been damaged. Demeter washed Persephone's wounds and rewrapped them. She fed Persephone a warm drink of herb-steeped water, and soon the girl fell asleep.

The earthquake was Persephone's earliest clear memory, but even by then she was aware that hers was an unusual childhood. Growing up as a mortal girl in a household of immortals made Persephone a curiosity. The women and men calling themselves her aunts and uncles were kind, wise, lively, and astonishingly strong. They never got sick, the way she sometimes did, and none of them had any scars like the ones the falling stones left upon the side of her face or her leg. The break in her leg bones had been serious, and left her with a limp. But her elders always assisted her, carrying things for her or scooping her up to ride upon their backs if she got tired. Her weight was nothing to them, even to the slightest of the women, little Hestia.

Persephone wondered often about who her father was. While she was little, her mother said he was someone who no longer lived here. Then when Persephone was seven or eight, Demeter explained to her, "Zeus is truly your father, but he already has a wife and can't act as a father to you."

"Oh," Persephone said. "I sort of hoped Poseidon was my father." Even at her young age, she could see the careless way Zeus treated women, and the irritation it caused Hera and plenty of other people. But Poseidon, who visited sometimes, treated Demeter tenderly, and was always willing to tell Persephone tales of ocean adventures.

Demeter only hugged her and said, "I think Poseidon would be happy to have you as his daughter. But he has his wife and their daughters to take care of. You're doing all right without a father, though, aren't you?"

Persephone couldn't deny it. She agreed, and that was more or less the last they spoke of it.

The mortal people who lived nearby sometimes dropped to the ground in a low bow before them, and brought them gifts. They called Demeter and her fellow immortals "gods" and "goddesses." Persephone accepted this, as she could see their strength firsthand, and that made them much more real and believable than the gods from the old stories people told.

On the whole she felt perfectly safe and happy among them, and after the earthquake, nothing dramatic happened until a day when she was eight years old. It was mid-day, and she was sitting drowsily on the front step in the sun, thinking of going inside for a nap. Then her uncle Hades jogged up to the house. She seldom saw him, as he was usually off somewhere thinking with his eyes closed. But today he'd clearly been more active. He was barefoot and shining with sweat, and his white tunic was splotched with dried mud, obscuring the purple geometric embroidery on its hem.

"Did you fall in the river?" Persephone asked.

Stopping to catch his breath, hands on his thighs, he shook his head. "I fell much farther."

"Where are your sandals?"

"They broke yesterday, so I left them. I've run a long way."

"Why would you run when it's so hot outside? I hope a wild boar was chasing you. I can't think of any other good reason."

He laughed, reaching out to pinch her ear gently. "Is your mother around? Let's fetch her and anyone else in the house. They have to hear this."

Demeter, Athena, Hermes, and Zeus were in at the time, and they came out when Persephone and Hades called for them. They clamored to know where Hades had been, as no one had seen him for at least three days.

To Persephone, his explanation sounded like something out of the stories Hermes made up to amuse her, and the others doubted him at first too. But the more he explained, the more they listened in seriousness.

In one of his trances several days ago, he had slipped into some other place, one that looked like the regular world but with no living people, nor towns nor anything else built by humans. Only animals lived there—strange, different animals—and, more importantly, the ghosts of people. The ghosts all flew fast, going the same direction, so Hades followed them. All night and day he ran, walked, climbed over hills, and splashed across rivers, guided by the stream of souls.

He came to the opening of a cave within a seaside mountain. All the ghosts were flying down into the cave's mouth, a thick swarm of them. He dropped rocks in and heard them splash far below, so to jump in would have meant a serious fall. He braided vines into a rope, and lowered himself in. What he found below was an underground river that led into a huge cavern full of grassy hills and pale flowers and trees that all somehow lived without the light of the sun. There the dead of all the world strolled and talked, sometimes alongside the souls of their pets.

Hades explored for at least a day, learning what he could from the souls who spoke the languages he knew. The dead told him that if the amount of evil a person committed in life outweighed the amount of good they did, then their soul was confined to a solitary cell in a cavern below this one, a darker realm lit by eerie fires, where they were beset by guilt and loneliness. But even those souls were released after a time, and then they, like the more virtuous souls, could linger here in the fields as long as they liked. When they were ready to be reborn, they followed the river downstream. Once reborn, they would remember nothing about the Underworld until they died again. For Hades, a living person, to enter this realm, was unheard of. The souls all regarded him as some kind of hero—or god.

"My rope vine had broken, so I couldn't climb back up the entrance when I was ready to leave," he explained. "So I went downstream too. The bank disappeared just past the cavern. I had to swim—or rather, get carried along through the tunnels. The river ended up shooting out the side of the mountain as a waterfall." He laughed. "I fell a long way and landed in the sea. It probably would have killed a mortal."

"But you were still in this spirit world?" asked Athena.

"Yes. The souls coming downstream with me all vanished. They got reborn, I suppose. I don't know how that works. But I swam to shore, sat and meditated again, and managed to slip back into this world."

The adults pelted him with questions, leaving Persephone no chance to ask any, though she had lots of them: What color were the ghost animals—green like the human ghosts, or a different color? How fast could the spirits go? Faster than a horse? Did the ghosts look scary, forever bearing any bloody wounds that killed them, or did they look normal?

What the others wanted to know was where the cave was located, whether he could carry things with him other than the clothes on his back when he switched to that realm, and whether he could do this switching trick again right before their eyes.

He said he had managed it a few more times, going back and forth, and it got a little easier each time, so he'd try to show them. They moved into the garden in their central courtyard, where Hades could sit without disturbance. He set himself on the ground in the shade. They brought him a cage containing a dove to see if he could bring a living creature along—something he hadn't tried yet. Then Persephone and the others withdrew to the edges of the courtyard to watch.

It happened quickly. Breathing deep with eyes closed, he was there one moment, then he winked out of sight. They all rushed to the spot and confirmed it: he was gone, as was the cage with the dove.

"Back here," he called.

They turned to see him standing a few paces away, holding the cage, where the dove still fluttered and cooed.

"Teach us how," Hermes commanded.

"I will, I will."

"Take me this time," said a number of them at once, pushing forward—Persephone included.

"Not you." Demeter pushed her back.

"I want to see the spirit world," she protested.

"Not until we know it's safe, transferring back and forth."

"The dove is fine."

Demeter took the cage from Hades and frowned into it. "It's a bird. Who knows whether its mind is still sound, or ever was?"

While Persephone pouted, Hermes leaped into Hades' arms, drawing up his legs and clinging to Hades' neck as if he were a maiden being carried. Everyone laughed, and Hades dumped him on the ground. Hermes stood, undaunted. "Seriously, bring me."

"Fine," Hades said. "No loss if *you're* damaged."

And though it made them laugh and therefore took them a while to settle down, Hades sat with Hermes encircled in his arms, and soon vanished once again, taking his friend along with him.

It took them a long moment to reappear, and when they did, Hermes was in the middle of protesting.

"—want to explore more!"

"They're going to worry," said Hades, "and will want to see us again first. We'll go back later."

The afternoon sped by in that fashion, Hades escorting each of them to the spirit realm for a look around and then back again. As more of the immortals arrived home for the evening, the news spread and Hades kept sharing the experience with each new person. But Demeter still forbade Persephone to cross over.

Finally, after she had been put to bed but could hear the adults still conversing around the hearth in the courtyard, Persephone crept to the doorway and watched. When Hades rose and wandered out alone, wine cup in hand, she stole after him and followed him into the front garden, where he stood looking up at the stars.

"Hades," she whispered.

He turned. "You're still up, little one?"

She ran to him. "Take me into the spirit realm."

He set the cup next to the door, chewing his lip. "I'm not sure. We don't know much about it, and if you were hurt…"

"If it starts hurting, I promise I'll jump away from you and stay here. Please, please. Just for a bit?"

He gazed at her, then smiled and took her hand. "I suppose it's probably safe. We've done enough practice runs today with no harm so far."

She leaped into the air in excitement, a leap lopsided as ever thanks to her weak leg, but she knew how to keep her balance on it. Hades sat upon the ground, and she climbed into his lap. He enfolded her in his arms and reminded her to keep very still. She breathed the scent of the herb garden and his warm skin, watching the house and its flickering oil lamps because she wanted to see them disappear.

And soon they did. A small jolt, like an earthquake, rippled through her, and darkness fell as the house and village lights vanished. But the glow of the stars took over, and soon she saw her first one: the greenish streak of a ghost flying past. With a gasp of wonder she crawled out of Hades' lap and began racing around, looking at the wild nighttime world.

"Careful." He caught her and drew her back to their starting point. "Remember all those large animals I talked about? They haven't bothered me yet, but I don't know what they'll make of you. Possibly a meal."

She bounced in front of him. "Can we go to the Underworld?"

"Of course not. It's a two-day journey from here."

"But some day?"

"Perhaps. If your mother allows it."

"I'll ask her every day until she gives in."

He laughed. "I believe you. But let's take you back now before she finds out." He crouched, motioning her to climb onto his back. She scrambled on, clinging to his neck, and he wrapped both her little hands in one of his large palms. "Know what?" he told her. "I bet you're the first mortal person ever to come here."

"What about the people who taught you to meditate? Didn't they say they'd seen this place?"

"Seen it. Sensed it. Never fully entered it like this, as far as I know."

Persephone wriggled into a more comfortable position against his back. "Then I want to be the first mortal person to visit the Underworld, too. Before I'm dead, I mean."

"Ideally long before then." He squeezed her hands, and the world shifted, and there stood the house and its bright lights.

And her shouting mother. Oh, dear.

CHAPTER EIGHTEEN

DEMETER WAS *NOT* PLEASED AT Hades using her daughter as the latest experiment in realm-crossing, and told him so in a tirade of lashing words. He backed off at once, apologizing, promising not to do it again without Demeter's consent. But Persephone was so excited, and begged so extensively to be allowed to do it again soon, that Demeter finally grumbled her forgiveness, and carted the girl back to bed.

Persephone did enjoy a few more jaunts into the spirit world, carried by Hades or eventually by her own mother as the other immortals learned the realm-switching trick. Though it had taken Hades years of meditation to discover the method, it was easily taught to other immortals once he described the right sensation to reach for. Soon they could all do it as easily as snapping their fingers. Persephone listened avidly to the instructions too, and kept trying during her afternoon nap with her eyes squeezed shut. But her body stubbornly stayed put in the living world. It seemed nature barred mortals from the ability to cross over.

And though Persephone asked time and again to be allowed a trip to the Underworld, no one ever organized the journey. Nearly all the immortals other than Hades seemed reluctant to go there, as if walking the fields of the dead was too unnatural, even for them.

Hermes was the only one besides Hades who didn't mind paying visits to the ghostly cave, and he frequently told Persephone about it when he returned. His stories of the gentle, glowing ghosts, the vastness of the cave, and the myriad tunnels that still lay unexplored made Persephone burn with interest to see it. But still Demeter put her off.

But Hades himself looked troubled when he returned one day, a few months after his discovery of the Underworld. Again he called together the immortals who were home at the time. Persephone slipped in among them, sitting beside Demeter in the courtyard's shade.

"I found...the place of punishment," he said. He glanced in concern at Persephone, as if not wishing to give nightmares to a child, but went on, "It's a bit like Tartaros, in the old stories—a deep cave, where those who have killed or caused a great deal of harm have been tied up. And...they aren't suffering bodily, but it's dark and stuffy and lit only by flames, and..." He looked around at his friends' alarmed faces. "Well, it's the natural way of things, I suppose, but it felt horrible to be there. To know it really happens."

The others looked pale with alarm and fear. Some of them in particular, Persephone thought, looked deeply withdrawn and stayed silent. Perhaps they were thinking of all the cruel things they had ever done, the way she was. Would they be among the punished someday?

"Hades," Demeter said, "I can't help believing it's quite unnatural, a living person visiting there. Even an immortal. I say this as your friend."

"I don't wish to go to *those* caves often, that's certain," he said. "But...what if they killed someone, and could tell us who, and we could tell the victim's families what happened, in case they didn't already know? Or, better still, what if I found some victims in the fields of the virtuous souls, and could help bring their murderers to justice in the living world?"

To Persephone it sounded admirable and heroic, more like the deeds of the legendary gods than anything the other immortals had done so far. But her mother and aunts and uncles looked dubious.

"It's a noble thought," said Athena, "but all the murders in the world? You'd never have time to track them all down."

"Of course not. But if I could make a difference for just one victim—one family—each day, or even each month, surely that's worth trying?"

The grown-ups debated it a long while, and soon led themselves into discussions of law and philosophy that Persephone couldn't follow. She crawled off to feed the doves the household kept in large cages, her mind consumed by images of the Underworld, both its beautiful and its terrible caverns.

Another day, a month later, Hades arrived with a cart of rocks that glinted and sparkled in various colors in the sunlight. At first Persephone didn't realize what they were, but her aunts and uncles did.

"Ah, what beauties!" said Hephaestus the blacksmith, crouching to dig his fingers into the rocks and lift up handfuls of them. "Where did you get them?"

"The Underworld." Hades shook the dust off his tunic. Ash or dirt marked his face and hands. "I was exploring, and found some caverns where gems completely cover the walls and floor. Silver and gold too—look." He picked up a larger, chunkier rock and handed it to Hephaestus. When Hephaestus turned it round to examine it, Persephone saw the sun flash off the gold streaking through it.

Hermes scooped up a handful of rough gems. "Have I told you lately how much I like you, Hades?"

"An amount equal to the value of those sapphires, I'm sure," Hades said.

"Now these make your cave worth something," said Hera, plucking a green crystal from the mix and holding it up to the sky to view the light through it.

"I brought back enough that you can make jewels for us all," Hades told Hephaestus. "If you're willing to take on the work, that is."

"I'd be delighted." Hephaestus was already sorting rocks, setting them on the ground in piles. "These are fine specimens. What do you think? Belts? Rings?"

Athena, watching from the shade of the porch, suggested, "Crowns."

"Agreed." Zeus sauntered closer. "We're immortals. Let us wear crowns."

Persephone slipped in between Hephaestus and Hermes to look closer at the gems in the cart. Quietly she picked up a purple crystal that appealed to her. She wasn't immortal and therefore wouldn't get a crown, but she could still admire the stones.

"That one's an amethyst." Hades had bent down behind her. "You can keep it. Shall we make it a necklace for you?"

When she nodded shyly, he added, "We'd make you a crown too, but the trouble is you're still growing, and soon it would be too small for you. For now you can have a necklace. All right?"

"Trying to woo my child with jewelry from the dead?" Demeter asked, walking up to them. She had been sitting near Athena, not joining the group around the cart until now.

Hades tilted his head toward her in deference. "With your permission. In fact, Demeter, I was thinking, for you…" He flicked his hand through the gems, found a few, and plucked them out. "Look at the amber color of these—it's almost like wheat. Since you're our expert on crops and plants, I thought some of these, with a few of these emeralds for a touch of green…"

"And some gold leaves," Hephaestus suggested. "Or gold wheat sheaves. I could hammer out a few of those." He picked the rocks out of Hades' hand and arranged them on his own palm to show her. "Yes, that'd be lovely."

Demeter hesitated, taking in the sparkling jewels. "Well…"

Aphrodite wandered up too, and draped her arm around Demeter's shoulders. When Demeter glanced at her, Aphrodite lifted her eyebrows in encouragement.

Demeter smiled. "Very well. You always do beautiful work, Hephaestus, and it wouldn't be gracious of me to refuse."

"Quite right." Aphrodite leaned over the cart, elbows on its edge, bosom nearly spilling out of her tunic. The attention of all the men, or so it seemed to Persephone, instantly transferred to Aunt Aphrodite. "Now, which would look best on me?"

LESS THAN A year after Hades discovered the Underworld, he moved house to live there, underground with the souls.

"There's so much to be learned and done," he explained to the group. "The few souls I can talk to sometimes have unfinished business I can help with. And the rest—well, I can learn their language. They say there's a common tongue they all speak, and I can study it if I live there."

"But it's so morbid," said Hera with a shudder. "Living in a cave, with ghosts."

"It's what I wish to do. I'll still meet the rest of you as often as I can, and tell you what I've learned."

The group began drifting apart as the other immortals also sought places where they could address their special interests. Poseidon, originally a fisherman and boat-builder, wanted to live on the sea coast rather than along the narrow gulf, and took his wife and daughters there. Athena was interested in the evolving forms of government being tried out in cities, and took up residence in the largest city in Greece. Aphrodite found a private island where she could indulge her interests with any companions she wished to bring home. Hermes kept roaming, unattached, turning up wherever and whenever he felt like it. Zeus and Hera stayed put, acting as the god and goddess of the region, the house becoming something like a temple or palace for supplicants.

Demeter took Persephone and moved south to a village on the Himeros River, in a region where the people's livelihood came from growing olives, grapes, and other crops. Demeter had been born into a farming family, and had always been adept at tending gardens and orchards. Now she taught Persephone the same skills, while assisting the local farmers with their crops and livestock.

When Persephone was twelve, she began growing anxious over the realization that she may need to marry soon. None of the boys and men she knew so far seemed quite good enough to merit leaving her mother for. "When am I supposed to marry?" she finally asked Demeter.

"If you wish, you never have to," her mother said. "You have a comfortable, healthy life here, and I can always protect you."

"And I'll learn things only the immortals know," Persephone said, relieved. "Like the secrets of the Underworld. It isn't far from here, is it?"

"It isn't, but we needn't go there. It's unnatural for the living to visit."

"But there are such wonders—like the pomegranate that made Hades learn the language of the dead overnight, and lots of other languages besides."

Demeter snorted. "Just one example of why I doubt his sanity lately."

"Hermes ate it too. He says it works. He remembers the languages and everything."

When Persephone had asked Hermes what he was like in his other lives, he had said, "A scoundrel, always. But this is the first time I've been immortal, so this is the only life I feel inclined to pay attention to. I'll leave the soul-searching to Hades."

"Hermes," Demeter pointed out now, "will try, and say, anything."

"What about the horses? You have to admit those are a wonder. Useful too."

"I use them when I must, but it makes me nervous to bring you along. It's only a matter of time before someone crashes into a mountain and gets their mortal companion killed."

After a couple of years living among the spirits, Hades had happened upon a combination of plants from the Underworld that, when woven together, fastened instantly to souls. Realizing there were ghost horses roaming the fields, animals accustomed to pulling chariots or being ridden by humans, he wove a harness and gained a new mode of incredibly fast transportation.

The spirit horses never tired, never needed feeding, and went wherever you wanted—though if left to their devices, they would point themselves to the Underworld. Within the year, all the immortals kept and used spirit horses to get around, even Demeter. But she drew the line at letting them carry Persephone to the Underworld itself.

"Look, if the Underworld were so horrible," the girl persisted, "it wouldn't have given us anything so good, and I'm sure Hades wouldn't live there. I just want to see it."

"Stop asking. The very idea gives me chills."

Her voice was sharp enough that Persephone did, in fact, stop asking, for many years. Nor did she see her uncle Hades much at all. Those gatherings of the immortals happened infrequently, and usually some of the invited guests were too busy to attend.

She kept the necklace Hephaestus had made for her, and wore it nearly every day. He had polished the amethyst and set it into a nest of gold and silver petals so that it looked like a violet, and hung it on a leather cord wrapped with threads of gold. She supposed it should be Hephaestus she thought of when she looked at the beautiful object, but whenever she closed her hand around the cool stone flower, she thought instead of the magical place it had come from, and wondered what Hades was doing and discovering there lately.

Violets were her favorite flowers. She no longer remembered whether they always had been—perhaps that was why Hephaestus chose that shape for her?—or whether she now liked them because of the necklace.

When she was sixteen, she accompanied Demeter to a spring equinox feast in Aphrodite's palatial home on the island.

Looking around the airy room, all pillars and flower arrangements, Persephone examined the people she had been accustomed to view as her aunts and uncles. Today, having not seen many of them for months or years, it struck her that they all looked younger than she remembered, and quite lovely.

Her gaze landed upon a young man across the room in a dark purple cloak, his beard clipped short, his curly black hair braided back and adorned with a wreath of ivy—much less showy than the bright spring flowers Persephone and the others wore in honor of the equinox. He stood apart from the others, squinting against the bright sun as he gazed out the window at the sea.

Soon he turned his head and noticed her. The brooding expression on his face evaporated as he regarded her, an appreciative smile taking its place. Truly, he was quite beautiful. They gazed at each other a moment longer than was proper. A pleasant flutter danced in Persephone's belly. Was he an immortal? Gold did seem to glint beneath the ivy, as if the vines were twined around one of the gods' crowns.

Then she recognized him. Hades.

She dropped her gaze, the recognition giving her a shock that radiated out to her fingertips.

Well, he wasn't *really* her uncle, so it wasn't incestuous to have admired him. Still, he might not agree, and her mother certainly wouldn't approve. Persephone kept her eyes averted, and let Demeter lead her to Aphrodite for a welcome hug.

The goddess of love, as she was already being called, was scented divinely with oils and flowers, with a few blossoms tucked between her breasts, just above the line of her tunic. She engaged Persephone in a conversation about local youths that made them both laugh immoderately. But Persephone kept stealing glances at Hades. What was it like to live in the Underworld? When could she pull him aside and ask him? Better yet, when could she visit?

Hades, conversing with Hermes, glanced at her a few times too. Each time, she felt her heart beat faster. Burying her nose in the cup of wine Aphrodite handed her, she began thinking up what to say in greeting to him, what kind of question might hold his interest.

She would have asked him about the Underworld even if he had still seemed to be her mature old uncle. But already her fascination with that realm was colliding and mingling with the fact that she had found him beautiful today. And she knew it was going to be very difficult, perhaps impossible, to regard him as her uncle ever again.

CHAPTER NINETEEN

GRRR, said the text from Sophie. *I'd just gotten to us meeting at Aphrodite's house when I was 16, then my alarm went off. Where'd the night go? I want back in!*

Adrian grinned. He had drifted off to sleep in his bed in the Airstream, but the buzz of her text message awakened him. The rising sun filtered through the window blinds. His breath made clouds in the air, as did Kiri's as she slept on her dog bed. He rolled onto his elbow and thumbed in a reply.

Now that you're there, you can remember it awake.

Yes, but that's very distracting and I have classes. Argh, I'm going to be thinking about it anyway.

I was just in those early days too, he answered. *The next bit is like a romancey chick flick. And don't tell anyone, but I totally love it.*

Everyone loves their OWN romancey chick flick. Even boys. OK, getting ready for class.

Update me often. This is fun.

I will. Bye.

Adrian settled onto his back, smiling. He lay in dog-scented chilly air inside a caravan, and would have to sneak into the living world again soon because he had nothing to eat for breakfast except some stale granola and a bruised apple, but happiness enfolded him. *Us,* she called Persephone and Hades. She craved more of their story. She was a part of it now.

Watching the dim orange sunlight spread onto the curved ceiling, he let his mind return to Aphrodite's house on that balmy spring afternoon.

THE GIRL ACROSS the room had dark brown hair, braided at the sides and tumbling loose down her back. A crown of purple and white flowers rested on her head, with similar blossoms tucked into the woven belt that gathered her gown around her waist. She might have been anywhere between fifteen and twenty. And that face...Hades stopped moving as he took it in. Full lips, sweet eyes, long graceful brows, smooth skin. Though she stood beside voluptuous Aphrodite and radiant Demeter, she outshone them both.

Hermes wandered near him, and Hades tugged on his cloak to get his attention. "Did we find another immortal?"

"Where?" Hermes followed Hades' gaze. "Her? No, you old fool, that's Persephone."

"That's Persephone?" He stared in amazement, trying to reconcile this goddess-like individual with the scrappy little girl who had crawled into his lap to visit the spirit realm. "What—how many years—"

"She's sixteen. I suppose you haven't kept in touch, being busy down there with your dead people."

"No. I suppose I haven't."

The young woman moved then, walking with Aphrodite, and Hades detected the limp she'd retained from her injury in the earthquake as a child. And when she turned to glance the other way, he noticed the scar marking the side of her face. None of it detracted from her beauty in the slightest. It only caused him a twinge at the reminder of her mortality.

"Got quite fetching, hasn't she?" Hermes sipped his wine, watching her. "Believe me, I've noticed. After all, we're not *really* her uncles."

Hades blinked at him. "You haven't..." He glanced again in alarm at Persephone.

Hermes snorted. "No. Demeter would castrate me and feed

my balls to a pig." He paused to frown in thought. "Wonder if they'd grow back? Well, I certainly don't want to try it. Regardless, our Persephone is of marriageable age. So, fair game, I would say, if *you* want to give it a go." He elbowed Hades.

"Enough, shut up."

But it was only a few minutes before Persephone drifted close enough that he could turn and greet her. "Persephone."

"Hello, Hades."

He took the hand she held out, and kissed it, as he would for any grown female friend. "It's been a long time. You've changed."

"So have you."

"Have I? That isn't supposed to happen."

She laughed. "You haven't *really* changed, I suppose. But you seemed older when I was a little girl." She gestured around to indicate the others in the room. "All of you look quite young to me nowadays."

"Ah. Then thank you. So aren't you and Demeter living in the south, same as me?"

"Yes. Along the Himeros. But above ground, unlike you."

"I'll have to come visit."

"You'd be welcome. I also wish to visit you, if I may." She looked over her shoulder at Demeter, who was in conversation with Artemis several paces away. "Mother still doesn't like the idea. But I think the Underworld sounds fascinating."

"Come anytime, if she can spare you. I'll show you around."

"I hear you even have furniture down there."

"Yes, I've got a very comfortable set of chambers."

"Do ghosts wander through them at all hours?" she asked.

"No, they stay in the fields."

Persephone sipped her wine. "Hermes told me of the pomegranate that grows there. Mother doubts the story. She thinks it only makes people see and believe things that aren't real, the way nightshade does for the priestesses."

"Oh, it's a much clearer-minded and less dangerous experience than nightshade. I've brought some of my mortal meditation experts there to partake, and none of them came to any harm. We all believe the memories are real."

"How amazing. I'd love to know who I used to be."

"So far none of my past lives have contained anything as momentous as immortality, but they have made me recover all the languages I used to know. That's the main way we can tell it isn't a hallucination."

"Knowing all those languages would be extraordinary. I wonder why Mother says she wouldn't touch the pomegranates?"

He glanced across the room at Demeter, who met his gaze with a cool nod. "Demeter has strong opinions about what is natural for a living creature, and generally it doesn't involve anything to do with the land of death."

"So I've noticed. Still, she doesn't mind using those horses to dash around." Persephone smiled. "All right, she's beckoning to me. Perhaps we can talk later."

"I hope so."

Persephone slid a violet loose from her belt, and slipped its stem into the chain securing Hades' cloak. "Come see me two days from now. I'll give you some of our vegetables, and you can tell me more about your caves. Hermes knows the way."

"Fine. I'll see you both then."

She was only curious and brave, the way young people always were, he told himself. Probably the appeal would diminish along with the novelty, after he'd explained the major points of the Underworld to her. Besides, Persephone was mortal, so he couldn't court her even if she encouraged it—especially not with Demeter in residence.

Still, as he made the rounds and talked to his friends, his spirit bobbed pleasantly and his mind already planned the things he would say when he arrived at her house.

Two DAYS LATER, Hermes climbed into the chariot with Hades in the Underworld, took the reins, and guided the horses up into the bright sunlight and over the land. He slowed to point out landmarks by which Hades could, in future, navigate to Demeter and Persephone's village. Between instructions, he hummed a naughty song about a boy trying to bed a girl, a tune he had made up himself and taught to drunken people all over Greece. Hades finally had to kick him to make him shut up.

They landed beside a bend in the river, coasting to a stop on a large flat rock. Next to them loomed a forest. Huge rabbits and spiral-horned deer bounded away, disappearing in the undergrowth. Hades and Hermes tied up the chariot and switched into the living world. The wild forest transformed into a tidy orchard of pear and pomegranate trees, their green leaves shining in the sun.

A stone house stood near, small but charming. Its herb and vegetable gardens overflowed with plants. Flowers and bushes grew in pots all around—beside the door, hanging from the eaves, and sitting upon the gently sloped roof. Sheep and goats bleated from a pen behind the house.

Hades walked with Hermes up the dirt path. From the house wafted the scents of apples, wood smoke, and a savory stew being cooked.

Before they could knock, Persephone came around the corner, her arms around a basket of vegetables.

Hermes and Hades nearly bowled each other over in jumping forward to take it from her.

"I've got it," Hermes said, while Hades said at the same time, "May I take this for you?"

She laughed, relinquishing the basket, and watching as Hades finally wrested it free from Hermes. "It's for you, actually, Hades. And you needn't worry. I carry such things all day."

She was less glamorously attired than she'd been for the equinox feast. Her hair was twisted into a knot and gathered back in a small net, and her gown was a weathered plain white wool with a grass stain at the knee. Still, she had a pair of violets tucked behind her ear, and with that face she couldn't possibly, in Hades' eyes, look less than divine.

He cradled the basket of vegetables in one arm. "Thank you very much. Where's Demeter?"

She folded her hands behind her back. "Off to help with a birth. There's a woman on the other side of the hills who's expecting twins, and arranged for my mother to attend her. She won't be back for a few days yet."

Hermes turned to him with eyebrows arched. "Well, I really must be going. You two have fun."

Hades managed not to glare at him. "Don't you need a ride somewhere?"

"We brought my horse, remember? I'll detach it from the team and be off." Hermes kissed Persephone on the cheek, his arm around her waist rather tighter than Hades thought necessary, then he turned and kissed Hades on the mouth. "Be good. Or not." Smiling, the trickster stepped into the other realm, leaving only a gust of wind swirling to fill the space where he'd been.

Persephone gazed wistfully at the spot. "I'd love to be able to do that."

"Perhaps someday we'll discover a way."

"I hope. Well, shall I show you around?"

She acted so natural about being there alone with him that he relaxed, forgetting Demeter and her possible disapproval. After all, as Hermes had rightly stated, Persephone was a grown woman, one who could have been married by now if she wished. (Did she not wish it, then? Hades couldn't help wondering.)

She showed him around the orchards and gardens, pointing out new plants they'd acquired from markets near the docks. Crouching, she touched a branch on a potted tree no higher than their thighs. Its leaves were glossy dark green and smooth-edged, and its flowers white and fragrant. "This one came from Asia. The man who sold it to me said it grows 'golden apples,' but clearly it isn't an apple tree. Those were just the closest words he could think of in our language. I can't wait to taste the fruit."

"Looks like it's thriving. You're excellent with these plants. I only know a few crops, the ones we grew on Crete. And, I suppose, the ones I remember from other lives, elsewhere."

"I'm sure the souls in the Underworld could tell us about lots of crops. What they use different plants for in their country, what to call them…"

"Indeed. You should come talk to them." The invitation was out of his mouth before he realized it.

She rose to her feet, beaming. "Agreed. Let's go."

"Hah. Your mother would sense you suddenly heading southwest, wouldn't she?"

"Only if she thought about it. Isn't that how it works?"

"Yes, but…"

"And haven't I heard that the hillside containing your cave is thick with oaks? So she wouldn't be able to track my whereabouts once I was there."

"True." He studied her not-quite-innocent smile. "I'm beginning to think you invited me here today because you knew Demeter would be gone."

She turned to the arbor beside her, curling a vine of a climbing flower around her finger. "Let's say I wanted to avoid an argument about it. The truth, whether she likes it or not, is that I'm an adult and can go where I wish. She wants to protect me, but she overdoes it. If I could switch realms, I'd visit the Underworld myself on a day like today, when she's not here. But I can't."

"I'd love to take you. It's only, she's my friend, and if she felt I'd betrayed her…" He thought of Hermes' suggestion involving pigs, and shivered.

"You talk as if she'd find out." Now looking fully as mischievous as Hermes ever did, Persephone pulled Hades' arm around her shoulders. Holding onto it with both of her cool hands, she stepped up close against him. "Come on, take me."

As if he could resist her, of all people, saying that.

"Gracious, woman, all right." Balancing the basket of vegetables in one arm and Persephone in the other, he swept them into the spirit world.

Chapter Twenty

Sophie stared at her laptop in Communications—her least favorite class so far, taken only because it was required for practically all students—and watched the cursor blink while she failed to take notes. The professor lectured on, his voice a background drone, and she knew she'd better start paying attention or she was going to have to do an extra hour of remedial textbook reading to figure out what he said. But the more dominant part of her mind danced and whirled in the Elysian Fields—did they call them that back then? No; the name was added in mythology later.

Communications couldn't possibly compare with this, with Persephone discovering the land where all the dead of the world converged and shared their knowledge and their bittersweet memories, their glow lighting the plants and trees, all of which contained magic that had lain inaccessible and forgotten for centuries...

Persephone drew her eager steps up short when she first saw all the souls. These were real departed people and pets. Would her beloved cat who died five years ago be here? Or the man from the village who died last week, whom Demeter and Persephone helped care for in his final illness?

She leaned closer to Hades both for support and warmth—the cave was chillier than the warm spring air above ground—and felt comforted when he hooked his hand around her elbow.

"One of the first souls I found down here was my wife," he said. "I asked the crowd if they knew of her, and they spread the word among themselves and brought her to me."

She now remembered hearing that Hades had been married, long ago, before offering himself up as the sacrifice at Knossos. Yes, that was why he volunteered, she supposed—he lost his wife and felt he had nothing to live for. "How old was she when she died?"

"Sixteen. I was the same age at the time."

The same age Persephone was now. She shivered. "How sad."

"By the time I discovered this place, however, I was—let's see—forty-five. It had been a long time, so it wasn't as painful as it might have been. And by then she had her parents to keep her company."

Forty-five when he discovered the Underworld. Persephone had been eight at the time, so now he was perhaps fifty-three, not that he looked it. Was that already too old for him to be interested in someone young like her, or did age not really matter for the immortals?

Hades added, "Our infant son, though, who died with her…" His voice went quieter, and Persephone's heart ached. She had utterly forgotten there was a baby who died too. "My wife had let him return to the living to be reborn, not long after they died. He was so young, he'd had no real life at all. It seemed only fair to give him one."

In the face of such grown-up concerns, she felt hopelessly young and useless. She wished she could at least find the courage to stroke his hand or face, the way Aphrodite or another self-assured woman could. "He's probably someone very smart and happy now," she said, hoping that might help.

He smiled, looking more thoughtful than sad. "I like to imagine so. Since he's of my blood, I could track him if I like, but…well, I never knew him really, and he has other family now. I've chosen to let him be. Ah—you were after the plants? Look at these." He led her to a vale between hills, where flowers carpeted the ground.

She knelt to examine them. "Violets, only they're red! And

narcissus that are purple." She sniffed them, finding the scent was sweet as she expected from those flowers, but with the dank smell of cave rocks beneath it. "You never see these colors in the living world, not on these flowers. May I pick some?"

"Of course."

She stood with her handful of flowers. "And the pomegranates? Where do they grow?"

"The grove's this way." It was a long walk, especially since she couldn't move as fast as he could, but they filled the time with her many questions and his answers. Finally the path brought them beneath the boughs of a forest so dark and thick she could only see as far as ten or twelve tree trunks in any direction, and nothing above but branches. The souls seemed to avoid the grove; she only spotted one or two wandering through it, and without their glowing light it was especially dark within.

"These aren't pomegranates." She studied leaves and bark as they walked over the crackling dry leaves and bumpy roots. "They're all kinds of trees."

"Yes—those willows are part of what we use to harness the horses. We braid them together with—"

"Ivy," she filled in. "I've examined the ropes."

"Very good. Ivy. Some of the tree trunks are covered with it."

"Ah. That's a pomegranate." She stepped off the path, reaching for one of the fruits above her head.

"Whoa." His hand closed around hers, stopping her before she picked it. "Do you want Demeter to know you've been here?"

She let her hand drop, with a pout. "If I eat the pomegranate, you'll tell her?"

"No, if you eat the pomegranate, she'll know, because you'll never act the same again. It's impossible, with the memories flooding your mind. Think it over. Don't do it on your very first visit."

She grimaced. Then, after a pause, she lifted her eyebrow. "You mean I can have more visits?"

He only smiled in answer. And there seemed no way he could be over fifty now, because that was the coy, radiant smile of a young man invited to come court her again.

"MOTHER, I'VE FOUND a new tutor. He knows lots of languages and plant lore from other countries, and I've arranged to go learn from him. Perhaps half a day every four or five days, as you can spare me." Persephone recited her story as she cut greens from the garden with a knife.

It was two days after Hades' visit, and Demeter had returned that morning after delivering the twins. She leaned on the door frame of the house, squeezing water out of her freshly washed hair. "Slow down, girl. What is his name? Where does he live?"

Persephone parted her lips to give the answer she had made up (though Hades had urged her not to lie)—the invented name, the tale of him being an elderly traveler from the north. But her tongue went limp at the idea of such untruth. She laid the greens in her basket and looked straight at her mother. "His name is Hades, and he lives in the Underworld."

Dismay clouded Demeter's eyes. She wrung her hair, twisting it tighter. "I might have guessed. The way you two were talking at Aphrodite's house—I suppose he invited you then."

"I invited myself." Persephone moved to the next row of greens. "And I've already been there."

Demeter growled, delivering such a hard shake to her gathered-up hair that drops rained upon the herb garden. "And it didn't appall you? You want to go back?"

"It's beautiful. Or at least, strange in a magnificent way. How can you judge it when you've never been there?"

"For most people, the fact that all the dead souls in the world dwell there is reason enough to find it appalling, and to stay away."

Persephone sat back with her heels beneath her. "This is the argument I would rather have avoided, and could have avoided by lying to you. But there should always be truth between us, you've said."

"Yes, and therefore I'm being honest too, and not pretending I like the idea of you spending your time under the earth, among spirits, with only one slightly insane immortal man for living company, when I do *not* like it."

Persephone climbed to her feet. Pain flared in her weak hip, and she winced and settled her weight on the other leg. "Why do you call him insane?"

"Precisely for reasons such as wishing to live among the dead when there's an entire living world that needs attention and is better suited for us all." Demeter stepped into the garden, closing her warm, damp hands upon Persephone's bare arms. "Darling, isn't it bad enough that mortality exists, and tortures even us few eccentric immortals by taking away everyone else? It's a frightening, disturbing thing for a living girl to want to spend her days with the dead when—" Voice weakening, Demeter checked her words, and cast her glance aside.

Persephone understood the unfinished sentence: *when someday all too soon you'll have to die and go there as a soul yourself.* She hugged her mother. Persephone's mortality tormented Demeter, as Persephone well knew. Their time together would be brief, in the span of Demeter's living existence. Now having seen the Underworld, Persephone felt no fear about returning there as a soul. But a parent could never feel anything other than grief about losing a child. Even Hades, remembering the lost baby son he had never known, had been affected that way.

She rested her cheek on Demeter's shoulder, breathing the smell of her clean wool tunic and sweet skin. "For goodness' sake," Persephone said, "I don't plan to live there. Only visit sometimes, and learn." She stepped back, smiling at her mother. "It's *this* world I want to learn about, and living people I want to help. The souls can tell us things the living can't, that's all. And the plants down there can do things no other plants can."

Demeter still wore a frown. "Then you and Hades…forgive me for asking, as you *are* a grown woman, but remember he's immortal and it's dangerous."

Persephone laughed, turning away to retrieve the basket of greens. "He's well over fifty, isn't he? I'd feel ridiculous. Plus I gather he only tolerates my interest in the Underworld for short periods of time, and wouldn't want to be burdened with me or anyone else beyond that. I suppose it is a bit insane, as you say."

"That's some relief. Then, as long as I get to see you at the end of each day…"

"Of course. I still live here, with you, and I wouldn't want it any other way." Persephone kissed her mother's cheek and moved past into the house, carrying the basket. At the moment, she even meant it. A comfortable home with a wise, wonderful immortal for a parent, and the freedom to visit the Underworld once in a while for novelty—the arrangement seemed perfect to her. Only at the darkest edges of her consciousness did she sense she might someday want more from it.

CHAPTER TWENTY-ONE

*J*UST *WALKING UP TO YOUR dorm*, said the text. *Let me in?*

Sophie's heart leaped in excitement, until she realized it was from Jacob, not Adrian. With the flood of romantic, ancient, mythology-colored memories distracting her today, Sophie had forgotten Jacob was driving up to visit this afternoon.

Groaning, she closed her laptop and stood up. She wasn't getting anything done on her Communications essay anyway.

"Something wrong?" asked Melissa, glancing up from her own computer.

"Jacob's here. I totally spaced and forgot he was coming."

"Should be a good kind of surprise."

Sophie only grunted, and walked out into the hall, texting back as she moved: *Yep. On my way.*

Jacob. Okay. Focus on Jacob now.

But her brain, it seemed, had been utterly reprogrammed. She kissed and greeted Jacob, smiled for him, and pretended to listen while he talked about university life. But her attention returned straight to Hades, whose image and actions kept unpacking themselves in her head.

Hades resembled Adrian more each time she dwelled on it. Not in every detail, but in the ways that mattered: a look in the eyes, a way of moving his head, a smile.

And this was not what she was supposed to be thinking about while spending time with her boyfriend.

Who was Jacob back then, or in those other lives?, Sophie pondered, staring at him as they sat across from each other at a pizza parlor. What would he learn if he were taken to the Underworld to eat the pomegranate?

Maybe she could swing it if she asked Adrian very nicely, but she doubted he'd be keen on the idea. Honestly, she didn't care for it herself. She didn't want to try to explain the Underworld to Jacob, nor share it with him.

In fact, as their food arrived, she realized she didn't even particularly want to share a pizza with him.

Surely it was just PMS or, likelier, the confusion of all this information flooding her head. When the novelty of Adrian and the Persephone life died down, she would appreciate Jacob again, she told herself. She partook of the pizza, and brought out smiles and remarks in response to Jacob's chatter.

After dinner they returned to her dorm room, which Melissa had tactfully vacated for a few hours. Jacob grinned and crowded her against her closet door. "Now this I have missed." He reached under her jacket and shirt, and she winced—his hands were cold from the evening air.

She returned his kisses for a few seconds, then turned her face aside. "I don't feel like it anymore."

She hadn't meant to add the last word. She intended only to avoid any physical shenanigans tonight. But it was a Freudian slip: all too true.

Jacob's reaction might have been comical if she hadn't felt so guilty. His mouth went agape, his eyes widened, and his hat, tilted back on his head to accommodate the kiss, looked like it was knocked back by the force of his shock.

"What do you mean?" he asked.

It was her chance to salvage the remark, laugh it off, apologize, and say she only meant she had cramps and wanted to sleep.

Or, if she was going to be brave, it was her chance to get this difficult task done. Reluctantly, she stepped up to the challenge.

"I mean I'm breaking up with you. I'm sorry."

Sophie sat in her desk chair and Jacob on the floor, as if his legs had given out on the spot.

Thus commenced the least enjoyable conversation she'd ever had, and it went on longer than she would have liked. Jacob kept demanding she tell him why—and asked more than once if Adrian Watts had anything to do with this. She said no, it wasn't for any other particular guy; she and Jacob just had different interests and she'd been thinking about ending it for a while now.

He kept pleading for her to reconsider, give him another chance. She stated, with sincerest apologies, that it would only be cruel to string him along, as she didn't love him anymore and didn't want to be his girlfriend. Why would he want to date some-one who felt that way?

Melissa returned, took a look at their haggard faces, and froze in place in the doorway. "I could go out a while longer."

Jacob stood with a sigh. "No. I was leaving."

"I'll walk out with you," said Sophie.

They didn't speak as they trudged to his car in the student-and-visitor lot. Lights buzzed on posts. The air was cold, a fog beginning to form. The marching band practiced in the football stadium nearby, horns and drums reverberating between campus buildings. An autumn smell of chimney smoke made her so nos-talgic for home that, already weakened by the breakup, she almost wept.

At his car door, he looked at her, his eyes miserable. "Can I call you in a few days? Talk it over?"

She folded her arms. "I guess. Just to tell me how you're doing. But I won't change my mind."

"You might. I won't stop hoping." He touched his palm to her face. "Who's going to look out for you now? I'm worried, babe. This Adrian guy…"

Irritated, she moved back. "Those people were insane, Jacob. *They're* the dangerous ones. I can't believe you didn't see it."

"How you could know that, or say that? They're only looking out for you."

"They aren't. If you want to keep me safe, don't talk to them anymore. I mean it."

He stared at her. "What are you talking about? Tonight I don't even know you."

"I'm still me. I'm just..." She sighed, looking past him at the lights reflected in his car window. "Please drive carefully."

Jacob opened the car door, looked at her a long moment as if trying to come up with an answer, then got in without a word. She stepped back as the car started. He pulled out from the parking spot slowly, and drove away.

Feeling shaky, Sophie walked back to the dorm. *I didn't do this for Adrian*, she insisted to herself, as she'd been insisting out loud to Jacob. But of course she did do it in part because of him, and did imagine how Adrian might react when she told him she was free. Panic and pleasure twisted in her belly at the notion.

Okay, she was romantically interested in him, but she was going to be smart about this and not tell him immediately, this very night. That would smack of rebound.

Instead, as she reached the glass door that let her into the dorm, she tapped the contact number for Tabitha's cell.

"Hey, lady," Tabitha answered. Thank God. She was somewhere quiet and answering her phone, not off partying on Capitol Hill with her cool new friends.

"Taaaab," Sophie wailed. She pulled open the door, entered the building, and leaned against the wall beside the stairwell. "I broke up with Jacob."

Tab moved straight into her voice of sincere approval. "Good. You're better off."

"Really? I feel awful. Did I do the right thing?"

"Dude, if you strung it out much longer I was going to have to do my friend duty and tell you he's not that spectacular. You can do way better."

"Thanks."

"You can tell me the reasons if you like. But I bet I can guess."

Sophie drew in her breath nervously. "You can?" She wondered if it was obvious even to someone in another city that the breakup might be connected to another guy, who actually was rather spectacular.

"You and Jacob were never a great fit. Especially lately. It wasn't working and it was hurting me to see."

Sophie let her shoulders relax. "That's about it, yeah. Although…never mind. Can we do a video call tomorrow when I'm less tired?"

"Absolutely. Hey, get your odd little roommate to go out for ice cream with you."

"Ice cream?"

"Or a pedicure. I'm fairly sure either one of those is standard therapy for a breakup."

Sophie smiled, remembering Melissa's tact this evening during Jacob's visit. "I guess I do owe her a treat for putting up with me."

"I love you, Soph. You're going to be fine."

"I love you too."

MELISSA ACCEPTED SOPHIE'S invitation to walk to the nearest all-night convenience store to buy ice cream. Sophie told her the bare bones of the relationship collapse on the way. With her usual calm, Melissa took it in.

"It's tough to break up," she said, biting into the ice cream bar Sophie bought her. "I've never regretted dumping the womanizing jerk I dated in high school, but still, it sucked at the time."

Sophie was surprised to learn plain, aloof Melissa possessed dating drama in her past. But then, it was hardly the biggest surprise in her life lately; and didn't everyone have romantic turmoil once in a while? Sophie murmured in agreement, sucking chocolate ice cream off the wooden paddle-shaped spoon that came with her tiny carton.

Late that night, she washed her face in the communal bathroom, ignoring the two girls chatting at the end of the counter. She didn't want Jacob back. She knew this breakup was for the best. But she felt like a failure—that was the closest she could pinpoint her abysmal mood. Not very long ago, she had thought Jacob was the love of her life, the best thing to have ever happened to her, the most perfect match and the closest male friend she could have hoped for. And she had been so very wrong. It made her feel idiotic, bereft, and just plain cruel. If there were some way to hug Jacob all night long and soothe him without getting his hopes up, she would have done so.

Tears filled her eyes and soaked into the washcloth she pressed to her face. The two other girls breezed out of the bathroom, their voices traveling down the hall. Sophie brought the washcloth into a stall, and wept into it as silently as she could.

Afterward, with rose-scented moisturizer cooling the skin around her stinging eyes, she slipped into bed. Listening to Melissa's steady breathing, she lay her palms flat on the mattress and steeled herself for another Persephone dream. Were these memories going to make her night even harder?

Possibly. For the moment, the thought of Adrian threw her into a panic. *Yeah, I'm free now*, she imagined saying to him, pointing her finger in his face. *But that doesn't mean I'm leaping into your freakish world and joining you in immortality, so don't get any ideas.*

Nonetheless, her dreams were about to put her right back into that freakish world. Oh, well. No helping it. She needed to sleep, and the sooner she sorted through these past lives and got over the shock of them, the better. Maybe it would even take her mind off Jacob.

All right, Persephone, she thought, in the tone of a prayer. *Help me through this. Show me what to do.*

Chapter Twenty-Two

Sophie sank her concentration into Persephone's life, delib-erately reducing the pace, as if pulling the reins of the ghost horses to slow their dash across the planet. Taking in a few weeks or months tonight would be enough; no need for digesting entire years. And considering this was the era when Persephone began studying the Underworld in earnest, there would be plenty of interesting memories to examine.

Persephone began her research on her next visit to the Under-world, bringing a pot of paint and a brush. She walked through the forest with Hades, asking him what each tree's magical prop-erties were, and marking their trunks accordingly.

"You've said 'I don't know' for most of these," she teased, painting an open half-circle on another trunk. The empty cup shape was her mark to indicate "don't know"—knowledge to be filled in later, as it were.

"How would I know?" Hades said. "There aren't many people who want to come to the Underworld and try eating the plants to see what happens. Nor would I ask them to. And I won't allow you to do it, either, so don't try."

Kneeling by the trunk, she looked over her shoulder at him. "Have *you* tasted them all?"

"Nearly all, and when I say 'I don't know' it means I haven't noticed any effect. But I'm immortal, and the effect on mortals could be quite different."

She rose, rubbing a wet spot of paint between her thumb and

finger. "We'll think of safe ways to test them. Besides, plants have uses beyond eating."

"Like the harnesses, yes."

"Exactly. Think what else we might discover."

Their discoveries over that first summer were sundry but not earth-shaking. Persephone coaxed Hades into allowing her to taste very small amounts of some plants, once in a while, to learn their effects.

The red violets, when eaten, made you go harmlessly numb all over for about a quarter of the day.

"Wish I'd had these when Mother pulled my sore tooth last year," Persephone said, touching her jaw in regret.

One tree's berries, when boiled, dyed cloth and other materials a permanent dark red, and left a deep stain on skin too. Persephone dyed one of her cloaks, and it took a month before all the red faded from her hands.

Around there, Sophie awakened, and faced her first morning as a single woman in five months.

Today I just recover, and study, she vowed. And she did — with a pleasantly long video chat with Tabitha later, in which she related the break-up discussion in detail.

It felt good just to see Tab's face on the video screen. She had rosy skin, playful blue eyes, a sheet of blonde hair cascading almost to her waist, and a plump figure that she clothed in dramatically contrasting solid colors. Today it was a fuchsia knit top with a plunging neck, and a black velvet wrap with a yellow sunflower pin on its shoulder.

"So here's what you do," Tabitha said. "Think of all his annoying traits, and how you're free of them."

Sophie pondered. "Always saying he was going to 'grab' food."

"Pointing at people when he said hi to them."

"The turquoise Converse that don't match anything he owns."

"His opinion that classical music is 'boring,' and opera is 'weird,'" Tabitha said.

"The way he won't eat any salads except the most boring iceberg lettuce ones. Not even the awesome ones *I* make."

Tabitha waved her hand grandly. "See? Completely incompatible with the daughter of produce. Hey, how are your folks and Liam? Any news?"

Sophie sighed. "Not really. Liam says Mom still spends a lot of time out of the house, but he hasn't figured out why. Dad acts like everything's fine as long as I text him every twelve hours. And Mom's supposed to come down and visit me soon, where I'm sure she'll act like everything's fine, too. I don't know."

Tabitha nodded in commiseration. "You remember how royally it sucked when my parents got divorced. I hope you and Liam never have to deal with that. But still—there is nothing, repeat, nothing, you can do. You're an adult, and you've got your own crap to deal with."

"Yeah." Sophie sighed. "It's just—her *kissing* some other guy… and he looked like a sleazy *banker* or something, with the haircut and the suit…"

"Honey, I know. But don't torture yourself with that. Today, just take care of you."

Sophie obeyed as best as she could. She finished most of her textbook reading and her worksheets. Then she laced up her running shoes and jogged to Avery Park and back. She'd taken up jogging in the last year, but had neglected it since coming to college. It did her good—it left her tired enough to sleep, and she dropped with exhaustion into Persephone's world.

Persephone and Hades were still experimenting with the Underworld's plants. One tree's bark yielded an effective substance for tanning animal skins in a fraction of the usual time it took, and with less of the obnoxious odors. Another, when fed to pigs, made them stay up all night and sleep all day in reverse of their natural habits; and, when fed to bats (captured in one of the more remote sections of the cave), switched their habits the other way.

"Day-flying bats." Hades shook his head, watching them flutter and swoop around outdoors in the noonday sun. "A lot of good that'll do anyone."

Persephone frowned at them, shielding her eyes from the sun. "The real problem, if you ask me, is that so far none of the edible plants do anything special unless they're eaten inside the cave. We can't be dragging people to the Underworld all the time for cures."

"Agreed. But I take it as a sign that we're not meant to export too much magic. The Underworld likes to keep its secrets close."

"Then back into the cave we go," she declared.

There was a whole half of the cave she never saw, though she knew it existed.

"The place where the evil go," she finally dared to say one day, as they walked the fields. "Where is it?"

Hades shot her a stern look. "Deeper. But I'm not taking you there."

"Why?"

"It's no place for a pleasant young person. Even *I* hate going there."

Dread chilled her, and she almost felt relieved that he wouldn't show it to her. But the need to know the truth pushed her to ask more questions. "Why? What is it like?"

He sighed. "They're alone, each separated from the rest, and though they'll talk to me if I wish, they're always sunk in horrible guilty thoughts. And the vines hold them there, all by themselves, until the Underworld decides to let them go. That's what disturbs me, really: seeing the cave as…as some kind of thinking, judging thing. I don't know what to make of it. Perhaps it's the great Goddess at work, and that's…frightening, in a way. Even if it's also good, in the larger scheme."

Persephone nodded, gazing down at the pale grass as they walked. "I feel no need to see it yet, then. Your description is enough." Then she looked at him. "The vines, you said? Vines hold them? Like the ones for harnessing the spirit horses?"

He glanced at her, guilt shadowing his eyes. "The same. That's how I learned to do it. I looked at the vines down there, which the Underworld twists together on its own. I didn't want to tell anyone, though. The others think me insane enough as it is, and if they knew I was using methods from the caves of punishment to capture horses for them…"

"I won't tell," she promised. "And I think it's admirable, actually. You took something dark and made something useful of it."

He gave her a soft smile. "Thank you for putting it that way, at least."

Upon awakening from that memory on a Friday morning, Sophie wandered to class in a morbidly thoughtful mood, recalling Adrian telling her about those caves of punishment, and wearing the same troubled look that Hades had.

Meanwhile, Sophie hadn't forgotten Jacob. She had kept him with her throughout the dreams; Jacob, angered and hurt, hovered in the wings like one of the Underworld's ghosts, even while she stepped into Persephone's skin and explored prehistoric Greece.

But it had to be admitted: after these considerations of life and death and divine retribution, breaking up with her high-school boyfriend looked a bit less momentous. It was survivable, at any rate.

She got through the day with a bit more grace than she had yesterday, and fell asleep that night looking forward to her dreams.

Time and again, Persephone reminded Hades it would be extremely useful for her to be able to speak the language of the dead, and converse with the souls directly about the plants and other topics. He taught her several phrases and words, which she picked up easily. But they both knew the faster way to fluency.

"I don't want any more mortals eating the pomegranate," he told her in mid-summer. They were lunching above ground, on the beach. "There have only been three, and they were all ancient wise folk. Even most of the immortals have turned it down—like your mother."

She glared at him. "So now you're hoarding *all* the wisdom? You won't let anyone else have it?"

"It isn't that. It's a burden, bringing all those past lives—and past deaths—into your mind. You're much too young to do that to yourself."

"Why should age enter into it? If I'm old enough to marry and bear children, why shouldn't I be old enough to know my other lives?"

"You're young and delightful." His voice gentled, and the sea wind ruffled his black hair. "I'd hate to see you darken your mind with all the tragedies that have ever befallen your soul."

She pitched an olive pit into the waves, and lay back on her elbows on the warm sand. "Does your mind feel darkened? You speak more of having been 'enlightened' by this realm, it seems to me."

"Now you're playing word games. Demeter would hate it if you ate the pomegranate. You know she would. You got your way in coming here so often; just leave it at that."

But Persephone didn't leave it at that. That afternoon, walking with Hades through the orchard, she spotted a freshly fallen pomegranate among the dead leaves. Under pretext of adjusting her sandal, she knelt so her gown's hem covered the fruit. As she stood again, she wrapped the pomegranate in the corner of her red cloak and picked it up, tucking it into the cloth bag she carried.

Of course, in order for it to work, she would have to eat it here rather than take it home.

She looked into the bag and made a sound of dismay. "Oh— my paintbrush. I must have left it by one of the trees." She began circling each tree trunk, pretending to search the ground.

Hades turned back on the path. "I'll check the farther trees."

"Thank you." As soon as his footsteps died to a far rustle, she dropped to her knees and took out the pomegranate. She dug her fingernails into its thick skin. Red juice dripped onto her hand and splattered onto her white tunic. Swearing in a whisper, she ripped loose a section of the fruit and sank her teeth into the tightly packed seeds. They tasted sweet and cool. She tugged free one more section and ate its seeds too, just to make sure the magic would take effect. A drop of juice ran down her chin and splashed in a large pink spot on her tunic's neckline.

Hades' footsteps crunched back toward her in the leaves. She wiped her chin, swallowed the mouthful of fruit, and shoved the rest of the pomegranate under the dead leaves.

"Nothing yet," he said. "You?"

"It's all right, yes, I found it." Rising, she held up the brush and stepped out from behind the tree.

"Ah, good." He halted, his gaze falling to her tunic. His solicitous expression turned to suspicion, and his hand lifted toward the pink spot. "What's on your…" She tried to cover it with her own hand, and instantly he caught her fingers and examined them—sticky with the fruit's juices, her nails stained and still wet. Clutching her hand, he looked at the ground, kicked aside a rise in the leaves, and uncovered the half-eaten pomegranate.

She pulled in her breath.

He pushed her backward and released her hand. "*Persephone!*"

It was the first time she had ever seen him angry, and being the cause of it sent a thrill through her—part fear, part triumph. Even in that muddled moment she understood she wanted to cause strong reactions in him. Ideally of a more pleasant kind, but anger was a start.

"I'm sorry," she said. "I take full responsibility."

"Yes, I should hope so."

"I mean I won't let you take the blame. I promise."

Growling, he turned and paced away, one hand buried in his hair. "How can I trust you down here? The magic is dangerous, and if you won't listen to me, I can't let you be here."

That was a threat that scared her and brought her close to tears. "Please let me come back. I won't sneak about anymore. I *will* be careful. I just wanted the knowledge, the languages…"

Still glowering, he swung toward the river and marched that direction. "Come. It's time to take you home."

She chased after him, but could barely keep up because of her limp, and for once he wasn't slowing his pace to accommodate her. Only at the river's edge did she catch up to him, as he unwound the rope that tied the raft. "Please," she said. "I'm sorry. Don't send me home forever." She closed her hands around his upper arm and laid her forehead against it, feeling the warmth and muscle through the cloth of his cloak. "Please."

He held still a moment, then took her arm and led her onto

the raft with him. He said nothing as he pulled the raft across the river, and lifted her up the other bank.

Tears pulsed in her throat as she followed him to the entrance chamber. Daylight glimmered from the mouth above. The warm breeze descending from outside swirled his cloak around him. He untied the chariot waiting there and stood aside to let her climb in.

Miserably, she did so.

Hades stepped in after her, but only gazed at the horses, his expression like a thundercloud.

"Can I come back?" she asked, voice quivering.

He sighed, and rubbed his face. The pause before he answered stretched far too long for her taste. "I suppose you'll have to. Where else will you be able to use the language of the dead?"

She breathed free at last. Leaning sideways, she kissed his shoulder. "Thank you. Really, I'm sorry. I'm too impulsive and I know it."

"You'll pay for it." He tied an extra knot in the willow-and-ivy reins. "Goddess only knows what kind of dreams you'll have now."

"I look forward to them. I'm sure they're worth gaining the languages."

"Foolish confidence of youth." He hooked his elbow into hers and snapped the reins. The horses leaped upward, and the chariot tipped Persephone and Hades nearly onto their backs as they flew into the sky.

They straightened out over the land and began the flight up the river. "To be honest," he said, "when I was your age I would have done the same. I suppose I did the nearest thing, volunteering as a sacrifice. Hoping to journey to the Underworld that way."

"That's much braver and more foolish than me. I wouldn't dare be a sacrifice."

"Let's hope you never are." His grave statement kept them quiet a while, then a snort of a laugh escaped him.

She looked at him. "What?"

Watching the horses, he shook his head. "It's like having a dog. 'What has she eaten now?'"

"*Not* very flattering." She tried to look stern, and failed when laughter overtook her.

Knives, blood, ceremonies. Beautiful chants under the stars, colorful murals on palace walls. A boy named Hades falling as voluntary sacrifice, his blood pooling down the steps to where she stood, only a few paces away, trying not to faint with horror. Then Rhea bringing her in secret to the court of the dead to witness his miraculous recovery…and after parting from him in Greece, the midnight squall at sea that sent the ship pitching onto its side, flinging her and everyone else overboard, the wet sails and beams trapping her under the heaving surface, saltwater invading her lungs…

Persephone awoke from her first memory-dream with a choked cry of terror, and Sophie did the same a moment later.

It was Saturday morning, and Melissa still slept, but the sky was light at the edges of their closed curtains. To calm and reorient herself, Sophie focused on real-world details: Melissa's family photos taped to her wardrobe door; Sophie's untidy stacks of books on the shelves.

Memory-dreams within memory-dreams. That was new. And confusing.

Closing her eyes again, she rubbed her eyelids, unable to hold back a shiver at the thought of young Hades being sliced open with a pair of blades. Hearing about it as history in Persephone's time was nowhere near as disturbing as seeing it firsthand as Tanis. Even when, as Tanis, she fully believed it was done for the good of some all-powerful Goddess, it had been utterly horrible to witness.

And she couldn't deny one of her reasons for being disturbed. Seventeen-year-old Hades, with his beard shaved and his curls cut to above his neck, looked more than ever like Adrian. The thought of watching him get sacrificed grieved her more than she expected.

Well, he was a friend. Quite a lot more than a friend. What

did you call someone you'd been usually in love with for the past seventy-five lives?

Sophie pulled her phone off her desk, and found it was 9:04 a.m. She sent him a text.

Did you know I was Tanis who helped you escape the palace after the sacrifice? Of course you knew. Well, I didn't till now. Freaked me the hell out.

She got out of bed and took her towel and basket of toiletries to the bathroom, closing the door quietly to avoid waking Melissa.

As she hung her worn red terrycloth bathrobe on the hook beside the showers, the phone buzzed from its pocket. She tucked the towel around her naked body and looked at the message.

Sorry you had to see that sacrifice. Always reckoned it looked even worse from the outside than it did from my point of view. So Persephone's eaten the pomegranate now?

Yes, she thumbed in. *Very sneaky of her. Me. Whoever.*

True, and I still feel bad for that dog comment, Adrian wrote.

Ha, she answered. *I plan to call you a potbellied pig someday in revenge.*

That'll teach me. So what are you up to today?

Studying mostly. You? she typed.

Same, kinda. If you can bring it elsewhere, want to study together?

Nervous pleasure warmed her belly. Her lip ran back and forth under her teeth, a smile emerging despite her stress. *Sure. What time?*

CHAPTER TWENTY-THREE

EW SOAKED THE GRASS, WETTING her high-top sneakers as she crossed the quad. The maple trees were turning brilliant yellow against the blue sky. The air was calm but cold, and smelled of smoke and damp forests. Southern Greece was decidedly warmer than Oregon, Sophie noted, wrapping her purple and blue scarf (knitted by her mom) one extra time around her neck.

She arrived at the newly chosen rendezvous spot and waited— between a hedge and a statue, near a lecture hall. Her backpack, stuffed with the laptop computer and a few books, dragged heavily on her shoulders. She wore the loose knitted cap that went with the scarf, but still shivered with cold.

A rustle in the hedge made her turn. Adrian emerged, pushing branches away from his face, and smiled. He wore a wool hat too, in gray rib knit, and had his flannel-lined coat buttoned up. On his back was a dark green pack with extra straps and pockets, probably intended for hiking. Dew sprinkled his boots and darkened his indigo jeans up to the knees, likely because the grass was higher in the other realm.

"Hi," he said. "Ready?"

She nodded. Stepping up, she slipped her arms around his neck. Her cheek touched the rough wool of his coat.

Adrian held her around the waist, and the world transformed. Hedge, building, and statue vanished. Wet tips of meadow grass poked at her thighs, leaving cold wet spots on her jeans. Adrian's hold went slack, but Sophie kept hugging him, on an impulse. It was cold, and he smelled good, and it had been a tough week and she could use a hug, was how she rationalized it to herself.

Adrian held still, as if processing the gesture, then responded, rewrapping his arms around her. He stroked her hat-covered head and let his hand settle between her shoulders.

After a few seconds, she let go, and he smiled, ducking his head. "Good morning," he said.

"Good morning. It's, uh, nice to see you…alive."

He smiled kindly at her and bent to pet Kiri, who had bounded over. "Yeah, the memories can be traumatizing sometimes. Sorry about that."

"Poor Tanis." Sophie patted Kiri's back. The wagging tail thumped her leg. "So this might count as spoilers, but does this connection thing between us keep going into the past? Before Hades and Tanis and all that?"

"Some, but not as much." He started strolling across the meadow. She followed. "We were drawing closer to each other over the years, but it really kicked off with the Persephone lifetime."

"And has been going strong ever since." She said it as an observation, thinking back over the many lives; but when he sent her another shy smile, she realized how romantic a statement it was. Clearing her throat, she squinted at the trees ahead. "So, are we studying in the Airstream?"

"Yeah, nah. Niko's brought me a generator, and he's setting it up. He's annoying, so we'll go elsewhere." They passed through the trees and emerged near the Airstream.

"Niko's here? I should say hi. I feel bad for trying to beat him up when we first met."

"Well, he did jump you. Beating him up was perfectly warranted."

At that moment, Nikolaos sauntered into view from the front end of the trailer. He wore full soccer-fan regalia in some team that favored bright red and yellow: jacket, nylon shorts, cap, and scarf. "Sophia." He waved a wrench at her in greeting. "Why, look. She does smile."

"Hi, Niko." She stopped before him, and they exchanged long, amused gazes. "Life sure has gotten interesting ever since you grabbed me."

"I thought it might. And for once I am not being an insincere wanker when I say it's wonderful to see you again. *Persephone*." He said her name in the proper Greek pronunciation, all slanted and exotic.

"*Hermes*," she responded in the same accent, then said in the proto-ancient-Greek tongue from her dreams lately, "For a complete scoundrel, you're not too bad."

Arms folded, he winked at her. Then his gaze moved to Adrian, and he hissed his breath inward. "Ooh, Adrian's going to grab this wrench and brain me if I charm you any further. Be off, you two. Ade, the generator's working fine. Just a few more adjustments to make."

Adrian did look a tiny bit annoyed. "Cheers. We're off to study."

Nikolaos yawned. "Think I'll nap in your bed while you're away, before I head to Brazil."

"As long as you take off your filthy shoes. And keep Kiri company. Put her out when you leave."

Niko whistled to the dog. "Come here, girl. Naptime."

He and Kiri climbed into the trailer, and Adrian led Sophie across the clearing to the bus and horses.

"Brazil?" she asked.

"Football match." Adrian untied the reins and got seated in the bus. "As far as I can tell, he spends most of his time gambling, hitting on people, and watching football."

Sophie slid her backpack to the bus's floor and sat beside him. "By which you mean soccer, I assume."

"Yes, although you Yanks are the only ones who call it that." He smiled, got out his phone, and tapped the screen. "So. We can do real world today if you like. As long as it's not somewhere we're expected to be. Where's a good coffee shop in another city?"

"Hmm. I've never been to San Francisco," she suggested.

"Me neither." He zoomed in on the map. "Let's look for a

park…good place to appear. Buena Vista Park. Not far from some big streets where there must be coffee. Shall we try it?"

"Sure."

He offered his arm, and she took it, holding on tight. With a snap of the reins, the horses shot up over the treetops and went supersonic toward the south.

Rivers snaked past and mountains scooted along between islands of white clouds. The wind was frigid, and Sophie tugged her cap down around her ears. "Does Niko sleep in your bed a lot?"

"No." He grinned at her, eyebrows diving down in the middle. "And what are you asking exactly?"

She laughed. "I have to wonder. He's always been bi, in the lives I can remember. And you occasionally have been too."

He returned to watching the terrain. "As have you. Usually when we were born into the opposite kind of body, though—me as a woman, or you as a man."

"True. But in this life I'm straight. With a lesbian as a best friend, if that gives me street cred."

"Really? Me too."

"You too what? Straight, or the lesbian best friend?"

"Both," he laughed. "My best mate Zoe—she's gay. Says girls smell better. With which I agree. As for Niko, he's certainly tried with me, but I'm not that desperate yet."

"I see."

Neither Zoe nor Niko was competition, then. Sophie's mood did grow more buoyant at that news. But she still hadn't told Adrian that she'd dumped Jacob, and nervousness frazzled her at the thought. She lowered her gaze to the backpacks at their feet. "What are *you* studying?"

"A lot of things. Adding to the catalog of safe places to appear and disappear. That usually means finding places like this park we're going to, and writing down the coordinates for a list we've got going. We all add to it when we can. Need as many safe spots as we can get. Really awkward when you wing it and appear in someone's kitchen or bathroom."

"Hah. Yeah, I bet. Or a brick wall—what happens if there's a wall where you want to appear?"

"Kicks you back out of it. Hurts, too. Could probably break bones if you were mortal. So, yeah nah, best to aim for outdoors when you switch."

"So mainly you're looking at maps today?"

"Only a bit. There's also my Underworld job. Talk to the souls, find justice that needs to be done. Research murder trials, report back to the souls who were killed and tell them how it's going. That sort of thing."

His words stirred her memory. "You did that as Hades too. We both did."

"Yep."

"Is it only murder trials? Or do you do other kinds of justice and unfinished business too?"

He sighed. "I'd like to, but…unfinished business is usually 'Tell so-and-so I love them,' and *everyone* wants that. I could never do it all. And if it's a crime that left the victim still alive, then obviously I'm not going to be seeing them down there—at least for a while—so they have to take care of their own justice. But murder victims, they're the ones who can't speak for themselves in the living world. And they're the ones I *can* speak to. So if they know who killed them, and can give me clues that I can report as anonymous tips, then I do that for them."

"Those are serious good deeds right there," she said, impressed.

"Well, I hope. In any case, that alone could keep me occupied forever. But I also ought to be researching Thanatos, which is boring and hateful but has to be done."

"Like tracking what they're up to?"

"Kind of. I've found people in the Underworld who knew Quentin, and Bill Wilkes too, though they haven't yet thought of anything I could use to make them stop what they're doing. Niko hasn't found where Quentin's living yet, but he's followed Wilkes around a little. He lives in Salem, and actually is a police officer."

"Wow. So the card wasn't fake."

"Surprise, eh? Also, I have emails to go through. Niko hacked into the account for Sanjay's guru a while back—the bloke in Thanatos who got him killed—and downloaded heaps of messages. We've been sorting through them for months, seeing if there's anything dangerous we ought to know, or anything useful to learn."

"You're a lot busier than I realized."

"Thought I zipped about the world all day on ghost horses, visiting pretty places, selling diamonds for spending money?"

"It did cross my mind," she admitted.

"It's a challenging business, this immortality thing. Especially in the Internet age. We have loads to do."

"Is that why you're trying to bring me on board? To help with the workload?"

She said it lightly, but he thought it over before answering. Keeping his gaze ahead, where the gray-blue waters of San Francisco Bay were sliding into view, he said, "I'm trying to bring you on board because I've never lived a life without you. And I don't want to start now."

The sweet declaration warmed her heart. But she kept the lightness in her tone when she responded, "So it's because of who I used to be? What if I'd been born into this life as someone horrible and obnoxious?"

His beautiful eyes met hers. "With that soul, you couldn't have been."

Sophie looked troubled, turning her head forward. Her lips were closed tight in a pensive frown, and the wind whipped a curly tendril of her dark hair around her face. Adrian glanced ahead too, slowing the horses and guiding them to a thickly wooded hill. He shifted his gaze between the ground and the GPS arrow on his phone screen, while his mind kicked itself.

What was he thinking, spouting sentiments like that when she'd only barely become aware of his existence? He may have had years to think it over, but she hadn't.

He brought the horses down between the trees. Pine boughs swiped the sides of the bus and scattered needles into the open windows. The bus landed. A flock of blue-green birds rose from the trees, croaking like frogs as they flew away.

"Look, I'm sorry." Adrian wound and unwound the reins around his hand. "You have your studies, and your family, your friends, your boyfriend, and I had no right to barge in and—"

"I don't anymore." She spread her hands symmetrically on her legs, and gazed at them.

"You don't what?"

"Have a boyfriend. Anymore. I broke up with Jacob."

Plenty of times he'd imagined her saying that, and had fore-warned himself not to cheer out loud. He succeeded—but in fact, found he was a mess of anxiety. What was the right thing to say here? None of the statements he'd come up with, in those imaginings, sounded appropriate now.

"Oh." He followed her lead and stared at his own hands. "When?"

"Wednesday night. It was something I'd been thinking about for a while, though."

"Even before Niko and I…kidnapped you?"

"Yeah. Even before that."

"Okay." He drew in his breath, feeling a bit steadier. "Then how are you feeling about it?"

"I'm all right." She folded one hand over the other. "Mostly I feel guilty. He was blindsided. But he'll get over it, and it's for the best."

Adrian nodded, and decided it was permissible to smile now. He did, rising and offering her his hand. "Probably what you need is to find some coffee and get some studying done, eh?"

She nodded, and grasped his hand.

Good signs. So many good signs.

CHAPTER TWENTY-FOUR

They switched into the living world and found themselves on a forest path, beneath a large pine tree with twisting roots.

Their sudden appearance startled a middle-aged man jogging by, who skittered aside and stared at them.

Adrian waved at him. "We're practicing a magic trick. How'd it look?"

"Pretty damn good," said the bewildered man, still jogging but slowing down as he examined them.

Sophie gave him a thumbs-up.

The man shot his gaze across the ground and up into the tree as if looking for hidden trapdoors, then lifted his brows and jogged on.

Sophie and Adrian burst into laughter.

"Oops," he said. "Always a risk."

"Magic trick? That's your excuse?"

He shrugged. "It *is* magic." Adrian glanced around. A city gleamed below the hill they stood upon, fog and sunlight wrapping around its skyscrapers. He had never been here before, but his GPS assured him it was San Francisco's Buena Vista Park.

Sophie, spotting the magnificent city view, beamed in delight and set off that direction.

As they walked down the hill, he asked what she was taking this term, and she related her course schedule, all prerequisites for the nutrition major.

"What were you going to do with your life before Rhea showed up?" she asked. "Before you knew you'd be… this?" They emerged from the park onto a residential street lined with expensive old houses, packed close together and painted cheerful colors.

"I was going to be a lawyer," Adrian said. "Not the kind everyone hates, but the kind who defends the innocent, the poor, all that superhero stuff. Maybe amongst the Maori in particular—my mum was part Maori. But I try to do it for the souls now instead, since I can't spend too much time in one place in the real world."

"I'd say it worked out. You became an actual superhero."

They turned a corner onto a busier street: Haight, according to the sign on a post. "I don't feel like one. Nor a god."

"No? Not even after all this time driving ghost horses and living with Hades' memories?"

"Hades had style. He was a mature, mystical guy. He's not supposed to be a young geek with a Kiwi accent."

Sophie snorted. "For one thing, you're not *that* geeky. For another, your accent is completely hot."

He glanced at her. "Really?"

"To American chicks, you know it is." She elbowed him. "Quit pretending you don't."

They chose a cafe and entered its warm and pungently coffee-scented interior. On the dark red walls hung mosaics made from ripped-up magazines. Strings of lights in the shapes of skulls and pumpkins framed the front windows.

As they waited in line, Sophie pointed to a small round table in the corner. "Go save that one for us. Tell me what you want and I'll order. My treat this time."

"Cheers. Er…" Adrian blinked at the vast and detailed menu hand-written on a blackboard above the counter. "Just drip would be fine."

"Sixteen ounce?"

"Whatever you're getting."

She nodded, and he picked his way between tables to the one she'd indicated, where he set up his laptop. Sophie arrived with the coffee, and for a while they browsed and typed independently, trading occasional remarks. Adrian read Thanatos emails referencing himself, dated a few months ago, but found nothing relevant in them. As far as he could tell, their assumptions were way off base—they seemed to think Adrian had some "recruiting" plan to bring in other immortals, and they were trying to figure out what it was.

No, he thought; at the moment he only really desired one person as a potential new recruit. Indeed, even if there was some coded message of importance buried in these emails, he could well miss it, given how his mind was more inclined this morning to dwell on remarks like: *'I broke up with Jacob'* and *'Your accent is completely hot.'*

Sophie's phone chirped. "My mom," she said, looking at the screen.

"Go ahead, answer it." Adrian got up. "I was about to take a break."

She nodded and accepted the call. "Hi, Mom."

He found his way past the counter to the restrooms, and when he came out, she was still talking, so he examined the food for sale on the chilled shelves under glass. A few minutes later, he brought a large, colorful salad and a walnut-studded brownie to the table.

"Okay, love you too," Sophie was saying into the phone. "Bye." She hung up and smiled at the salad. "Beets and blue cheese?"

"Thought it looked good. Getting near lunchtime." Sitting down, he handed her one of the two forks. "Hungry?"

"Yeah. Thank you." She gathered up a forkful of salad greens, blue cheese, and a pear slice, and crammed it into her mouth. "Mmm."

Adrian speared two beet slices and ate them. "How's your mum?"

"Oh…" Sophie swallowed her bite. "Fine, she says."

He glanced quizzically at her.

She grimaced, picking up a pecan. "I feel—that is, I almost know—she and Dad are having problems. And I'm terrified they might get a divorce. But they haven't said anything and I'm too scared to bring it up. Just now I tried 'You guys doing okay?', but all I got was 'Fine, honey.'"

Adrian scooped up some salad greens. "What makes you say they're having problems?"

A spiraling lock of hair slid down to touch her cheek. She pushed it behind her ear. "I saw her kissing another man a couple months ago. Some guy in a suit. They were in a parked car." Sophie turned away, squinting at the front windows.

Adrian winced. "Crap."

"It's hard to ask her something like that. Especially since she called to talk about my breaking up with Jacob. Guess she heard it from his folks."

"Did they get on well with him, your parents?"

"Yeah." She sighed. "Dad loved watching football with him. Sorry—American football." Adrian smiled at the correction, and Sophie resumed, "Anyway, Mom's coming down to visit me next week. Just the two of us. Maybe I'll get more of an answer about her and Dad then."

"Hope so."

She nodded, and focused on eating salad for a minute. He did the same.

"Of course," she added, sounding a bit wry now, "if they knew what I was up to lately, they'd have even bigger problems."

"It's tricky, the relly question." Catching her confused glance, he clarified, "Relatives. Family."

"Oh, right. Just like the old days. Demeter trying to keep us apart." She smiled.

"How far have you got in that?"

"Not too far. No making out with Hades yet. Though I know it happens eventually."

"Mm," he said in casual agreement, thinking, *And wait till you get to the fabulous sex.*

"Is she one of them? The new immortals?" Sophie sounded interested.

Adrian looked up, diverted from his arousing thoughts. "Who?"

"Demeter. Is she one of the ones you can sense? Track? Do you know who she is?"

He hesitated. Sophie looked so animated, so intrigued by the notion of finding her long-lost mother.

Catching his expression, Sophie added, "I know. You said you wouldn't tell me yet how many there are these days, or who they are. I just wondered, since souls who were close to each other tend to end up close again in other lives…I thought she could be some-one I know." Her voice turned sad again.

Adrian relented. What the hell. "She is. We do know."

Her eyes locked onto his. "Who is it? My mom?"

Slowly, he shook his head. "Close."

She blinked, looking confused.

"Your dad," he said.

CHAPTER TWENTY-FIVE

SOPHIE NEARLY JUMPED OUT OF her chair. Forcing herself to remain seated and not cause a scene, she gripped the edge of the table. "Why didn't you tell me?"

"There was no reason to tell you. He doesn't know. None of us have approached him."

"Well, were you going to?"

"Maybe. Eventually. We're being extra careful these days, as you know."

"But—this is important. This seems like the kind of thing you should have told me." Beyond that, she couldn't articulate why she felt betrayed.

"I'm telling you now." Adrian stayed patient, watching her steadily.

She relaxed her fingers on the table's edge. Her mind tried to reconcile the images: strong, feminine, beautiful Demeter, the same soul as her weary, mustached dad. Given their protective attitudes toward her, actually, she saw the resemblance.

"What does it change?" Adrian continued gently. "Your mum and dad are still your mum and dad."

She gazed at the scenery photos that had taken over her laptop as a screen saver. "Who was my mom, back then?"

"I don't know. Honestly, I don't. It isn't the largest number of people, those we can track."

"You have to trade blood somehow? Like you and Rhea in the sacrifice, or pricking your fingers and pressing them together?"

"Or share blood with someone as a parent. Or of course… sleeping with someone."

"And you can sense Demeter's soul?"

"Yes."

"So did you two…"

"The blood trick," he promised. "That's all."

"Well, that's a relief." She picked up her fork again and stabbed a leaf of salad. "Now I'm wondering what he would do, if we brought him to the other realm, got him to eat the pomegranate. I honestly don't know if he'd like the whole deal."

"I don't *plan* to approach him." Adrian peeled the plastic wrap from the brownie, broke it in half, and handed the larger section to her. "I don't think anyone else will, either. Rhea doesn't think anyone new should be made. That's why she was brassed off at me when I brought you there."

Sophie smiled, remembering Rhea lecturing Adrian. "Has she forgiven you?"

"Yeah." He bit into his half of the brownie. "She comes and sees me once or twice a week. We've given her a mobile phone, but she hasn't quite got the hang of using it. She did tell me she'd enjoy visiting you, if you're willing."

"Oh. Of course." Sophie took a bite of the chewy brownie, pondering how Rhea looked the same now as she had in Persephone's time. Could it really be…? As the truth dawned on her, she looked suddenly at Adrian. "She's been in the same body this whole time?"

Nodding, Adrian pulled a walnut out of the brownie and popped it into his mouth. "The only one who has. As far as we know."

"But how long was she alone like that? How many years—centuries—"

"Longer than anyone can imagine." He ate the last corner of his brownie. "She slept for most of it, mind you. Only awakened recently. We spoke to her, as Grete and Karl, you know."

Sophie gasped as the memory burst back into her mind with clarity. "We did! We were still down there when she woke up.

I'd skipped over so many of those recent memories, I didn't even know till now…"

"I was about ready to leave, and be reborn, and you soon did the same. But we made her promise to come find us, once we were grown up, and once she was able to navigate the modern world." He smiled. "So it was predestined, really, you and me being introduced in this life."

Sophie shook her head in wonder, ruminating upon that while she finished her portion of brownie.

Wiping crumbs off his fingers, Adrian lifted his chin toward the windows of the cafe, where the sun was brightening the street. "Looks like it's warming up. Shall we walk?"

They packed up their computers and went out onto the street. Adrian insisted on taking all her heavy books into his pack, promising he wouldn't notice the weight. People strolled past, some in comfortable dark coats and others in bright colors, drinking from paper coffee cups or tapping the screens of their cell phones. Skyscrapers peeked between the Victorian buildings.

Adrian looked around in interest. "I miss cities. Lately I'm always in the wilderness."

She turned into a side street full of tiny shops. "Then let's explore."

They spent the afternoon browsing the neighborhood—clothing, antiques, music, books, kitchenware, imported gifts with Chinese or Japanese script on their labels, anything that took their fancy.

They talked all the while. Sophie told him more about Tab, and he shared stories of his friend Zoe—who, she learned, was blind. "It was something to bond over," he said, "both of us disabled in our way. I still feel protective of her, and I want her to become immortal, because—well, she deserves it, and then surely she'd be able to see. But she's highly stubborn and won't even eat the pomegranate. If only she'd eat it, she'd at least be able to see in her dreams."

"Do you know who she was in Persephone's lifetime?"

"Yeah, I do." He glanced apologetically at her. "Shouldn't tell you yet, but before long you'll know."

"Fine, no spoilers. Feel like dinner?"

They found a pizza place on one of the side streets adjoining Castro, and each devoured three slices of a thick pie topped with pepperoni, artichoke hearts, and olives.

The sun sank, and the air was cold again when they came out. Sophie and Adrian retrieved their warm hats from their backpacks and put them on.

As they walked to Buena Vista Park to find their starting point, Sophie asked, "So. Aphrodite. Is she one of the people you can sense?"

He chuckled in a manner that suggested he'd been awaiting and dreading this question. "Yes. I can."

"And? Have you met her? In this life, I mean."

"Yeah. She came and found me. She was just curious."

"So if she came and found you, she must be immortal too. Only immortals can do the sensing-tracking thing."

He admitted this with a nod.

"So what's she like?" Sophie prodded.

He gazed at the sidewalk. "She's quite beautiful. It'd be silly to pretend otherwise. But we're not…involved. She's about thirty years older than me."

"But I bet she looks twenty-three," Sophie pointed out. "And you'll both live forever."

"Well…yeah. But no one ties down Aphrodite."

"Plenty *want* to."

Adrian gave her another glance, his face in shadow as they entered the park in the twilight. "Look, you may remember, when I was Hades…there *was* a time or two, mostly before I knew you—Persephone, I mean. But Aphrodite gave such times to a lot of people."

"Gosh. How generous." Sophie sounded icier than she meant to.

Adrian bowed his head. His boots kicked up leaves as he walked. "I'll also admit," he finally added, "that even in this life, when Freya—that's her name now—came and found me last year…well, for old times' sake, being friends and all, just this one time…" He let the sentence die off, allowing her intuition to fill in the blanks.

Sophie wasn't prepared for the arrow of jealousy that penetrated her stomach. She narrowed her eyes at the city lights. "Lucky you."

"You have to understand." Adrian sounded hesitant, maybe even miserable. "Before, being disabled and all, I hadn't…been with anyone. I wasn't really *able* to. I knew that in other lives she was always a friend, someone I could trust, and I didn't know how long it might be, how many years, before I could meet *you* properly, if I ever would, so…I need to shut up now, don't I."

Sympathy washed away most of the jealousy. Sophie despised herself for not even considering how limited his experience might have been when he was confined to a wheelchair. "Sorry," she said. "I didn't mean to be a bitch. It's none of my business. Of course you're free to…I mean…I had a boyfriend till, like, Wednesday, so it's okay."

Oh, my God, she thought. *We're talking like we have claims on each other.* Frightening, sort of, but mostly exhilarating.

He glanced at her as they waded through a layer of sweet-smelling pine needles. "You doing all right about that? Jacob, I mean."

She nodded. "The first day or two was a little shaky. But today I've felt mostly good."

The fading evening light wrapped him in shadows, but the shine of his eyes reached her vision clearly. "Good," he echoed.

Reaching the same tree where they'd startled the jogger earlier, Adrian slipped his arm into hers to draw her near. She laid her hands on his shoulders, looking away, suddenly feeling shy. He transferred them into the spirit realm, where darkness cascaded around them—no city lights, and a multitude of trees to block the sky. The brightest thing around was the gentle glow of the ghost horses.

Adrian reached into a coat pocket and lit up the darkness with his cell phone. "Let's see if I can drive us out of here without hitting a tree."

They climbed into the bus, and he navigated them out of the forest, only letting the horses pick up serious speed once they got over the treetops. The sunset silhouetted the hills in a crisp line. Frigid wind made Sophie's eyes water. She slid close to Adrian.

He settled an arm around her, and they rode in silence a few minutes. Then he said, "You know, even though it was Aphrodite, and it was lovely…well, this time around, I kind of wish I hadn't."

Sophie smiled. He didn't have to say such things, but she appreciated the gesture. "Seriously, it's all right."

"Just would have liked it to—I don't know, mean more." He adjusted the reins, tilting the bus leftward. The faint gleam of a river swept past; the smell of wet earth surrounded the bus, then vanished. "You absolutely don't have to answer, but have you… well, I suppose you've had more experience?"

"In some ways. But, as it happens, not that *one* thing."

"Ah. Probably smart."

In a silence cozy and shy, huddled together, they descended to the meadow in Oregon.

Using their cell phones as flashlights, they picked their way through the damp grass. When they reached the newest stake with the orange flagging, Sophie shut off her phone's screen and tipped her head back to gaze at the night sky. "Wow. I haven't seen so many stars in years."

"Yeah." Adrian looked up. "That's one benefit of hiding out in this realm."

A soul streaked by, a mile distant, like a pale green meteor, and they fell quiet in respect.

"Well." He set his hands on her waist. "Suppose I should take you back. You have classes tomorrow."

She reached up and twined her arms around his neck. His face was warm against her temple. He didn't switch realms at once; they lingered in the embrace. She turned and lifted her head. She could barely see a thing in the darkness, but finding his lips by touch would be easy enough, especially as he wasn't turning his head away. In fact, he was lowering it, and then she was kissing him.

He transferred one hand to the back of her head, holding her there. She sank into the warmth of his lips, and breathed the scent of his hair and the fresh outdoors. The kiss stretched a handful of seconds, long enough to set her tingling from head to feet.

As the kiss ended, he hugged her close, resting his chin on top of her head. "Ah, Sophie Darrow." He tipped up her head and kissed her again. "You're magnificent."

She burrowed happily into his arms, and the world swung and wobbled around them. Lights glared into existence. The statue loomed up beside them. Cars and voices murmured from all around. Sophie peeked out from the front of his coat to find the spot near the hedge, where they'd started.

With reluctance, she let go of him. "I'll text you. Maybe we can hang out tomorrow."

"I'd like that."

"And I'll keep you updated on the dreams. Those seem to be getting interesting."

"Oh, they are. Enjoy." He smiled even wider—truly he'd been smiling ever since the kisses. As had she.

But as she remembered that first taste of Persephone's memories, both of them ghosts, walking grief-stricken in the Underworld, her smile faded. "I guess it has to get grim eventually, though."

He granted that with a nod, but assured her, "Not just yet. You should have a while of mostly good stuff first."

"Cool." She sauntered backward, managing not to run into the statue. "Goodnight."

"Goodnight."

Sophie strode across the lawn, glancing back over her shoulder a few times to see if she could catch one more glimpse of him, but he was wisely staying hidden. Regret stole across her happiness—but then, she did want him to be careful, for both their sakes.

The grin spread across her face again, and her feet moved

faster and faster until she was jogging so swiftly and easily it felt like flying.

PUMPING BOTH FISTS up toward the millions of stars in the spirit realm, Adrian laughed out loud. Then he sprinted across the field, in the dark, and was met halfway by Kiri, who barked and wagged her tail. He scooped her up, all forty kilograms of her, and held her in the air above his head, where she wriggled in protest. Setting her down, he rewarded her with the pizza crusts wrapped in a napkin that he'd carried home in his pack.

He knelt and stroked her head as she gobbled them. "You're going to see a lot more of Sophie. You like her, don't you?"

Kiri lifted her muzzle to bestow a pizza-crumb lick upon his cheek.

"Yeah," he answered. "I like her too."

Chapter Twenty-Six

Jacob texted Sophie that evening: *I feel like crap. How about you? Will you please just tell me I might get a second chance?*

Sophie didn't flinch at doling out a refusal. A woman who'd been kissing the lord of the Underworld could handle anybody.

I don't see us getting back together. I'm sorry, but it's best if I don't lead you on. You'll get over me and find a better match. Really you will. I want you to be happy. Take care.

Setting down her phone, she engaged Melissa in a conversation about the horrible music choices of some of the people in their dorm—generally the ones with the loudest speakers. Then, sleepy after all that hiking up and down San Francisco's steep hills, she changed into pajamas and got into bed.

From her pillow she sent Adrian a text: *Just felt like saying goodnight again. So, goodnight. :)*

He answered in under a minute. *Goodnight, beautiful.*

Smiling, she closed her eyes and reached for Persephone's memories.

Persephone's dreams unfolded, awakening her mind to lifetimes of other experiences.

"It's strange, but—well, enlightening, to use your word," she told Hades. She packed soil around the young apple tree she was transplanting into the Underworld. "Water, please."

Hades hefted the clay jug, filled from the underground river, and tilted it to water the soil. "Gives you an insight into other people and places that no amount of traveling or study could."

"I feel I've aged fifty years. A *hundred* and fifty. Suddenly I know what it's like to have done all these things I've never done— lie with people, give birth, see my children married. Die." She spoke the last word softly, brushing wet soil off one of the leaves.

"I know. I can hardly treat you as an innocent anymore."

He sounded rueful, and she looked up at him. "Is that a bad thing?"

He set down the jug, clearing his throat. "Children and youths are charming when they're innocent. But I suppose it's better that I don't have to worry *too* much about damaging you."

Demeter, of course, was quite ready to place the blame at his door. The next day she found Persephone beside the hearth, wiping away tears while laying out herbs for drying. "It isn't onions you're working with," said Demeter, "so no tears are warranted. Who's the scoundrel and what's he done to you?"

Persephone laughed, rubbing her eyes. "It's nothing like that. I was...thinking of something I'd heard lately, about a young mother who died."

In truth it was one of her own memories, three or four lives ago. The death of her mother in a terrifying raid by an invading tribe, in some land she couldn't even name, had shaken her out of her mid-day nap, and still haunted her.

Demeter studied her. Persephone kept her gaze lowered, smoothing out mint cuttings. "Did Hades feed you one of his pomegranates?" Demeter's voice was cool and hard.

Persephone laid down the handful of dill she held. "No. I stole one and ate it. He didn't want me to."

Demeter exhaled a furious breath and began pacing.

"Mother," Persephone entreated. "If you would only try it, you'd see it's marvelous, amazing—"

"So marvelous it leaves you weeping over the herbs by yourself? Yes, it sounds wonderful."

"Some of the memories are sad of course, but on the whole it's fantastic. The languages I know now—the new ways to prepare food—" She grabbed two of the herbs and held them up as if this would change her mother's mind. "Look, I'm going to try something new tonight with the lamb. You'll see."

Demeter shot her a look. "You realize this doesn't make you immortal. You're still every bit as vulnerable as before."

"Yes. But worlds smarter."

"Worlds more *tempted*, I would think."

Persephone set aside the handful of herbs. "Stop worrying. Just wait till you taste this lamb."

But Demeter had a valid point. Those "lying with people" memories fired up Persephone's mind and body rather too thoroughly. Being trained in healing, she already knew how the basic process worked. But she remained a virgin, having only been kissed, and then not seriously—unless Hermes had naughtier motives when kissing her in greeting or farewell, which indeed he might, from what she heard of him. Still, it wasn't Hermes, but her latest friend and tutor in the Underworld, whom she kissed and touched in her imagination.

Did that remark about not viewing her as innocent anymore mean he thought of her the same way? The idea made her blood spread hot through her. Of course he wouldn't dare—a mortal girl; it was too dangerous. There could be no serious future in it. But perhaps a dalliance, some playing around...? Gods above, her mother would lock her up if she knew about such thoughts.

Persephone resolved to behave as long as she could stand it. Truly it *would* be healthier to get over her crush on Hades and maybe, someday, marry someone else and have that man's children...but the idea only made her dreadfully sad.

HADES KNEW HE loved Persephone within a month of her theft of the pomegranate. It was exactly as she said: now that she had eaten the Underworld's fruit, she possessed the wisdom and experience of several lifetimes. She had been Tanis, and many other people besides. Accordingly, he let himself stop viewing her as an oblivious virgin, even if technically she hadn't lain with anyone in this life.

Being around her now was nine parts bliss and one part torment. And he wanted it to last as long as possible. In the chariot or when switching realms, she pressed her body so close against him. She felt warm and sweetly curved, and smelled delicious, like an apple ripe for plucking. Every day, more and more, he longed to touch her, arouse her, pin her to the ground beneath him.

But of course he couldn't say, or do, a thing about it.

At the end of her visit one day, as they flew back to her house, something in the fading twilight and the ocean scent from downriver made him think of his sea journey with Tanis. As the chariot descended to the ground, he finally said, "If Tanis had survived and come back, and had been willing to stay...well, I know it never ends well, a mortal woman and a man of my kind, but I think I would have tried all the same. I was quite fond of her. I thought you...she...should know."

Perhaps it was only the jolt of the chariot landing that made Persephone lean against him. But she answered, "She would have been pleased. She felt the same about you."

Hades eased the ghost horses to a stop, and climbed out to tie the reins to a tree.

When he lifted Persephone down from the chariot, she lingered with her hands on his shoulders. They gazed at each other. "You know, she *has* come back to you," Persephone said.

"I'm glad of it." But he could never ruin Persephone's life. So he let go of her and looked away, chuckling as if the whole thing were amusing. "I was much younger then, of course. More foolish."

"Are you truly fifty-three now," she challenged, in the playful tone he already knew well, "or are you the sum of all the years you've lived in all your lives, since you can remember them all and benefit from their wisdom?"

"If the latter is the case, then I'm quite ancient indeed."

"And in that case so am I."

Yes, he thought. *But still mortal.* With great effort, he smiled calmly at her as if romance had never entered his thoughts, and pulled her back into the living world where she belonged.

When he returned to his chariot alone a short time later, he leaned against it with a gust of a sigh, thinking, *Just what I need. To be in love at last, and for it to be someone I cannot be with.*

PERSEPHONE KEPT VISITING Hades, trying to learn about plants and languages rather than dwelling on the charms of her immortal friend. The botanical experimentation continued, Persephone bringing down saplings and seeds to grow in the cave's magical soil, to see what resulted. Hades tested the flowers and fruits himself before letting her near them. If they caused his tongue or skin any burning sensation, the plant was relegated to non-edible status, and they looked for other uses for it. If they didn't harm him, Persephone placed a small amount on her skin as a first test, then held some in her mouth if that went well, then swallowed a tiny amount if no ill effects occurred.

The testing worked on the whole: she only got sick from the plants a couple of times, and one time was at least interesting. Along with developing a fever, she saw the world in far brighter than usual colors while lying dizzy on the ground. Hades, however, was deeply alarmed by her illness, and didn't let her eat any new Underworld plants for nearly a month after that.

One variety of olive made her able to command dogs by using yips and growls she suddenly knew by instinct—which made both Hades and her laugh helplessly. The ability wore off after a day, though.

Some of the fruits seemed to speed healing, but not to the cure-all levels she dreamed of discovering.

And what if she found a plant that would let a mortal woman safely carry a child to term when the father was immortal? Well, that would be hardest and most dangerous to test, but she could dream. She kept raising new plants, never giving up hope.

Plants did grow faster than usual in the Underworld, but months or more still elapsed before most of them were mature enough to bear fruit. So while Persephone and Hades waited for the orchard to produce its next marvel, they spoke to the souls, using the answers and their own memories to expand another of their projects: mapping the world.

Choosing a large, mostly-flat wall of light brown limestone in the cave, Persephone painted the shape of Greece and the surrounding Mediterranean as they knew it, in dark blue paint that dried purple. The sea was as long as her arm, its southern edge at the height of her waist. "Up here, the north countries." She dabbed in a swath of land for the mountains and the cold plains. "Off east, the Himalayas, and India and Asia somewhere beyond that. To the south, we know, is Africa…but how far does the land go?"

"Quite some way, to judge from what the souls have said. I remember living down there and making the journey as a soul myself, but I'm not sure where I was." Hades circled his palm toward the southeastern side. "Pretty sure there's another sea here. Hotter and sunnier."

"What I want to know is what's beyond *this* sea." Persephone sketched in the strait that led from the Mediterranean out to the great western ocean, and let the waters trail away in a few vague waves of blue paint. "Some of the souls speak of flying all night across it when they come here. But then, some say they come *west* across such an ocean, and that's what I don't understand."

"Yes. Souls like these people." Hades gestured to a small group of souls watching them curiously, men and women with straight black hair, brown skin, and clothing made of animal skins that didn't quite match any animal they had seen in the Mediterranean region. "It seems obvious," he added, "that the living world is bigger by far than we've all guessed."

"Agreed." Persephone studied the map. "Some of the lands I'm remembering from past lives, well, they're like nothing I've seen or imagined before. But they're out there somewhere."

"Hermes took one of the horses last month and flew west as far as he dared, but even he lost his nerve after seeing nothing but ocean for so long. He turned around and let the horse take him home."

Persephone slid the brush back into the jar of paint. "Then let's try it ourselves."

"Absolutely *not*."

"Oh, come on, we have to get out of the cave sometimes. And you're a much safer horseman than Hermes."

He fidgeted, glowering at the map. "We can try going some of these places. But not all the way across the great ocean."

Persephone beamed, for in truth she had got what she wanted: to travel with him, even if only for day trips.

As that first winter turned to spring, and then into summer, they took their secret chariot journeys—south across the sea to the hot sands of Africa, east to the feet of the giant cold mountains, north over dark forests to the seashore where white cliffs rose on the island opposite them. They risked switching into the human realm on most visits, and sometimes even got lucky and found they spoke the local language, or some older version of it, thanks to their past lives. Touching those exotic trees and stones, walking among people who viewed Hades and her as astonishingly outlandish in their lightweight Greek tunics and fine Underworld jewels, and breathing the spices and smokes of other lands—it all enchanted Persephone. Only her first visit to the Underworld rivaled the thrill she felt at setting foot in faraway countries.

Best of all was being with Hades. She held his arm to ease the stress on her weak leg as they walked, and cuddled in his protective embrace as he flew the horses high up to mountaintops, the evening star sparkling and the world spread out like a perfect map below them.

Demeter knew nothing of their visiting other countries, but Persephone's growing preoccupation didn't escape her notice.

Persephone felt no surprise, only a dismayed sense of inevitability, when her mother brought up the topic again, shortly after Persephone had returned from an outing with him.

"I sensed you northward today," Demeter said, in the middle of their quiet dinner. "I thought you were with Hades. Where were you?"

"Oh. I was with him. We were on an errand. Visiting another

village a soul had mentioned." They did such things sometimes, delivering important messages from the departed, but in this case it was a lie: she had been much farther north with him, several countries away.

"Are you in love with him?" Demeter asked.

Persephone dipped her flat bread into the stew. "Goodness, Mother. That's abrupt."

"Well, are you? You have that look about you lately. And naturally I worry."

"I…don't know." When she glanced up to find Demeter looking as stricken as if she had just announced she was pregnant by Hades, Persephone added, "I know it's unwise and there's no possible future in it."

"Then why do you continue seeing him?"

"I've told you. It's a fascinating place. I enjoy what I'm learning and I have many projects there."

"Does he love you? Has he tried anything?"

"He's said and done nothing." Unless you counted certain gazes and compliments, and the lingering way he had taken to holding her lately when given the chance…but even Persephone wasn't sure she could count those.

"My dear, perhaps it would be better to seek new interests, if—"

"Mother, I don't want to talk about it."

It was only another day, however, before Demeter confronted her again, and that time Persephone liked the conversation even less.

CHAPTER TWENTY-SEVEN

𝕳 ADES LOOKED UP FROM REPAIRING the raft at the underground river to find Aphrodite strolling toward him, her slim white tunic nearly glowing in the dim cave, her pretty face making an expression of amused dismay. "Gracious, it's dark in here."

He stood up, smoothing his cloak. "Aphrodite. What brings you down to this world?"

Smiling, she stroked his cheek. "Wish I could say it was my insatiable needs, but in truth I'm on an errand. Demeter's waiting for you outside the cave."

That surprised him even more. "Oh. Why?"

Aphrodite shrugged. "She wished to speak to you, but didn't have the nerve to come down here. So she brought me."

Already he began to suspect something was wrong—something to do with Persephone. "I'll go right up."

Aphrodite walked with him to the entrance chamber, and remounted the spirit horse she had ridden down there. Hades climbed onto one he kept saddled, and they both flew up into the summer sun. Demeter waited there, seated several paces off on a boulder, her head turned toward the sea.

"I've done my part," Aphrodite said, and sent an approving glance up and down him. "Come visit me more often, won't you?"

He felt a small thrill of flattery, and guilt along with it—as if it were a betrayal of Persephone to admire Aphrodite. He did give the goddess of love a smile, but, too unsettled about Demeter's errand, he only waved goodbye in response and watched Aphrodite fly off. After tying up his ghost horse to a tree, he approached Demeter on foot.

"Demeter," he said. "What can I do for you?"

She turned, and rose. "Hades." The sea wind stirred her hair, bringing out the gold in its dark depths. "Thank you for coming up to see me."

"Won't you come down to the cave? I promise it's perfectly safe, and I know you've never seen it." He invited her mainly as the duty of a gracious host, but also as a challenge, to see if Demeter could be as brave and inquisitive as her daughter.

She put that question to rest at once. "No. I'd rather not, thank you. The reason I came…" She laced her fingers together at her waist. "It's a bit awkward. Persephone's a grown woman, of course, but she hasn't had much experience in the way of suitors, and less still with immortal men."

Defensive statements readied themselves on Hades' tongue, but he held them in reserve, letting her speak.

"Lately she's sensed that you may be attracted to her," Demeter continued. "And it makes her uncomfortable."

Hades' heart plummeted. Still saying nothing, he let his gaze slip past her, unfocused, to rest on the blue of the sea.

"She likes you very much," Demeter went on. "As a tutor. And she feels she may have accidentally given you the wrong signals, for which she's rather embarrassed, and therefore allowed me to come speak to you instead of trying to explain it herself." Here she paused, as if inviting him to respond.

Twisting his tongue in his dry mouth, he attempted an answer. "I had no idea she felt this way, or rather, no idea that I was making her feel…I promise, I haven't attempted anything."

"I know. She assures me of that. Still, for a long time I thought she wouldn't marry, and now she does seem to be thinking of it, and…Hades, we both know—we *all* know—it isn't possible, a mortal woman with a god."

He gazed at the endless waves. "Indeed. I would never wish to harm her." That, at least, he could say with fluency, as it was true.

"So, although she's enjoyed the Underworld very much and

may still wish to visit on the rare occasion, we've agreed her regular lessons with you should come to an end."

He hadn't thought it possible for his heart to sink further, but it did. "If she wishes."

"She does. It's for the best." Demeter sounded apologetic.

"All right."

She turned briskly toward her white spirit horse, reined to a pine branch. "Thank you for understanding. I'm sure we'll see you again at a gathering before long."

"Goodbye. And...do apologize to Persephone for me. For everything."

She climbed astride the horse. "I will. Goodbye, Hades."

She sped away. The souls kept streaming into the Underworld, barely visible in the bright light of day.

He didn't wish to hurt Persephone. It was for the best. All this was true. Nevertheless, he stormed to the top of the cliff, and for the rest of the afternoon hurled boulders into the sea until even his immortal muscles ached in defeat.

"My dear, I happened to speak to Hades today," Demeter told Persephone, as they rinsed the clay plates and pots after dinner, in the back garden's water basin.

"Oh? How did that come about?"

Demeter peeled a wet scrap of grape leaf off a plate and flicked it into the garden. "I was visiting Aphrodite, and she had some errand to see him, so I went along. I assume she wished to arrange a personal visit from him. They do such things from time to time, I've heard."

Hearing that was like getting nicked with one of the knives she was rinsing. Persephone had heard such gossip too, but had wished to disbelieve it. Not that she could deny Hades such visits, considering Persephone and other mortal women were an unsafe prospect. If anything, it was honorable of him not to look to mortals.

It still hurt. Persephone merely said, "Ah," set aside the knife, and picked up the next.

"It would seem, darling," continued Demeter, "that he suspects you fancy him. And flattered though he is, he wishes me to tell you that he must turn you down."

Now it was more like getting stabbed outright. Wiping grease off the latest knife, Persephone answered, "Oh my. That's dreadfully embarrassing. I promise, I haven't thrown myself at him, or anything of the kind. I don't know why he said that."

"Men aren't always as dense as we think. They do sense attraction, especially men who've been alive several decades and have figured a few things out. And, my dear, I'm afraid he isn't interested."

But surely he is, he must be, Persephone wanted to wail. However, mistaking uncle-ish affection for love, in her wishful naïveté, was entirely possible. Setting the knife onto the drying cloth, she dragged a pot toward herself. "That's fine," she said, her voice as light as she could make it. "What future could we have had anyway?"

"Exactly. So he's suggested you cease your regular lessons in the Underworld, and take up something new, among the rest of us. Just to get your mind off this awkwardness. You could still visit him from time to time, naturally."

A knot of grief and humiliation swelled in Persephone's chest. She kept speaking casually, though it became difficult. "All right. I'd like to see how my plants are coming along in the Underworld, but only once in a while, as you say."

"As for what you might do up here, I have an idea." Demeter dried her hands on the cloth draped over her shoulder. "Aphrodite would love to share some of her knowledge with you. Regular meetings with her could be very interesting indeed."

"Yes, that they would be." Persephone turned aside, drying her own hands, wondering if she could possibly face Aphrodite without withering in miserable envy.

"I realize you already know such things from your past-life memories," said Demeter, "but even so, there are plenty of arts only she could teach you. And who knows? Among her acquaintances you might well find a mortal lad you fancied."

The cure for one crush was another, was what Persephone supposed this idea encapsulated. But almost at once, a different possibility dawned on her, and fortified her spirits.

If anyone could help Persephone in her current predicament, it was Aphrodite. The goddess of love needn't be a rival, and likely wasn't. Aphrodite put no exclusive claims on any man. And as Demeter had obliviously stated, there were pieces of knowledge only Aphrodite could supply. If Persephone could learn those… well, it left her a morsel of hope, at least.

Persephone dried the knives with the cloth. "Lessons with Aphrodite. All right. I admit my curiosity is piqued."

"Oh, I was jealous. So jealous." Adrian wiped a spilled drop of coffee off the table with a paper napkin. It was Sunday, and Sophie was enjoying lunch with him, this time in Ashland, Oregon. The small, busy restaurant was decorated with wide-brimmed and feathered hats upon the walls, as befitting a town famous for its Shakespeare festival. All the tablecloths were purple with a pattern of black cats—perhaps for Halloween.

"I can't believe she did that," lamented Sophie. "Does that mean my dad would do that? Interfere with one of my relationships?"

Adrian rested his chin on his hand, gazing at the cat design. "Protecting your daughter from a known danger is understandable. I know the feeling."

"From past lives, I hope."

He laughed. "Of course. No children in this life yet."

"Oh, good. Me neither. So, those lessons with Aphrodite…" Sophie looked out the window they sat next to. Rain streaked the glass, obscuring their view of the green hills. "Those are coming back to me today, and uh, wow."

"Did I mention really, really jealous."

"Right, because her, um, assistant was Adonis." The vision

bloomed in her mind: the beautiful young man about Persephone's age, hair lightened nearly to gold by the sun, naked body patiently stretched upon the pillows for Aphrodite to demonstrate upon, and later for Persephone herself to try some acts with.

Due to having indulgent parents, Adonis hadn't married yet, and due to being charming and pretty, he had landed the role of Aphrodite's latest mortal plaything. After meeting Persephone, he didn't mind sharing some of his love-goddess time with her, though it was clear to Persephone that the majority of his adoration belonged to Aphrodite.

Adrian sat back, folding his arms. "The things you did with him. Day after day. And you were jealous about me visiting Aphrodite a couple of times." He shook his head with mock disappointment.

She laughed, but her mind flashed straight to the idea of doing such things with Adrian. He wore a white T-shirt today under his black coat, and it made his skin look especially warm and delicious. She could imagine the heat of his body through the cotton, the feel of the rivets and belt loops on his black jeans as he lay on top of her to kiss her...

Okay, yeah, they had only hugged today so far, but she was going to have to kiss him before they said goodbye, for sure.

Not that there weren't serious risks. She sipped her coffee and set the mug into its saucer, her amorous thoughts dwindling. "That problem with mortal women getting pregnant by immortal guys—the miscarriages, deaths—is that still an issue?"

He sat forward again and picked up his coffee. "Well, none of us have tried yet, but we have to assume so. These days, I suspect there'd be fewer deaths, given we have modern medicine, but... we don't know."

She nodded. "I suppose that's one of the things to study and figure out." She took another sip of coffee. "But not today."

He smiled gently. "No, not today."

"So...I still can't get past the notion that we don't know each other from *this* life well enough."

He nodded. "I agree."

"We know, like, everything from past lives, and that counts for something. But it's not like we'd even have met if it weren't for Rhea, and the pomegranate, and all."

"I've wondered about that. In the past, our souls always found a way to each other, and I figure they eventually would have this time too."

"Or else Rhea was meant to be the way."

"Maybe." He sent her a shy smile, and bowed his head. "But… okay, there was this one time, before I ever met Rhea. Someone had given my dad and me a box of peaches. Like, way more peaches than anyone could need at once. So I Googled recipes for things to do with them. I was trying to learn to cook, with the hope of maybe living on my own someday. And I found your blog. You'd put up this video.…"

Sophie laughed, remembering. "When I was juggling peaches?"

"Yeah. While talking about how to make a pie. For a second, anyway."

"Hey, I got four in the air before I dropped them."

He leaned his temple on his knuckles. "I watched it three or four times in a row. I thought…you were the cutest thing I'd ever seen."

Sophie's crush leaped a few steps ahead, landing within reaching distance of love.

"And then I thought, 'Oh well, she's in America, I'm never going to meet her,'" Adrian added, and glanced at her. "Still, I made the pie the way you said."

"How'd it turn out?"

"Pretty good. Well, I messed up the crust a little. But the fruit part tasted great. I used your suggestion of less sugar and more spice."

"The whole world would be better off if people used less sugar and more spice."

His boot tapped her leg. "Spoken like a nutritionist."

She rested her elbows on the table. "So when you learned who

I was—who Persephone was these days—you must have been surprised it was, you know, the peach girl."

He shrugged. "I was and I wasn't. As I started remembering past lives, it became evident we kept finding each other. I couldn't sense you at first, not before becoming immortal, so I had to ask Rhea who you were. She knew; she could sense you. And she told me your name, and there you were online. It was only a few months after I'd seen that peach post, and I had checked your blog a couple of times since. Finding out it was you—you were her—I don't know, it mostly felt right. Surprise, then relief. Someone who was clearly a good person, not to mention around my age. And hot." He glanced at her with a grin.

"Is that when you started commenting on my blog?"

"Yeah. I didn't say anything till after I found out."

"You erased all your comments lately," she accused. "I went looking for them."

"I had to, in case it endangered you to be associated with me. Way too late, of course. Thanatos already noticed. But I figured I might as well not leave them up."

"But now I don't *have* them anymore. I wanted to see what we said."

"Oh. I kept them." He leaned down and pulled his laptop from his pack on the floor. "Saved each page. Want to see?"

"Yes!" She happily scooted around the table to sit beside him on his bench, and for the rest of the hour they read their old comment threads. In each of Sophie's posts, she began with a fruit or vegetable recipe or nutritional information, and wrapped up with something going on in her life at the time, usually related somehow to the featured food. Kiwi Ade had commented regularly on both the food and the daily-life parts, and their discussions tended to go back and forth for two or three comments apiece on each post. They somehow got onto the topics of music, television, movies, political news, and once even mythology.

"Maori, though, not Greek," Sophie observed.

"Yeah. Mum's about half Maori, half other South Sea Islanders.

Dad's white—British ancestors mostly—but with black hair like us."

Tenderness blossomed in her mind as she remembered his words about his mother's death, the first day they'd officially met. Sophie had been so shaken by the video of Grandpop, she'd barely been able to process Adrian's story at the time. She interlaced her fingers with his, ready to offer more comfort today. "You said you still see her, in the Underworld?"

Adrian nodded. "Haven't been down for a while, though. Been over here instead."

"You should take me. I could visit Grandpop again, and maybe meet her…and I want to see the place again, now that I'm remembering so much."

He squeezed her hand. "Of course. Anytime you like."

She gazed at their thumbs sliding against one another. "Why didn't you come find me a long time ago?"

"Would you have wanted me to?"

"Yeah. Of course."

He took a while to answer, tapping his thumb up and down as if counting something. "When I was disabled, I tended to get pity from people a lot. I was used to it, but I didn't want it from you. I didn't want to risk it. So I thought I'd wait to see if the immortality fruit worked. And if it did, I'd try then."

"But you *didn't* try then. You've been immortal how long now, a year? And you only just came for me."

"Not quite a year. But yeah. When I ate the fruit, life suddenly got very complicated. I had to explain everything to Dad, and make up a story for the other people I knew. Niko and Sanjay and Freya were eating the fruit and going through their changes… and just when I was getting up the nerve to approach you, Sanjay got killed. And we all went on high alert and started being very careful who we spoke to. Soon after that, someone shot me, and I had to move into the other realm to avoid putting Zoe or Dad or anyone else in danger. Rhea was upset about all the violence, so we promised her, no new immortals for a while, maybe a year; till we felt safer. I spent a while building the bus, making sure I could drive it safely, making the Underworld livable—bringing in furniture and all. But…I really wanted to meet you, and they knew it. Niko kept tempting me. 'She'd like you. She'd be into it. Let's go see her.'"

"And eventually you gave in."

"Yeah." He leaned back against the wall, pulling her with him, their shoulders together. "I said, 'All right, bro. When she goes to uni. Will you help me?' And of course he was delighted to help." Adrian grinned. "Been a while since he'd pulled off a good heist."

They clung together on the short flight back to Corvallis. The bus's speed vaporized the rain into a mist that sprinkled them from all directions. Laughing, they endured it, coats buttoned up, wool blanket wrapped around them both.

Adrian landed the bus in the meadow. The rain pattered on the metal roof, and fell straight through the glowing horses, who twitched their ears calmly.

"Back to homework?" Adrian asked, with a regretful smile.

"Yeah." Sophie gazed at his eyelashes, dampened and thickened by the mist.

"Maybe tomorrow if you—"

Sophie cut off his pleasantries with a long kiss on the mouth. He turned to embrace her, one hand at her waist, the other cupping her face. The hand on her waist felt warm from being under the blanket; the other cold from holding the reins. They kissed for a full minute or two, shifting closer, fingers slipping into each other's hair.

Finally separating, breathless, they rested a moment with their noses together.

"Do they say 'snog' in New Zealand?" Sophie asked.

Adrian grinned. "Occasionally. Could say 'pash.'"

"Pash? Were we 'pashing' just now?"

"Oh yeah, that was a choice pash. Sweet as, bro," he assured, treating her to what she assumed was his broadest Kiwi accent.

She laughed in delight. "What are you doing the rest of the day?" she asked, reluctant to let go of him.

"Work. Got a spreadsheet full of anonymous tips to call in to various police precincts. Promised the murdered souls I would, but haven't got to it yet. Some Underworld god I am."

"Still. Once again, I am impressed. You do important work."

"Suppose. If the tips lead to an arrest and conviction, then yeah, it'll change someone's life."

She sat up, straightening her damp coat. "All I've got going on is a Communications essay. Which definitely will not be changing lives."

"Much less morbid, though." He sounded like he was honestly trying to cheer her up. She repaid him for the attempt with another few kisses.

But after they said goodbye, and she set off in the drizzle toward her dorm, she let herself dwell on the unspoken invitation in his eyes: *Come be an Underworld god with me, and you could change lives, too.*

"I'm thinking about it, honey," she whispered. "Give me time."

CHAPTER TWENTY-EIGHT

ER CLASS THE NEXT MORNING plodded drearily compared to the time spent with Adrian. She gazed at the diagram of a molecule her chemistry teacher was sketching on the whiteboard, and thought how she could blow open the professor's world by bringing him various Underworld substances to examine under a microscope. For a moment it excited her: a future in which she became a scientist of some variety, and also became immortal and married Adrian and used her expertise to understand and explain the magic of the spirit realm.

Yeah, except before she got to do all that, someone might strap Adrian and Sophie to bombs and kill them.

She got up at the end of the lecture and trudged out into the cool air with the other students.

"Mind if we talk a little?"

Sophie looked over in alarm. The voice was female, and she feared it might be Quentin or some other Thanatos representative. But it was Rhea, wearing a long gray raincoat over a black paisley-patterned dress, walking with hands in pockets as comfortably as if she were one of the students.

Sophie beamed. "Hi. How'd you find me? Never mind. Dumb question. Yes, please, let's talk."

Among some tall trees near the library, they found a hidden spot where Rhea wrapped her arms around Sophie and transferred her into the other realm. Sophie glanced around for

Adrian's trailer or for Adrian himself, but Rhea said, "It's just us today. Adrian's at work in the Underworld."

Abashed, Sophie ducked her head. "Oh. That's fine."

"I imagine you have a lot of questions." They began strolling along the hillside.

"Not as many as I had the first day. But yes, I do have some."

"You've probably realized that the main reason I didn't want to bring you into the secrets yet was because of Thanatos. They've become dangerous. We had agreed, no new immortals for a while, until we better understand the threat."

Thinking of her father, who unknowingly possessed a former goddess' soul, Sophie nodded. What if he regained his youth and strength, and was rewarded by Thanatos blowing up their house in Carnation and killing her whole family? She shivered. "I wouldn't want to put anyone in danger. And I hate these Thanatos people, from what I've seen of them."

"I'm sorry they've bothered you. Keep doing as you have been: saying nothing about us. Not in person and not even under other names on the…" Rhea hesitated. "Website?" She gave Sophie a questioning glance, as if asking whether she'd chosen the right newfangled word.

"The Internet. The web. Online. Right, I'll keep quiet."

Rhea smiled. "I can't fault Adrian for pulling you in. We all think you're wonderful. And clearly he loves you, as he always did."

Happiness bloomed in Sophie's chest. "I don't know about now," she admitted, "but I believe he did in past lives."

"Of course he does now. I can see him catch fire when he talks about you." It would have sounded odd to Sophie, except she recognized the direct translation of a phrase people used to say in the pre-ancient-Greek she and the others once spoke. It was the equivalent of saying someone's face lit up.

"I couldn't stay angry with him," Rhea added, "when he waited so long to meet you, and when it makes him so happy to be with you."

She could get addicted to hearing such things. Sophie basked in it a moment, then returned to business. "He's been great. But I'm glad you came to see me. I've been curious about *your* life. My memories don't seem to cover it much."

"I can tell you some things." Rhea paused at a large fallen log covered in moss, tested its surface with her long fingers, then sat upon it.

Sophie joined her, setting her backpack on the ground.

"To begin with 'How old am I?,'" Rhea said, "the answer is I don't know exactly. But it's over four thousand years."

"Holy cow."

"I wasn't awake for most of them. When the other immortals were killed, and I was the only one left...well, I tried being the Underworld goddess a while, the way some of you used to be, but I found it too lonely. Finally I resolved to sleep. There is—or rather, was—a fruit in the Underworld that killed mortals and put immortals into a deep slumber. The sleep could last months."

Sophie circled her fingers in the moss. "I remember that. Sort of. It was some kind of berry I planted."

"Yes. It still grew there at the time. I ate that and then crawled into a tiny cave and slept. Every time I woke, I ate more—I had brought dried berries with me. They work just as well whether dried or fresh. I grew weaker and weaker, going so long without other food, until finally I stayed asleep in a sort of...what do they call it?"

"Coma?"

"Yes, a coma. Then one day, I heard someone speaking of Hades and Persephone. It was a pair of the souls, wandering near the cave where I lay. The names resurrected me. I awoke and managed to crawl out from under all the rocks and dirt and hair that had piled up on me."

"Hair?" Sophie repeated.

Rhea flashed a grin. "My hair had grown while I slept. I was still alive, after all. It grows as long as my ankles before each hair falls out and starts fresh. So years and years' worth of long, long hair had fallen out and grown and fallen out again, and was wrapped all over me like a nest." Sophie supposed her face must have displayed her horror, because Rhea nodded wryly upon glancing at her. "I was a terrible mess. I'm sure I looked like an animal."

"What year was it by then?"

"Adrian tells me it was around 1990, though I wasn't able to make sense of modern calendars for a long time. I can only guess, looking back. When I woke and crawled out, I spent a while wandering in the Underworld, listening to the souls and trying to understand how long it had been and what had been happening in the world."

"Could you still understand the language?"

"Yes. The language of the Underworld is the only tongue that never changes. All the living languages were so different I didn't recognize a single one anymore. After getting myself cleaned and clothed and fed—which was an adventure in itself—I returned and sought out some of the souls I knew from before, the ones who were in the Underworld at the time, because that was the only language I could understand."

Sophie smiled. "Like us. The other day I finally remembered talking to you, after my lifetime as Grete."

Rhea grinned. "Precisely. I wouldn't be surprised if it was your two voices who awoke me."

"So all the time we were growing up, you were planning to come find us, when we were ready."

"I was. But before that, I had plenty to do. I needed to learn about the modern world, which took much more study than I expected. Learning English became important in particular. The souls told me that would be the most useful language to know in the world now. Also, it was what you and Adrian spoke."

"He was the first you found," Sophie said.

Rhea nodded. "After harnessing a ghost horse, I went and looked at several of the souls I used to know—you and him and others. I wanted some of the old gods to eat the pomegranate and remember who they were, so I could talk to them, even though I didn't know of a way to give them immortality. I didn't want to revive the memories in all of them; not necessarily the ones who became troublesome, causing the rift with the mortals. But the ones who did more good on the whole, certainly you Underworld gods—I wanted your company again. However, when I saw all of you, for a time I almost gave up my idea of the pomegranate. You had your own lives, and why should I disturb them? But Adrian caught my sympathy and for him I made the exception. He couldn't walk and never would. He was a young handsome man and should have had a full life ahead of him, but was confined to pains in some places and couldn't feel anything in others. Knowing what he used to be, I thought I would do the one thing for him I could."

"The pomegranate."

"It was one of the only things still growing in the Underworld that I knew how to use." Rhea looked at Sophie, her face troubled. "I didn't know at the time that it would cause him to remember the immortality seeds. I thought I was only giving him memories, some pretty thoughts. But it turned out there was brilliant, powerful knowledge in those memories. And when we did grow the immortality fruit, neither of us had any idea what trouble it would cause. We didn't imagine a group like Thanatos existed, or that anyone remembered us at all. I only wanted one of my friends back. And I wanted to improve his life."

Sophie kicked at the wet grass with her sneaker. "You did. And mine too. I only wish Thanatos *didn't* exist."

"The part of me that used to sacrifice people to the Goddess to help the island of Crete would not mind dragging all its members into this realm, one by one, and letting the lions eat them." Rhea smirked. "But Adrian and the others remind me that this is not how things should be done."

Sophie saw the appeal of the idea in a flare of bright hatred against the murderous group. But the god of the Underworld was right: answering murder with murder wasn't the correct policy. "He does spend a lot of time trying to bring killers to justice. To make the world better." Sophie heard the pride in her own voice.

"Yes." Rhea spread her hands at her sides, stroking the moss. "Well, those are the main things I wanted to make you understand.

I do not wish to fill the Earth with immortals; I only brought some back out of love. Love—for each other and for life, for Earth herself—is why we wish to exist. Thanatos may think they act from love for humankind too, but they do not. Like all such groups, they're based in fear. There are certainly dangers in our magic. But we would never be as destructive as those people are."

Sophie breathed the chilly, fragrant air, and listened to a bird chirp its flute-like notes. "I was starting to understand all that. But I was still afraid. I'm not as scared now. I'm glad you told me."

"I thought telling you would be wise." Rhea chuckled. "In case you imagined Adrian was only a strange magical boy trying to seduce you for his own reasons."

Sophie grinned. "Isn't he?"

"Well, yes. But he's more than that." Rhea rose, and gave Sophie her hand, pulling her up. They walked back along the hillside.

"Since you mention the sacrifices…" Sophie said. "Even when I was a junior priestess, they seemed awful to me. Did they seem that way to you?"

"Of course. They were horrible. They were meant to be. That's why they're called sacrifices. Everyone suffered to gain something for the land." Rhea shrugged. "We thought that was how it worked."

"How does it work?"

"You mean, is there really a great Goddess controlling it all?" Rhea smiled. "I have no idea. I like to think there is. There are too many secrets and mysteries we still don't know. *Someone* must."

"I can't imagine who knows, if you don't. I hope she's up there."

They walked in silence a minute, then Rhea remarked, "The Underworld has lost a lot of its magic plants since the old days. It needs an expert like Persephone. Especially a modern Persephone who knows her fruits and vegetables."

Sophie smiled. "I don't feel like an expert."

"Considering you didn't know anything about the Underworld a month ago, you're learning quite fast."

Rhea took Sophie back into the living world. The row of tall trees by the library bounced back into place. The quiet roar of campus swirled around them.

Rhea lingered with her hands on Sophie's arms. "You have a lot of memories yet to sort out, and meanwhile I know you have your studies. I'll let you return to them. I hope to see you again soon."

"Thank you. I hope to see you too."

With a motherly smile, Rhea drew Sophie forward and kissed her forehead, then let her go. "Goodbye for now."

"Goodbye." While Sophie crossed the street, she noticed a middle-aged man sitting on a bench near a bus stop. He had a stocky build, and thinning black hair streaked with gray. His smartphone rested on his lap, and he glanced from its screen to Rhea. For a moment Sophie smiled, thinking Rhea's beauty had attracted the man's attention. Then a chill flashed through her. Stepping onto the curb, just a few yards from the man, she glanced back in time to see Rhea move behind a tree trunk and vanish. Sophie looked at the man to see if he'd noticed. His watchful gaze moved straight to Sophie's eyes. He tucked his phone into his pocket and rose from the bench.

Sophie rushed away, suddenly sure this was someone in Thanatos. She veered aside and jogged up the steps of the nearest building. Inside, her damp sneakers squeaked on the marble floors. A glance over her shoulder confirmed the man was following, ascending the stairs. She darted down a side hallway and made two more turns inside the building, tugging her pepper spray out of the side pocket of her backpack as she moved.

She found a different door that led outside, and burst out. She looked around swiftly. The man was nowhere in sight. Through a steady rain, she ran all the way back to the dorm, pepper spray in hand.

CHAPTER TWENTY-NINE

*M*AYBE *I* SHOULD TELL ADRIAN *about the guy,* Sophie thought that night. But telling him would mean removing her mouth from his, and skewering his romantic mood with a spear of stress. Which didn't seem necessary, especially since she had no proof the man had been following her at all. He could have been a random professor, who happened to be returning to his office inside that building. Until a more concrete threat emerged, she opted not to worry Adrian.

She had meant to study with him in the Airstream that evening, and talk about Rhea's visit. Which she had, for a little while. Then she'd gotten up to fetch a binder, and on her way back to the table she had paused to look at the spreadsheet of murder victims' names and details on his screen, which he began explaining to her. While he spoke, she straightened the hood of his sweatshirt against his shoulder blades, then laid her palm on the back of his neck. Adrian's words began to falter. As soon as she began stroking his skin, enjoying the warmth, he dropped the spreadsheet explanation entirely and pulled her down onto his lap, engulfing her in a kiss. And there she had stayed.

They hadn't gotten a lot of studying or talking done since then, but Sophie finally decided to broach a semi-serious topic—not regarding the man who may or may not have been in Thanatos, but on a subject more important to her mind lately.

"So how do we handle this?" she asked, still planted on his lap, their arms folded around each other.

"Handle what?" Adrian sounded cautious, though hopeful excitement kindled in his eyes.

"Seeing each other. Or—hanging out. Whatever we're calling it," she amended. However, from the look of sweet surprise that brightened his face, he didn't mind the phrase "seeing each other."

"Oh. Um, as we have been, I'd say. Lie to most people. Meet in safe places only. Until you…decide."

"Either to join you or go our separate ways," she clarified gently, but there was no way to make that statement sound exactly gentle, she realized.

He lowered his gaze and nodded, his hands resting motionless on her waist. "Though, going on like this could last us a while. No rush, really. You'll want to take your time, a decision like that."

"It doesn't bother you? Us being…you know, close, affectionate, when I haven't chosen on the immortality deal?"

He lifted his eyes again to hers. "That'll never bother me. Any time I can have with you is…" His eye contact faltered, in shyness it seemed, and he looked out the dark window. "I've been obvious enough, haven't I? You do realize I want *you*—not just your company, or your friendship, or to have you as an ally. It's the same totally-smitten kind of thing it's been in every other lifetime so far. You know that, right?"

Sophie felt she could easily have jumped to the top of the highest tree around, even without being immortal. "I was getting that impression. And I'm, uh, feeling pretty smitten myself."

He smiled, moved a lock of her hair out of her face, and cupped her cheek in his hand. "Good."

A new relationship, she thought giddily, and at the same time a very old one; and this time one that was complicated, dangerous, and impossible to explain to most of the world. But all she could feel at the moment was complete bliss, and the utmost gratitude for whatever fate had landed her here, on Adrian's lap in a trailer in the spirit world. She kissed his lips for a long moment, to seal the pact, then snuggled close to him in a hug, feeling his arms slide tight around her.

The intimate scent and contours of his body were too delicious to resist. She decided it was time to apply a few tips Aphrodite had given Persephone, in her latest memories. She nosed aside a stray curl below his earlobe, and pressed kisses to his neck in a slow trail downward to his shoulder. His hands flexed against her spine, and he tilted his head in encouragement. His pulse tapped fast in a vein in his throat, tangible to her lips as she drew aside the collar of his sweatshirt and kissed his collarbone and his warm shoulder.

Soon she was breathing fast, and so was he—evidently being immortal didn't make you immune to that symptom—and the evening was slipping by in ever more pashing and tight embracing and no studying at all.

Finally she looked at the clock and said in half-despair, half-amusement, "I have to finish my paper."

"Sorry." He grimaced, looking guilty but irresistible with his distracted eyes and kiss-moistened mouth. "It's late. Should you—do you—"

"I should probably go back."

He nodded, diplomatically.

Getting safely back to the dorm without letting the situation skid out of control deserved bonus points, she thought as she dropped into her bed well after midnight, after finally finishing her paper. A few more days, at least, should pass before certain anatomy got groped or clothing got unfastened. But knowing he wanted her, and being free to show she felt the same, was the stuff of pure happiness.

Her dreams wandered through a few more awkward but interesting lessons with Adonis and Aphrodite, and she allowed the memories' pace to meander so she could benefit from the goddess's wisdom. Ideally she could attempt another of those tips next time she and Adrian "studied."

Veering out of her afternoon class the next day, answering a text from Adrian suggesting exactly that, she bumped into someone.

"Sorry," she said, looking up, then stopped. "Jacob."

"Hey." He stood with hands in his coat pockets, looking sheepish and depressed. His eyes were dull and his jaw blotchy, as if he'd been hasty in shaving this morning.

"What are you doing here?"

He squinted down the street, as students flowed around them. "I…just wanted to see you. I knew you'd say no if I asked to come up, so…ah, I probably shouldn't have come. But I did, so, can we have coffee or something?"

"Look…"

"As friends." He gazed at her, his eyes softening, becoming so familiar it weakened her defenses. "Please? You're not going to make me drive straight back to Eugene, right?"

Ashamed to have been in the middle of arranging another date, she slid her phone into her pocket. "I guess I have an hour."

They sat with mugs of coffee in a sandwich shop, and caught up on the news of each other's family members and friends. (Sophie left Adrian out of her account, of course.) But she was only halfway through her coffee before Jacob heaved a sigh, sent a puppy-eyed look at her, and asked, "Can't we try again?"

She rotated the mug on the table, her appetite vanishing. "I told you. I don't think so."

"We're good together. I know we've had fights sometimes, but everyone does. I'm sorry about all the times I annoyed you. I'll do better. Can't we clear the slate and start over?"

Immediately Adrian's voice filled her head, somber and sweet: *We don't know of any other way to clear the slate. You're stuck with these memories.*

There was no question whose voice she'd rather hear, who she'd rather share a table and a life with.

She looked directly at Jacob. "I'm sorry too. I really am. But no. It's impossible."

This time he didn't put up much of a fight. Evidently he could see she meant it. Within five minutes, they dumped their mugs in the bin for dirty tableware, and left the restaurant. The sun was setting, and thick clouds darkened the city. Streetlights gleamed between trees; cars and bikes traveled with their lights on.

Sophie walked Jacob to his car, since it was only parked a block away.

He unlocked it, and gazed at her. "If you ever change your mind…well, I'll be here."

I won't, she thought. But she answered with a nod, and said, "Drive safely."

She watched him drive away, then checked her texts. Another had arrived from Adrian. *Sweet. See you at 7 then. We'll make sure you get your homework done. ;)*

Raindrops began pattering around Sophie. She moved beneath the awning of the nearest restaurant, and entered a reply: *It's ok if we take a few breaks from homework. ;) So um, weird: Jacob just visited. Hasn't given up. I sent him back to Eugene just now.*

Ah, he responded. *Well it can't be easy, losing a treasure like you. Whole thing wasn't too awkward, I hope?*

A bit, she wrote. *Mainly I just wanted to be with you instead.*

Aw, you're the best. I've missed you all day.

She smiled, re-reading his words, feeling warm all over despite the cold wind and the rainy darkness. *Thanks. See you soon. I better get dinner now.*

His *See you* arrived as she walked out into the rain; she glanced quickly at it, then tucked the phone deep into her pocket to protect it from the wet. She turned onto a campus sidewalk that ran under a row of trees, and hurried toward her dorm's dining hall.

Halfway along the street, a shadow leaped up next to her. Startled, she skittered aside, but the man seized her and dragged her off the sidewalk. Panic flashed hot through her; she kicked and yelped. A clammy, rough hand covered her mouth.

"Give me your phone," he growled into her ear.

She tried to scream, but the sound was trapped in her throat. She kicked again, hitting the man's shins, but not hard enough to make him let go, and somehow he had her arms pinned and her body tilted off balance. He twisted her forearm to the point of wrenching pain, and repeated, "Give me your phone."

"Mm-hmm," she whimpered, as if acquiescing.

Carefully drawing one arm free, she slid it into her coat pocket.

And pulled out the pepper spray instead, firing a hissing stream of it over her shoulder, straight into his eyes.

He screamed, began coughing, and let go to claw at his face. The cloud of chemicals stung Sophie's eyes and nose too, and she stumbled away, tears streaming from her burning eyes, coughs overtaking her throat. It was torture—she could only imagine what the man felt like, having the stuff right in his eyes. But the bastard deserved it. Time to call 911 and get him locked up.

She had her phone in hand and the digits dialed. But as the dispatcher answered, a car screeched to a stop next to the sidewalk, and a man in dark clothes reached out from the passenger side, grabbed her assailant, and hauled him into the vehicle. The door slammed and the car took off. Sophie, coughing, eyes blurry, squinted after it to get a license plate or at least a make, but couldn't see anything clearly enough.

It wasn't Jacob's car, and neither guy was Jacob. That much she could say with certainty, though she loathed that the thought entered her mind.

"Hello? Do you need help?" the dispatcher asked on the phone.

"I was just attacked," she rasped out. "On the street. He got away."

"What's your location? Someone will come as soon as possible."

A few instructions and answers later, a police car and ambulance arrived with lights flashing. A medic sat Sophie down on the tailgate of the ambulance and helped her rinse the pepper spray out of her eyes, and gave her water to drink. One male and one female police officer took down her report.

"Did you get a good look at him?" the woman asked.

"No, not at all. He was a little bigger than me, definitely stronger, but I couldn't see much."

"Did you recognize his voice? Could it be anyone you know?"

"I don't think so, but..." Sophie blew her runny nose, and wadded up the tissue. "There's a woman who sort of threatened me the other day. I have to wonder if she's connected to this."

"What's her name?" asked the male officer. He flipped open a smartphone, ready to run a criminal search, Sophie supposed.

"Betty Quentin. I think she's a retired professor—not a professor here; from somewhere on the East Coast. But I saw her here a few days ago. We talked in a coffee shop. That was the first and only time I ever met her."

"And why did she threaten you?"

Sophie hesitated. "I'm not really sure. I got the impression she was kind of unstable. She got crazy pretty fast."

"What did she say?" the woman asked. "What was the threat?"

Sophie realized too late that she couldn't truthfully explain it. *She'd* become the mentally unstable one in their eyes. "Something about…how she wanted me to join her cult, and it'd be dangerous to say no. I don't even know what the cult is." There; that seemed safe enough.

"We do get types like that around campus," said the policeman with the smartphone. "We'll see if we can find her. But my hunch is this was unrelated. Attempted mugging and assault; some guy with an accomplice. They were looking for someone alone to grab, saw you, and went for it. Good thing you had that pepper spray."

"But just now, a few minutes ago, I was having coffee with my ex-boyfriend, and these cult people have bothered him too. So I thought, if they followed him or something, and then saw me…"

The two cops exchanged a glance. "You were with your ex-boyfriend tonight?" the man asked.

Sophie saw where this was going. "Yeah," she said reluctantly.

"Was the breakup recent?" asked the woman.

"About a week ago."

"So, possibly some bitter feelings on his side?"

"He wasn't one of the two guys who attacked me. And I really don't think he'd have anyone else do it. But these people, if they followed him, without him knowing…"

"What's his name?" asked the smartphone cop. "We can at least ask him if he saw anyone hanging around."

Sorry about this, Jacob, she thought. "Jacob Nealon. He's a freshman at U of O."

"Okay. We'll look into it. But like I said, chances are it was just a random attack. Can we take you somewhere? Back to your room?"

She nodded. "I have some people to call."

CHAPTER THIRTY

I DO NOT LIKE THIS," SAID Adrian—after a tightly bit-off string of swear words. "Not one bit." He drew in a long breath, exhaled, and gathered her into his arms. "But you're safe. The police are on it. You did well."

They were in the Airstream, its interior lit by a small bedside lamp and the pair of candles on the table. From her dorm room, she had called her parents first. Meanwhile, Melissa sat at her desk, gathering the story by overhearing Sophie tell it, and looking quietly concerned. The news incited her parents' terror and fury, and she had to spend a long while soothing them and promising to be extra careful. The most difficult part was convincing *them* to be careful too. They saw no reason why anyone would bother them or their lowly fruit stand, but Sophie now possessed heightened fears about the possibility. Finally, having secured their promise to watch out for suspicious people, she wrapped up her call, and barely reached her study date with Adrian on time.

She hadn't told him about the attack until he arrived. He had looked at her reddened eyes and asked in alarm what was wrong. She'd told him as they walked back to the trailer, and now they sat together on his bed, in their silent hug.

She rested her head on his chest, comforted by the gentleness and warmth of his embrace—though, she found when she tried to shift, his arms were as rigid as an iron cage around her. "Relax," she said. "I'll be okay."

His muscles loosened. "Sorry. But… 'random attack'? I don't

247

believe it. Not with Quentin warning you the other day, and Jacob being there five minutes before it happened."

"I really don't think he'd arrange anything like that. But yeah, if they followed him, it makes sense. That reminds me." She lifted her head to look at him. "Yesterday, after Rhea talked to me, I saw a man watching us. He even followed me when I went into a building, but I took off a different way and lost him. I figured it was just my imagination. But now…"

He sighed. "Yeah. They're onto you, all right."

"Do you think it was that Wilkes guy? The one on the business card?"

"Could be. If Quentin's using him as a contact, I wouldn't rule it out."

"I thought of mentioning him to the police, but…he *is* a cop." She frowned. "Does this mean we can't trust any of the police?"

"Oh, we can trust most of them. That is, most of them aren't in Thanatos. The cult is a small group. But they have members in several different useful positions—religious leaders, cops and other officials, academics, and so on. Still, no, I doubt it would help to mention Wilkes. All he did for sure was hand out his cards, and he could easily deny doing that, or say he hands them out all the time during investigations and doesn't remember everyone he gives them to. He'll know how to cover his tracks, being a cop."

"Is Niko still keeping an eye on him?"

"Yeah, a bit. He's also looking for Quentin, but can't find her yet. She could be using a different name, and might not even be in Corvallis. Thus no luck so far. But I'll ring him tonight and tell him what happened, so he can look for any hints that Wilkes or Quentin were involved."

Sophie nodded, thinking about the assault. "The guy who grabbed me was after my phone. Not my purse. That's really what makes me think it's Thanatos."

"Yeah. Bet they wanted to find my number on it and lure me out."

"They'd have to search under 'David.' Not sure they're that smart."

Adrian smiled wryly. "Likely not." He touched the puffy skin around her eye. "Poor love. It was good work, the pepper spray, but it hurt you too." He settled the lightest, softest kiss upon one eyelid and then the other.

The tense knot eased inside her. Hollowness still remained, though: her stomach growled. She looked up at him. "Hey, I skipped dinner. Do you have anything to eat around here?"

"You're in luck. I bought groceries today. Salami, bread, pasta, salad, biscuits."

"Does biscuits mean cookies?"

"Yep."

"Ooh. I *am* lucky."

While Adrian rose and began heating water for pasta, Sophie's phone buzzed.

"Hmm," she said, looking at it. "Text from Jacob." She opened it and winced as she read it.

You called the cops on me?? Real nice. I'm sorry someone jumped you but I had NOTHING to do with it. I can't believe you'd even think that. Had to spend an hour answering questions, making me feel like a criminal when I HAVEN'T DONE ANYTHING. You can forget what I said about waiting for you. You are freaking crazy. Good riddance.

Rage and hurt filled Sophie's chest, choking out her breath. She scooted her thumbs over the screen, ready to fire back all her defenses—who was the attacked party here?—then she stayed still, reconsidering. The rage subsided; she breathed again.

The police surely told Jacob that all she'd done was mention his name, as part of the circumstances regarding where she'd been right before the attack. A good friend would get that, and would make sure she was all right, not complain about being interrogated. *Good riddance*, she thought. *You said it, man.*

"What's he say?" Adrian asked, from beside the stove.

Sophie sighed, and began tapping menu items. "He is not amused."

"Ah. You calming him down?"

"No." She tapped another button that came up on the screen.

"I'm deleting all the texts he ever sent to me, and taking him off my contacts list."

Adrian poured the pasta into the boiling water, stirred it with a wooden spoon, and lowered the heat on the burner. Finally he cleared his throat and said, "Okay then. Tomato sauce all right with you?"

AFTER DINNER, FINDING herself exhausted, she returned to the dorms. Adrian walked her to her door, despite her protestations. With scarcely a word to Melissa or anyone else, Sophie went to bed.

Her dreams continued through Persephone's phase of lessons with Aphrodite, which involved plenty of laughter but always carried the undercurrent of loneliness from missing Hades.

In the morning, after Sophie's first class, someone called on her cell. It was the male police officer who had talked to her last night. Jacob was almost certainly uninvolved in the attack, he said, and they couldn't find any Betty Quentins staying in the area. They doubted she was involved either, so far. They'd issue a public warning that a pair of unknown assailants were on the loose, and they'd keep looking for them.

"Thank you," said Sophie, and hung up with a sigh.

But that evening she was feeling rather better about the world, as she leaned against the kitchen counter in the Airstream, with Adrian pressed up and down her front, his arms around her, their mouths involved in what she figured definitely counted as "pashing." A small lightbulb glowed above the kitchen sink. Rain poured against the windows. Their computers sat open but neglected on the table.

"If you'd just let me steal you away for good, to live in this realm forever," he murmured, "I could keep you safe. I'm merely pointing that out."

"Mm-hm. No problems with that arrangement." She wriggled into a more comfortable angle, and nibbled his damp lower lip.

His hands roamed around her waist. "None at all. Can't think of any problems. This whole situation, it's quite low-stress."

She broke into laughter and hugged him closer, not only for the wry humor but for the delicious way his accent turned "stress" into "striss." Resting her forehead on his neck, she thought of Thanatos, and then of Demeter's treachery, and sighed. "Why do people want to keep us apart?"

"Scared. Jealous. Both." He groaned suddenly, sounding annoyed.

Puzzled, she tilted her head at him.

"Niko's coming," he said. "Just sensed him. Another person getting between us, temporarily at least." He let go of her and moved to the door right before the brisk knock sounded. "Hey," he said, opening the door.

"*Kalispera*," greeted Niko—"Good evening" in Greek, as Sophie now knew. He stepped in, wearing a dark red fleece and snowboarder-style knit hat complete with earflaps. Every inch of him dripped with rain. He took off the hat and tossed it onto the kitchen counter, glancing from Sophie to Adrian. "You weren't in the middle of getting each other off, were you?"

Adrian cringed. "Charming, Niko."

Sophie sat at the table, near her computer. "We were waiting for you," she told Nikolaos. "So you could watch."

Niko grinned, and told Adrian, "I like her."

"What do you want?" Adrian asked.

"Some gratitude. I spend all afternoon lurking around Bill Wilkes' house in Salem, in the drenching rain, waiting for a chance to dive in there and download his hard drive, all because you ask me to, and do you even thank me?"

Adrian folded his arms. "Thank you. Did you succeed?"

Niko whipped a small portable hard drive from his pocket and held it up.

Finally smiling, Adrian took it from him. "Ah, sweet as. Let's have a look."

"I already did," Niko said as Adrian plugged the drive into his computer. "You might be interested in the little vacation Mr.

Wilkes took back in February. Seems he heard it was summertime in New Zealand, and decided to warm up his toes in Wellington."

Adrian stopped in the middle of clicking through files, and looked at Sophie, then at Niko. Then at Kiri, standing nearby, sniffing Niko's wet shoes. "He's the guy who shot me and Kiri?"

"Yes, to judge from the email he sent Quentin that very night, saying something like, 'Found our friend. Delivered the message. As suspected he's recovering fast, and left for his other home.' 'Other home' is apparently their oh-so-clever code phrase for the spirit realm."

Sophie imagined Wilkes shooting Kiri and Adrian without warning in the park at night. She'd heard the story already, but having been assaulted herself now—possibly by the same man— made it twice as horrifying. Fear chilled her stomach, then the temperature raised itself to simmering hatred. "If I ever see him, I'm pepper-spraying him and kicking his head in."

Niko looked up from petting Kiri to grin at Adrian again. "I *really* like her."

Adrian sighed, gazing across the table at her. "Thanks, love, but that wouldn't be the greatest way to show you're unaffiliated with us."

"Fine," Sophie grumbled.

"He's right, I regret to say," Niko added. "Your best course is to lie, lie, lie. I say that as someone with the greatest respect for lying. It's saved my life many times. But pepper spray, that reminds me…" Niko drew a small black plastic bag, wrapped around something rectangular, from the inside pocket of his coat. "Present for you." He handed it to Sophie.

She unwrapped it. "A flashlight?"

"Not just that." Niko turned it in her hands, and showed her a button on the side. "A stun gun. Press this end against the next freak who grabs you, push the button, and zap. Million volts. Down he'll go, and it won't hurt you. But if someone *does* grab it from you, they can't kill you with it, at least."

"Yikes." She lifted her eyebrows, examining the weapon. "Well. Thank you. I admit, I'm sort of looking forward to trying it on these douchebags." She glanced at Adrian. "Was this your idea?"

He looked guilty. "Kind of. Though I hope you never have to use it."

She unfolded the instructions she found in the bag, and glanced over them. "When you're friends with dangerous immortals, guess this is part of the deal."

"Indeed. So." Adrian drummed his fingers on the table, exchanging a look with Nikolaos. "It was Wilkes who shot me. Now what? I can't turn him in for it. There's no evidence. Kiri and I were fully recovered in hours, and we didn't report it back when it happened."

"We'll keep watching him," said Niko. "Turn him in if he does try anything." He pointed at Sophie. "For example, if he lays a single finger on you, darling. 911. Or rather, stun gun, *then* 911."

"I will," said Sophie. "But we still aren't sure how much he knows about me, and my hanging out with you guys or Rhea. Right?"

"Well..." Adrian clicked on files again. "We might get a hint. Niko, did you find anything in the messages?"

"Yes, the most recent ones have Wilkes seeing Sophie yesterday in company of someone who 'resembles Ms. R,' though it doesn't mention the disappearing and reappearing."

"So it *was* Wilkes who followed me," she said, feeling queasy again.

"And a week or so back," Niko added, "Quentin and Wilkes got rather excited about some 'texts' and 'meetings' between some girl and some troublemaker. That'd be you two, is my guess."

She shivered. "So they know we're texting each other? How?"

"Let's see your phone." Niko held out his hand.

Sophie handed it over. "I've already checked for spyware. I didn't find anything."

"That's the thing about good spyware. You wouldn't notice." He tapped at the phone's screen. "Usually, for spying on texts, someone would have to get hold of your phone physically, and install something." He lifted his gaze for a moment to examine her. "Who's been close enough to do that?"

"Well, *you're* the only one who ever actually *stole* my phone," she retorted.

Nikolaos laughed, glancing at Adrian, who still gazed at the files on his computer. "Only in the service of love, and I swear I didn't tamper with it. Who else?"

Adrian met her eyes briefly, then looked at his screen again. She cleared her throat and hedged, "I suppose…Jacob might have. My ex-boyfriend. Thanatos did approach him."

"Mm-hm. I'd consider that." Niko danced his fingers across the phone, eyes rapidly taking in information. "And who do you live with? Girls in the dorm?"

"Melissa's my roommate. But she hardly pays any attention to me. And I keep the phone pretty close."

"Looking at these emails," Adrian suggested, "they possibly haven't read the actual texts. There isn't much detail. Just 'From what source says, it sounds like they've met, and exchanged texts.' And if they knew the exact times Sophie was going out to meet me, surely they would've simply followed her straight to me, and grabbed me then."

"Right." Niko held up her phone. "So my guess is, someone's watching you from a distance, or from fairly close, even; and they occasionally had a look at these while you were asleep or out of the room. You probably don't have spyware transmitting your every text to someone else. That is, I don't see any. But just in case, let's do a little factory reset, shall we?"

"Go ahead. I don't think I have any important stuff to back up."

"Brilliant." While Niko touched the options that sent the phone into its reset operation, Sophie squinted at him.

"Do I want to know why you're so informed about spyware?" she asked.

Nikolaos gave her a charming, dazzling smile. "No, my dear. You do not."

Ugh, said the text from Sophie the next morning, arriving in the middle of Adrian's breakfast. *Sore throat. I'm getting a cold. Damn dorm food and its lack of nutrition!*

His spirits sank, mainly out of sympathy for her, but also (he had to admit) because it would mean less making out for a few days, and he had thoroughly enjoyed those kisses lately. Shoving aside his hormones in guilt, he typed back, *Oh no. Poor thing. I'm sorry.*

Guess it wasn't just the pashing making me feeling lightheaded. ;)

No, that isn't amongst my powers, sadly.

I'd say I hope you didn't catch it, but I guess you can't get sick.

Yeah, he texted, *that is one of the perks.*

Okay, I've decided. Sign me up.

Ha. Why not think about it a little longer. Anything you want me to fetch you in the meantime?

No thanks. I'll take it easy today and soak up some Persephone as therapy.

Do that. Feel better soon. xo.

CHAPTER THIRTY-ONE

ERSEPHONE DIDN'T SEE HADES AGAIN for over a month. Their next meeting was at a feast at the autumn equinox, at Zeus and Hera's palace. Demeter and Persephone both attended. By that point Persephone had gained enough poise from her tutoring sessions with Aphrodite that she was able to greet Hades with a cool smile. Still, her heart pounded, reminding her full well that her crushed pride had not recovered.

"Hello, Hades."

"Persephone." His smile was cordial as well, though his gaze soon slipped away from hers.

"How is the Underworld? I've been meaning to visit, to see my plants."

"It's fine. They're doing well. One in particular of your fruit trees has grown quite tall."

"Good. I'll be curious to hear what it does."

His glance moved to Aphrodite, who stood across the room with her arm around the waist of her guest—Adonis. "And how are your new lessons?"

"Quite interesting."

"Dare I ask what she has you doing?"

"We've only lately begun any 'doing.' Before that it was mostly explanation—things like anatomy, and the way everything should work, and how to practice independently so I can be ready when it's time." *There*, she thought. *Try not to think about that, I challenge you.*

It seemed to work. He took a few moments to answer, rotating his wine cup in his hands and frowning at it. "When it's 'time'?" he echoed.

"She says by the spring equinox I should be fully educated. She promises I can find a husband at the festival there, after she's done with me." Would that spark any jealousy from him, any at all?

He only peered at Adonis and looked away. "Meanwhile I suppose that lad has something to do with the practicing and the anatomy lessons."

"Yes." She laughed, an imitation of Aphrodite's carefree laughter. "I suppose the gossip is everywhere. Adonis does come to our sessions. He adores her, but she makes him no promises, and chances are he'll have to marry soon too. He's quite well born. His father owns a huge swath of vineyards, and they make the best wine in the world."

"Hm. Well, do take care to watch out for diseases."

"Don't worry. Aphrodite's teaching me about those too."

Zeus strolled to them, embraced each of them in greeting, then led Hades away to show him the latest building improvements added to the palace.

Persephone spent as much of the evening as she could with Adonis and Aphrodite, flirting and laughing. When she dared look at Hades, she often caught him watching her, looking preoccupied. They said goodnight to one another at the evening's end with exactly the same kiss on the cheek and farewell that they gave everyone else.

Through the winter Persephone kept expanding her anatomy horizons with Aphrodite and Adonis, and tending to the home and garden where she lived with Demeter. And in secret she kept aching for the immortal man in the Underworld.

Finally one day Aphrodite divined the problem.

Hades had been at Aphrodite's house, just leaving when Persephone arrived. They exchanged startled glances, outside in the winter sun. He was wrapped in his wool cloak, lately adorned with embroidery of gold and rubies at the hem. He had cut his hair to chin length, so it fell loose in its curls rather than being tied back in braids and twine as it used to be. He looked magnificent. Persephone glanced at the door, where Aphrodite leaned against the frame and waved, looking a bit rumpled.

Hades and Persephone exchanged greetings, then Adonis came strolling up the road, and Hades made his farewells and escaped into the spirit realm.

Persephone endured the lesson in a whirl of distraction and envy. At the end of it, Aphrodite sent Adonis out, kissing him and saying she needed some woman-only talk with Persephone.

"He'd have been jealous," Aphrodite confided after Adonis left. She leaned toward Persephone, adjusting the cushion she sat upon. "All that time down in the Underworld, did you and Hades…?" She tilted her face in curiosity. The jewels on her necklace winked in the sunlight from the window, as if they were listening too.

Persephone shook her head. "Nothing at all."

"You both seemed shaken to see each other here, right after he'd been—well, you understand. And darling, you must know that even if Hades comes to me occasionally, there is no reason on Earth for you or any other woman to be jealous."

At that, Persephone had to laugh, somewhat hopelessly. "We're *all* jealous of you, Aphrodite. We can't help it."

Aphrodite pushed at Persephone's knee with affection. "But you don't have to be! Especially with Hades. He hadn't visited me for years until today. And it's only a service between friends, since the poor immortal men can't be quite as free with the mortal women."

"I know." Persephone lifted her hand to her face, fingertips tracing the bumps of the scar that ran up her cheek and into her hair. "Which is why it was useless, even if I did have a bit of a crush on him."

"I wouldn't say 'useless.' There are precautions you can take, if you wish to avoid pregnancy. Even with an immortal lover."

"The herbs don't always work. Demeter and I grow some to make the tea for women in the village, and it isn't foolproof."

Aphrodite rested her elbow on a higher pillow, and leaned her head on her hand, squinting at Persephone. "Tell me what you put in it."

Persephone reeled off the ingredients.

Aphrodite waved the recipe away. "No need for all that. Just use cloudhair flowers from the spirit realm. Seeds only. It *does* have to be from the spirit realm, mind you, but if it is, it works every time."

"But does the woman have to be in the spirit realm for it to work?"

"Not at all. I've stored the seeds for over a year in this realm and it's still worked for myself and everyone else. You eat a small handful of them right after sex. I suggest chewing mint along with the cloudhair seeds, though, because they taste awful, and make you feel sick if you eat them by themselves."

"All right. I'll tell Mother. We'll improve the lot of the local women."

Aphrodite smiled. "And your own lot, should you wish to seduce Hades after all."

Persephone's face went hot, and she adjusted the jeweled belt she had taken to wearing, in Aphrodite's style. "Oh, he isn't interested."

"I wouldn't say that. I would guess quite the opposite, the way his eyes follow you every time I see you together. And the way he oh-so-casually asked about you today."

"Did he?"

"Yes. I daresay that's the main reason he came here: to get news of you. The rest was just consolation."

Hope and despair fought for predominance. "But Mother spoke to him, and he *said* he wasn't interested."

"Darling. Isn't it possible he said that to avoid alarming your mother? Or even that she bent his words a bit, when speaking to you later, in order to kill your affections quickly and humanely?"

Persephone *had* dared to hope such things, but... "It doesn't matter," she lamented. "Even if we were lovers, we couldn't have children, and I'll still age when he won't. I'm already eighteen. I need to marry someone else. Someone mortal." She ended sounding so wretched that Aphrodite stayed quiet a while in thought.

"Love is cruel, crueler than sex. But give it a chance when it might make you happy, for if you turn your back on it, you'll regret it forever."

Persephone regarded her with a new reverence. She knew of Aphrodite's wisdom when it came to matters of the body, but her solemn look and well thought-out words made her realize that Aphrodite truly merited the title "goddess of love." And for the first time, Persephone wondered what Aphrodite had suffered in past years to make her so familiar with the cruelty of a broken heart. Perhaps someday she would ask. Still…

Persephone shook her head. "I'm mortal. I need to accept it. I'm lucky even to know such people as you and him. I should be content with that."

HADES KNEW PERSEPHONE had to marry someone else. And he hated it. But what could he do?

At best he could hope she might take him as a lover on the side someday. But even among the rather liberal Greeks, who worshiped Aphrodite more fervently every year, an extramarital affair carried a whiff of disgrace for a woman, and disgrace was the last thing he wished to bring upon Persephone. He would have made her his queen. In an instant. If only she wished it.

Why had she been so cruel? She knew he wanted her, so why would she flaunt her amatory lessons with Aphrodite and that young brainless sprig? It angered and confused him, but he went on loving her all the same.

He kept making his trips to the mortal world to deliver justice for the souls, at least in Greece and nearby countries, where he could communicate with the people. More and more people recognized him lately, and bowed to him in reverence or fear—sometimes hitting the ground completely like supplicants before the great Goddess. Given that the justice he delivered was frequently in the form of dragging a murderer before the local courts, which often enough led to public execution, he supposed he understood the fear. Besides, the rumors of Tartaros, which was what people had taken to calling the hell-like caves beneath the fields, had spread and become embellished until the stories were even worse than the reality. Some citizens avoided speaking Hades' name, he was told by his fellow immortals, because they thought it might invoke him to appear, kill them on the spot, and drag them beneath the earth. As if such a thing could ever happen.

But he couldn't laugh it off. Hearing himself called "the god of death" dismayed him. What woman would want to marry the god of death? He tried to spread it around that he was actually just the king of the dead, but people rarely grasped the distinction.

On one of his errands, less than a month after running into Persephone at Aphrodite's house, he encountered a skinny dog, limp and trembling, lying beneath a tree. It was a male, with a sleek tan coat and dark brown ears that folded back fondly as Hades knelt to examine him. The dog's curly tail, showing a fluff of white fur, thumped the dusty ground. A large patch of hair was missing on his neck, where the skin was marred with deep, inflamed wounds.

"Poor fellow." Hades stroked the soft ears. "Looks like you got in a fight with someone much bigger than you. I expect I'll see you in the Underworld soon if no one takes care of you."

He looked around, but found only farmlands and a few houses. He carried the dog to each door, but the inhabitants shrugged and said they'd never seen him before. Finally, unable to leave him, Hades brought him to the Underworld.

"Persephone had a few plants that helped with infection," he told the animal as he carried him into the orchard. "Let's see if I can do it right."

He must have chosen the right leaves to wrap around the wound, for soon the dog perked up and began eating better and walking around, though with a limp. Somewhat whimsically, Hades named him Kerberos, after a fearful dog-like monster that was supposed to guard the gates of the dead, in the stories the Greeks told. Hades kept Kerberos with him nearly all the time. It eased his loneliness.

Hermes visited him in the Underworld a few days before the spring equinox festival, cajoling Hades to come to it.

Hades wandered across the fields with him, Kerberos limping along at his side. "No one wants the god of death at their fertility festival."

"Sure they do. I've heard plenty of girls sighing over your tasty darkness."

"Tasty darkness. Really."

"You wouldn't think they'd want the god of thievery and mischief at their festival either, but I've received a *lot* of invitations." Since Hades made no reply, Hermes added, "Look, just because Persephone's likely to be married to Adonis by the end of that day is no reason for you to stay down here and mope."

Hades flinched. "Is it settled, then?"

"Oh, nothing's ever settled about these festivals. But everyone expects that's how it'll go. They both ought to marry soon if they're ever going to. They know each other and get along…it would work. It doesn't mean you're out of the picture, though."

"Yes, it does."

"Not when she obviously prefers you."

"She doesn't. Demeter came to me and said Persephone didn't want me, and wished to stay away from now on."

"Oh, *Demeter* said?" Hermes snorted. "Demeter, who's never wanted Persephone anywhere near you, who would say anything to keep her daughter above ground and out of the hands of an immortal man? You never guessed she might have been…what's the nice way to say this…*lying*?"

The hope that spiraled up in Hades' heart was the cruelest emotion yet. "It still couldn't work," he snapped. "I couldn't give her children, not without endangering her."

"Adopt some. She wouldn't mind."

"She's mortal. She'll age. There are other dangers, other problems…just, no. It's better we stay apart."

"Oh, yes." Derision seeped from Hermes' voice. "You only

have a certain number of years you can be together. Much *better* you don't use them."

"You must have other people to irritate today. Don't let me keep you." Hades strode ahead, leaving Hermes to find his own way out.

Making matters worse, that night Kerberos came down with a fever again, and the redness and inflammation returned to his neck wound, which reopened with an alarming amount of bleeding after the dog scratched at it too deeply with his hind claws. Hades located a different type of leaf that Persephone had discovered was good at stopping bleeding, and it did work for that. But nothing seemed to work in fighting the infection and fever this time. In grief, Hades carried Kerberos around the orchard, looking at the plants in hopes of a new treatment.

"I'm sorry, boy," he told the dog. "I don't know which to try. I don't know a thing without her."

He felt pathetic. Hugging a dying dog among a bunch of fruit trees in the land of the dead, ready to collapse weeping like a child. Hades sank to the ground and sat beside the row of the newest trees, cradling Kerberos in his lap. He wiped a tear off his face while the dog wriggled, trying to sniff one of the trees.

Hades moved him closer to let him smell what interested him. "What, you like those?" Kerberos licked a fruit that had recently ripened. The little tree had grown from one of Persephone's saplings, and had just produced its first fruits—only two of them. Hades knew from his memories that they were oranges, and that they came from Asia.

"Dogs don't eat fruit, you fool. But I suppose you can try if you want." Hades picked the orange and tore off a scrap of the peel. Its sweet fragrance filled the air. As he uncovered the flesh, he found it the strangest color: blue like the midday sky. "Well, that's different." Detaching a wedge of the blue fruit, he ate a bite himself, and found nothing amiss with it. He held out the rest of the wedge on his palm.

Kerberos gobbled it up, his muzzle and whiskers tickling Hades' hand. After swallowing it, he licked Hades' arm, then curled up in his lap and lay there shivering.

Hades petted him sadly. "Yes. Sleep a while. We'll see how you feel later."

He carried the dog across the river on the raft, and through the tunnels to his own bedchamber.

CHAPTER THIRTY-TWO

IT WASN'T IDEAL, SOPHIE THOUGHT as she let her mother in, to see your parent at a time when you were obsessed with a memory in which your parent had messed up your love life.

Just to confuse her, of course, Demeter was now her father, not her mother. But her current mother was still causing problems in relationships—not Sophie's, at least, but the one between herself and Sophie's dad, which was almost as upsetting.

"Hi, Mom." She hugged her, smelling her perfume and feeling the coolness of her raincoat.

"Hey, sweetie. It's so good to see you." Her mom hugged her an extra few seconds, then looked anxiously at her face. "Still feeling sick?"

Sophie sniffled, and nodded. "Sore throat started yesterday. Now I have a stuffy nose on top of it."

Her mom laid her hand on Sophie's forehead. "Yeah, you're a little warm. Well, that's why I came bearing soup. We'll skip going out, and eat in your room."

It almost shamed Sophie how readily and comfortably she submitted to her mother, letting herself be taken care of as if she were a kid. But, hey, Mom knew how to do this. She urged Sophie to sit on the bed with a blanket on her lap and pillows behind her back, served her a bowl of soup brought in a carton from a restaurant nearby, and brewed mugs of herbal tea with the electric kettle Sophie kept in the room.

Even Melissa, who was still healthy, found herself given tea

and homemade cookies when she returned from class. She obediently sat and ate while Sophie's mom drew her into the conversation.

The talk was all about home, putting the little town of Carnation and the gray Washington skies foremost into Sophie's mind
again. Her dad was manning the fruit stand today, with help from
a hired high school kid, and since it was October they had ship-
ments of pumpkins to unload and arrange. Sophie had assisted
with the task so many times she could almost feel the bristly stems
in her hands as she listened. She ached to be home again, where
things were simpler and no one wanted to hurt her. Adrian and
ancient Greece seemed surreal, impossible, for the time being.

But then, perhaps home wasn't so much simpler. When Melissa left for her next class, Sophie finally found the strength to ask
her mother for the truth.

Gazing at the honey-thickened inch of tea at the bottom of her
mug, she asked, "Are you and Dad getting a divorce?"

Rather than act shocked, amused, or angry, her mother stayed
quiet a few seconds, then set her own mug on the desk. "No. But
you must have seen or guessed something that makes you wonder."

Good, Sophie thought. She and her mother were treating each
other like adults, then, despite the mom-and-sick-kid act. "I saw
you kissing a man. In the car, by the library, a few months ago.
And you text someone a lot now, which you never used to do,
and you're gone more than usual, more than your classes would
need you to be."

"You've been wondering for a few months? Honey, you could
have asked me sooner." Her face looked pale, her wavy hair dark
beside it. She laid her hand on Sophie's foot, through the blanket.
"Have you heard of the term 'companionate marriage'?"

"Not exactly." Sophie already began to guess what it meant,
though.

"It means different things depending who you ask, but in our
case it means we're staying together because we care about each

other, we love you kids, we want to keep the house, the fruit stand, et cetera. But, romantically…"

"You can see other people." Sophie kept her hands clenched around the mug.

"Yes." Several silent seconds passed, then her mom added, "He's a nice man named Sam—"

Sophie twitched and looked away. "I don't have to know this."

"But he understands I'm not leaving Terry. I promise you I'm not."

Another sign they were being adults: Sophie's father had become "Terry" instead of "your dad."

"I assume Liam doesn't know any of this," Sophie said.

"No. He's twelve. I don't think he'd get it."

Sophie nodded, swishing the honeyed tea back and forth. "I won't tell him."

"Does this make you feel better, at least?" Her mom sounded anxious. "Is there anything else I can answer?"

"I guess it does make me feel better." Sophie put on a weak smile. "Except for the whole fever and cold thing. That's still making me feel like crap."

Late that evening, while Sophie was in the middle of explaining the visit via alternating texts to Tabitha and Adrian, her cell phone buzzed. Her dad was calling.

She answered, with a measure of reluctance. "Hey, Dad."

"Hi, hon. I had a talk with your mom. Sounds like she told you a few things."

"Yeah. I…it's fine, I swear."

"Is it really?"

"Well…okay, it's weird. But I think I can get used to it." *I hope*, she added silently. This did seem the kind of thing that could send a daughter to a therapist if she dwelled on it too much.

"I want to reiterate what she said," her dad went on. "We are good, we are not splitting up, and most of all, we love you guys."

"I love you too. I just…worry you're not as happy as you could be."

"Aw, you're fresh out of a breakup, sweetie. I know it's hard to imagine being happy without a smokin' romance. But it is possible."

Sophie lifted her eyebrows, dryly amused. He had no idea the flood levels of smokin' romance inundating her life these days. "Sure, maybe," she said.

"When you get all tired and middle-aged, you'll see. Having you and Liam to love and be proud of—well, that's enough for this old guy's life."

"Dad, you're not *old*."

"Tell that to my back. It's yelling at me for lifting pumpkins all day."

She chuckled, which made her cough. "So…are you, you know. Seeing anyone?" God, did *that* feel weird to say to Dad.

"Nah. Not interested. It's your mom who's still got the, uh, inclination to do those things."

If this was a way of saying, "She's got a higher sex drive than me," Sophie really didn't want to continue the conversation. "Oh. Well, I'm glad I know the truth." She coughed again. "This cold's kicking my butt. I better go to bed."

"Get better soon. Goodnight, honey."

Shortly after hanging up, she wrapped up her text messaging as well, sending Tabitha a goodnight, and Adrian too. Right now she felt uneasy on all fronts.

She could cross one concern off her list, yes. Mom and Dad weren't divorcing. But it only caused her to add double underlines to another major concern: Sophie mattered in a gigantic way to her parents. Dad's life was complete only because of Liam and her. In short, one thing she *couldn't* easily do was become immortal, vanish into the spirit realm, and write off most of her earthly relationships. Sorry, Adrian.

But even as she acknowledged that problem, an ache spread under her ribs, the same way it had felt when Persephone was trying to give up Hades.

And she already knew *that* resolution hadn't stuck.

"HAVE YOU HEARD the rumblings against Zeus?" Demeter asked Persephone, as they walked toward a patient's house. It was a few days before the spring equinox, and rain was turning the road to mud. The women wore extra woolen cloaks draped over their heads to keep dry.

"No," said Persephone. "What's wrong?"

"Only what we've all expected for years. He can't stop seducing mortal women. Maidens and married ones alike. And though he claims he's careful, two girls have died in the last year in miscarriages. Those who manage to escape pregnancy still end up with broken hearts and irate families."

"Oh, no."

"Hera's no help, of course. She takes the arrogant stance, claiming it's all jealous lies on the part of girls with a crush on him. And Zeus dodges responsibility, says the pregnancies could easily have been caused by other men."

"Which, I'm sure," said Persephone with a sigh, "does not make the families any less furious with him."

"Quite the contrary. It's starting to make all the immortals look bad."

"How are things with the others? Apollo, Athena, Artemis, Poseidon...?" Persephone added the name as casually as she could, more aware now of the tenderness of unsatisfied love.

"I gather they have contented followers on the whole. But even they hear grumbles and insults more often these days. Artemis said there's an unruly pack of men who jeer at her for not wishing to take any of them as lovers, and an arrow hit her while a group was out hunting recently."

"Gracious."

"She wasn't hurt, of course, not for long. And the man who fired the arrow swears it was a mistake. But she suspects it wasn't. As to Poseidon, his mortal wife lately got accosted by a bunch of bitter old women wanting to know why he couldn't perform miracle cures for them, or protect their sons and grandsons from dying at sea." Demeter shook her head. "They've only known of us for ten or twenty years, yet already they're completely misinformed about what we are and what we can do."

"Well, they call you 'gods.' And you encouraged it. They want you to be the gods in the stories."

"Wonderful. Let them tell us how exactly we're supposed to climb up onto the clouds and grab hold of a lightning bolt, let alone raise the dead."

That was all it took: one mention of the dead, and Persephone's mind slid straight to the Underworld, forgetting its speculation on whether her mother still loved Poseidon.

They trudged along, the mud squelching beneath their deerskin boots, water seeping in between the stitches to chill Persephone's feet.

"In short," Demeter added, "it's not a good time to align yourself with immortals. Know that if you wish to marry Adonis, I'll miss you terribly, but I'll be pleased that you're safe and taking on a normal life."

"Oh, Mother, the people don't bother me. And they love *you*. We're safe, I dare say."

"They don't all love me. Didn't I tell you, some wench yelled at me a few days ago? 'How much grain for the village could that fancy gold crown buy?' She was not asking in friendly jest, I promise you."

Persephone linked her arm into Demeter's. "Then I'm sure she was drunk."

"Well, yes. That she was."

They both laughed.

But the central message wasn't lost on Persephone: marry Adonis, not Hades.

If Hades honestly didn't want her, there was no choice at all. In her time spent with Aphrodite, her head full of outlandish seduction ideas, she entertained notions that she could sway him. But the rest of her days, such as now…well, why would he want her? Look at her: a limping mortal with mud all over her feet, and maybe fifteen years left before wrinkles and gray hairs overtook her. What a prize.

She bowed her head, and plodded along in the rain with her mother.

Sophie groaned upon awakening. Pain rushed back into her consciousness, throbbing at the back of her throat and deep inside her nose. Sweat dampened her pajamas, thanks to her fluctuating temperature. She hauled herself upright to blow her nose.

It was 9:00 a.m. on Saturday, and Sophie had the room to herself. Melissa had left last night to visit her parents for the weekend. Of course, Sophie thought, the one weekend her roommate was gone, she was so ill she could barely function, and therefore couldn't realistically use her room for a hot date with her gorgeous new boyfriend.

She staggered to the bathroom, figuring she'd feel better after a shower, and might be able to face a study session at the library. But, as with yesterday, dragging herself to the dining hall for breakfast was enough to make her dizzy, and all she could stand to swallow was a few bites of oatmeal and a cup of chamomile tea.

Bringing toast and an orange back to her room, she flopped into bed and resigned herself to feeling miserable.

Well...mostly miserable.

How you feeling? Adrian texted, shortly after she returned from the dining hall.

The sight of his name, his simple three words of concern, made her feel like she could survive the day.

Been better, she answered. *Goddess of phlegm, they call me.*

Ha. Nice. Want anything today? Soup?

Nah. Thanks, but I look and feel gross. Talking to you helps, though.

Good. Text me whenever you like.

I will. She set the phone down at her side, and picked up her Chem textbook.

Adrian pocketed his phone and got up to make coffee in the Airstream's little kitchen. He didn't need caffeine, technically, nor did it affect him anymore, but coffee's smell and taste comforted him, reminding him of lazy afternoons studying with Zoe, or Saturday mornings reading across the kitchen table from his father, back when he was a mortal. Back before he became cut off from the world.

Outside in the wilderness, a clean blue sky glimmered behind the row of evergreens. Splashes of yellow and red along the hillside signaled foliage changing color for the winter. Dew, or possibly an overnight rain, had drenched everything and bent the meadow grasses over.

Autumn. Demeter searching the Earth desperately for her kidnapped daughter, and in her grief letting the world's plants die and the weather turn cold. Or so the mythology had it.

While the kettle heated, and Kiri chowed down on her bowl of dog food on the floor, Adrian leaned on the counter and thought of Demeter, and what Sophie had told him about her father lately. As Demeter or as Terry, that soul put the happiness and safety of her (or his) daughter first. Adrian sympathized with that.

The problem was, he put Sophie's love and companionship first among his own priorities, just as he had with Persephone. Even knowing what a lonely, difficult, dangerous existence this was, he wanted her in it with him, living centuries if not forever.

Selfish perhaps. But everyone was allowed a vice, and desiring her seemed like it was destined to be his.

CHAPTER THIRTY-THREE

*H*OW YOU DOING? SAID THE text from Adrian. It was dark outside now, and Sophie had just slurped down an overly salty but somewhat nourishing cup of chicken noodle soup.

Surviving, she texted back. *Extreme stuffy head. Fever of 101. But conscious.*

Sorry. Sounds awful.

Yeah. But these memories do help. Distraction, at least.

They are that. And some nicer ones should come soon.

Finally the making out with Hades part? she guessed.

Perhaps…and now I'm blushing.

She smiled, blew her nose for the nine hundredth time that day, and tapped in a response. *Sweet. OK, I'll try to sleep soon. Hope I feel good enough tomorrow to see you.*

Me too. Take care.

Night.

Sophie wasn't sure what awakened her in the middle of the night—a faint sound, perhaps, or the sensation of someone moving near her. But when she opened her eyes in the nearly-dark room, she saw the solid shape of a person sitting on the edge of her bed.

She gasped, and flew into an upright position, grabbing at the desk lamp and switching it on.

Quentin.

Sophie could barely breathe, let alone shout.

Professor Quentin smiled pleasantly. She wore a lavender rain jacket and a black OSU baseball cap. Her cane leaned on her knee, her hand wrapped around it. "Hello, dear. We need to talk." She lifted her other hand, showing Sophie's pepper spray, which evidently Quentin had picked up from the desk. Quentin chuckled. "I've got this, in case you're looking for it."

"How'd you get in?" Sophie's voice was only a squeak. Her cold had moved into the laryngitis stage, apparently. Great timing: just when it would've been useful to scream.

"Oh, that was easy."

Sophie shot a glance at the alarm clock. It was 12:30. She scrambled out of bed, her legs shaking. "But you'd need keys. I…."

Professor Quentin chuckled. "I have my ways. But that isn't the point." She lowered her chin, keeping her pale blue eyes fixed on Sophie. "I know you've been in contact with Adrian. And the woman too—Rhea, if that's really her name."

"Out. You need to get out."

"I told you, you don't want to be in this fight, sweetie. Where's your cell phone? Hand it over and let's end this now."

Under her pillow. It was under her pillow, all too close to where Quentin sat. And the stun gun was in her backpack, hanging next to the door. Damn it. Sophie moved back to the bed and sat upon the pillow, trying to make it look like she was too weak to stand. Her hand crept under the pillow's edge, behind her. "Look, I'm sick, and you have to leave."

"I imagine he's seduced you by now," said Quentin. "Into believing him, I mean, though possibly he's seduced you in the usual way too. But imagine the problems, if you haven't already. Say you have children together. Won't you want them to live forever too? Then what about their spouses, and their children? It's inevitable. You'll want more and more of his kind. A whole race of them will soon exist, and then what?"

"I told you, I don't know what you're talking about. Go." Sophie captured her phone and surreptitiously pulled it out, keeping it behind her back.

Quentin gestured conversationally with the leather-wrapped canister of pepper spray. "Some government's sure to get their hands on this magic fruit, this fountain of youth. It'll become a commodity. What if the next version of the Nazis get hold of it?"

They wouldn't, because no one would let them into the Underworld to eat it, which is the only way it works, Sophie thought. She tucked the phone up her pajama sleeve and stood, moving toward the door. "Really, you need to go. You'll catch my cold if you stay."

"That cold. How do you know it isn't something he gave you? Something from that other world?"

"It's a cold. I've had them before."

The professor squinted at Sophie. "But think of it. Microorganisms no one's been exposed to in all these centuries. Plagues, incurable diseases, horrors we can't imagine. He could be unleashing all that onto us, going back and forth between worlds."

"If it never was a problem before—" Sophie stopped, realizing her error too late.

Professor Quentin smiled dryly. "So he's been showing you those pretty pictures of the past. Hallucinations, dear. Some attribute them to demons, but I'm not as religious as all that. I'm sure neurotoxins are enough of an explanation. His world and powers are *real*, but there's no guarantee they are what they seem to be."

"You're making no sense."

"The Underworld—that's not necessarily the real afterlife. The past lives he's described might be total fictions. And so on."

Sophie thought of Grandpop's ghost, the dreams, the rides in Adrian's bus, the giant lion that had almost eaten her…could they all be hallucinations?

Last week, she'd found a piece of long grass latched to her coat, topped with a tassel of reddish grain. Nothing like that grew on campus. It had ridden over from the spirit realm. Her gaze darted to it, still lying across her desk as a souvenir.

Fury won out over fear. To think, this woman had made her doubt all of it—doubt Adrian—even for a second.

Sophie reached for the doorknob. "If you're not leaving, I will, and I'll fetch my R.A. and have her throw you out."

"I wouldn't open that door. Hand me your phone. Now."

Quentin's eyes gleamed as she watched Sophie, and she lifted the pepper spray.

"Trust me, you don't want to use that. Hurts like hell if you're anywhere near it."

"And you trust me, you don't want to go out into that hall. Let's have the phone."

Defiantly, Sophie pulled the stun gun out of her backpack— from a distance, she figured, its dark rectangular shape probably looked enough like a phone. "You want the phone? Come get it." She opened the door and walked into the hallway.

A tall man in a ski mask and dark clothes leaped at her. She managed to scream this time, though it was only a throaty croak, and she threw herself aside, crashing hard into another door. The man lunged at her again, and this time she was ready: she met his leg with the stun gun and stabbed her thumb against the button.

A crackling buzz reverberated in the hallway. The man gave a strangled cry and crashed to the floor, limbs twitching.

Footsteps thumped behind the door Sophie had bumped into, and someone opened it: one of the girls who lived across the hall. "Holy crap!" the girl said, and dashed back to her desk to grab her cell phone.

Sophie dived into the girl's room, not wanting to be left alone, still peering out into the hall.

"Hello? Whitney?" the girl said. She had evidently dialed their R.A. Meanwhile her roommate, in bed, rubbed her eyes groggily. "There's some dude on our floor. I think he broke in."

Quentin sauntered out of Sophie's room, leaning on her cane. "Goodbye, then, dear," she told Sophie on her way past. "I'm truly sorry you've chosen the wrong path."

Sophie knew she should jump on the lunatic, zap her as well, try to detain her for the cops, something. But Quentin was elderly enough that Sophie feared the weapon might kill her, and she wasn't ready to commit murder. In addition, a wave of weakness and nausea overcame her and she slid to sit upon the floor.

Quentin walked on by, into the stairwell. Sophie leaned against the wardrobe in the other girls' room and closed her eyes.

"Thanks, Whitney." The girl hung up. "She'll be right up. What the hell did you do to that guy? Taze him?"

Sophie nodded, resting her head on her knees.

"Wow. You're bad-ass," said the girl in admiration.

Sophie didn't answer. What she longed for, even more than eradicating Thanatos from the face of the Earth, was to get Adrian here right now, seek reassurance in his strength and closeness.

But the next half hour went by in a flurry of activity.

Whitney, the R.A., arrived just a few minutes before the cops, and went pale at the news. Learning that a cult nut-job had somehow gotten into one of the student's rooms, with a violent accomplice in the hall, was probably high on the list of an R.A.'s worst nightmares. While they waited for the cops to arrive, Whitney noticed Sophie's nausea and illness, and had Sophie lie down in her bed again, and drink from a water bottle she brought her. Meanwhile, the girl from across the hall was happy to take the stun gun and point it at the dude in the hallway, covering him in case he got any notions of violence again.

The initial electric shock sufficed, though: he was still on the floor, immobilized, when the police tromped in. They slapped handcuffs on him and carried him out. Sophie caught glimpses of it all through the open door, as she lay curled in bed, sipping water.

The police came in to get her report. She sat up in bed, and this time insisted they add Bill Wilkes' name to the list of people to interrogate—even if he *was* a cop.

Taking her statement lasted ages, or so it seemed. Finally they left, promising her they were scouring the area for Quentin and any other accomplices. They also strongly suggested she change her lock.

"We'll do it tomorrow," Whitney promised Sophie. "Will you be okay tonight?"

Sophie nodded. "Thanks, Whitney."

"Call if you need anything. Any hour. I'm so sorry—I don't know how this happened."

"Not your fault." Sophie waved wearily, and watched as Whitney left to file her own incident report.

After retrieving her stun gun from the enamored girl across the hall, Sophie locked her door, sat against her bed, and finally dialed Adrian.

He answered after three rings, his words slurring in sleepiness. "Hey. What's up?"

"Professor Quentin was here. In my room. Watching me sleep."

"What?" Instantly his voice changed to full-alert mode.

"Warning me about you. Threatening me." Her breath came sharp on the next inhalation, and she realized she was on the verge of crying.

"Bloody—where is she? Are you all right?"

"Yes. She's gone now. My R.A. was here, and the police, and… I stun-gunned a guy in the hallway who tried to grab me. But Quentin got away."

"A guy in the—? All right, I'm coming over there."

"You can't."

"Yes I can." He sounded like he was speaking through clenched teeth. "I can threaten that woman right back, and I will."

"I said, she got away. The cops are looking for her. I only called you to tell you."

"God, Soph. How'd she get in? This is bad."

"Maybe she knows a locksmith, or copied someone's key; I don't know. We're changing the locks tomorrow. But I might never feel safe again."

"Me neither." He sighed, sounding wretched. "What are you going to do the rest of the night? Will you be able to get any sleep?"

"I don't know. She probably won't come back now, or even tomorrow, but I'm freaked out. If I could go home, I would, but it's too far. And there isn't anywhere else."

"Yes there is." His voice lowered and warmed. "Come stay with me."

CHAPTER THIRTY-FOUR

SOPHIE STUFFED A CHANGE OF clothes into her backpack, her mind in a flutter. Even without the Thanatos issue, the problems of staying overnight with Adrian would be enough on their own to worry her. Was it actually dangerous, with spirit-realm microbes floating about? Would she be disgusting and snore all night with her cold? Would he try to cuddle with her even when she was disgusting, or would he not want to? Which would be worse?

Adrian had said he was going to come all the way to the dorm to meet her, since it was the middle of the night and she was sick. He overrode her protests by assuring her he had a disguise of some kind, which Nikolaos had provided for him a while back.

So, on top of the other concerns, Sophie also worried she'd burst into nervous giggles at the sight of whatever this disguise was.

Her phone rang.

Sophie answered. "Hello?"

"I'm downstairs," said Adrian. "Do you want to come down? Or buzz me in?"

"I'll come down. See you in a minute." She hung up and grabbed her pack. Dizzily, blowing her nose on the way, she hurried down the staircase and stepped out the glass door. Night air gusted into her face, rattling leaves on the shrubs. No one was around except a guy leaning on the wall, holding a cigarette. He had straight hair to his shoulders, brown streaked with bleach-blond. He wore a black fedora, glasses with thick dark rims, and a typical emo-kid long black raincoat.

Oh, *no*. She stopped, closed her eyes a second, then looked at him again. Giggles overtook her. She leaned back helplessly against the window.

Adrian slid the unlit cigarette into his coat pocket, and stepped back into the shadow of a high hedge. "Pull yourself together. Let's go."

She followed. "You look—this is—" She grasped a handful of the wig, then fell against his chest, unable to do anything but laugh.

He hugged her. An extra swoop of dizziness, and the cessation of the university noises, told her they had switched realms.

She lifted her head, trying to see his face in the darkness. "Don't ever go blond."

"Deal. I was only ever going to wear this disguise in extreme emergencies. Like when a murderer threatens my girl." He removed the glasses, and her adjusting vision could make out the shine of his eyes, and the concern in them. "You all right? Really?"

Her laughter faded and her emotions teetered back to the verge of tears. She leaned on him. "No. I'm a wreck. And so tired."

Adrian stooped and lifted her, tucking an arm under her knees. She hugged his neck and he carried her across the fields, moving branches out of the way so nothing scratched her. At the Airstream he transferred her to one arm while he opened the door, then climbed in with her. It was warm inside; the generator was humming. Two small lamps shone, one above the sink and one on the wall above his bed, at the end of the trailer. He set her on the bed, and took her backpack and coat, pushing them into a tiny open closet. He removed the pieces of the disguise and shoved them onto the top shelf. Sophie curled up on the blankets, watching him.

Kiri thumped her tail on the floor. Sophie held out her hand, and Kiri leaped up to snuffle it.

Running his hand through his flattened curls, Adrian sat on the fold-down bench that served as the only seat in the small bedroom, other than the bed itself. "Okay. Tell me what she said to you."

Sophie did so, dully recounting all the threats and disturbing suggestions Quentin had made.

Adrian listened, gaze steady on her face, his knuckles pressed to his lips and his dark eyes burning with anger. When she was finished, he dropped his gaze to the floor and sat motionless a while. Then he rose and kissed her on the forehead. "You did the right thing getting out of there. But it's okay to lie in the future and say you've had nothing more to do with me."

"I will." She reached out for his hand. "But I do want more to do with you. I know it's real, everything you've shown me."

"Good." Adrian squeezed her fingers and let go. "Tell me what you need—for now, or for morning. I'll get it. Tea? Orange juice? Vegetables?"

"Right now I just need rest. But for breakfast, I guess some kind of herbal tea, maybe with rosehips or echinacea. And apples and almond butter, if you don't have them."

"What kind of apples do you want?"

"Aww. People don't usually ask me what kind of apples."

He gave her a half-smile. "We in New Zealand are apple experts, I remind you."

"I know it. We in Washington import them when ours aren't in season. I like Honeycrisp best, but if you can't find them, Fuji are fine."

"Anything else? Are you warm enough?"

She nodded, drawing his blanket up over herself. "I'll be all right."

"Kiri'll stay with you. I won't be more than an hour or two. Call right away if you need anything."

He went out. Sophie lay with her eyes closed, comforted at being in his bed, in a realm out of reach of lunatics like Quentin. Kiri snoozed near her, getting up once to drink from her water bowl in the kitchen, then returning. Outside, the generator hummed and some kind of wild dog or monkey yipped in the distance.

It's a strange realm, but it's my realm, she thought, letting Persephone's identity steal over her in her exhaustion.

She heard the click of the Airstream's door opening, and the rustle of a plastic bag. Sitting up, she saw Adrian enter. Her phone indicated that an hour and a half had passed since he left—it was almost three in the morning now. She must have fallen asleep.

He set the plastic bag of groceries on the kitchen counter and walked to her, still in his flannel-lined coat. Dirt was smudged across his shoulder and chin. "How are you doing?" he asked, sitting on the edge of the bed.

"Not bad." She thumbed the dirt off his chin. "How'd you get all dirty? Did you fall over or something?"

"No. I, uh—"

He moved his right hand behind his back. Kiri whined and lifted her muzzle to sniff it.

Catching a glimpse, Sophie gasped and seized his hand to drag it into view.

It looked like a car had run over it, was her first horrified thought. It was crushed and bloody and mangled. His cuff was wet with blood, and a few red drops had fallen on his jeans and stained them.

"I'm fine," he protested.

"How is this fine? What did you do? Did you find Quentin?"

"No. I wanted to, believe me. But I didn't even know where to look, so…after getting the food I took out my aggressions on some rocks in the spirit realm."

"Some rocks."

"The smaller river over there, I think it's the Marys River. I started picking up boulders and throwing them down into it, just to smash something, and…" He sheepishly covered his injured hand with the other. "One of the really big ones slipped and landed on my hand. Probably broke just about every bone in it. Stupid."

"Oh, my God. Doesn't it hurt? It does. You're pale." She laid her palm on his cheek, finding it clammy.

"I'll recover. It'll be fine by morning." He picked up a black T-shirt from the floor, and wrapped it around his hand.

She set her fingers on top of it. "You were this mad because some woman was a bitch to me?"

"No." Adrian gazed at his lap. "I was mad because she's right."

"Are you insane?"

"She *is* right. I thought of all those things myself, or most of them, those two years I was waiting for the immortality fruit to grow. I told myself it wouldn't be a problem, it'd be fine, we'd work it out. I'm stubborn and selfish."

"You're not. She's crazy."

"At first I thought it'd be enough if I could just have you. If I had to pick one person to bring into this with me, then of course I'd pick you. I told myself that was all I was trying to do. One real companion isn't so much to ask for, is it? But wouldn't we eventually want our best mates and closest relatives to join us? Then wouldn't they want *their* loved ones to join us too? Numbers would multiply in no time."

"There's a whole other realm for us—for you. There's room. We wouldn't be overpopulating the living world."

Adrian flexed his injured hand carefully inside the T-shirt, and winced. "The more of us there are, the harder it becomes to keep secret. The likelier it becomes that the wrong people *will* hear about the fruit and steal it."

"Then why not hide out in the other realm? Hardly ever go to the living world at all?"

He didn't lift his face. "It comes to that, eventually. Closing the door on the world you know, only seeing it in quick visits, never living properly in it again. That isn't what you'd want, is it?"

When he put it that way, Sophie realized it was pretty much how Adrian lived now. She laced her fingers into his, on the uninjured hand. "There still has to be some way to compromise, to be a part of both worlds. You said it yourself: most people wouldn't mind immortals existing. They might even protect us. Thanatos is the extreme—the crazies." Her throat rasped as she spoke, her cold reasserting itself. She took a moment to cough and clear it.

Adrian glanced at her. "Right, go back and forth. Bringing new plagues to humankind."

"I don't have a freaking *plague*. I have a cold."

"That's the one thing that didn't occur to me in those two years. Didn't occur to Rhea either, because she doesn't think in modern terms—germs and all that. But it's completely possible. Likely, even. Weird giant animals evolved out there. Of course different bacteria and viruses would have too."

Though fear shivered through her, she adopted a brave tone. "All right. If I get worse and look like I'm about to die, rush me to the orchard and feed me the blue orange."

"That's my plan. Though it would mean turning you into one of their targets."

"Whatever. I already am. That's the choice I made." When he glanced at her cautiously, she added, "I came running straight to you and your realm, didn't I? I never called the cops on you for kidnapping me. I've been choosing you since day one."

He leaned over and hugged her, cradling her head with his cloth-wrapped hand. Then he moved back to kiss her softly on the lips. "That doesn't have to be your final answer," he said. "But thanks." Suddenly his expression brightened. "So you know it's a blue orange?"

Sophie paused, thinking about it. "Yeah. I do. Though I haven't totally unpacked the memory yet."

"You will soon." He rose. "Want some tea?"

"Sounds good. And you can tell me about New Zealand."

"New Zealand? Why?"

"Because I want to know everything about you. The things the memories *can't* tell me."

He rolled his eyes. "I got good marks in social science, bad marks in maths, my favorite color is green, and are you falling asleep with boredom yet?"

She plumped the pillow upright and settled her back against it. "Make that tea. And wash the blood out of your coat before it dries that way."

CHAPTER THIRTY-FIVE

A CLOUDY GRAY LIGHT FILTERED THROUGH the Airstream's drawn curtains. Almost seven a.m., said the vintage analog clock set into the wall.

Sophie was alone under the blankets. Rising onto her elbow, she found Adrian and Kiri asleep on the floor. Kiri was curled up on her dog bed. Adrian's head shared the edge of it; he lay on his back with his knees drawn up to fit the small floor space. He still wore his jeans, boots, and green flannel shirt, as if he hadn't intended to fall asleep.

His right hand lay across his chest. She leaned down for a closer look at it. Though smudges of blood marked his skin, his flesh was whole and unbroken, the lines of his finger bones perfect. Incredible.

To avoid waking him, she stepped over him and tiptoed to the tiny bathroom, and slid the pocket door shut. Adrian's coat hung over the one towel rack, its sleeve damp from where he'd washed out the blood. She moved it to the edge of the bucket-sized tub, wondering with a smile how Adrian fit in that, and spent several minutes making herself feel more human again with the help of warm water and a washcloth.

After blowing her nose enough to use up nearly a dozen tissues, she could breathe more freely, though the noise must have woken up her companions. Dog toenails clicked on the floor, and Adrian murmured something. A moment later, he said from outside the bathroom door, "Sophie?"

"Hi. Yeah." She glanced in the mirror—oh well, dark shadows under the eyes, no fix for it now—and opened the door. There he stood, looking anxious and adorable with sleep-disordered hair. "Sorry," she said, "I'll get out of here for you."

"No, take your time. I was about to take Kiri out. Just checking on you."

"I'm okay. At least, my throat feels better, and I don't think I have a fever anymore." They both smiled. "Just a cold. Told you," she accused gently.

Adrian pulled in a long breath, as if a weight had lifted off him. "Good."

"How are *you*?" she asked.

"Me?" He held up the hand that a boulder had smashed last night. "Fine. Good as new." Eyes twinkling, he echoed, "Told you."

He hopped out of the trailer with Kiri, and Sophie employed her low store of energy in slicing up an apple and starting the coffee maker for him. Then she sat at the table and nibbled the apple slices with a spoonful of almond butter.

Adrian returned, washed and changed in the bathroom, and came back to the kitchen with a fresh shave. Too bad her stuffy nose couldn't detect smells today, she thought. The scent of shaving cream on his jaw would be a treat. He offered oatmeal to supplement her apple slices, and she accepted.

Along with the bowl of oatmeal, he brought her a cup of herbal tea, and sat across from her.

"Thanks." She blew on the tea to cool it. "Bet you don't miss being sick."

He shook his head, chewing a spoonful of oatmeal. "I remember it well enough, though. And if I work myself up to it, I can still *feel* sick."

"How? Like if you're upset about something?"

"Yeah. Stress mostly." He tossed a self-conscious glance at her. "Like the day we first grabbed you. Thought I was going to hurl."

"How come?"

"It was so *wrong*. So illegal. I don't do stuff like that."

"I've been wondering about that." She sipped the tea, and found it still too hot. "There had to be some other way for you to approach me. We knew each other online. Why not explain it in an email or something?"

"You'd never have believed it. You'd have thought I was insane, and fed my address into the spam filter."

"Okay, then what if you just said, 'I'm going to be in town; let's meet up,' and then pulled me into the other realm?"

"Which is nearly kidnapping itself." He lifted an eyebrow. "And would you have agreed to meet me in real life?"

"Of course. Well…" She frowned at the window. "Maybe. You never know with Internet people."

"Right. I wasn't sure you'd agree. And you were moving to university, where you wouldn't be watched so closely. So I thought, best just appear and get it done."

"Which you did. Barely two minutes after I'd finished moving my stuff into the dorm."

He folded his hands around his mug, gazing at the black surface of his coffee. "I couldn't wait any longer. You'd been in my head all those months—a couple of years almost. It was driving me mad that you barely knew who I was."

Sophie scraped up a spoonful of oatmeal and swallowed it, unable to taste anything through her congestion. "That's sounding more like the original myth. The 'I must have her though she barely knows me' Hades."

Adrian rested his temple on his knuckles and examined her from a tilted perspective. "What would you have done? If we'd been the other way round?"

"If I were immortal and had all the memories, and you barely knew who I was?" She picked up her mug and thought about it, watching a flock of other-world birds flap across the sky in V formation. The imagined scenario crystallized easily: the loneliness, the longing for him, the need for him to know the truth. "Yeah. I'd totally have kidnapped you, too."

Sophie returned to the dorm at midday. Setting her backpack down, she noted the room already felt less like home than the Airstream did—and anywhere that Quentin had invaded would creep her out forever, she was certain. But she couldn't just *live* with Adrian, certainly not yet. She'd told him so, when he protested he really didn't like her wandering around on campus with madwoman Quentin on the loose.

"I have to go to class," she'd said. "I promise I won't walk through any dark alleys. And I'll carry my stun gun and use it if she comes near me, even if it does kill her."

He looked dubious, but released her into the living world— after a sweet, long kiss, and a moment of leaning his forehead against hers.

Her lips curved in a dreamy smile. She indulged it a few seconds before coming back down to Earth. They did face a few problems. Not only did some deranged people want him dead, and were happy to drag Sophie into the battle, but she had a major decision to make regarding living forever.

Then there was her family.

Coming home for Halloween?? her little brother texted, as she walked to class. *What's your costume??*

Sophie sighed. Her costume, indeed. Goddess of the Underworld, maybe.

Don't know yet. On both questions. What's yours? she typed back, settling herself into the wooden desk in the lecture hall. Other students milled around her, and she glanced uneasily at them, wondering if Quentin had sent anyone to assassinate her or at least spy on her. Hard to tell.

The Scream remember?? Liam answered.

Of course. Forgot.

U should come back. Wilsons are having a party.

A Halloween party—or any other party. Could she ever attend one of those in the real world with Adrian? Would that ever be safe? She began to grasp the depth of isolation his life involved, and the complications hers would acquire if she became his girlfriend.

Well, even if he couldn't accompany her, she could go to these things alone if need be. But that wouldn't be as much fun.

I might, she texted back to Liam. *I'll let you know soon. Shouldn't you be in class? Not texting?*

Lunch break! What abt u??

Class just starting. Bye. Love you.

And though he was a twelve-year-old bad-ass skateboarder, Liam texted back, *u2*.

CHAPTER THIRTY-SIX

SOPHIE ATTENDED CLASSES THE NEXT week, caught up on assignments, banished her cold with plenty of nutritious soups and teas, and endured a whirl of confusion about immortals and Thanatos.

Whitney got Sophie's lock changed, and issued new keys to Sophie and Melissa. (Melissa looked wide-eyed and petrified when Sophie told her about the crazy woman in the room at midnight, and vigorously nodded in approval of the new locks.) Sophie took to sleeping with the stun gun under her pillow too, just in case.

In her dreams that week, her control slipped and gave her memories she'd already seen, from other lives. Adrian said that happened sometimes when you were ill or exhausted. He also said she could find the shut-off switch if she liked, and just have normal dreams for a while. She tried that, and succeeded: for a couple of boring but restful nights, she returned to "ordinary" dreams, such as riding a Ferris wheel with Abe Lincoln and her eighth grade math teacher, and arguing about which Lord of the Rings movie was best.

Meanwhile, Quentin remained at large, hiding out, no one knew where. Nikolaos was scouring the city for her, still to no luck. But no one bothered Sophie that week, perhaps because of the extra police attention, and her habit of fighting back. The police checked in with her the day after the break-in. Bill Wilkes, they said, had a solid alibi: he was working a night shift in his own district, in Salem, when the incident occurred. Furthermore, he claimed no knowledge of Quentin or Sophie.

"But if they dug into his emails—" she said to Adrian on the phone, frustrated.

"I know, I know. But they'd have to get a warrant to do that—keep in mind *we're* reading his messages illegally—and at the moment they don't have a strong enough connection with your case to get one. Which sucks."

She scowled. "You said it."

The man she had zapped with the stun gun remained in custody. According to the cops, he claimed he'd been hired as backup for this break-in job, but he didn't personally know anything about the people involved or what they were after. He had nothing against Sophie and didn't even know who she was. So he said.

"Could that even be true?" she asked Adrian—again in the utmost frustration—as they took a walk in the spirit realm on a mild afternoon.

"Sure, it could be. I wouldn't doubt if Thanatos made a habit of hiring criminals off the street to do their dirty work. Makes it harder to find out the real brains of the operation, if the people caught don't know anything about the cult."

"Grrr." Sophie borrowed a page from Adrian's book, and picked up a rock and hurled it as hard as she could against a tree.

Throwing rocks didn't particularly help. But Adrian draping his arm around her afterward did.

"We still have this realm," he reminded her. "We're the royalty of the Underworld, love. They come to our domain when their lives are over, whether they like it or not—and if they were bad enough, they definitely will *not* like it. So in a sense, we always win in the end."

Appeased, she wound her arm around his hips. "True. By the way, when are you taking me back to the Underworld? We can ask around for more dirt on Quentin and Wilkes, visit your mom and my grandpa. And besides, I really want to see the place again."

"Do you? Then, sure. Whenever you like."

"How about this weekend?"

He smiled. "It's a date."

ADRIAN PICKED UP Sophie on Friday after her classes. A chilly October sun drifted between puffy gray clouds. They climbed into the bus, and she stashed her backpack beneath the front seat.

Adrian couldn't help wondering how much different this overnight stay was going to be from the night she'd spent in the Airstream. She seemed healthy again, and their kisses had certainly grown steamy lately. But, he reminded himself, this trip was about business, and letting her revisit the Underworld. Nothing more.

Not that he'd argue if she invited him to sleep beside her in the bed.

He picked up the wool blanket and unfolded it. "Where'd the dreams take you last night?"

"Nothing new. Some memories I'd already seen before, from when Persephone was younger. The cold must still be messing with me."

"You seem better today, though."

"I am. No more plague." She smiled.

"Good. Ready to cross international boundaries?"

"Ready." She scooted close and kissed him.

He savored the taste and texture of her lips for a minute before pulling back. "Here. It'll be cold." He swooped the blanket around her. In tugging it down over her shoulder, he accidentally swiped her breast. They exchanged bashful smiles. "Sorry."

"It's okay." She picked up his hand and drew it straight back to her breast. "This is allowed."

He swallowed, transfixed, as he watched his fingers spread over her chest. She wore a thick ski coat, which rather disguised shapes, but he still could feel the softness and curves. A second later, he decided he maybe shouldn't be going for it so eagerly, and let his hand slide to her waist. Kissing her once more, he murmured, "Thank you. I'll keep that in mind."

They took off in the bus, Sophie nestled under Adrian's arm.

Clouds and rain splashed past, then a cool autumn sunshine took over on the plains.

"I don't offer that to every guy who's driving me somewhere nice," she mentioned. "Just in case you wondered."

He chuckled. "I didn't expect so. I wouldn't do it to every girl who offered, either."

"With you it's different. I feel like I've known you forever."

"You have. Or near enough."

She snuggled closer, and was quiet a few minutes. "Meant to tell you, I looked up Thanatos," she said. "Obviously the cult doesn't have a webpage. But the Internet says Thanatos was the god of death in Greek mythology. I thought people called Hades that."

"Sometimes. More accurately Hades is the god of the Underworld. Thanatos is the actual god, or spirit or something, who causes death. Not that there ever was an immortal named Thanatos."

"I was wondering," she said. "I couldn't remember one."

"No, the cult of death is all them. Those few crazy, bitter mortals."

They swept out above the Atlantic, its humid marine smell engulfing them. "I'll do anything I can to keep them from hurting you." She sounded scared, her voice small.

Adrian kissed the top of her head. "I'll do the same for you, love."

And sadness swamped him, for Persephone and Hades' enemies *had* destroyed them eventually, and she still had that memory to live through.

But not today. That was how people got through life, he supposed: by acknowledging death and telling it, "Not today."

THIS TIME WHEN Adrian brought Sophie into the fields of luminescent souls, he got to watch her beam and look about in joy and recognition. He let her take the lead. Atop one hill, she poked at the grass with her sneaker. "A tree was here. A willow. Guess that was a long time ago. But…ah ha. These rocks don't change much, do they. There was a good seat right here." She circled the pile of boulders and found the bench-like ledge.

Then she turned to face him. "Okay. Grandpop and your mom. Ready?"

"Yep." He hooked an arm around her waist and walked back through the fields with her. "Who first?"

"Your mom. That way in case I cry again when I see Grandpop, I won't have to meet her all puffy-eyed afterward."

Adrian's mother sat atop a tree-dotted hill in sight of the orchard. Seeing him approach with his arm around Sophie, his mother stood up and smiled, awaiting them.

His mother had long, wavy black hair and tan skin. She had died young enough that she still looked youthful as a soul, with her favorite flowery summer dress setting off her petite figure.

"That's her, in the purple dress?" Sophie said. "Oh, she's pretty. How'd you know where to find her?"

"She's usually on this hill. It's the highest one around. She always liked tramping when she was alive."

Sophie laughed. "She liked what, now?"

"Tramping. Walking about, outdoors?"

"Oh, you mean hiking."

He grinned and elbowed her. "Sure, tease the Kiwi."

They reached his mother, and she stretched out her arms with a smile, though of course he couldn't embrace her. "Ade, sweetie! You're back."

"Hi, Mum. Had someone to fetch. This is Sophie."

He had of course told her about Sophie by now, and she beamed to see the reincarnation of Persephone in person at last. "Welcome. It's so good to meet you."

"You too." Sophie shyly kept her hands folded before her. "I've never met anyone from Adrian's real life until now. Almost seemed like he's been—you know, supernatural forever."

"Oh, he's a real human, all right. I toilet trained him myself."

Adrian splayed his hand over his eyes. "*Mum*."

From there she did, at least, take them to more acceptable topics, surrounding his young life and the unusual transformation he'd recently undergone.

"I'm the luckiest soul here, hands down," she said, smug with maternal pride. "To have *my* son be the one who runs this place."

"It runs itself. I just hang out here. Because I'm weird."

But Sophie linked her arm into his and pressed her side against him, as if she were proud too.

His mum then asked Adrian if he'd seen his father lately.

"A few weeks back," said Adrian. "He's all right. Just lonely."

"You could bring him here for another visit," his mum said.

Sophie looked at him in surprise, and he realized he'd never told her about that. "It was a long time ago," he told Sophie. "Just after I'd eaten the orange." Then, to his mum, he answered, "I'll see if he wants to, but he seemed kind of disturbed about the first one. This still doesn't match his idea of heaven."

"You get him here," she declared. "I'll get the message through his thick head."

"I don't know, Mum. I don't want to be the cause of a...posthumous divorce." While he paused to think about whether that was the right term, Sophie and his mum looked aside and smiled at someone else. He turned to find the soul of Sophie's grandfather strolling up to join them.

"Heard you were here," he said, with eyes only for Sophie. "Hello, sweetheart."

Sophie, as it turned out, didn't cry this time. She smiled and made introductions, and launched into the complicated explanation of what she was doing here, including who she'd been in a past life.

Adrian let the two of them drift aside to talk in privacy while he and his mum chatted.

Finally he and Sophie said their goodbyes to their relatives for the time being, and walked down the hill. Sophie slid her arm around his waist while still in full view of Mum and Grandpop. Warming at the display, he draped his arm around her as well.

"I told Grandpop about Mom and Dad's companionate marriage thing," Sophie said. "He said he sort of already knew, or guessed. He tells me they'll be all right."

"Does that make you feel better?"

"I don't know. He might have just said that to relax me."

Adrian looked aside at her downcast profile. "There's only so much you can do, you know. Keep being their loving daughter. That's all you ever signed on for."

"It's still weird to me, is all." She glanced up at him, swaying closer. "Only because I can't imagine being in a marriage like that." She smiled. "We sure weren't, when we were married to each other in past lives."

"Mm." Nearing the river, he stopped to kiss her. "Indeed. Romantic chemistry much?"

"Whole big vats of it."

Just wait till you see, he thought. Indeed, remembering some of those memories made it hard to keep from tackling her on the grass here and now. *Please, Goddess, let her get to those soon.*

"So, out of curiosity…" She sounded sober now. "The orange. Where are you growing it?"

"Oh. Over here. Same spot as it used to be."

He handed her the flashlight and again let her lead the way, to see if she remembered. She did, or near enough. They walked through the orchard, emerging on the other side, almost to the upstream curve of the river. There she stopped and knelt by the tiny tree. It was barely knee high, and its leaves shone glossy in the beam of the flashlight. Only one fruit was left now, a small orange just ripening. Adrian, Niko, Sanjay, Freya—they had all plucked and eaten the first round of fruits, and now this orange was the last.

Sophie touched the orange lightly and quickly with her fingertips, as if it were hot, then pulled her hand away. "So that's it. Immortality."

"That's it. Saving it for you, when you're ready." His fingers and toes tingled. Would she eat it today?

She touched the three white blossoms on the tree. "More fruit soon, maybe."

"Yeah. Another couple of months or so."

"Good." She rose. "Then I have time."

He nodded, not sure whether to feel relieved or disappointed.

"So." She looked at him, clear-eyed and businesslike again. "How do we put out a call for souls who have dirt on our Thanatos peeps?"

He let go of her and waved his arm toward the fields of souls. "You know the language. Give it a try, Persephone."

CHAPTER THIRTY-SEVEN

"OKAY, SO, NOT A LOT," Sophie said as they returned to the river's raft a couple of hours later.

"Yeah." Adrian unwound the ropes. "Quentin and Wilkes and the others were weirdos in their youth and unpleasant later on, but nothing technically illegal. At least, not that anyone's thought of. God, I wish I had evidence linking them to Sanjay."

"I assume he keeps asking around on his own behalf, since he's always down here."

"He does, but so far he can't find proof we can use either." They settled onto their knees on the raft, with Kiri alongside them, and Adrian steered them across the river. "What now?"

Sophie sighed. "I'm hungry. Maybe food will cheer me up."

"Dinner in Greece, then?"

Her mood surged upward. In this lifetime, she'd never been to Europe at all, on the living side. Seizing his wrist, she said, "Ooh, yes, yes, yes."

THEY SWITCHED REALMS, entered a nearby town, and enjoyed a late dinner at a small restaurant. Neither of them knew modern Greek from any of their past lives, but Adrian had picked up enough from hanging around the region that he could communicate with their waitress, and both Adrian and Sophie knowing Ancient Greek—or something like it—did help a little.

Their table was outdoors on a deck, under a string of lights cased in white paper globes. The sea shimmered and whispered at the edge of town. A street musician played an accordion somewhere nearby. Sophie drank it all in, mesmerized. Meanwhile, Adrian gazed at her in adoration: the shine of the globe lights in her eyes, the way she wrapped her pita around the olives and feta to form a little package to bite into, how she teased him for taking apart his own food into its component pieces before eating it, the silken shadows of her neck and cleavage.

"Think they'd be honored to know they've got Hades and Persephone in their restaurant?" she asked after the waitress removed their plates. "Or scared?"

"Possibly neither. Greece has gone almost totally Christian—Greek Orthodox, you know. They don't care about us old-school types anymore."

"Oh, I don't know. I bet they still consider us family." She smiled out at the sea. "It feels familiar to me, to be here. The way that wind smells...mmm."

Upon returning to the Underworld, Sophie yawned and leaned against him. "I know it couldn't be that late in my own time zone, but I'm super sleepy. Must be the ouzo."

"At least it does something to you. I think I'd have to inject pure grain alcohol into my veins to feel anything nowadays, and even then it'd only last a few minutes."

"But you and the other immortals were always drinking wine, back in the day."

He shrugged. "It was the thing to drink at the time. If you could afford it."

"Which of course you could." She yawned again. "Okay if I take a nap?"

"Sure. I'll make up the bed for you."

In the bedchamber, in the light of a fluorescent camping lantern, he unzipped the duffel bag in which he kept sheets and blankets, and spread them over the mattress.

Sophie looked up at the gauzy black canopy he'd draped atop the four posts. "You had a canopy in the old days, too. Different material. And white back then."

"Yeah. Keeps pebbles and things from landing on you. And the shop did have white, but I figured black would look better down here. In the old days, black cloth was practically impossible to get, otherwise I'd probably have used it."

"Pink might be nice," Sophie mused. When Adrian shot a glance at her, she grinned. "Totally kidding."

He exhaled in relief, placing a hand over his heart. "Thank God."

She sat on the mattress and toed off her shoes. "Goddess," she corrected through a yawn.

"Indeed." He shook open a comforter and settled it over her legs.

She pulled it over herself, lying back on the pillow. "You going to sleep too?"

"Not yet. I'll read a while."

He sat beside her with the lantern, the extra pillow stuffed behind his back, and opened a novel. Within minutes, Sophie was asleep, breathing steadily. He brushed his fingers against her warm hair, as lightly as possible. In the old tongue they used to speak, he whispered, "Sweetest of dreams, darling."

THE MORNING AFTER feeding Kerberos the blue-colored orange, Hades awoke to the dog planting his front paws upon his chest and licking his face. Hades grunted, pushed him aside, and sat up. "So you're feeling better."

He squinted at Kerberos in the dim light of the two ghost dogs he had leashed to a metal ring on the wall. In the perpetual darkness of the cave, they served not only as company for Kerberos, but as night lighting. They were also cleaner and more convenient than oil lamps or flames in the fireplace. (His bedchamber did have a hearth, with a narrow but sufficient vent up to the outdoor air.)

Standing on the goatskin mattress with tail wagging, Kerberos gazed at Hades, panting, looking very much like he was grinning.

Hades examined the dog's neck, but couldn't even find the

wound. The fur grew smooth all around his throat, and the skin looked healthy when Hades pushed aside the tan hairs to search through them. "Interesting. Let's remember that blue orange. Looks like a keeper."

As Kerberos ran around beside him the rest of the day, Hades noticed the dog was moving faster than ever, and no longer limped. In addition, the gray hairs that had sprinkled his muzzle when Hades found him were now replaced by dark brown ones. Could that little orange tree restore youth as well as health? Excited, he turned and began striding toward the cave's entrance, intending to find Persephone and tell her. But upon remembering she was planning to marry Adonis in a few days' time, he stopped and remained in the Underworld. The news could wait a while. Best to see how Kerberos fared, and perhaps find willing test subjects another time.

Later, in his bedchamber, he picked up the half-peeled fruit from where he had left it wrapped in a cloth, and ate another slice himself. Cure-all though it may have been, it did nothing, as far as he could tell, to ease an aching heart.

An earthquake struck on the morning of the spring equinox. The shaking and rumbling awakened him. Clumps of dirt and rock from the cave's ceiling fell and clattered on the floor. Kerberos leaped barking onto the bed. Hades latched his arm around the dog and scrambled backward with him until they met the wall, where they waited, breathing fast, as the earth thundered and jolted around them. Then, finally, the quake died away.

With Kerberos beside him, Hades seized the willow leashes of the ghost dogs to light his way, and rushed out of the bedchamber. He paused a moment to look across the river and make sure the souls in the fields were all right. They were. They apparently couldn't have cared less about trivialities like earthquakes. That accomplished, he commanded Kerberos to stay in the Underworld, then ran to his chariot and soared out into the sunlight.

He had to know if Persephone was safe. That was his central burning thought as he sped the horses toward her village. Damn his pride and idiocy. Hermes was right: Hades and Persephone only had a limited number of years they could be together before age took her away, and Hades wanted her with him for as many of those years as she could spare. If she was still alive, not killed beneath a collapsed stone roof or chimney, he would tell her he loved her, even if she turned him down. Silence on the matter was no longer an option.

And if she was in fact dead? Fear and grief gripped his throat.

Then he'd still tell her. In the Underworld, where her soul would be. She could be there now. Perhaps she would even consent to stay there and keep him company a while before being reborn…

He landed near the site of Demeter and Persephone's house and switched realms. Their house stood intact, a scattered pile of firewood being the only sign of the earthquake. But it was silent, no one inside. Glancing at the sun, he found the morning farther advanced than he had realized. The earth rumbled again, gently, sending a quiet aftershock across the fields. He ran faster to the village, where he was grateful to note minimal damage and injuries. Catching the attention of an old woman walking by, he inquired after the lovely local goddess and her daughter.

"They're off to the festival, like all the young folk," she told him with a salacious chuckle. "Saw them heading out after the quake, looking fine indeed."

He nearly melted with relief. He thanked her, tugging a ruby off his cloak's hem and placing it in her palm, then dashed off again. He wheeled the horses back toward the Underworld.

He'd still tell Persephone he loved her. Absolutely, no question. But this was the spring equinox. The least he could do was bathe and put on fresh clothes first. An armful of her favorite flowers from the Underworld wouldn't hurt, either.

PERSEPHONE WAS FRANTIC. She moved across the sunny meadow as fast as her limp allowed, her hair and gown adorned with flowers, her hands picking blossoms from the grass and thrusting them into her basket. On her red cloak she could smell the incense from the morning's opening ceremony, after which the priestess—with the special sanction of Aphrodite, beside her—had set the youths free. The day was meant to be dedicated to people chasing each other, letting themselves get caught by those they liked, securing marriage vows, or just fooling around together. A bonfire and feast would follow tonight in the clearing near the village, with amorous activity continuing out in the dark forests and fields. It was the most felicitous and raucous celebration of the year, and this was the first time Persephone had chosen to participate. But she couldn't bend her mind to any feeling except panic.

She had split off from the group and angled across this meadow in the hopes of finding Hermes or Aphrodite or some other immortal. She needed someone to take her to the Underworld to make sure Hades was all right. If the earthquake had caved in the tunnels, and the whole hill of rock had fallen upon him—good Goddess, even an immortal couldn't move that mass. He could be pinned there in agony, and who knew how long before anyone could get him out?

She hadn't dared even mention Hades to Demeter, let alone ask her to go there. Her mother had checked the house for damage, declared it sound, and shooed Persephone off to the festival to enjoy herself. Meanwhile, Demeter set off to visit the nearby villages to see if anyone needed a broken bone set or a wall re-erected.

Persephone suspected herself of overreacting. Earthquakes carried a strong terror for her, given her childhood injuries. But the Underworld surely was protected by its magic and could never be damaged, not even by a big earthquake, which this had not been, compared to the one from her childhood. Even so, she would not rest easy until she knew he was safe.

No. She couldn't rest then either. It was time to be honest. What the rumbling of the ground this morning had told her was plain: her greatest fear was losing Hades. If Adonis were killed, she would be sad, but not agonized like this. She didn't love Adonis. She loved Hades, and one way or another, she would tell him.

Her peace with Demeter, the comfort of aging with one's mate, the possibility of bearing her own children—she was willing to throw all that away for the Underworld and its quiet king. Goddess forgive her.

She reached the edge of the meadow, where a forest of oaks and olives took over. A red violet caught her eye, already plucked and lying across the strands of grass. She picked it up and examined it, then brought it to her nose. The Underworld was the only place she'd ever seen such a flower. Nearby she spotted another one, lying plucked like the first. She gathered that too, moving closer to the trunk of a large oak. At its base lay a showy purple narcissus. She stooped and picked it up. She glanced around in confusion; then, with a sudden hopeful suspicion, she looked up into the tree.

Hades, seated high above her on a branch, grinned shyly and waved. In his hand he held a bouquet of Underworld flowers. He leaped out of the tree and landed in front of her—a fall that would have broken the ankle of a mortal man, but which he performed with catlike strength and grace.

"Hello," he said. "I climbed the tree to look around, and when I saw you coming, I thought I'd lure you in with these."

She laughed and took the bouquet as he offered it to her. "Thank you—oh, I'm so glad to see you." Heedless of the flowers, she threw herself forward and hugged him. "The earthquake—I thought—if you'd been crushed under the mountain or something—never mind, it's stupid. Of course the Underworld wouldn't cave in, and you're immortal, but I was worried."

He held her, stroking her braided hair. "You were worried? Not half as worried as me. I flew straight to your house, but you were already gone and the neighbors assured me you were all right. So I came here."

He had rushed all the way to her house to check on her? His cloak felt clean and fresh against her cheek, and the narcissus tucked into his gold crown smelled delicious. Was he spruced up for the equinox festival? For…her? She drew back to look at him, then lowered her gaze, arranging the flowers in her basket. "So you do care a bit after all?"

His face grew grave. "What did your mother tell you? I have to know."

Her cheeks warmed with a blush, but determination carried her forward. "She said you knew I loved you, and that you were sorry but you weren't interested. And that's all right. But I want you to know, I—"

Hades' angry growl cut her off. Planting hands on his hips, he scowled across the field. "Hermes was right. Gods, I'm an idiot." He looked at her. "You do know she told me the same thing in reverse—that *you* weren't interested, and wanted to stay away from *me*."

Persephone stared at him. It made perfect sense. She had suspected it without wanting to believe it, but now... "*Damn* her!" Persephone threw down her basket. Flowers spilled across the ground. She stormed back and forth. "How could she?"

"I do see her point. There are dangers for you..."

"Damn the danger, and damn you too if you think I'm that cowardly! I've thought through all the problems, and found ways around most of them, and I'm willing to ignore the rest." She stopped in front of him. "So forget those. Tell me the truth. Did you want me to go away?"

"Never," he said softly.

Her heart pounded. "I didn't want to leave you. Mother was right, I loved you—I still do. I've tried to love Adonis, but I can't— I don't—"

She was saved from having to explain further by Hades pulling her forward and kissing her. She twined her arms around him, and they staggered a few steps to the tree. Hades leaned back on it, lifting her off the ground. Her mind was ablaze; her body suddenly felt light and free of pains. They kissed each other's mouths, necks, shoulders, until the kisses smoothed away all the turmoil caused by words and wasted time.

Finally he let her slide down until her feet met the ground. "I love you," he said at last, his voice quiet and rough. "And if you marry Adonis or anyone else, they'll start calling me the god of insane jealousy, as well as the god of the dead."

"We must make sure that doesn't happen." She slid a fingertip down his nose and chin and chest. "Oh, dear, Mother will think I'm with Adonis today. Too bad."

His eyes took on a naughty sparkle. "Poor boy. Where will he be, then? Nursing his broken heart?"

"His heart won't break over me. We were classmates, that's all. I'm sure he'll be with Aphrodite if he needs any consoling. Or any of the hundred other girls who have their eye on him."

Hades stroked her bare shoulder where her cloak had fallen back, and touched the crown of flowers in her hair. "Then why did you make yourself look so beautiful, and come to this festival?"

She flicked her fingernail against his gold crown. "Well, why did *you*?"

Catching her around the waist, he drew her close again. He kissed her ear and neck in a way that sent heat rushing through her. "I was going to steal you away if I had to. Don't you know how you've tortured me? Being so brilliant and gorgeous, living alongside me, then leaving me...taunting me with lessons on seduction with other men..."

Persephone took hold of his hips and pulled herself tight against them. "I didn't want him. It was you I thought of, during all of it." She kissed his mouth, their tongues meeting for a moment. "I only wanted to learn it for you. I thought you were beautiful when I was sixteen and saw you at Aphrodite's."

"Two years ago today," he murmured. "I've wanted you from that same moment. Oh, how we've wasted our time."

Abandoning the task of bringing her flowers back to the village to help decorate for the festival, Persephone left the overturned basket on the ground and moved deeper into the forest with Hades.

"Oaks," he noted, glancing at the trees. "Good. Won't be easy for the others to track us."

The sun broke through the thin white layer of clouds and warmed the air. Persephone and Hades removed their cloaks and spread them on the ground as a blanket. There they lay, kissing and touching, speaking throughout, enraptured with the luxury of being in total honesty with each other at last.

They untied their belts and flung them out of the way, and unpinned and pulled aside each other's clothes to give their hands more room to explore. She kicked off her sandals to run her bare feet up and down his legs. So long she had wanted this, and it lived up to every hope. Details she couldn't have foreseen fused fantasy with reality, making the experience so sweet that tears pulsed behind her eyes at some moments. At other times her emotion overflowed into words of giggling nonsense.

His lips were softer and his beard rougher than she had imagined. He laughed and teased more than you might expect from the god of the Underworld. His mouth tasted delicious, like spring water drunk from a wooden cup. Though his immortal muscles caged the strength of a warhorse, his skin felt nearly as silken as her own, especially in intimate places. Any shyness she retained about being younger and less experienced was swept away by his obvious desire and appreciation, along with his wish to please her—at which he was quite skilled.

She arched up against his fingers at one particularly adroit stroke. "Mmm…you know, I do have those seeds with me." She found the cloth pouch on the string around her neck, and swung it before him. "So really, whenever you're ready…"

After a reluctant pause, he shook his head. "I won't take chances with your life."

"But it *works*. Aphrodite promises. Come on, she knows these things."

"Then maybe someday when I'm braver. But today I want to *enjoy* you, not endanger you."

This only made her feel young and fragile again. She let the pouch drop onto her shoulder, turning her face aside. "I want to be able to give you what *she* can, at least."

Hades hugged her close. "You already give me what no one else can: the company of the woman I love. I'd rather do nothing but lie here with you than do the most debauched things with Aphrodite."

Appeased, she wriggled against him. "Well, you'd better do more than just lie here."

He rolled her onto her back, his comfortable weight landing on top of her. "Don't worry. I'm going to make very good use of you." He paused, looking down at her throat, and untangled the pouch's string from the leather cord of her violet necklace. "Is this the Underworld amethyst you chose when you were little?"

"Yes. I've worn it every day since. That's how much I like you and your world."

He let go of the necklace and settled down onto her. "Ah, my darling. We'll make you a crown, as you deserve, with all the precious stones that can fit upon it."

"Not strictly necessary, but tempting." She latched a bare leg around him, and they went on kissing. He had pulled his tunic up entirely and draped it backward over his shoulder, and now only a few folds of her robes remained between them. She unfastened the pins holding them in place and slid the fabric away. They both sighed in pleasure at the feel of their skin touching all the way from head to legs. After enjoying it a moment, he slid down to her side again so he could resume caressing her. She repaid the favor.

"Oh well. You're supposed to get deflowered at this festival," she murmured, "but this is perfectly acceptable."

He glanced down with a lifted eyebrow at what his fingers were engaged in. "I have to say, you're looking fairly well deflowered from this angle."

She laughed. "Feeling it, too."

Her strokes brought fast breaths from him now. "This will do for me if it will for you," he said. "Will it fulfill your maidenly spring-equinox fantasies?"

"Quite. As long as we can do it again later, with variations."

"Agreed." He bent to kiss her throat, moving his hands with more determination.

Footsteps crashed through the leaves. Laughter floated toward them. Another couple was approaching, one lover chasing the other into the forest. This was still the living world, after all.

At that moment the earth rumbled again—a more violent

shock that made the trees sway and threw the young couple to the ground. The earth jolted and cracked open under Hades and Persephone, and she fell into the chasm.

"Hades!" Persephone screamed, scrambling for a foothold in the crumbling dirt. He reached down and caught her arm, his fingers digging into her flesh as he pulled her back up.

She caught one last glimpse of the young couple, who watched them from their startled crouch on the ground, before a stronger tremor knocked Hades off balance too, and he fell into the crack alongside her. He wrapped her in his arms and switched them to the spirit realm even before they rolled to a stop at the bottom of the trench.

Wild, huge trees crawling with vines and shrieking with birds took the place of the living-world forest. The aftershock died away, and the earth went still.

Hades pulled Persephone out of the ragged rip in the ground, and they collapsed naked at the base of a tree, laughing, in each other's arms.

"We're having a most exciting day," he remarked.

"Very." She trailed her fingers up his chest. "Shall we finish this in the Underworld?"

"Let's." And, as she had left her sandals behind in the other realm, he picked her up and carried her across the twigs and rocks to his chariot.

Demeter was going to be furious. Persephone's life was taking a sharp turn and would never resemble the ordinary again. She might gain worshippers and enemies. She knew all that, but, winding her arms around Hades' neck as he held her, she chose him gladly and regretted nothing.

CHAPTER THIRTY-EIGHT

ADRIAN BORROWED THE LOOSE HALF of the blanket to keep his legs warm, and kept reading. Sophie had been asleep about an hour, and Adrian was considering lying down to nap too.

She whimpered. She must have been dreaming—her eyes were still closed. But when she twitched and tensed, and whimpered again with brow furrowed, he closed his book. She could be getting a later or earlier scene than she wanted, and there was no shortage of upsetting memories she might be dreaming of.

"Sophie." He laid his hand on her shoulder. "Soph. It's okay."

She pulled in a breath, and her eyes opened. Regarding him hazily, she reached up and slid her hand along his neck.

"Bad dream?"

"No." She pulled him down, rolling to face him. He lay alongside her and hugged her. "Good dream." She kissed his neck, and Adrian realized with lovely shock that she was twisting rhythmically against him.

He sank into the mattress, nuzzling her ear. "Spring equinox festival, by any chance?"

"Oh, yes."

"Finally." Suddenly quite warm, he pushed the blanket down with his elbow, exposing Sophie's throat and kissing it. "Good dream indeed." His mouth traveled along her collarbone.

"I didn't get to finish it, but now I'm remembering the rest of it. Mmm."

Yes, Adrian really didn't need this blanket anymore. He was

toasty warm all over. Blazing hot even, some places. "I woke you up in the middle of that? Sorry."

Sophie hooked her leg over his. "Then you better finish what you started."

Adrian gave in.

He couldn't hurt her, he reasoned, by kissing and embracing her in bed. Nor by letting his hands wander like they had in the bus this morning. Maybe she hadn't specifically given him permission to slide his hands under her shirt and bra this way, but she seemed not to mind. On his part, he didn't mind her pushing up his sweatshirt and T-shirt to stroke his skin. Or her unbuttoning his jeans to give her hand more room. And he really, really didn't mind her wriggling out of her own jeans to let him explore too.

Finally he forced himself to stop her. He pulled her hands into neutral territory between their chests, and closed his own around them. "In that memory I did refuse to do a certain act," he said. "Which I'd still refuse. And I'm sure a health-conscious modern woman like you would never, um, let a substance into her body that might kill her."

"No," she assured.

"So then…"

Her full lips curved into a smile. "One of those workarounds?"

"Good plan."

It had to unleash some invisible magic, he thought; Hades and Persephone, joining together again within these black and holy stone walls, for the first time in millennia. As they indulged in enjoying one another, how could they not be reactivating some power within the Earth itself? Surely they were at least bringing autumn storm clouds rolling and thundering over the Mediterranean.

But probably every boy felt that way when finally in bed caressing the girl he loved.

WITH JACOB SHE'D been so much more self-conscious. She'd been reluctant to let him see her naked at all. Sophie liked her own body, knew it to be healthy and attractive enough; but even so, unveiling it for the critique of a teenage boy daunted her. When Jacob wheedled her into allowing him a look, then professed himself totally wild about her, her relief and gratitude were enough to make her love him for the short term.

But with Adrian it was a different world altogether. Clothes seemed unnecessary once the desire overtook her. Even afterward, lying naked with him felt natural, like something long awaited and finally fulfilled.

Likely it was the memories—they'd known each other's bodies as lovers in so many lives, and so many circumstances, youth through old age. But it surely had something to do with this life too, with the endearing knowledge that not long ago Adrian had been stuck in a less-than-satisfying body himself.

"So until you ate the immortality fruit, you couldn't do this kind of thing?" Her head rested on his shoulder, their arms and legs cozily interlaced.

"Couldn't feel a thing below the waist. I could've tried pleasing someone else, and wouldn't have minded giving it a go. But I never had the chance."

"Hm." She brushed her cheek back and forth on his collarbone.

"Don't feel sorry for me. I got cured. A lot of people never do. And even before that, once I ate the pomegranate, I did have the memories, the dreams. In the dreams I could *almost* feel everything. It made me happy." He kissed her head. "So you see, I was grateful to you before you knew I existed."

"It wasn't *only* me you could be grateful to. Other people in the past have, ahem, helped you out."

"True, but you've always been my favorite." His embrace tightened, and his voice became both bashful and suggestive. "I've been over and over those memories. Had to be sure I'd know how to make you happy. Hope it worked?"

"Oh, yes. You did a very good job studying your, um, technique." She giggled, as did Adrian a second later.

He sighed in contentment, the exhalation washing across her cheek, warm and intimate. "I can't believe we're finally here again, like this." He switched into their ancient tongue, and repeated Hades' words: "The company of the woman I love."

Without a qualm, Sophie answered in the same language, "I love you."

He lifted himself to his elbows to look in her eyes, his face tinted blue by the camping lantern. "I love you, too," he said in English.

"I know. You said so."

"Well, I didn't *exactly* say so. Wanted to make sure you knew."

She rolled her eyes, and hugged him so he tumbled down across her chest. "So…is this unfair of me, when I haven't even decided about joining you?"

"Unfair? No." He shifted over, letting her breathe more easily, while keeping his body fitted snug against her side. "Of course I'd want you to think about it a while, and I do want to be…as close to you as possible while you think about it."

"Because that way you can influence my choice?"

"I admit there's a touch of that." He kissed her shoulder. "But I just want to *be* with you. Whenever I can."

"Sounds wonderful." While she snuggled into his arms again, she allowed herself a moment of girlish exultation: she and her new boyfriend were crazily in love, and he was the Greek god of the Underworld, complete with magic and everything. And she was his rightful queen, and could become immortal herself as soon as she was ready. No, it could *not* get much more romantic than that.

For the rest of the weekend they lingered and slept in the bedchamber, explored the Underworld, and visited beaches in living-world Greece. Adrian also took her to the site of the house where she and Demeter used to live, though naturally not a stone of the house itself remained. Now a modern village stood there, small cars puttering down the bumpy streets by the river.

She'd been able to direct him here herself, in the bus. She remembered the way, and knew the house had been here, but the living world had utterly changed since then.

As they walked a path overlooking the river, Kiri padded beside them, sniffing bushes. Sophie watched her. "So she *must* have been Kerberos, right?"

Adrian crouched beside the dog, and received a lick on the face. "I wish she could tell us. But I have to think she was."

Eventually the real world intruded again, and Sophie had to return to campus—woefully behind on homework, but incandescently in love.

Adrian loitered a few minutes behind the dorm with her, holding her and giving one "last" kiss after another. Promising to meet again no later than tomorrow, they finally parted.

Sophie knew their location wasn't exactly invisible to outside eyes; there were windows and paths within sight. But she hadn't realized she'd been spotted by any of her acquaintances until Melissa asked, back in the dorm room, "So who's the guy you were kissing?"

To buy time, Sophie chuckled, pretending to read her texts. "Oh, you saw that? When?"

"Just now, behind the dorm. I was walking back from dinner."

"His name's David." Sophie had thought up her cover story already in case it was needed. Which apparently it was. "He's the friend I stayed with, the night the crazy woman broke in. He's a geography major."

"And now you two are a thing?" As usual, Melissa sounded about half a shade up from utterly bored.

"Yeah. I guess we are. We weren't before, but it sort of happened."

"Good. You look happy. Both of you." Melissa nodded, as if having solved a sudoku puzzle, then moved to her desk to wake up her computer.

Sophie spread out her latest chemistry worksheet and gazed at it, but her mind drifted all over the globe, and the past and future.

At what point would she tell her family about "David"? How would she introduce him, bring him into the daily reality of their farmhouse back in Washington, without incurring risk to Adrian and herself? How could she *not* introduce him without making her family suspicious? Could she even tell Tabitha? She was itching to fill in her best friend about the fabulous new man in her life, but how much could she safely reveal?

In short, how long could a mortal girl go on dating a Greek god before serious trouble intervened?

Trouble, it seemed, waited all of three days. Wednesday evening found Sophie occupied in the same fashion as the previous few nights: tangled in a cozy and exciting roll in the blankets with Adrian, both of them missing most of their clothing. The October wind smacked twigs against the exterior of the Airstream, and occasionally Kiri barked calmly from outside to remind them she was still hanging around.

Adrian lifted his mouth from Sophie's to call, "Kiri, go run. It's okay."

"Poor dog," Sophie said.

"Eh, she's having fun. Though not as much fun as me." Grinning, he dived back into their tangle. His tongue slid along her teeth, then her neck, breasts, belly…

His cell phone rang from the pile of clothes on the floor. With a groan, he grabbed it, glanced at the caller's name, and answered. "Yes, Niko?"

Lying beside Adrian, Sophie could hear Niko's voice, thinned and transmuted through the cell. "So I'm near you, but in the regular world, and the two of you are pretty close together, feels like. *This* time are you getting each other off?"

"Do. Not. Disturb," Adrian warned, spreading his hand possessively over Sophie's hips. He settled down on his elbow, phone between their heads, allowing her to listen in.

"Oo-ooh." Niko's answer was a lascivious sound of appreciation, dropping from high pitch to low. "Well done, Ade. Fine, I won't show up, even though you *said* I could watch. But listen, did you get my email a few minutes ago?"

"No, I've been *busy*."

"Haven't you, though. Well, I thought you might be interested to know what popped up in Wilkes' messages."

Sophie and Adrian exchanged a troubled glance. Nikolaos had swiped Bill Wilkes' email password along with the copy of his hard drive, and had shared the password with Adrian. But Adrian told her he'd checked it this morning and hadn't found anything new to worry about.

"What was it?" Adrian asked.

"From Quentin to Wilkes: 'The plan to fetch K.A. sounds good.' Let's assume that's Kiwi Ade. Then, 'We'll have one less to worry about if we can find our woman friend at her meeting.'"

Sophie pulled up her knees, cuddling close to Adrian. He shifted his arm to wrap it around her body in a comforting hold. "So you reckon they'll try to catch me when Sophie goes to meet me one of these days?"

"I'd count on that, yes."

"Did they say when?"

"No, but likely soon. They're probably looking for the next good opportunity. I'd also count on them having the kind of weapons required to take you out." While fear congealed into a ball in Sophie's stomach, Nikolaos went on, "I haven't been able to get in touch with Rhea yet."

"She feels far off. Maybe Greece or around there."

"Yes, but rather than leave to fetch her, I'm going to stay close for the next few days, just in case, and so's Freya. She's coming to stay with me."

"Okay." Adrian drew in his breath, and stroked Sophie's side in reassurance. "Cheers."

"*You* could always fetch Rhea, you know," said Niko. "No harm getting you out of the way and making them wait."

Adrian nudged Sophie's forehead, very gently, with his own. "No, I'd rather stay."

"Yes, I thought you would, you stubborn arse."

"But it'll be good to have Freya near."

"Good in lots of ways." The lechery had returned to Niko's tone. "You're not the only one who can hang out a 'Do not disturb' sign, laddie."

"Too much information, bro," Adrian said, but a smile lifted the corners of his lips.

"Keep me posted." Niko raised his voice. "Bye, Sophie."

"Bye, Niko," she answered.

Adrian hung up, and set the phone on the floor. He cradled Sophie in both arms. She lay listening to his steady heart, her body cold with dread.

"I might as well stay tonight," she murmured. "We're safe here."

"Sure."

But what about tomorrow? she thought. *Or the day after, or the week after that, or some day next year when they least expected it...?*

CHAPTER THIRTY-NINE

"I F IT SOUNDS LIKE THEY were hoping to attack today, or at least soon," Sophie said the next morning, "then I shouldn't meet you. I'll only go to classes, and normal public places like that, and stay in the dorm the rest of the time." She sat across from Adrian at the Airstream's table, coffee and cereal between them.

He looked sober and stressed. "I hate it, but yeah, a couple days apart might be wise. We have to assume you'll be followed. Watched. They'll be looking for any time you meet one of us and disappear. So you mustn't do that. Still—" He leaned forward, pointing at her in lawyerly fashion. "Do what a normal person would do if she saw someone stalking her. Call the police. Tell someone. Confront these people, make a scene. And if they lay hands on you, zap them and scream and all that. Although...I don't know, be careful. They'll probably be armed."

She nodded and turned her gaze away, watching a long-tailed bird swoop from one treetop to another. She did want to fight them, as bitterly and viciously as she could, but what if fighting got her hurt, or killed? What if she and Adrian dodged the assassins this time, but next week Thanatos sprang a new plan on them, catching Adrian off guard and killing him?

Then at least Niko or Rhea or someone could take her to the Underworld to see him. But to be unable to touch him, to know he was confined to that cave with his emotions diminished until he felt like becoming reincarnated, and began life again as an infant somewhere...no, that was unbearable.

She turned her face farther away, as if following the bird's flight, in order to hide the tears welling into her eyes. But the sharp catch in her next breath gave them away.

Adrian came around the table, sliding onto the bench seat beside her and enfolding her in his arms. "Don't worry. Please don't. Their plan's not very good, you know. Think of the strength we have on our side. How easily we can escape into this realm. I don't think Wilkes even knows we're reading his email. And Niko's going to shadow him and see what he can find out. If he sees Wilkes about to attack me or you, he'll stop him. He wouldn't let anything happen to us."

She steadied her voice with another deep breath. "Do they know about Niko?"

"We don't think so. Even if they suspect he exists, he's so good at aliases that they'd never recognize him, or know where to look for him."

"But how is shadowing them going to be enough?"

"Ideally, he'll get them caught with weapons they shouldn't have, or trespassing somewhere they shouldn't, and they'll get arrested. That's why it's important you call the police if they touch you or threaten you. Then you could get restraining orders, even if they don't get locked up. They'd never be able to explain to a judge why they were lurking around you and behaving like that."

Sophie sighed, resting in his embrace. "They'll find another way. Other assassins. They always do."

"Listen." Adrian swayed her back and forth in his arms. "We're the smart ones here. We're going to win, nearly every time. All they have on their side is surprise and violence—and they're not even very good at those. We've eaten the pomegranate. We have the knowledge of thousands of years."

"Great, so I know how to milk a goat. And make my own barley bread."

"Those could come in handy. You never know."

Finally she smiled, and he chuckled, kissing her on the ear.

"I'm going to miss you tonight, though," he said, voice husky. "Right now, that's what I hate them for the most."

She had a class in half an hour. It was time to leave. He walked her to the newest switchover spot, and kissed her on the lips, his hands framing her face. A tear spilled from her closed eyes, and he wiped it away with his thumb. "We always get back together," he told her. "Always."

She opened her eyes. The beauty and familiarity of his face pierced her heart. "I'd rather it was in this life, though." Her voice quivered.

"It will be. I'll be careful. So will you. Lie, lie, lie, just like the trickster says."

"Lie?" She cleared her throat. "In that case, I don't love you."

He smiled. "I don't love you either." He hugged her and switched realms. With a puff of cold air that smelled of grass and car exhaust, the living world hummed to life around them. They stood under a huge rhododendron, near the edge of campus.

Sophie straightened up with a deep breath. "Do not let them get you. Whatever happens."

"I promise. You stay safe too."

She nodded. "I promise."

Adrian glanced aside as a bicyclist zoomed past on the nearest street. "Better go." Looking miserable, he kissed her once more. "Bye."

"Bye." She kept her eyes locked on his until he vanished.

It'll be okay, she repeated as she walked to class, wrestling down the tears. *Knowledge of centuries. We always get back together. It'll be okay.*

Then why didn't it feel okay?

Adrian leaned against a tree in the spirit realm and closed his eyes, feeling her walk away from him, the strength of her signal fading from a vibrant nearness to a modest gleam.

He heard a rustle of trotting feet and a canine grumble. Opening his eyes, he held out his hand to let Kiri lick it. Appeased, she sat at his feet and gazed at him, as if asking what they should do now.

What he should do. Good question.

Simple. Stay in this realm, smash his mobile and get a new one Sophie didn't know about, and never approach her again. Not so much as a comment on her blog. Then she'd be safe. Thanatos would sniff around her a while, but they'd eventually realize she didn't know where he was, and they'd leave her alone.

But it was much too late for that. She'd eaten the pomegranate. It would be psychological torture to leave her now, when she could remember it all but was physically unable to break through into this realm.

Besides, he lacked the strength to stay away from her. Existence without her—especially now that she loved him and wanted to see him—wouldn't be worth enduring. Far better to risk his life to be with her whenever he could.

But risking hers as well?

Bloody hell, why wouldn't she just eat the orange and join him over here?

That was a sore point. A few days ago, after he and Sophie had returned from the Underworld, Niko had texted him, *Felt like you two went overseas. Orange cocktail for your girl, then?*

Adrian had gritted his teeth, and had been forced to answer, *Not yet. She's thinking about it a while.*

Pity, was all Niko had said, and then presumably returned to larking about the world, free as a jailbreaking bird.

Adrian knew he shouldn't resent her for hesitating. He couldn't expect Sophie to give up her entire earthly life just for him, a mere few weeks after they'd officially met. Besides, her eating the orange wouldn't solve all their problems. It would only swap one set of problems for another.

As he considered ripping a few limbs off the nearest tree in frustration, another familiar signal strengthened in his mind. Nikolaos was near—and so was Freya.

He turned in the direction the signals streamed from, and within seconds, a white spirit horse streaked down from the sky and skidded to a stop, plowing up a spray of wet grass and dirt. The two riders, sharing a saddle, slid off and called hello to him.

It wouldn't surprise anyone, Adrian thought, that Aphrodite had been reborn as a curvy Swedish blonde. Though Aphrodite's hair had been black and her skin olive-toned, somehow he recognized her easily as the same soul. The eyes gave her away—the same shape and expressiveness they'd displayed in every life. She now wore jeans and hiking boots and a blue parka instead of clingy robes and jewels, but she still moved like Aphrodite too, all swaying hips and graceful arms.

She strolled up to Adrian and kissed him on each cheek. She smelled like woodsy, smoky vanilla, a scent he supposed was meant to allure (and usually did, surely), but which only went as far as calming him a bit right now.

"Oh, my dear." Her Swedish accent rounded her words. With her warm fingers she smoothed back his hair. "It looks quite serious for you."

He felt a second's flash of alarm before glimpsing her smile and realizing she only meant he was quite seriously in love.

Niko, having tied up the horse, walked over too. "Told you. They're right back in the thick of it. Full marital bliss. Quick work, Adrian."

"It's not a conquest," he snapped. "It's—" Adrian exhaled and looked at their spirit horse. "Why are you here? I thought you were tracking Wilkes and Quentin."

"Still can't find Quentin," Niko said. "I have a hunch on some rental houses; we'll be checking those out. Wilkes is still in Salem, with nothing exciting showing up in his email yet. So we came to say hello. To the world's grouchiest person. Because that's such fun."

Adrian knew he ought to apologize, but stress and worry delayed the words. "Thanks for coming," he finally muttered. "I wish I were freer to move around over there, so I could just handle it myself."

"If it means protecting Sophie, I'm happy to help," Freya assured. "I can't wait to meet her. I do hope she joins us."

"Yeah, hasn't she shown any interest in that orange?" Niko asked.

Adrian folded his arms, staring past the horse. "She wanted to see it. But not eat it yet."

When they murmured in pity, or possibly disapproval, he burst out, "You two wouldn't get it. You got to live decades first, have a career, have kids if you wanted, see them grow up and leave the house. She's *eighteen*. If she joins us now, that's it for a normal life. No big events in the real world, no Christmas with the family, no watching her brother graduate high school, no going to her best friend's wedding, no sitting at her parents' bedside when they're dying. Because Thanatos would expect her to be at all those things, and they'd target her, and possibly blow up everyone she loves along with her. Can you blame her for wanting to think it over a bit before joining her weird brand-new boyfriend in his wasteland of ghosts and freakshow animals?"

Freya and Niko, receiving his diatribe, looked more sympathetic than offended.

Niko, in fact, looked impressed. "That may be the most I've ever heard you talk all at once, Adrian."

"Of course we get it, dear." Freya caught Adrian's hand and stroked it. "It's all right. The tree's still growing and making new flowers. She has time. Plenty of opportunities."

"And in the meantime," Niko said, "we'll catch the bastards. So let's do it." As he and Freya turned away, Niko punched Adrian on the shoulder. "You worry too much, mate. We'll fix this. You'll see."

Texts to and from Adrian kept Sophie going that day. As agreed upon beforehand, the messages were vague. When Sophie said *Boring day so far*, she knew Adrian would understand it meant she hadn't seen anyone following her. And when he answered, *Same here. Saw friends briefly*, she knew it meant he had checked in with Niko and Freya.

They said nothing of substance; no plans for next time they'd meet, not even, "I miss you and I hate this," though Sophie longed to say it.

She slogged through the day, barely able to focus in classes, itching with paranoia every time she was outside. Rain poured down during most of the hours, hindering her ability to spot anyone suspicious in the crowds. Coats, hats, and umbrellas disguised the populace. Once or twice she thought she saw someone who might be Wilkes, but wasn't sure.

As night fell, and she sat in her dorm room, depressed at the idea of sleeping alone, a text arrived. "Customer Disservice" was the sender. After a moment, she remembered it was Nikolaos. He hadn't texted her directly before, but Adrian had forwarded her the contact.

Look out your window, love, it said.

She leaped up and peered out through the rain and darkness. There, under a lamppost, stood a middle-aged guy under a bright red umbrella. He wore a business suit, his paunchy belly stretching out the jacket, and his hair was gray and thick and combed back. He waved at her. It took her a moment of squinting, then she recognized Niko under the disguise. Tonight, deprived of Greek gods and aching for them, she felt unusually delighted to see him.

Hi! I'll be right down, she answered.

"Just going to get some fresh air," she told Melissa, who was studying at her desk.

"It's pouring," Melissa said.

"Yep, I'll…bring an umbrella." Grabbing her purple umbrella, Sophie darted from the room, down the stairs, and out into the wet, breezy night.

Niko sauntered over, meeting her beneath the shelter of the dorm's overhang. He looked ridiculous to her eyes, but surely would pass as a parent or professor to any casual onlooker.

"Hi, Uncle Joe," she said, not that anyone was out there listening.

"Hello, niece." He switched to the ancient language that was Persephone's mother tongue. "I just wanted to assure you I haven't seen any indication that anyone's moving in on you tonight. Nor on Adrian, not that they could reach him. He's safe in his caravan, scowling and being prickly."

For the word "caravan," she noticed, he substituted English. That was a word the old language didn't have.

"Good," she answered, using the old Greek-ancestral tongue as well. "Is Wilkes following me? I thought maybe I saw him."

"No, he's been stuck at home all day. Strangest thing. His car battery—" (he also resorted to English for those words) "—disappeared completely."

Sophie grinned. "How very strange."

"Yes. Can't imagine how that happened. Then, while he was dealing with that, a fire started in his laundry room."

She covered her mouth. "Niko!"

"Uncle Joe," he corrected sternly. "No one was hurt, so calm down. Kept him busy all day, though. Not a chance to drive here and disturb anyone."

"But isn't he going to suspect someone's messing with him— that we know his plans?"

"He might, yes." Niko sighed. "Adrian's angry at me for that. We're supposed to be like the Allies in World War Two, I guess, and let attacks happen so no one knows we're decoding the Nazis' messages. I'm not a big fan of that approach. I'd have messed with him a lot more if left to my own devices. I had plans for a whole cage of ferrets..." Niko's voice trailed off as he looked away, forlorn at the rejection of his glorious ideas.

"What about Quentin?"

"Freya's been looking for her. Surveillance on one rental house after another in Corvallis. Haven't found her yet."

"I don't suppose you could set *her* house on fire when you find it." Such sentiments were unlike Sophie, but she couldn't help feeling them when it came to Quentin.

"I just might. Well, we'll check in tomorrow, darling. Can I bring Ade a kiss back for you?" Without awaiting permission, he leaned down and kissed her juicily on the cheek.

She wiped it off. "Yuck."

He nodded in commiseration. "Isn't that the kind of kiss uncles always give, though? Now, Freya's been complaining that today's surveillance was absolutely the most boring thing she's ever had to do, so I'd better go make it up to her with a much more exciting night."

"Again yuck," said Sophie, but she smiled.

With a wink, he walked off.

Despite Niko's assurance, she felt uneasy as she reentered the dorm. The divine liar, thief, and trickster evidently wasn't above arson. And he remained the only person she knew to have gotten hold of her phone. Was there any chance he was the exact person they should suspect? A chill crawled through her body.

Pausing on the landing in the stairwell, she dialed Adrian's number.

"What's up?" he answered, sounding tense.

She resorted to the language of the Underworld this time. "Are we sure we can trust Nikolaos?"

He took a moment to answer, then said, also in that language, "Of course. I mean—trust him, no, never entirely. He does what he wishes, even when it's reckless and wrong. Like that fire tonight—did you hear?"

"Yes. He just visited. Told me about it and took off."

"Well, he definitely is irritating, but he wouldn't sell us to the enemy."

"Are we sure?" she said. "I'm trying to think of anyone else who might have betrayed us, and there aren't many possibilities."

"What could they offer him that he doesn't already have? What could possibly make him work for their side? We know he's immortal. We know they hate immortals. There's no way. No."

"Then…" She slumped back against the wall. "If it was Jacob spying on my phone, which I guess is the likeliest, then I don't know what I'm supposed to do about it. He's in another city, and I already dumped him."

"Nothing. Tonight you don't have to do anything. Except do your homework and get some sleep."

"Sleep." She grunted a laugh, and switched the phone to the other ear. "I'm still avoiding the dreams. I know there's drama later—Demeter finding out, trouble with immortals and the rest of the world—and I don't want to go there yet. So when I do visit Persephone, I've just been replaying that one day. The spring equinox." She smiled fondly. "It's been good. Suppose I should move on, though."

"You're in control. Dream what you like."

"You're the only thing I want to dream of."

"You're the only thing I have dreamed of, for years."

The soft words washed over her, bringing love and loneliness at the same time. "I'll miss you tonight," she said, still in the Underworld tongue.

"You too, my love."

CHAPTER FORTY

WHEN SOPHIE CAME BACK TO the room, Melissa glanced up from reading something on her phone. "Not seeing David tonight?"

Lie, lie, lie. A good policy, in case dorm gossip was getting back to Thanatos.

Sophie shook her head, sliding her phone into her pocket. "I don't think it's working out. It's…too weird."

Melissa nodded, as if she totally knew the weirdness guys brought to your life. "A good night's sleep ought to help."

It might, Sophie thought, except her dreams lately took the form of an endless buffet of vivid, emotional scenes from real human lives. At the last moment, drifting off to sleep, her mind reached for Adrian. And perhaps because of Niko's mention of the Nazis, her dream settled upon the gentler moments between Grete and Karl. She let herself rest in those: coffee in the shop with pictures of trains on the walls, their laughing conversations, his shabby black coat and beautiful young eyes, the heat of his body when he stood close to her outside once, beneath the eaves during a rainstorm. The sadness, the love, the faint comforting hope that goodbye might not be forever.

THE NEXT DAY, Sophie got the call from Niko as she left her last class of the afternoon.

"Wilkes has left Salem," he said, in the old proto-Greek tongue. "I'm trying to follow him, but traffic's getting in the way."

"You're driving?" She did hear something like the low roar of engines behind his voice.

"Trying to, but everyone and their dog is getting on I-5. Rrrgh, I hate having to do this like a bloody mortal."

Dread made Sophie feel alert for the first time all day. "I'll watch for him. I'll be ready."

"Call us if he shows up."

"I will. Thanks, Niko." She hung up, and for a moment almost burst into tears of stress and exhaustion. Someone was coming, now, today, probably intending to hold her hostage and kill the love of her life.

But then she took a deep breath and held her head high. *Don't start crying. Start doing.*

Wise words. She and her friends could defeat this. They could.

She strode back to the dorm, glancing around for enemies, heart thumping. *Bring the battle*, she thought. *Let's do this.* Salem was less than an hour's drive from Corvallis. It would happen soon. They'd catch the assassins. They had to.

But an hour passed, and then two, and the battle hadn't arrived. Night fell. She had dinner at the cafeteria with Melissa, who ate little and stayed silent except to complain that her cramps were tying her insides into macramé knots.

During that half hour, Sophie's phone lit up with texts between Niko and Adrian (cc'ing Freya and Sophie), all in their best attempts at writing proto-ancient-Greek in English characters, which made it harder than usual to understand. But, Sophie figured, it also made a pretty good secret code.

Lost him on the road, Niko said. *Driving around Corvallis looking for him or his car.*

Damn it, Adrian said. *Couldn't he have switched cars?*

Yes, he could have, especially if he picked up a helper and some weapons. Maybe an SUV or van, to hide them better. But I don't know what he switched to, so it could be anything.

I'm coming to the living world to help look for him, said Adrian.

No you are not, said Niko. *You're the target and they know what you look like.*

Sophie put down her fork and tapped "reply." *Would you both shut up*, she wrote in her own version of English-lettered proto-Greek. *It's me they'll come after, so just stay near and wait for me to tell you when they show up.*

She's right, Freya weighed in. *They'll make a move on Sophie, and we'll be there, more of us than they expected.*

More of us to blow up at once, Adrian said.

And risk killing innocent students too? They wouldn't dare, said Freya.

But Sophie wasn't so convinced. Adrian's words stuck in her mind and destroyed what was left of her appetite.

Across the table, Melissa shoved her plate away with a sigh. "Everything is gross. Ready to go?"

Sophie tucked her phone into her pocket. "Yeah."

They dumped their trays at the bins, and walked out into the night. The wind blew spatters of cold rain at them. Wet leaves smacked down onto the pavement.

Melissa turned pained eyes up to Sophie. "Will you go with me to the drugstore? I need meds for these cramps."

Sophie deliberated. Walk the streets in vulnerability, tonight of all nights? Or was it better to go somewhere the opposition wasn't expecting her, and confuse them? Well, Adrian and the others could track her wherever she was, and perhaps outside was actually better, as they could reach her more quickly. "Sure," she told Melissa.

They turned their backs to the wind and headed toward the shops at the edge of campus. Sophie tapped a text to her immortal friends on the way: *Going to drugstore with roommate. Quick trip.* Having sent it, she put her phone away, closed her fingers around the stun gun in her coat pocket, and resumed glancing around for suspicious SUVs or vans.

They approached a lecture hall, its windows darkened, and Melissa veered toward it. "Let's cut through here."

"Wait. Why?" Sophie strode after her, not fond of how they

were heading into an especially dark region, between that lecture hall and the next, beneath tall trees.

"I thought I saw someone I knew." Melissa marched onward, shoulders stiff in her puffy gray coat, ponytail whipping in the wind.

"Melissa, I don't think this is safe." Sophie held the stun gun tighter, ready to yank it out and electrocute anyone who looked at her wrong. She followed Melissa beneath the shadows of the trees.

In the dark between the buildings, Melissa stopped abruptly. Sophie almost bumped into her.

"That's right," the man's voice said. "Stop right there. Hands up."

The gleam of the gun was what Sophie spotted first, advancing out of the darkness.

Suddenly her stun gun didn't seem so terribly useful. She slid it up her coat sleeve, out of sight as she drew her hands into view.

"Hands up. Don't move," a second voice said, another man.

She and Melissa both raised their hands slowly.

"Oh, God," Melissa breathed.

Now Sophie made out their forms, two men in ski masks and long dark coats, both armed. The stocky build of the shorter one, and the fact that some dude was pointing a gun at her at all on this particular night, made her pretty sure it was Wilkes. The other guy was tall and broad-shouldered, and he pointed a handgun of some kind at her too.

Terror engulfed her—insides turning to water, hands and feet going numb, tongue sticking to the top of her mouth, all of it. At the same time her mind snapped into high gear, thoughts whirring faster and clearer.

Had anyone ever pointed a gun at her before? Not this life. Maybe a couple of times in previous lives. Didn't matter right now. What she noticed was that even though she knew where she'd end up if she died, she still felt the fear of suffering a painful or lethal wound, and grief on behalf of her family and friends, who would be in an agony of mourning to lose her.

She either had to call Adrian and the others right now, or escape, maybe by fighting back. But with her hands up and two guns pointed at her, she could hardly do either; attempting to could get her shot.

Two guns, *both* aimed at her? Yes. Both men seemed more focused on Sophie than on Melissa, though Melissa obediently held still with hands raised too.

And Melissa had veered straight over here.

Anger gave Sophie the courage to speak again. "Told you this wasn't safe," Sophie said to Melissa. "Why'd you want to walk over here, I wonder?"

Melissa acknowledged her with a flicker of a glance in Sophie's direction, but didn't answer.

"No talking," said the one Sophie assumed was Wilkes. He stretched out a hand. "Give me your phone."

Sophie's fear dashed straight from herself to Adrian. "I... didn't bring it."

Wilkes beckoned to the other guy, who lunged forward and grabbed Sophie, hauling her around with her left arm bent painfully up behind her. His body felt armored and bumpy—under his coat he probably had an arsenal strapped to him. Grenades maybe, and who knew what else. He twisted her arm harder, and when she screamed, he knocked her in the side of the head with the grip of the gun, hard enough that pain reeled through her skull and colored lights flashed in her vision. "Quiet," he said, and she felt him yank the phone out of her back pocket. A second later, he frisked down her arms and legs, found the stun gun up her sleeve, and confiscated that too.

Crap.

"We heard you might have one of these," the tall guy said. "Cute."

He let go of Sophie, who dropped to her knees. Cold mud soaked through her jeans, and she hung her head, gasping, trying not to throw up from the nausea that the head blow had caused her.

Would they dare detonate a grenade here on campus? Sure,

she figured. Between two buildings empty for the night, with one guy holding Sophie hostage at a distance while the other blew up the immortals—they could probably do it without hurting anyone except their targets.

As soon as her head cleared, she vowed, she'd take the first chance she saw. Someone would walk by soon. It wasn't late at night yet. She'd scream her loudest, even if they stunned her or shot her for it. These bastards needed to get caught, and she still doubted they'd actually kill a mortal girl for their cause. They'd probably only use her stun gun against her, or shoot her in the leg or something—either of which would hurt like hell, but she'd endure it if it meant saving Adrian's life and throwing these guys in jail.

Besides, a wound was nothing a blue orange couldn't cure.

She kept her head down, surreptitiously watching the sidewalk across the lawn.

"David, was it?" said Wilkes above her, evidently looking at her phone. "Ah, lots of calls tonight. That must be the one."

Sophie didn't answer, and neither did anyone else, but he must have dialed the number, because soon she heard him say, "Adrian? We've got your girlfriend. Come alone unless you want her to get hurt." After a pause, he said, "South side of Burke Hall," and hung up. "Here's what's going to happen," he told Sophie. "I've got a grenade. He's going to strap it to himself. I detonate it by this button."

Sophie glanced slowly over her shoulder, just far enough to glimpse the dark shapes of the grenade and remote detonator clipped to his vest, under his coat. The gun, meanwhile, stayed pointed at her head. She turned her face forward again.

A detonator. Which worked on electrical signals of some kind, and therefore could, for all she knew, get triggered by a blast from a stun gun. Just as well that they'd taken it from her, and that she hadn't tried zapping him earlier.

Still…crap.

"Okay," she whispered.

"Gun stays aimed at you till it's all over. Another thing: it's fine with me if this goes off and kills us all. You, me, him, your roommate, whoever."

"No. Please. I'll help you do this if you let me live." *Lie, lie, lie.*

"Good girl."

Over my dead body will I help you, she added to herself—accepting that the phrase could become literally true tonight.

CHAPTER FORTY-ONE

ADRIAN TURNED AND SPRINTED AWAY from Sophie's location even before responding. He had to get a look at the situation from farther off before appearing right in the middle of it. Kiri yipped in alarm, and ran with him.

"Where?" he asked the man calling from Sophie's phone. Adrian could find her, of course, and was already quite close to her—he had been shadowing her all day, right next to her, one realm away. (*Fine, I'm a stalker, FINE.*) But if Thanatos didn't know he could track her, so much the better.

"South side of Burke Hall," said the voice.

"I'll come. Don't hurt her." Allowing the tremor of fear into his voice was easy. Genuine, in fact. He could likely defeat these thugs, especially with Niko and Freya's help, but Sophie could also get injured or killed in the struggle. And that was the absolute last outcome he wanted.

He disconnected the call and hit Niko's number.

"Yes?" Niko answered.

"Get here now, now, they've got Sophie, both of you, come *now*!"

"On our way." Niko hung up.

Adrian put his phone in his pocket and turned around. He stroked the dog's head. "Kiri, *stay*."

Kiri whined, but sat obediently, her gaze glued to him.

He sensed Sophie maybe twenty meters away. He didn't know

the campus map well enough to be sure where he'd end up when he switched over, but it was time to risk it. He switched realms.

Something slammed him sideways, knocking him onto the wet grass and leaving his shoulder throbbing. He glared up at the looming brick wall of the building. Rubbing his bruised arm, he climbed to his feet, glanced around, and deduced Sophie and the assassins were on the opposite side of the structure. As he crept around the corner in the shadows, he became aware of Niko and Freya approaching fast. Soon they burst into sight a few meters from him, sending misty rain gusting out around them.

They looked toward Adrian and paused. They wore college student disguises, jeans and parkas and sneakers, along with baseball caps and shaggy but realistic wigs.

"We go in first," Niko told him quietly.

Adrian nodded. Tricksters excelled at diversions. Even buying Adrian a few seconds of confusion would be valuable.

"Be careful," he said. Getting Niko or Freya killed wasn't what he wanted either.

Niko gave him a nod, and linked his arm into Freya's. "Darling," he invited, and they set off around the perimeter of the building.

Adrian trailed them, far enough back to stay hidden, close enough to hear and see. Reaching the corner of the building, in the shadow of a tree, he pressed his back to the wall, and peered around into the dark space between this building and the next. What he saw nearly made him bolt in and start snapping necks. Sophie drooped on the ground on her knees, head bowed, with Wilkes (or at least it was probably Wilkes) pointing a gun at her, in an image straight out of a prisoner-execution nightmare. Adrian clenched his jaw to keep from making a sound.

Nearby he spotted the second assassin, gripping a gun and using it to cover both Sophie and another girl, who stood frozen with her hands raised. She was probably Sophie's roommate, and equally deserving of being rescued. But all he could think of was how to grab Sophie and get her out of there.

At that moment Niko and Freya arrived, pretending to stumble upon the scene like innocent pedestrians.

Freya shrieked, very twenty-year-old-girl-ish. "Oh, my God! What's going on?"

"Holy crap," Niko rumbled, in dumb-young-dude tones. "Are you guys getting mugged?"

"Back off," the younger thug said. "Leave or someone gets hurt."

"Call 911!" Freya flailed her arms in a show of panic. "Oh, my God, I forgot my phone. Do you have one?" She was shouting the question at the roommate, it seemed, who furtively nodded but didn't move.

The younger assassin, in the long coat that probably hid all kinds of deadly explosives, raced toward Freya and Niko. "Shut it!"

But the pair darted apart, faster than your ordinary mortal, and vanished from sight.

The assassin whirled around, looking for them.

Freya reappeared beside Melissa. "Over here."

Niko, meanwhile, reappeared directly behind the assassin in the long coat, locked his arms around him, and they both vanished.

Wilkes pointed his gun at Freya instead, shouting, "She's one of them! They both are!" But of course, his accomplice was out of hearing now, tussling with Niko in the other realm.

Freya shoved Melissa and said, "Run."

Melissa bolted past Adrian, yanking out her phone on the way.

Wilkes turned, swiftly and expertly, and fired the gun at Freya. She fell with a cry. Adrian and Sophie both jolted in shock. Wilkes pointed the gun back down at Sophie, and called to Freya, "He made a big mistake doing it this way. You're all going to be dead."

Yeah. Adrian remembered that threat, in that voice, from a night he lay bleeding on the ground in a Wellington park.

He pulled in his breath. Time to act.

Adrian memorized Wilkes' location and the position of his arms as they pointed the gun down at Sophie. Then he switched realms and strode forward the requisite number of paces. Moving through the spirit world, he heard the snarls and grunts of Niko fighting the other assassin, and Kiri's frustrated barks from where she still sat, obeying her "stay" command. Adrian only had time to glance at all of them before reaching his target and slipping back into the living world.

Adrian appeared right behind Wilkes. He seized both of Wilkes' forearms and yanked backward, snapping his bones. Wilkes screamed and dropped the gun, which bounced off Sophie's elbow.

"No," Adrian clarified, "*you* made a big mistake."

Sophie shoved away the gun with her foot, leaped up, and kicked Wilkes so hard in the crotch that the force knocked Adrian back a step too.

Grunting and choking, Wilkes fell to his knees. Adrian pushed him onto his back and tore the ski mask off. As he suspected, it was indeed Wilkes—he recognized him from the online photos they'd found, even with Wilkes' face now contorted in pain.

Adrian was on the verge of a false-cheery *Good to see you again; meant to repay you for shooting me in February*, when Sophie shouted, "He has a grenade! Look out!"

Adrian looked down to see the round shape strapped to Wilkes' body beneath his coat, and the small black box on the other side that Wilkes was trying to grasp, even with his broken arms.

Adrian sucked in his breath, realizing it was a detonator. He seized Sophie and hauled her away in a giant leap, switching realms as they hit the wet ground. An explosion like a hellish orange firework burst into existence just before they leaped out of the living world, and he heard sirens for a brief second. Then they landed in the spirit realm, and a new sheet of flame and heat knocked him backward.

Shielding Sophie, both of them coughing, he stumbled away from the fire until they were at a safe distance. "Are you okay? Are you okay?" he asked her, realizing he was nearly shouting.

She nodded. They both stared at the flames engulfing a patch of forest. Kiri sprinted toward them from the side, and Adrian knelt and hugged her. "Thank goodness. Where's Niko, girl?"

Kiri whined, looking at the fire. A fresh wave of panic hit Adrian. Yeah, he could sense Niko—straight ahead, in the flames. Adrian scrambled forward. "Niko!"

No answer. A few seconds later, Freya's voice called the same. "Niko!"

Adrian and Sophie turned.

Freya was bent over in pain, her hand braced on a tree. Blood drenched her jeans; a bullet hole loomed black on her thigh. But she'd be all right. Sophie ran to her and got her arm beneath Freya's, letting her lean on Sophie. The two women gazed at each other a moment, with shaky smiles; a reunion between long-parted friends. But then Freya looked at the flames, and at Adrian, her face shifting to horror. "They detonated one of the grenades?" she said.

He nodded. "Kiri, stay," he said again, his voice uneven. Then he turned and dived into the fire.

The smoke choked him, and the grenade's chemical fire began devouring his clothing and searing his skin. But he stuck to his one reliable sense, the one pointing him toward Nikolaos, and rushed forward. He tripped over branches and rocks, and what he thought was a log but felt...fleshlike. He glanced down. Between ripples of fire and gusts of hot wind, he saw a blackened, bloody mess—what was left of the assassin. Squeezing his eyes shut against the horror and the heat, he plunged to his right, where he sensed Niko's soul.

What if it *was* only his soul? That was what you sensed, when you could track someone. Ordinarily souls departed straight for the Underworld, but Niko would know enough to stick around a few minutes and wait to tell his friends what had happened if he had died...

But then Adrian's feet crashed into someone's legs, and he fell, and his hands landed on hot flesh, and clothes that had been mostly burned away, and he knew he had Nikolaos, there in one piece, soul within body even if unconscious.

Adrian threw him over his shoulder, and darted out of the fire. He burst into the coolness of the forest and gasped a breath of air. He dropped to the ground to smother all the flames on both Niko and himself with armfuls of wet dirt.

Freya and Sophie limped over too, Freya wincing as she landed on her knees beside Niko.

The burning bushes sent bright orange light flickering across them, showing that only a few scraps of Niko's clothes remained, and all his hair had been burnt away. Wounds and burns studded his body, probably not only from the flames and the burning chemicals, but from the grenade's shrapnel.

Freya stroked his head, tears running down her cheeks. "Oh, my poor dear. You scared me. But you're going to be fine, you know."

Nikolaos drew in a rasping breath, and his eyelids fluttered, but he didn't regain consciousness yet.

Adrian sat back against a log, trembling. Sophie moved over next to him, embracing him, shaking even worse than he was. Kiri circled the group, then sat by Adrian and devoted herself to licking the burns on his arms and neck.

Sophie and Adrian sat hugging each other until Adrian recovered his composure, and looked at her. "We'd best get you back so you can give the police your report."

"Yet again," she sighed.

"Will you guys be all right?" Adrian asked Freya.

She nodded, cradling Niko's head on her lap.

"I'll be right back," Adrian promised. He helped Sophie to her feet. "Guess we better walk a good distance out of the way first. Who knows what Wilkes' grenade did to the area."

"So." Sophie took a long, shaky breath as they waded through the damp forest undergrowth. "It was Melissa."

"What was Melissa?"

"Spying on my texts. It must have been. She led me straight between those buildings tonight. They must have recruited her somehow."

Anger surged up in Adrian. "That explains how Quentin got in, then. Copy of the roommate's key."

"Yep."

They walked in bitter silence a few paces. "Bitch," Adrian finally said.

"*Stupid* bitch," Sophie agreed.

He glanced back at the dwindling fire, and stopped. "Here's probably good." She nestled up to him, and he embraced her and switched them into the living world.

They almost fell off a curb—they were standing right at the edge of the sidewalk, in a group of onlookers gaping at the grenade-fueled fire engulfing a tree between the buildings. In the confusion, no one noticed or remarked upon Sophie and Adrian's sudden appearance. The noise and flashing lights of fire engines, ambulances, and police cars surrounded them; hoses sprayed water and extinguishing foam upon the fire.

Adrian spotted Melissa, looking terrified, talking to a group of police officers. He nodded toward them, and told Sophie, "Suppose you better go. Say you ran off and just now crept back, or something."

"All right. I'll call you as soon as they let me go."

They paused to look in the direction of the fire. "Suppose that's the end of Wilkes, then," Adrian said.

Sophie shuddered. "Yeah."

"We'll be sure to visit him in the Underworld."

Sophie sent him a troubled glance, and he realized that not since her Persephone days had she seen Tartaros—the caves of punishment. He softened his gaze, and smoothed her disarrayed hair. "Don't worry about it. Go on."

Sophie nodded, straightened her shoulders, and walked toward the police.

Just before he slipped into the other realm, Adrian caught Melissa's eye. He was almost certain she was watching him as he disappeared.

CHAPTER FORTY-TWO

SOPHIE LEANED BACK ON THE crackling paper covering the hospital examination table, closing her eyes. When the police learned she'd been bashed on the head in addition to being awfully near a grenade detonation, they'd insisted on sending her to the emergency room.

After examining her skin, looking into her pupils, and asking a lot of questions, the medical team had decided there was nothing wrong with her aside from a few minor burns, a mean bump, and some soreness that would last a few days. She could leave as soon as she felt rested enough to do so. She was now waiting for Adrian so she could go to the Airstream and sleep. The dorm room was not an option, not anymore.

Her phone had been incinerated along with Bill Wilkes. So she had borrowed the hospital's land line to call home and tell her parents that someone tried to mug Melissa and her. *Yes, Dad, I did what he said and didn't endanger myself. No, Mom, he didn't get my credit cards; just my phone. Yes, Dad, he got killed. No, I don't know why he was carrying a grenade. Yes, guys, I'm fine. Really. You be careful too, all right?*

Only with great diplomacy did she manage to convince them not to come driving down here tonight like lunatics. Life would proceed normally, she assured them.

She'd wait till tomorrow or the next day to tell them she was moving out of that dorm room and finding a new place to stay.

She had given the police her report. Someone had tried to mug her and her roommate, she said. No, she had no idea who they were, except they were probably connected with the people who broke into her dorm room and also grabbed her recently. Yes, there'd been two guys, but one took off in pursuit of some other people who tried to step in and help, and he never came back. No, she didn't know who the people were, or where they'd gone. She'd never seen them before.

But perhaps, she told them, they ought to ask her roommate who the assailants were. Because it seemed like Melissa recognized them.

It would be terrible to be thrown in jail at Melissa's age. But that's what you asked for, Sophie reasoned, when you joined up with a murderous cult.

A middle-aged female nurse stepped in. "Your friend's here."

Sophie got up, picked up her mud-stained jacket (nice match for her mud-stained jeans and sneakers), and checked out at the E.R. desk.

Adrian, in blond-streaked wig, hipster glasses, and long black raincoat, leaned by the door in a secluded corner of the waiting room. Sophie walked to him and caught him up in a long hug.

"I've missed you," she said, then wrinkled her nose. "Though you smell like burned leaves."

"And that's *after* a shower." He sighed. "Missed you too. Huge amounts. Come on, let's go."

As they walked outside into a new rainstorm, a girl called, "Sophie!"

Melissa came running up, evidently from her parked car where she'd been waiting.

Sophie stared her down coldly.

"I need to talk to you," said Melissa.

"So you can report back whatever I say to the evil cult people? I don't think so." Sophie pulled on Adrian's arm, moving them forward a few steps.

Melissa leaped in front of them again. "I didn't tell them everything. They *are* evil. You're right."

"Aren't you supposed to be in jail right now?"

"I'm not in the cult. I told the police everything, and they're going to...see if charges need to be brought against me." Melissa's voice wavered in fright. "I'm not supposed to leave town until the investigation's done. But I swear, I didn't realize how far these people would go till they broke into the dorm room. I don't want anything more to do with them."

"Then tell them that, and call the police if they come near you again. But I'm moving out of the room, and I'm done with you." Sophie tried again to pass by, and Melissa seized her arm.

"I want in on the immortality thing."

Sophie and Adrian both paused, looking at her.

"I didn't tell the police about that," Melissa continued. "But I know about it from reading your texts, right? Plus I knew that very first day, when you disappeared into thin air with that other guy, something weird was going on. Something huge. So when that old woman came to me and said she wanted my help keeping an eye on you, I made her tell me why."

"The old woman told you an immortality story?" Sophie hoped they might still keep it secret—lie, play dumb, all that—and possibly Adrian agreed, since he hadn't said anything yet.

"Yes. So I started getting looks at your texts," Melissa said, "when you were in the shower or asleep or whatever. And the messages were about Hades and Persephone and another realm, and immortals, and it sounded like something you could join. So I want to join too."

"People pointing guns at you? Setting off bombs? Getting you killed?" Adrian finally spoke, not even trying to disguise his accent. "That's what you want in on?"

"If I could be immortal? Of course. Who would say no to that?"

Sophie stayed silent, largely in shame. She'd said no all these weeks, and look what danger it had put everyone in.

Adrian answered after a moment, "You'd be surprised. People like that old woman, they're really not keen on the idea."

"I don't care about them," said Melissa. "Listen, like I said, I didn't tell them everything. I wanted to know more about it— about you guys. I gave the cult a few messages so they'd tell me

things too, but I didn't give them much that would help them."
She looked at Sophie. "But she did get a copy of my key. She said
it was just to look at your stuff when neither of us was there—that
no one would be hurt. I didn't like doing it, but she was really
persuasive. Then she broke in, and I started getting scared and
didn't want to talk to them anymore. But they pressured me into
luring you out tonight. One last 'favor.' They were going to 'show'
me how dangerous Adrian was. I was going to turn them in as
soon as they did anything stupid, I swear. I wanted them off my
back. I didn't know they'd bring *guns*."

Sophie sighed, wiping rain off her forehead. "No, I have to
move out. This isn't something I can get past."

"But I want in on it! Please. I'm on your side, really. What I saw
tonight—" Melissa's desperate gaze latched onto Adrian. "The
way you guys can appear and disappear, how strong you are—I
know it's all real. Please, tell me how I can do it."

Adrian slipped his arm around Sophie. "You mistake me for
someone who's recruiting. Sorry. We need to get going."

They set off across the parking lot. Behind them Melissa called,
bitterly, "But you're recruiting Sophie."

Sophie and Adrian kept walking through the rain, and didn't
look back.

THE MORNING FOUND Freya and Niko sitting opposite Sophie
and Adrian at the Airstream's table, devouring bacon sandwiches.
Niko and Freya had spent the night in Adrian's bed in the caravan, since they were the ones most in need of recovery. Sophie
and Adrian had slept wrapped up together in sleeping bags and
blankets in the back of the bus—not at all a bad arrangement.
Adrian let himself think back to some of it, his blood warming at
the memory. He twined his leg around Sophie's beneath the table.
She nudged it affectionately.

This morning Niko looked whole and healthy again, and fully
normal. Normal, that is, aside from the fact that he'd had to throw
away his burned clothes and borrow some of Adrian's (which

were a bit too short for his limbs), and that his head was shaved to get rid of the patchy burned hair.

"You look better, you know," Adrian told him. "Without your ridiculous fluffy hair."

"I shall grow my hair fluffier than ever just because you said that. But it's a good thing you dragged me out of that fire before it burned up the rest of me."

"You wouldn't have died," Freya assured.

"I certainly could have. It's quite likely. I was a meter or two away when the grenade went off, and it still did that. Imagine if I'd been any closer." Niko popped a spare slice of bacon in his mouth, chewing it up contentedly. "I hate being a soul, being dead. You know what I hate most about it?"

"No sex?" Sophie guessed.

"That's what I hate *second* most about it. No, what I hate most is—"

"That you can't lie," Adrian cut in.

Niko lifted his eyebrows at him, impressed. "You do know me. Exactly right."

"And no bacon," Freya added.

"No bacon. Such a tragedy. So, guess what?" Niko pointed to Adrian's computer, in its satchel on the floor. "Found something this morning, when I went looking into Wilkes' emails."

"He's dead," said Sophie. "What could you find now in his emails?"

"Quentin's address. Here in Corvallis."

"Seriously?" said Adrian. "How?"

"It was from a message back in September, one Quentin sent to him. I'd overlooked it before, because it was titled 'Tech support' and did in fact look like a daft old person seeking help with her broadband Internet. But when I looked closer into it today, I found it was actually about the Internet in a house in Corvallis she was intending to rent. And deep in the attached documentation was the house's address. 4028 Kings." Niko bit into his toast and said to Adrian with his mouth full, "You want to get her or should I?"

"I'll do it," Adrian said. He had gone numb all over with the determination to make the woman pay.

"Are you sure?" Sophie asked, looking anxious.

Adrian nodded. "I'll be careful. I'll make it a surprise attack— like the kind they use—so she won't have a chance to grab any explosives."

"But what'll you do?"

"Tie her up and call the police and vanish a few seconds before they get there. And tell her 'Don't mess with us' while we're waiting."

Sophie thought it over, then nodded, and turned back to her breakfast. "I wouldn't mind coming along to help." After last night, she'd surely had enough of Thanatos and was ready to see some counterstrikes.

But Adrian shook his head. "I'm not endangering you again. This won't take long, don't worry. She's just a mad old woman. I think I can handle her."

"Speaking of mad old women," Niko said, "has anyone heard from Rhea?"

"No." Adrian took out his phone and frowned at its lack of new messages. "She hasn't answered any of my calls."

"Nor mine," said Freya. "I bet she lost her phone or forgot how to charge it or something."

"Can't sense her, either." Niko sighed. "So she's behind an oak forest, evidently, not that that narrows it down."

"Might be in the Underworld," said Adrian. "We'll look there. We'd better make sure she knows about last night. But first, I pay Quentin a visit."

ADRIAN STOOD ON the sidewalk outside Quentin's rented house in Corvallis, a small, gray-blue, one-story affair on a modestly busy street, its yard studded with juniper bushes. Adrian was wearing thin knit gloves to avoid leaving fingerprints, and now used them to wipe off the surface of the handcuffs procured from Niko one more time, just in case.

Adrian switched into the spirit realm, strode forward the right number of paces, and switched back. The ground tossed him upward a short distance, resolving into carpet under his boots. He recovered his balance and looked around. He was in a sparsely furnished living room, with a half-full mug of tea on the coffee table and a crocheted blanket crumpled on the sofa. An elderly woman's voice droned in one-sided conversation in another room. He stepped quietly toward her, and placed his back against the wall next to the door.

"Yes, that would be fine," she was saying. "I plan to be out of the unit by then."

She re-entered the living room, and shouted in surprise upon catching sight of Adrian. He seized her in both arms. He stole her cell phone, dropped it, and crushed it under his heel, then dragged her into the spirit realm.

They stumbled down onto the bumpy ground, fir trees looming overhead, the wind breathing chilly across the land. Adrian hauled her wrists behind her and clicked the handcuffs onto them. She struggled, but Adrian held her firm.

"Let's make this short and sweet," he said. "I'm getting you arrested today, and am hoping you spend the rest of your life in jail. But just so we're clear, in case you do get out, or in case you try to get friends on the outside to do your work for you, I want you to understand something. You bother Sophie Darrow or her family again, ever, and I find you, bring you here, and abandon you. You'd never get back. You'd die here. You're done putting mortals in danger. Understood?"

"But especially Sophie." She sounded tough and completely remorseless, despite being planted on wet ground in the spirit realm in handcuffs, flannel pajamas, and pink socks.

"Especially Sophie," he confirmed.

"You don't call this putting mortals in danger?"

"This I call justified."

"Threaten me all you like. We won't stop, you know. Whether I'm locked up or not, we'll find a way. And I'm old, Adrian. I don't mind dying for a good cause."

"There's nothing good about your cause, and you *will* stop. Didn't last night show you that your club isn't even very good at what they're trying to do?"

She chuckled. He felt the sound in his arm, locked against her throat. "Oh? Then you don't know?"

He yanked his arm tighter. "I know Wilkes and his mate got themselves killed, while we're all safe. Good enough for me."

"*Are* you all safe? Have you accounted for everyone?"

His flesh went cold. Rhea, who hadn't answered them, and whose soul could be in the Underworld to judge from her blocked signal...

He pulled Quentin back into the living realm. The upward bump of the floor's reappearance made Quentin topple over as he let go of her. She landed on her knees with a grunt of pain. He walked to her land line and dialed 911.

"I've found Betty Quentin, who's wanted for unlawful entry and arranging assaults on Sophie Darrow at OSU," he told the dispatcher. "She's at 4028 Kings, and I've tied her up."

"And your name?" the dispatcher asked.

"Just come." Adrian hung up, distracted by worry about Rhea—not to mention his own involvement in law-breaking now.

"This won't do you any good," Quentin told him.

"The threat still stands."

"And I still don't fear death."

"Don't you?" He bent over her, heart pounding in rage and fear and the thrill of saying something so unlike himself. "Then let me explain something. When you die, you come to *my* realm. And the more harm you do up here, the longer you stay in the darkness down there."

"If that's the nonsense it sounds like, I'll fight you because you're insane and dangerous. If it's actually true, then all the more reason we need to get rid of evil creatures like you."

There was nothing more he could say. She thought he was evil and would always think so. It was useless. She was the police's problem now.

Meanwhile, he needed to make sure Rhea was all right.

He stormed to the window and looked out. The sound of a police siren moved closer. Within a minute, the car with its flashing lights pulled up in front of the house. He unlocked the front door to make it easier for the cops. Then he glanced briefly back at Quentin, verifying she was still confined in her cuffs. She stared into his eyes, undaunted. Adrian plunged into the spirit realm without another word.

CHAPTER FORTY-THREE

OW SOON CAN YOU LEAVE? said the text from Adrian.

Glancing with guilt around the lecture hall, Sophie balanced her new cell on her thigh, and texted back, *Class is about to end. Free soon. Is Quentin arrested?*

Yeah, but please hurry. Worried about Rhea now.

Worried herself, Sophie jogged back to the dorm as soon as class was over. She hadn't entered the room since leaving for dinner with Melissa before last night's attack, nor had she seen Melissa. She would rather have avoided the dorm today, but needed to collect her clothes and books for the weekend.

Melissa entered when Sophie was almost done filling her backpack. Pausing tensely in the doorway, she said, "Are you staying a minute?"

"No." Sophie stuffed in an extra T-shirt and zipped up the pack.

"Please. I could help you guys. If you need allies—"

"Allies like you, who needs enemies?" Swinging the pack onto her shoulder, Sophie bumped past Melissa and left.

On the way, the police called her cell. They'd captured Betty Quentin; they just wanted Sophie to know. They would keep Sophie informed about the arraignment and further details. Sophie thanked them, and hung up.

Adrian waited for her beside the football stadium, the giant structure silent and deserted today. She jumped into his arms, and he whirled her into the other realm.

"What have you found out?" she asked as they climbed into the bus. Kiri waited within, lying behind the front seat, and thumped her tail on the floor upon seeing Sophie.

"Well..." He wrapped his arm around Sophie, snapped the reins, and they shot off. As they flew, he explained his visit to Quentin, and the ominous hint she had dropped.

"All we can do is check the Underworld," Adrian concluded. "Freya and Niko took off a few minutes ago. They'll meet us there." He sighed. "I should have just got Quentin arrested, and said nothing else. Threatening her was stupid of me. It did no good."

"It wasn't stupid." She leaned her head against his chest. The contact eased the hollow fear inside her. "Or at least...even if it did no good, I'm glad you said it."

"But acting as if I own people's souls, when I don't..."

"Own them, no. Stopping them from hurting others, that's fair. That's making the world a safer place."

"That's exactly what she thinks *she's* doing." Adrian sounded defeated.

With no answer to that, Sophie rested against him, watching plains, mountains, and finally ocean sweep past under the bus.

Upon arriving in the Underworld, they hurried through the entrance tunnel and stopped at the river's edge. An unusually thick swarm of souls milled on the other side. A solid figure pushed through the glowing masses and emerged: Nikolaos, looking at them with an expression more somber and distressed than Sophie had ever seen on him.

"Oh, no," she breathed.

Without a word, Adrian retrieved the raft and guided them across. On the other bank, the crowd of souls parted for them. In the middle stood two souls, the center of all the curiosity: Sanjay and Rhea.

Feeling sick, Sophie drew in her breath.

Adrian took her hand—his palm felt clammy—and they walked forward.

In front of Rhea, Freya sat on her knees on the white grass, streaks of tears on her beautiful face.

Rhea gazed at them with kindness and sorrow, all of it subdued, the placidity of the dead. "I went to visit Sanjay's widow," she said. "I brought her here from time to time, to see Sanjay. But somehow they found out I was coming, and captured me as I walked up to her house. They knocked me out quickly; I'm not sure how. It was a tingling pain all through me. And that was the last I knew before finding myself in the spirit realm as a soul."

Adrian swallowed. When he spoke, he sounded tight-voiced, as if his jaw were injured. "Probably a stun gun of some kind. Something strong enough to…" His words faltered and stopped.

Sophie closed her eyes for a moment, imagining the rest: once they'd knocked Rhea unconscious, they were free to throw her into a furnace, or feed her into some kind of grinding machinery, or strap a bomb to her… She shuddered. How they killed her didn't matter. It had worked; that was enough.

"Why didn't you tell us where you were going?" Adrian shouted. "We have to check up on each other, make sure everyone's all right. It's easy these days, but you never did answer your phone, or tell us half of what you were doing…" He let go of Sophie's hand and spun away, staggering in a circle, hands over his face. The crowd of souls drew back to give him room, as if in respect for their king.

"I'm sorry, Adrian," said Rhea. "You're perfectly right."

"We were even tipped off," said Niko quietly. "If only we'd been smart enough to notice."

Adrian looked at him, his eyes bleak and questioning.

"Quentin's email to Wilkes," Niko said. "'We'll have one less to worry about if we can catch our woman friend at her meeting.' They were talking about Rhea. The message was about two attacks, not one. 'The plan to fetch K.A.' meant you, but that one meant her."

Adrian sank to the ground at Sophie's feet, drawing up his knees. "We're the ones who are sorry," he said to Rhea, without looking at her. "We failed you."

"You didn't. I'm proud of you. Look at what you've all become, in such a short time. I'm so glad I brought you back."

"And we repaid you by letting this happen." Adrian's voice had gone gravelly. Sophie sank down beside him on her knees. He stared ahead, his eyes full of tears.

"If I can make a request," Sanjay said, "could someone please tell my wife what's happened, and check that she and the kids are safe too?"

"Better than that, mate," Niko said. "We'll fetch her here for you. You can tell her yourself."

Sanjay nodded his thanks, and Niko extended his hand to Freya, who still sat upon the grass. "Up for a bit of travel to India?"

She sniffled, nodded, and took his hand.

"We'll be careful," Niko assured everyone. "Oh, and Ade, we asked around for Wilkes and his mate, but they aren't up here, so, as expected…" His glance slid off toward the distant reaches of the cave, and he nodded in that direction.

Adrian acknowledged the remark with a slight lift of his chin.

Sophie began remembering the way now: a tunnel, at the far wall of the fields, leading down, down, down. To Tartaros. The sickening feeling strengthened in her stomach.

"See you soon," Niko said, and left with Freya.

Sophie slid her hand beneath Adrian's. "Do you want to stay, or walk?"

He said nothing, but grasped her fingers and got up.

Blinking away the tears that had risen in her eyes, Sophie paused to tell Rhea, in the old tongue they used as priestesses on Crete, "The world grieves to lose you. Your murderers will not go unpunished."

As Persephone, queen of the Underworld, she had said it to souls. She remembered it now, another whisper from a time later in Persephone's life. Now she spoke it not only as one friend to another, but as goddess to goddess.

Rhea inclined her head in thanks. "Go and live, daughter. I'll linger here a good while yet."

Adrian seemed to pick up energy, in a cold and determined

way, as they walked. He led her straight across the fields, toward the passageway to the deep caverns they had eventually named Tartaros, in accordance with the legends people used to tell. Kiri trotted beside them.

Trying to quell the chills she felt, she asked, "What's the point of us looking for them down there?"

"Information." His voice remained tight. "They might have some. And now they can't lie."

Sophie understood that, and accompanied him without further questions. But she had to wonder if temporary vengeance played any part in Adrian's motives: did he merely want to stand before Wilkes and humble him by showing him that he had, indeed, dared an attempt upon the king and queen of the Underworld?

Sophie saw the appeal in that, too. But she wasn't convinced it would do any good.

They reached the entrance after walking in silence for several more minutes. It was invisible until you stepped up close to the wall and looked behind a thick stalagmite that concealed it: a jagged, narrow crevice rising from the floor to just a foot above Sophie's head. Adrian switched on his flashlight and led Kiri and Sophie inside.

Blackness engulfed them for the first few minutes, as the tunnel descended in various large steps and steep slopes. The air grew warmer and stuffier as they negotiated the neglected path. Down and down they walked, deeper into the silent Earth.

Then a small spurt of flame, blue tipped with orange, shot out from the wall a pace ahead, startling Sophie. Adrian squeezed her hand to comfort her, and switched off his flashlight. He led her forward, and in a moment, the flame winked out, and another took its place, farther down the tunnel.

The cave sensed them, and was lighting their way as they proceeded. Sophie knew it in her bones, as part of her ancient memories. But although the Underworld was a friend to her, it had been ages since she'd seen such strong proof of its *aliveness*. It made her heart beat fast in alarm and wonder.

Soon they reached a place where the tunnel opened into a

small cavern. A ring of flames burst up around the arched stone doorway, ushering in Sophie, Adrian, and Kiri. From the small cavern, dozens of narrow tunnels branched off, and within them lay a honeycomb of cells each—Sophie knew—containing a condemned soul. Soft moans and sighs echoed from the multitudes, blending in the close air.

She looked at Adrian in entreaty. All she wanted was to leave.

But he picked up a scrap of a willow-and-ivy rope from the ground—several lay scattered around them, dropped by souls on their way out as the cave released them—and he wound it around his hand, leaving a short length dangling. He waved the loose end into the flames around the doorway, where it ignited like a candle wick.

"Fates who guard these souls," he said in the Underworld tongue, "guide us to those we seek: Bill Wilkes and his accomplice, who died yesterday in an attempt upon our lives."

Sophie remembered this procedure now, too. Since the souls were all in solitary confinement down here and couldn't speak to each other, you couldn't send out a call among them when looking for someone. Instead, the living cave would guide the seeker, if the right protocol was observed.

A new flame burst from the wall in one of the adjoining tunnels. Adrian dropped the burning rope, stamped out its fire, and walked toward the flame. Sophie and Kiri accompanied him. Down the tunnel they walked, following flame after flame that shot out ahead of them to guide them forward. They passed hundreds of cells, into which Sophie was, at first, too scared to look. But eventually she took a glance, and then longer glances, and soon made it a point to send a compassionate look into the eyes of each soul they passed.

No one looked terrifying or dangerous, only unhappy. The cells were all the same: tiny hollows in the rock, with open doorways that had no bars or barriers. But the cave chained each captive to the wall with a willow-and-ivy vine around the waist so they couldn't escape before their time. Aside from the rare occurrence of another soul or an immortal guardian walking past, they had nothing to look at in their cell but a single flame rising from the floor, and in it, Sophie recalled as a whisper from Persephone, they saw the harm they had done and the consequences it had caused. To feel joy or contentment was impossible here.

The trail of little flames stopped after five or six turns among the passageways. In the cell below the last flame, Sophie beheld the soul of Bill Wilkes, tied to the wall.

She felt slightly sick again as his eyes met hers, though he displayed no malice; only depression. A second flame burned on the opposite side of the corridor, two cells down, and she stepped aside to glance into that one. Indeed, there stood Wilkes' taller accomplice—some man in his twenties or thirties with bristly blond hair and small, blue eyes.

How strange, Sophie thought, that she didn't even know this man's name, nor anything about his life, and not much more about Wilkes, but they had assaulted her and tried to kill her beloved friends, and now she was viewing their souls in the afterlife.

Her life had indeed changed in the last couple of months.

Adrian ignored the accomplice and looked at Wilkes. "Who killed Rhea?"

"I don't know their names," Wilkes said. "Street criminals. The guru found them."

"How can we find them and have them arrested? And have the guru arrested?"

"You probably can't. The plan was to incinerate her along with hundreds of dead bodies, so if they carried that out, there's no proof of a murder or any crime at all."

Adrian sighed in frustration. "How do we stop them? Quentin's been arrested, but is this going to continue?"

"Of course. It will always continue." Wilkes sounded defeated, not triumphant. "The group has plans for every setback. And Quentin probably won't stay in jail long. We have a plan in place for that too."

Adrian scowled down the corridor a while. Then he looked coolly at Wilkes. "What else did you do, other than come after us? To end up here, it must have been pretty bad."

Wilkes' face grew sadder, stormier. He gazed at the flame on the floor of his cell. "Murder—a man I hated; I got away with that. Poisoned him. Even he didn't know who did it. Violence; beating people. Seeing prostitutes, girls I knew were underage—"

"I don't want to hear any more," Sophie interrupted softly, addressing Adrian.

"Enough," Adrian commanded Wilkes.

Wilkes lifted his face and looked at the two of them. "So you really were Hades and Persephone."

Sophie turned away from his gaze. Yes, Wilkes would have all the common Underworld knowledge now. A lot of good it did him.

"I suppose you won this skirmish," Wilkes added. "But it never ends, you know."

"We didn't win. In here, no one wins. All I know is you should try to do better in your next life," he regarded the ample gauge of the ropes holding Wilkes, "which appears to be in a long time." He turned away. "We'll be sure to tell Quentin you said hello."

Sophie, Adrian, and Kiri left the caves and climbed up the sloping tunnel. As the flames disappeared behind them, Adrian switched his flashlight back on. His features looked hardened and gloomy in its cold blue light.

"At least they're where they belong," Sophie said, hoping it might soothe him.

"But like he said, we can never stop Thanatos, not really. And what good does it do, being locked up in Tartaros? It doesn't *work*, evidently. You've seen how the world is. Evil people are everywhere."

"They forget when they're reborn," Sophie said.

"Exactly. What's the point, then? What is the cave doing? How am I supposed to help out, be some kind of god down here, when I don't even know?" He sounded completely desolate.

On top of Rhea's death and the violence they underwent last night, trying to work out the secrets of the universe was surely too much to ask. Sophie curled her arm around his, and leaned her cheek on his shoulder in consolation, unable to provide any answers herself, and feeling equally lost in the face of such questions.

They emerged into the fields, where the collective glow of the souls seemed almost bright after the tunnels. Sophie slid her arm around Adrian's waist. He sighed and leaned his head aside to touch hers. They stopped beneath a large pale-blue willow growing in a valley.

He sniffled, and swiped his palm across his eyes. "I was just this nice disabled kid, you know?" he said, his voice wobbling. "I was going to be a lawyer…"

From her pocket she pulled the cotton handkerchief he had handed her that first day, when she had watched the video of Grandpop. She had washed it and kept it, and frequently carried it. Now she handed it back to him. He glanced once and then twice at it, and chuckled in a broken way. He wiped his eyes with it, then hugged her again.

Sophie stroked his back, feeling his warmth and the perfection of his body through his flannel shirt. Her heart accelerated in anticipation as the decision took hold of her. "I want to eat the orange," she said.

Adrian pulled back slowly to look at her. Interest and wonder displaced the grief in his eyes. "Really?"

"Yes. This is where I'm needed."

"But…your family. Your life."

"I had to grow up and find something else to do with my life eventually." She smiled, through a tinge of panic. "I never guessed it would be this, when I left for college. But this is the most amazing thing anyone could do with their life. Besides, you guys are an endangered species. I want to help."

"By becoming endangered yourself?"

"Being in love with you, I already am in danger. I at least want to be able to defend myself next time, instead of having to call you in to do it."

He looked almost joyous, but hesitated. "I just…you said you wanted a long time to think about it."

"I've *been* thinking about it. Melissa was right. I'd be crazy not to accept immortality when someone offers it."

He exhaled a laugh of surprise and happiness, and caught hold of both her hands. "All right. If that's your decision."

"It is. Let's go."

"Right now?"

"Right now." Holding his hand, she turned toward the orchard, and they began walking.

"Sophie, this is Marilyn with the police department; we spoke yesterday. It's about eight a.m. on Saturday now. I need to inform you that the suspect Betty Quentin escaped from custody sometime during the night. Obviously we're investigating how that happened, but we also wanted to put you on alert, as the primary victim of her crimes. Our guess is she'll try to lie low rather than go after you or anyone else, but it's safest to consider her dangerous and to be on the lookout. So please call back with any questions, and we'll be in touch soon."

TO BE CONTINUED…

Afterword

It doesn't take much research to find that there is no one "proper" way to tell any of the Greek myths. People developed their own favorite versions in different areas, with contradictory details cropping up between one story and another. Therefore, in taking a Greek myth and turning it on its ear, I figure I'm only adding to the longstanding tradition of creating a version of events I personally am fond of.

The ancient myths usually tend to agree that Hades kidnapped Persephone, completely against her will, traumatizing her and breaking her mother Demeter's heart. But for reasons I can't fathom (maybe I simply longed for a prettier story?), ever since I was a teenager I wanted to see a version where Persephone loved Hades, and he loved her too. (It's possible he did in the original myth, and just had an unhealthy way of showing it. We don't get a lot of glances into Hades' mind in those old stories.) But in rewriting the myth that way, it became clear that if Hades wasn't the villain in the triangle, Demeter would have to be—or nearly so. However, it didn't feel right to portray the benevolent goddess Demeter as an evil person or even really an enemy. So I hope I've found a way to cast her in the role of romantic obstacle and overprotective parent without completely ruining her reputation.

As for matters of history and prehistory: It's possible, and even likely, that I made lots of factual errors in my depictions of the historic Mediterranean. I relied on Professor Wikipedia probably too much, and I take full responsibility for any mistakes. Though I did try to give some authentic flavor to the setting, I ultimately didn't worry too much about accuracy, since, let's face it, this is a novel about magic pomegranates and flying ghost horses. That said, here are a few research notes that might interest readers:

Placing the ancient-Mediterranean action at "roughly 3,700 years ago," or around 1,700 B.C.E., puts us in the height of Minoan civilization on Crete. Like me, you can read on Wikipedia that ritual human sacrifice does seem likely to have taken place there (we don't know under what circumstances), though in most ways the Minoans were a highly advanced civilization for their time. The palace complex at Knossos underwent several partial destructions and reconstructions over the centuries, but it seems that it remained the power center of the island for quite a long while. Though I'm unsure what the construction status would've been for the palace at the exact time of the story, I chose to depict Knossos at its full glory, complete with the beautiful frescoes glimpsed by Hades on his way out.

The Minoans of that time wrote in hieroglyphics and also in a script archaeologists call Linear A (which modern scholars have not entirely deciphered), and spoke a language we don't know much about either. Thus I took liberties in making up language and writing-system tidbits as needed for the story. Same goes for mainland Greece: my story takes place centuries before any existing written records appear there, and the language of Ancient Greek as we know it still hadn't developed. That's why I call the tongue "proto-ancient-Greek" at times.

The "cloudhair flowers" mentioned by Aphrodite as birth control are inspired by Queen Anne's lace, which is said to have been used for that purpose in ancient Greece and other places. However, they wouldn't have called it "Queen Anne's lace" back then, of course, so I made up a new name.

As to oranges, it appears they and most other citrus fruits have been cultivated for millennia in Asia, but weren't introduced to the Mediterranean until the 15th or 16th century A.D. So Persephone acquiring orange seeds or seedlings in ancient Greece is unlikely. However, I liked the idea of borrowing an Asian fruit and thus fusing East and West for the secret to immortality (the meditation technique that leads to switching realms is also originally an Eastern secret in this book). In addition, I liked the idea of the "golden apple" being an orange, because I'm told that the Greek language and several others derive their word for "orange" (the fruit) from the phrase "golden apple."

Then I made the fruit's flesh blue, just to be contrary.

Further etymological fun: the word "grenade" is French for "pomegranate." It was really just a fortuitous coincidence, as I was planning to have Thanatos deploy grenades even before I knew that, but I liked how the word relations turned out.

- M.J.R.

ACKNOWLEDGMENTS

I owe special thanks, first of all, to my beta readers:

- Kate Wharton, not only my sister but a talented and hilarious screenwriter who knows how to pace the action and helped me do it better. Thanks for being so positive and encouraging.

- Jessica Chambers, who took time out of her home renovations to read this and catch my awkward wording details and the plot moments that made no sense. Jess's novels always show the proper way to handle a large and diverse cast--something I hope I can learn from her.

- Beth Willis, for a fabulous and thorough list of "LOL"s and "squee"s, along with good sound grammatical advice. She even liked my first version from way back in college, so she's pretty much my ideal audience. But she has her own appreciative audience and you should join them: look up Beth Willis Music and swoon over the woman's voice.

- Dean Mayes, who commented on the first full draft and caught some Kiwi dialect problems. But he's Australian and I'm American, so it's likely we still missed a few between us. Also, Dean's own novels reminded me of the importance of dogs, which inspired me to invent Kiri and Kerberos.

A huge thanks to my editor, the incomparably friendly and supportive Michelle Halket, who encouraged me by expressing interest in this book even before seeing it, and whose suggestions helped deepen the emotion and romance and ended up making me love the story more than ever. And thanks for helping me keep my poise and professionalism (or as close as I could manage) when dealing with the marketing side of things!

Thanks to my sister Peggy Hawkwood, who pored over the Greek mythology book with me when we were kids, and liked my story so well in its early days that she acquired fans for me among her friends even before this version was ready. Also thanks to Rich Mulvey for answering my questions about technological espionage, and for general IT and moral support, and framed photos of Greek beaches. And thanks to Kirsty Harrison Skok on Facebook, whom the lovely Michelle Murphy introduced me to, for answering a brief flurry of my questions about Kiwi dialect and slang.

And, for that matter, many thanks to everyone on my Facebook author page for cheering me on when I posted updates about writing this novel. Your enthusiasm for yet another Persephone book in the world spurred me along toward the finish line.

Most importantly: immeasurable thanks to my husband Steve, who is always the person most inconvenienced by my obsession for writing novels, but who acts as a wonderful sounding board for my ideas nonetheless, and provided cool and useful facts on everything from botany to how GPS works. Also my sons, the wonderful and brilliant pair, who put up admirably with Mommy's habit of staring at the computer screen. And my parents, a god and goddess to me in their own ways, wise and lively and funny, always taking their children's side against the world.

I am so lucky to have you all.